Books by Roberta Gellis

A Mortal Bane
*A Personal Devil**

*forthcoming

A Mortal Bane

ROBERTA GELLIS

TOR®

A TOM DOHERTY ASSOCIATES BOOK
NEW YORK

This is a work of fiction. All the characters and events portrayed in this book are either products of the author's imagination or are used fictitiously.

A MORTAL BANE

Copyright © 1999 by Roberta Gellis

All rights reserved, including the right to reproduce this book, or portions thereof, in any form.

A Tor Book
Published by Tom Doherty Associates, LLC
175 Fifth Avenue
New York, NY 10010

www.tor.com

Tor® is a registered trademark of Tom Doherty Associates, LLC.

ISBN 0-812-57236-X

First edition: September 1999
First mass market edition: September 2001

Printed in the United States of America

0 9 8 7 6 5 4 3 2

To my husband, Charles,
whose help, patience, and understanding
have kept me sane throughout the vicissitudes
of writing and publishing.

A Mortal Bane

Prologue

⟐

Only a thread of moon remained, and the hair-thin crescent cast no light on the path. That made no difference to the blind woman whose staff swept back and forth, pausing infinitesimally as it touched the grass verge on either side. She knew the way so well that she could have trod it easily without the staff, but the sturdy oak rod gave her confidence. There was little protection for a whore, especially a blind one, in London in the year of Our Lord 1139, and she could wield the staff quite effectively against anyone who came close enough to strike her or seize her. She was not afraid now, however. The path between the Old Priory Guesthouse, where she plied her trade, and the church to which it had once belonged was through a walled garden.

The next sweep of her staff scraped gently on a hard surface. The blind woman pulled the staff back toward her, took another careful step, and stretched her hand toward the gate that opened the wall between the garden and the churchyard. The latch lifted; she went through and continued up the path until the staff touched the verge more quickly on the left than on the right. That was where the walk turned around the apse of the church. The blind woman adjusted her direction, took another step.

"Who is there?"

She stopped abruptly, recognizing the voice of the sacristan of the priory and knowing he would not welcome her, an excommunicate whore, into the church. In the next moment her keen ears picked up a soft thump and then the sound of running feet. She stood where she was quietly, her lips curved into a gentle, amused smile because she was sure the monk had come across a young couple sheltering in the dark of the porch for a caress or two. She listened intently for the footsteps of the sacristan pursuing them, but she heard nothing except the soft sound of the door closing.

After awhile she started forward again. Either the sacristan had gone back through the church, intending to catch the intruders as they came around to the front, or he felt he had startled the pair enough to discourage them and had gone into the monastery. It would be safe for her to go into the church now and pray for a little while. Priests said she must give up the life she led before God would listen to her prayers, but that made no sense at all. For what could she pray, born without eyes as she was, except not to starve—and was that not why she whored? Better to go on whoring and pray for forgiveness.

The path turned again, more abruptly, and the staff scraped against another hard surface—the first step to the north porch of the church. She brought her foot to the staff, mounted the step, mounted the next, and brought the staff forward to judge whether she was clear of the wall of the porch. The staff did not touch the stone step. It did not swing freely. There was something large and soft lying on the porch. The blind woman drew in a sharp breath, recalling the thud she had heard and that she had heard only one set of footsteps running. Could the meeting have been for a purpose less innocent than a kiss? Could the sacristan, who had a sour temper, have struck one of the young people without realizing he had caused serious harm?

The blind woman knelt, felt immediately that it was indeed a person lying on the porch floor, slid her hand toward a shoulder gently, intending to help the person up . . . and froze. Surely her sensitive fingers knew that cloth, the embroidery on that tunic. Holding her breath, she brought her hand up, touched thick, curly hair, a shaven cheek, a long, fine nose, lips . . . oh, yes, she knew those lips! Shaking now, she reached out to turn the face more toward her and her hand struck what did not belong, could not possibly be part of the man or his clothing. The breath she had held quavered out in a low, terrified whimper.

A knife hilt! And around it, something wet, sticky. The odor struck her now. Blood. He was covered with blood. He was dead! She did not dare cry aloud. Oh, God, if he was dead, she was dead also. Who would believe that she had not quarreled with him, buried a knife in him? She rose to run, but her feet were tangled. Then she would have screamed had not her throat been locked with terror, until she realized it was her own staff across her feet. She snatched it up and fled.

One

Magdalene la Bâtarde, whoremistress, she who had been Arabel de St. Foi until her husband died of a knife in the heart and she had fled before she was accused of murder, lifted her head and looked away from her embroidery frame. The bell at the gate in the wall had sounded faintly through closed doors and windows. She frowned. From the color of the light making the oiled parchment in the window glow, it was nearly sunset. All her clients were already in the house and in the beds of the women with whom they had appointments.

She sat still a moment longer. The Old Priory Guesthouse was not a place where men came casually from the street. But when the bell sounded again, she shrugged and rose. It might be a messenger, or a client who had a sudden need and intended to stay the night. Money was money and every silver penny might be important. Nonetheless, she was anxious, and she thought again as she went to the gate that she should hire a man or a boy to open gates and run errands. As she lifted the latch, she sighed. She could afford that now, since most of her clients were men of wealth or importance and they preferred to be known to as few as possible.

She was shocked to discover that the man at the gate was no common messenger and that she had never seen his face before. Although she kept her expression calm, Magdalene could feel the blood beating in her throat. Anyone recommended to her house would have been told that an appointment was necessary, and hers was no common whorehouse and was not marked in any way to attract passersby. Strangers, who did not know she had powerful protectors, were dangerous. Her fear was diminished, however, when she saw that the man looked more shocked than she felt.

"Who are you?" he asked.

The French he spoke was good, but the accent was not that of France or of England. Magdalene drew an easier breath. Either this was a traveler honestly lost or someone had deliberately sent him here to embarrass him. A mistake or a joke, Magdalene thought, divided between irritation and amusement. Some men never grew up and thought it great fun to send innocent foreigners to her costly whorehouse. Well, it was not this poor man's fault.

"I am Magdalene la Bâtarde," she said. "And this is the Old Priory Guesthouse." But she had been examining his horse, a well-kept, handsome animal, and his cloak, which, although a sober dark gray, was of exceptionally fine cloth, lined with fur and richly embroidered. The purse at his waist seemed plump, and she suspected there was a large pouch suspended from a strap across his breast, but it was pushed to his back where the cloak hid it. "Please come in," she added, pulling the gate open wider and stepping back. "If you are lost, I can set you on your way, and if you desire rest or entertainment, I can provide that also."

"The Old Priory Guesthouse?" he repeated as he led his horse in. "Is that not the church of St. Mary Overy? I was told one could see it from the foot of London

Bridge and that the Bishop of Winchester's house was behind the church."

Magdalene frowned and her full, beautifully shaped lips thinned. "Someone has a strange sense of humor— or wishes to besmirch Henry of Winchester's reputation. It is true the Bishop of Winchester owns this house, but he has never personally set foot in it. The Bishop of Winchester's local dwelling faces the front gate of the priory."

A wary expression had widened the stranger's large, dark eyes and tightened the corners of his mouth as she spoke, but his face cleared and he laughed when she came to the last sentence. "Ah," he said, "that was how the confusion came about. My traveling companion told me that the bishop's house was behind the church and, if one rides across the bridge, a house at the front of the priory would look to be behind the church."

"That is possible, I suppose," Magdalene said, and shivered suddenly. She had come out without a cloak because she expected to do no more than take a message from someone's hand or let a client in. She had thought she would be able to scold the client in comfort by the fire while he waited for one of her women to be free. "If you like," she went on, huddling her arms around herself, "I will send my servant to guide you to the bishop's house, but she is rather deaf and it will take me a few moments to make what I want clear. You may wait here if you prefer, or you may come in." She smiled. "I assure you this is not the kind of place where men are seized upon and robbed or forced to stay."

He laughed again at that. "With a face like yours, madame, I should think you would have more trouble driving men away than keeping them."

"I thank you," she said stiffly, stepping aside so he could lead the horse past her, "but I no longer take clients. And there is no one free to serve you at the moment. You would have to wait—"

Illumination and amusement changed his expression

again. "Ah, it is a special kind of guesthouse. I understand." He laughed again. "That is why you thought my friend might be trying to besmirch the bishop's reputation." He hesitated and frowned, glancing up at the church spire. "How close the church looks. Is there a short way to reach it from here?"

"Yes, there is," Magdalene replied. "But I do not like to stand at the gate as if I were soliciting custom. Let me fetch my servant if you do not wish to come in."

"I will come in," he said, his expression thoughtful. "Where do I leave my horse?"

"In the stable." Magdalene gestured to the right, where a well-built stable was backed against the stone wall that encircled the house. "I am sorry there is no one to help you, but I have no manservants. Our clients prefer to do for themselves. The door of the house is open. Just walk in when you have settled the horse."

He set off, and Magdalene closed and latched the gate. She glanced once toward the stable and then hurried back into the house. Inside, she walked to the fire in the hearth on the west wall and stood beside it looking into the flames as she considered the stranger. She then sat down on a stool, turning her embroidery frame so she could face the door. She had not yet pulled her needle from the cloth where she had set it before rising to open the gate, when the man came in. He stared around at the room, surprise plain in his face.

Magdalene suppressed a smile as she rose and asked if she could take his cloak. Most of her clients had been using her facilities for years; they were familiar with and accepted the comfortable appearance of a family solar. It was not until someone new entered and registered amazement that there were not beds in the corners with grunting couples in them, or near-naked women sitting or lying about, that Magdalene was reminded of how different her house was from the usual kind of stew. After a second glance around, the man undid the handsome brooch and handed her his cloak, which she laid on a chest under the window.

"I have just bethought me," he said, "that Richard de Beaumeis did not say this was the Bishop of Winchester's house. He called it the Bishop of Winchester's inn."

"Richard de Beaumeis!" Magdalene repeated, beginning to laugh as she returned to her seat. "Oh, that wicked young man. It was pure mischief to send you here with that explanation. Richard de Beaumeis attended school in the priory, and he knows very well what kind of guesthouse this is. He has availed himself often enough of our Ella's company."

The man laughed also. "He told me that he had attended the priory school. He said nothing of the extra-curricular activities he enjoyed."

"Naughty!" Magdalene sighed. "He has an antic sense of humor I never suspected, but I fear he has done you an ill turn. There is no decent inn to which I can recommend you on this side of the river. Of course, if you do not mind the plain food, the prayers, and the early hours, you may ask for lodging in the true priory guesthouse"—she smiled and shook her head—"which is now on the grounds of the priory. Or, if you have business with the Bishop of Winchester, who is in residence just now, I am sure you will be made welcome—"

"No," he said, "I have no business with the bishop, but I do have an appointment for a meeting on this side of the river, not far from here, around Compline. So, if you will have me, I think I will stay here."

"We are rather costly, I am afraid," Magdalene said. Her guest shrugged and waved a hand at the surroundings. His appreciative glance took in the floor bestrewn with clean, sweet-smelling rushes, the scrubbed table with a long bench on each side and two short ones at head and foot, the grouping of stools near the hearth, one with a lute on it and the two others with sewing baskets beside them. At the north end of the room there was an open corridor, and on the wall at each side, a set of shelves holding pewter and wooden platters and cups and some drinking horns. The lowest shelves held several large hard-leather vessels and sealed crocks.

"I had expected that," he said. "But I will want to stay the entire night, since I have no place else to sleep."

"You will be welcome to stay. I must lock the house and outer gate at dark, but your woman will let you out and wait to let you in again." She rose to her feet and gestured to the group of stools. "Please, do sit down. We do not serve meals unless they are specially ordered ahead of time, but I can give you wine, ale, or beer, and bread and cheese, possibly a slice of pasty or some cold meat if you are hungry. I must see what is in the kitchen."

"Wine, if you please," he said, clearly restraining a shudder at the thought of ale or beer.

Magdalene smiled and fetched a pair of stemmed pewter drinking cups from the shelf. Having set them on the table, she filled them from a polished pitcher and brought the cups back. She was amused again when the man sipped gingerly, as if he expected something unpleasant, then smiled and drank more deeply. It was good wine, she knew. It was supplied by William of Ypres, mercenary captain of all of the king's paid men. He had been her patron and protector for almost ten years and had uses for her house that had little to do with her skill and beauty or that of her women.

For that matter, most of her regular clients supplied their own wine, which was stored in the guesthouse cellar, each cask marked with a sign only she and her women would associate with the owner. William, because of those other purposes, sent more than he would ever drink, and some was for her own use. It was from that store that she had drawn the pitcher earlier in the day, so she felt free to offer it.

"Something to eat?" she asked.

"I thank you, no. I had my dinner at a friend's house not long before I arrived here. The wine is very good."

"A gift from a friend," she said.

Plainly, this client was not prepared to tell her his name or anything more than that he had come from somewhere in or around London. She had answered as she did, also naming no names, to indicate that she could be trusted, but she did not mind that he did not respond. If he came again, he would learn that secrets were generally kept quite secure by the women of the Old Priory Guesthouse. However, Magdalene had the feeling that this man was not settling in England. He had an air of "passing through" about him.

"We have been having a pleasant spring," she said, setting her cup down on the floor beside her and looking at the design she was embroidering.

"It is colder than I like," the man replied agreeably, resting his cup on his knee and smiling at her. "London never changes, though. Each time I come, I am surprised to find it just the same. It seems to me so large and busy a city would change more."

"Perhaps you do not notice the changes because it is so large and busy. For example, if a street changed from housing pepperers to housing mercers, likely it would look much the same to a passerby."

As she spoke, Magdalene rapidly made the tiny chain stitches that outlined a leaf and then began to fill it with green silk. If it had been larger, she would have chosen a darker green for the central vein and a medium color between that and the leaf itself for the smaller veins. As it was only one of many similar very small leaves on a tree, she did not trouble. Thin as her needle was and fine as her thread, there was no room for greater detail.

"I suppose you are right," he replied and then leaned forward. "That is very fine work you do."

"We are recorded as a house of needleworkers," Magdalene said with a smile. "That is less out of any desire to deceive than to escape having to mark the house as a stew. And that is to avoid men walking in from the street, expecting to be serviced and disturbing our clients. When a man has paid five good silver pennies for his pleasure, he does not expect to be rushed, annoyed by noise, or suffer any inconvenience."

The guest whistled and shook his head. "I should think not. You told me you were costly, but five pence . . ."

"That includes lodging for the night, stabling and feed for your horse, and such an evening meal and breakfast as we ourselves take, but if the price is too much, please accept the wine as a friendly gesture, warm yourself, and go free as you came. The priory is close, will lodge you safe, and is very easy to find. Just ride down the road to the first turning to the right. Take that until you come to another turning to the right. Take that and in a few yards, you will see the gate."

He laughed aloud. "You do not chaffer over your goods? Ah, well, you cannot blame a man for trying. No, it is not too much. I will stay."

"I do not wish to be rude," Magdalene said with an apologetic smile, "but you are plainly not a resident of Southwark or of London. I am afraid—"

"You want me to pay in advance?" His hand went to his full purse without hesitation and he emptied part of the contents into his other hand. Having picked out the coins, he handed them to her.

"I am very sorry to seem so untrusting," she said, slipping her hand through the slit in her skirt and finding the pocket tied around her waist, "but we see so few strangers in this house. Usually one client brings another."

The man shrugged. "A decent inn would cost two pennies, and the companions I would find in my bed— even those with only two legs—would be less pleasant."

Magdalene laughed. "I promise you will find no companion with more than two legs in any of our beds, and

you may bathe if you like also. Your woman will help
you. They are all equally skilled."

"For the price, I imagine they must be," he remarked,
but there was no sharpness to his voice, rather, a good-
humored acceptance. "What I cannot understand is how
such an establishment came to be in this place."

"That is easy enough to explain. The order of nuns
that founded St. Mary Overy was very strict. The nuns
would not permit men, except their priest, into their
convent walls. When the order failed and the brothers
took over the convent, they found a guesthouse outside
the walls to be hard to manage. Moreover, a wealthy
guest, who came often, found it inconvenient, so he
contributed a sum that permitted the brothers to build a
new and more comfortable guesthouse inside the walls.
Since the brothers had no more use for this house, it
fell back into the hands of the then Bishop of Winchester."

"And he felt that what the priory needed was a
whorehouse sharing its wall?"

Magdalene could not help laughing at the wry expression and tone. "It was not the current Bishop of
Winchester who made the decision, so I never knew the
man, but I can understand his problem. He could not
rent to anyone who had a trade that was noxious or
noisy, and in any case, there are few who would find
this house useful or convenient, having no place for a
stall on the road, two rows of small cells for sleeping,
and no area fit for a workroom. And the building is too
good to throw down. It is stone-built, with a good slate
roof. Moreover, there are not many who could afford
the rent for such a building—"

"Ah, you pay a good rent, do you?"

Magdalene cast her eyes up to the ceiling and sighed.
"Indeed we do, and—" She stopped speaking and
cocked her head, then nodded. "I think that will be Sabina's client leaving. He likes to get home before dark,

and the light is almost gone. I will get some torches for us now."

She rose and took from the highest shelf several torchettes made of rounded blocks of herb-scented wax, each with a many-stranded wick, affixed to a wooden holder. These she set into iron loops on the walls, one at each side of the room and one near the door, before she lit them from the fire with a wax-tipped spill. As she moved about, she noticed her guest looking at the corridor with considerable interest; Magdalene turned away to take candles down from the other end of the shelf. If he expected to see someone who frequented the establishment, he was doomed to disappointment. All guests were shown out through the back door just so they would not need to pass any other client waiting in the common room. He seemed to realize this, because a second brief glance told Magdalene that he was smiling, too, and had lifted his wine cup to his lips. A few moments later, footsteps came down the corridor. Magdalene set the candles into the holder on the table but did not light them and returned to her seat.

"I am here by the fire, Sabina," she said to the tall, slender woman who entered the room, "and we have an unexpected but most welcome guest."

"Welcome, indeed," Sabina said, turning toward them and coming forward slowly.

Magdalene's gaze flashed toward the man and saw his eyes widen, but she was not sure what had surprised him. Sabina was very beautiful. Her skin was flawless, its delicate pallor almost luminous, and although her thick hair did not reveal its rich red highlights in the dimmer light, it still flowed in waves and curls over her back and shoulders down to her hips. Moreover, her short nose and her full lips, turned up at the corners in the bare hint of a smile, gave that loveliness a look of saucy merriness. Still, the man might have expected beauty for the price she had set, so likely it was the fact that Sabina's eyes, although her head was turned in their direction, were closed. The doubt was settled when he jumped to his feet and extended a hand, not to take her arm, but to touch it gently.

"Let me help you find a seat," he said.

Sabina smiled and raised her hand to take his. "Thank you, my lord. Not only are you kind, but you know how to offer help to a blind person. My seat is the one with the lute. Since I cannot embroider, I make myself useful in another way. Would you like me to sing or to play?"

She allowed him to seat her, although Magdalene knew she was perfectly capable of finding her stool and removing the lute from the seat without knocking it to the floor. And when he said he would like to hear her, if she was not tired, she laughed in a low, musical murmur.

"We are not overburdened here," she said. "If I were tired, I could have gone directly back to my room. My ears are keen. I heard that Magdalene was talking to someone. I came because I was willing to entertain you in any way you desire."

"Then I would like to hear you sing," he said, and when they had decided on a song, he settled back to listen with clear pleasure.

By the time the song was done, two other women had entered the room. They stood quietly by the table, and Magdalene grinned when she saw her new guest look from one to the other with astonishment. Each was as beautiful as Sabina in her own way, but totally different. One was tiny and as dark as a Moor. Magdalene had always assumed Letice's parents must have been Saracen captives taken in the Crusade and brought back to England as slaves instead of being ransomed. Her skin was a warm olive-brown, her almond-shaped eyes black, and her hair a raven curtain that hung to her knees, so dark and shining that it shimmered with glints of green and blue. The other was her opposite, with milk-white skin stained with crushed strawberry on the cheeks; large, round, cornflower-blue eyes; and a pursed, cherry-red mouth. Her hair was golden and fell into curls and ringlets to her waist.

When the song ended and the women saw the guest's eyes on them, they both curtsied. "I am Ella," the blonde said, coming forward with a broad smile. "I am so glad you could come."

The dark woman came forward, too, but said nothing, only nodded her head in greeting and took a seat beside Magdalene, reaching down for her sewing basket.

"And what is your name?" the man asked the dark woman.

"Her name is Letice," Magdalene said, "and she is mute, so I am afraid she cannot make light conversation. However, she is a very skilled . . . embroideress and dances exquisitely. She is expressive enough about what is important here."

Letice looked sidelong at the guest under her long lashes, and her lips parted a trifle. "So I see," he said.

Magdalene chuckled. "I will go and tell Dulcie to bring our evening meal now. Why do you not go to the table with the women and speak with them a little. That should make your choice among them easier."

He shook his head. "Nothing can make a choice among three such beauties easier," he said as he rose, but then he bent to touch Sabina's hand. "That was a lovely song, Sabina. May I show you where the table is?"

"Oh, she can find it herself," Ella said in her little girl's voice as Magdalene started down the corridor. "We are never allowed to move anything lest Sabina bump into it. She—oh, Letice, stop! You know Magdalene promised that I could light the candles tonight."

Magdalene heard Sabina replying, reminding Ella that she had nearly set her hair afire the last time, and then, as Ella began to whimper, suggesting that if she would allow Letice to tie back her hair, Letice would let her light the spill, but she must be very careful. Magdalene sighed with relief. There would be no need to explain to their guest that Ella was simple.

She found, when she returned from making clear to Dulcie that there would be five at the table and nodding approval of the dishes the maid suggested, that she would not need to assure her guest that Ella was not being used against her will either. Having required the guest's help to light the candles—as evidenced by his removing his hand from hers just as Magdalene entered the room—Ella frankly rubbed herself against him to display the virtue that made her so popular as a bed partner: her wholehearted and single-minded delight in sex.

"Ella, my love, we do not urge ourselves on guests," Magdalene reproved gently.

Ella sighed and moved away. "But he is such a pretty man," she said. "Sabina does not care how they look. She does not need to look at them."

Sabina laughed. "But I know how they look all the same, love. My fingers tell me. And there are so few who know how to help a blind woman without pulling and pushing at her. What is more, he has a lovely voice. So do not be a greedy little bird. We all want this one."

"Now, now, you will make the poor man blush," Magdalene said just as Letice came forward and touched the tip of a pointed finger to the guest's lips, following the gentle touch with an even gentler kiss. "Sit down, all. You are getting in Dulcie's way."

As the maid stepped through the corridor door and went to lay five large rounds of stale bread on the table, two at each long bench and one at the head, the man handed Sabina to a bench and sat down beside her. Ella, pouting only a little, sat on the other side of the table, while Letice went to the shelves and took down five cups, three knives, five spoons, and a ladle. She placed the ladle at Magdalene's seat and left no knife at the guest's or Ella's; he had his own, and Ella would not touch a knife.

Dulcie returned with a pot of stew and a pasty, which

she placed by Magdalene's position at the head of the table. Meanwhile, Magdalene had brought a crock and the polished pitcher from the wall shelves and proceeded to pour ale for her women and herself, and wine for the guest. Then, before she sat down, she served everyone a portion of thick stew, which she dumped on the trencher with a slice of pasty beside it. Letice cut up Ella's food and there was a short silence while everyone tasted the meal, broken at last by the guest's compliments on the fine ragout.

"Dulcie is a good cook," Magdalene said. "She came to me from a cookshop in Oxford. They could not keep her because she could no longer hear the orders. To me, her deafness is not important. In some ways it is a nuisance to have to shout or use gestures, but on the other hand, she cannot overhear what might be better unheard."

"That is a comfort to some, I suppose, but not to me," her guest said. "There are very few who would be interested in anything I had to say."

Oh dear, Magdalene thought, this is a man who is concealing an important purpose and is not accustomed to doing so. A more practiced deceiver would never have denied a need for secrecy but laughed and agreed that all men had secrets. Magdalene kept her eyes on his face, careful not to glance at the pouch on its broad strap, which he had not set aside with his cloak. That pouch. Did it mark him a messenger?

"No, no," she protested, laughing lightly. "Every man has things of interest to say. If you tell Sabina how lovely she is, she would hang on every word, I am sure."

"And that would be a kindness," Ella put in, "because, you know, she cannot see herself in a bowl of water or a plate of polished brass."

"You are a sweet creature to think of that," Sabina said to Ella, "but I am sure our guest has more amusing subjects to talk about."

"Truly, very little. In fact, I would be happy to hear any news of England, since I have been absent for some time. It is clear that the king is not in London. Has there been more rebellion that has carried him out to the field?"

"No, thank God," Sabina said. "I do not know whether you were here when the Scots came down into Northumberland, and even to Yorkshire, but a great battle was fought at Northallerton, which was a victory for the English."

Magdalene wondered, as Sabina told of the battle of the Standard and how it was Queen Maud who had traveled north to negotiate a truce, whether their guest could be a royal messenger. He certainly seemed interested when Sabina said the king was at Nottingham and assured him the news was reliable and had come to her from a well-informed client. But the man did not dress like a courier, nor was his bearing that of a man accustomed to wearing armor.

Almost as if he had heard her thought, the guest said he was glad to hear the country was at peace, because he had some traveling to do, and without asking directly, he drew from Sabina the information that King Stephen would likely be fixed at Nottingham for a little while. The king, Sabina added in explanation, was examining the treaty Queen Maud had made with King David of Scotland. Letice tapped her knife and spoon together and everyone except Sabina turned to look at her. She made a few gestures; Magdalene nodded.

"Someone told Letice that what is delaying the king's confirmation of the treaty is the dissatisfaction of the barons of the north."

"They are the most affected," the man said, but his eyes were on Sabina's hand as she walked her fingers over the table toward her cup.

Wondering if he were feigning lack of interest, Magdalene enlarged on the theme. "The barons do not like the terms, which might give the Scots some advantage if the treaty were to be broken, particularly because the truce arranged by the pope's legate last November did not hold. But since Waleran de Meulan's twin brother, Robert of Leicester, was involved with the queen in the making of the treaty, it is likely that Stephen will approve it anyway."

The man shrugged. "It is the business of the English and the Scots," he said, making his indifference clear. "What is of more interest to me is that Letice can say what she needs to say, even without a voice."

"Sometimes," Magdalene replied, "but only to those who know her well. I have been thinking about teaching her to read and write—"

"Teaching her to read and write!" the man echoed, looking shocked. "What for? And who would teach a whore such things?"

So for all his courtesy, he has a churchman's attitude toward women, Magdalene thought. "What for?" she repeated. "To ease her spirit. So when she is bursting with a thought and cannot find a way to say what is in her heart, she could write it. And who would teach her? I would." She laughed aloud at his expression. "From whom did *I* learn? Why, of course, from a churchman who did not wish to pay me in coin. I have found it a useful skill." Then she laughed again. "I am sorry that you cannot read him a lecture on the evil of teaching deep mysteries to such fallible creatures as women, and whores at that. He is some years dead, poor man. He kept his purse strings drawn tight, but I liked him anyway."

"Because he did not think you weak and fallible?"

"No, because he knew what I was and found me no worse, if no better, than the rest of humankind."

He shook his head, smiling. "I cannot complain that what he did would not much help to save your soul when I am here—which surely will not help to save mine."

"That is easily amended," Sabina said, faultlessly

using her knife to spear right through the chunk of meat on the last piece of gravy-soaked bread. "If you are troubled, you have only to follow the path in the back garden to the gate in the church wall. It is just on a latch. You can go through, around the apse of the church, and into the north door. Cross in front of the altar to the south door, which leads into the monks' quarters, and I think you will find a bell that will summon a priest."

"How convenient," the man said, his full lips twitching. "Is the offering expected as high as the price here?"

Magdalene shook her head. "I, who have been treated with forbearance, can ill afford such a jest. The prior of the monastery is a gentle man of tender conscience. He has never been here himself and I believe him of a perfectly pure life, but I imagine that he writhes with the pain he thinks such sinners must feel and wishes to provide relief. If bad conscience draws from those who sin among us a substantial offering, well, it is not *exacted* by the church."

Before he could answer, Ella said suddenly, "One of the brothers told me I was excom-com-communicate and damned. He was very angry." Tears stood in her bright eyes. "Is that terrible bad?"

"For some, it might be," the man answered gently. "I do not think it applies to you, my child."

"Thank you," Sabina whispered in his ear. "She is truly an innocent. She does not understand the demands of her body, only obeys them. And I do not believe she has the power to control herself any more than an infant can control its bowels."

He squeezed her hand, and found Magdalene was smiling at him. He raised a brow. She nodded. He smiled at Letice, leaned across and touched Ella's cheek.

"Perhaps next time," he said to her, and then turned to Sabina. "Are you ready?" he asked. She nodded, smiling.

Ella and Letice retired to their rooms almost as soon as the door of Sabina's chamber closed behind her and her client. Magdalene took her embroidery, pulled the candles close, and sat working for some time to make sure that the new client would take no undue liberties with her woman. There was no indication that the man would turn nasty, but anyone who arrived without a recommendation from a known client made Magdalene uneasy.

There was something else about the man that made her uneasy. She was certain he was foreign, and his interest in the whereabouts of the king implied that what he carried in the pouch might be for or of interest to King Stephen. Normally, what she and her women learned from or about their clients, except for public news, was kept secret. They might discuss it among themselves, but they did not sell information or spread it with gossip. However, Magdalene was indebted for many favors and kindnesses to William of Ypres, and William was being supplanted in King Stephen's favor by Waleran de Meulan. So, should she send William news of this man's coming?

She sighed and raised her head, blinked smarting eyes. She did not know his name or even from where he came, though from his accent, she suspected Italy. Would her information be of any value? She blinked again and rubbed her eyes. She was, she decided, too tired to think the matter through and there was no need to do anything until morning. Possibly by then, Sabina might have learned enough, or the man himself might say more during breakfast. Finally she rose, walked silently down the corridor, and pressed her ear to Sabina's door.

After a moment she heard Sabina laugh and her client exclaim over his own laughter, and she smiled and turned back to the common room. There she carefully put away her work and extinguished the candles on the table and the torchettes on each side of the room, replacing the one near the front door with a fresh one, which she left burning.

There was light enough when she left the door of her room open to undress, fold her clothing onto the chest that stood against one wall, and slip into bed. Because the client seemed a good man and clearly desired privacy, she was troubled by her intention of mentioning him to William, but William was an old friend.

Her doubts kept her wakeful until she heard soft voices in the corridor. After a while she heard the key scrape in the lock, but she did not hear Sabina's footsteps returning. Surely he was not taking Sabina with him? Magdalene lay listening anxiously and then snorted gently at her own silliness. Probably his meeting place was close . . . even in the church itself, and he had told Sabina he would not be long away. The evening was mild. Likely Sabina had decided to sit in the garden and wait for him rather than chance she would fall asleep and not hear him knocking, which would cause him to ring the bell and wake the whole household.

A meeting in the church and churchly opinions, Magdalene thought sleepily, and the very sober, but rich clothing. A church messenger? The idea was somehow satisfactory; her eyes closed, her breathing deepened.

Two

It seemed only moments later, but it could have been hours, when Magdalene was startled awake by a clatter, a thud, and then Sabina's voice, thin with terror, crying her name. She sprang from her bed, grasping at the bedrobe that hung from a peg nearby on the wall, but did not stop to draw it on.

A shadow blundered into the wall, and the thin, breathless, despairing cry came again. "Magdalene!"

She dropped her bedrobe, caught at Sabina's groping hands, and drew the girl into her arms. Sabina was panting and shaking, totally disoriented by fear.

"He is dead," she whispered. "Dead."

"Who?" Magdalene whispered in return. "Who is dead?"

Sabina's voice rose to a thin wail. "He. He. The man I lay with."

"Your client is dead?" Magdalene's voice also rose. "He died in your bed?"

A hand grasped Magdalene's shoulder and squeezed hard. She only barely prevented herself from shrieking with shock, managing to swallow the cry because the hand had released her. Letice ran to shut Ella's door.

Magdalene closed her eyes and swallowed, whispered, "Thank you," when Letice returned. But Letice put her hand on Magdalene's mouth and drew her and Sabina from the corridor into the common room.

There, where the still-burning torchette gave better light, her eyes widened and her mouth opened with shock. She touched Magdalene and then seized Sabina's hands, which she raised into the light and held before Magdalene's eyes. Magdalene drew a gasping breath. Sabina's hands were covered with blood.

"What happened?" Magdalene whispered, beginning to tremble herself. In her mind rose an image of her own hands also stained red with fresh blood. "Did he try to hurt you so that you had to turn the knife on him?"

"No, no, I did not," Sabina whimpered. "I did not. Oh, God help me. If you think I killed him, who will believe me?"

"I will believe anything you tell me, Sabina—" Magdalene had reason enough to say that with passion; no one would have believed her, either. "But if the man is dead in your bed—"

"No! Not in my bed. On the church porch."

"On the church porch?" Magdalene echoed.

From Letice, standing beside them, came an audible sigh of relief. Then, as if released from a paralysis of fear, she dragged her eyes from the dark stains on Sabina's hands and garments, snatched up a half-burned candle from the table and lit it at the burning torchette. Seeing her hurry down the corridor puzzled Magdalene, but not enough to draw her mind from the wonderful fact that the dead man was on the church porch, not in Sabina's bed. There was no reason for anyone to associate him with her establishment.

She drew a breath of relief so deep that it stretched her chest and abdomen, which made her aware of a stiffness on her skin. A glance showed her that she was marked with splotches of drying blood. Her eyes fixed with loathing and horror on the marks, and a scream struggled in her throat, but at that moment Letice came back. Magdalene realized Lettice had come from the kitchen with water for washing the sticky mess from Sabina—and from herself, too. She pushed away the memories that were twisting her mind.

"Come," Magdalene said softly, leading a shaking and sobbing Sabina to the bench at the head of the table. "Sit down before you fall. How did you come to find the poor man?"

Sabina drew a deep breath, straightened her back, and released the hold she had kept on Magdalene. "He asked to be let out just after the bells rang for Compline," she said, "and of course I closed the door behind him so he would not think I was trying to hear where he went. But he had told me he would not be long, that his meeting place was near, so I thought I would wait in the garden. It was lovely, not cold, and I could hear the service being sung in the church. So after all was quiet and I was sure the brothers had gone to bed, I thought I would just step in and say a prayer."

She had been speaking quietly, but suddenly she huddled in on herself and began to shiver. "It is forbidden! So I was not allowed—"

"Sabina," Magdalene interrupted sharply, "do not be such a goose. Do you think God would have a man murdered just to warn a whore away from a church? That is the work of the devil, not of God. Besides, you pray in the church all the time and the place was never before strewn with dead bodies."

Sabina, who had been crying quietly, sniffed and lifted her head. "No. But it was so horrible. I was laughing, you see. I had heard the sacristan cry out 'Who is there?' and then someone running and I thought it was a pair of lovers Brother Paulinus had frightened away. After I heard him close the door, I went to the porch, and . . . and . . ."

She shuddered and began to cry again, and Magdalene

patted her shoulder comfortingly. After a few moments she asked, "Are you sure he was dead?"

Sabina sobbed harder. "There was a knife sticking out of his neck, and blood, so much blood, a whole pool . . ."

She started to raise her hands to her face, but Letice seized them and pushed them into a basin she had set on the table. The bottom was black with wood ash, and Letice used one hand to rub that over Sabina's and the other to prod Magdalene and point to the candles. Magdalene nodded but went to check the shutters before she lit the candles. She knew the Watch kept an eye on her house and did not want them to notice lights glinting from the windows on this night.

When the candles were lit, Letice examined Magdalene carefully and helped her wash away any spot of blood that Sabina's hands had transferred to her body. Magdalene then put on her bedgown, and she and Letice went over every inch of Sabina, her gown, her undertunic, her cloak, her shoes, her staff, which Letice had found lying in the corridor, even the tips of her hair, cleaning all as well as they could.

"There, love, there," Magdalene soothed. "You are clean. Your clothes are clean. Forget this. Forget the man. No one will ever know he lay with you. We are not to blame if the person he met killed him, and we must not be called guilty so that the real killer can escape."

"But—"

"No. Put it out of your mind. There is no way for anyone to connect him with this house at all, unless by misfortune he was seen leading his horse—oh, my God, his horse! It is still in our stable."

The three women froze. The horse. All realized that the horse could not be led out into the street and driven away. The clattering hooves would surely wake someone and attract the Watch.

"The beast cannot be loose in the streets while the

body is on the church porch," Magdalene said slowly. "We will have to get it into the churchyard."

"How?" Sabina cried, shaking more than ever. "It is impossible! Oh, forget me. Let me confess that I found him and let them do what they will to me."

Magdalene slapped her gently and then shook her. "This is no time for hysterics, even though you have cause enough. First of all, we do not abandon our own. Not in this house! Secondly, no one will do anything to you if you obey me."

Letice sat down beside Sabina and put an arm around her, but with the other hand she pointed toward where the stable was, then cupped her hand and blew into it.

"Yes," Magdalene said. "As Letice points out, even if you sacrificed yourself, you silly girl, the horse would not disappear into thin air. It would still be in our stable." She stared at the floor for a moment, then said, "Letice, go wake Dulcie. She will have to stay with Sabina while you and I move the horse."

Between signs and words repeated several times, though not so loudly as to wake Ella, the situation was explained to the maid. Dulcie did not seem surprised or frightened, and Magdalene suddenly wondered if the cookhouse she had come from was in a place where dead bodies were not uncommon. The question seemed answered as Dulcie calmly examined Sabina's clothes and said they would need washing or the stains Letice's wiping could not remove might set. Not to worry, she said to Magdalene, she would make sure no one knew she was washing clothes. The garments would soak well under pots and dishes, and dry hidden behind herbs near the fireplace. Then she gave the half-fainting girl a rough hug and led her away toward her room.

One problem solved. Magdalene told Letice to put on shoes and take a cloak, and followed that advice herself. Then she found a dark lantern on the bottom shelf. She lit it, but the thread of moon and starlight was enough and they did not need it to find the stable. Carefully closing the door, Magdalene unshuttered the lantern completely and then stood stock-still, staring open-mouthed at the disorder.

The horse was there, calmly lipping up some of the oats that had fallen from the bin in which they were stored. Clearly, someone had been searching through the feed for something hidden beneath it. Around the beast's feet was fresh hay strewn from bales broken when they had been tossed here and there. The saddle was hanging half off the rack on which it had originally been placed, and the saddlebags now lay on the ground open, their contents scattered over the floor.

"Oh, heaven," Magdalene whispered, raising the lantern and looking around. "The murderer must have been here searching for . . ."

Letice cocked her head on the side.

"For what?" Magdalene asked the question aloud for her in case she had guessed wrong, and when Letice nodded, answered it. "I have no idea. I wonder if . . . no, this is no time for wondering. Let us gather up everything that belongs in the saddlebags and rid ourselves of this sign of guilt."

As Letice gathered, Magdalene stowed as neatly as she could manage, although her hands began to shake from time to time. She did not waste any effort over excessive neatness however, partly because she did not know how neat the guest had been but more because she wanted the bags to seem to have been searched. When she had closed them and was about to lift the saddle to the horse's back, Letice stopped her, pointed to the horse, and made an arch with her hands. Then she walked the fingers of the left hand into the half arch that her right hand maintained and showed them getting stuck.

"You are right," Magdalen said. "I think we can get the horse through the gate, but certainly not wearing the saddle. You will have to carry the saddle while I lead the horse."

It was strange, Magdalene thought as she slipped the bit between the animal's teeth and fastened it to the halter, how everything tonight conspired to bring back memories of her life as Arabel de St. Foi. First the blood. . . . She pushed that thought away. And now the more pleasant memories of being mistress of her own small farm, of saddling and riding, dealing with horses. . . .

Silly beasts, she thought affectionately, so beautiful but so brainless. Everything frightened them. She paused as she was about to set the lantern down in a clear corner and close its shutters so she could open the stable doors. It would be hard to persuade a horse to pass through that low, narrow gate, especially in silence. It might balk or whinny. Magdalene bit her lip and then unwound the scarf that she had automatically used to cover her wealth of honey-gold hair. What a horse could not see would not cause it to balk. With soothing words and slow motions, she put the scarf over the horse's head so that its eyes were covered.

Except that Magdalene kept glancing at the moon and cursing herself for not remembering when it had risen and what hour its present position indicated, they had no trouble. The horse followed the pull on its halter docilely, and once Magdalene had pulled its head down level with its shoulders, passed through the gate without difficulty. On the other side, she removed her scarf and led the willing animal, who smelled fresh grass, into the graveyard. There she resaddled it, Letice helping as she could, leaving the girth somewhat loose, as a man might do who wished to ease his horse when he dismounted for some time but intended to continue his ride later.

Then Letice handed her the saddlebags. Magdalene gave Lettice the rein and started to lift the bags—and a light appeared in a window in the second-story dorter. Magdalene dropped to the ground, pulling Letice with her but keeping hold on the horse so it would stand still. Both huddled down on the ground, praying that if a monk on his way to the privy saw the animal, he would be too sleepy to do anything about it.

In a moment the light winked out. Magdalene jumped up and swung the saddlebags over. With shaking hands, she tried to fasten the straps to the loops on the saddle. One was half tied when she heard a bell. It was a faint, small bell, but she feared it might be the bell that woke the ringer to sound Matins, or worse, that the monk who made the light had seen them and was summoning others. She and Letice fled, silent, clinging to each other until they had latched the gate in the church wall behind them.

When they came near the back door, Letice pulled very gently on Magdalene's hand. Although she was shaking with fear and fatigue, Magdalene shook her head. "I am sorry, love," she murmured. "I know you are tired, but we must put the stable to rights. You know some of the monks wish to be rid of us. If Brother Paulinus decides he could accomplish that by saying the poor man came from this house, the stable must not look as if any animal had been there."

Letice sighed but followed without any further urging. Together they heaved the displaced bales into position, raked the hay and any soil in it out to the manure heap at the side, and swept the grain from the floor. When they were sure no one would guess that an animal had been stabled there that night, Magdalene took up the dark lantern, blew out the candle in it, and they returned to the house. Dulcie was waiting. She had emptied the wash water and put the bowl away, dried the table, straightened the benches, and put out the candles, so there was no sign of disturbance or disorder.

"Poor creature's asleep," Dulcie said. "Cried herself t' sleep. A strange sight it be t' see tears oozin' out from under those closed lids. Poor child. As if she didn' have enough trouble of her own."

"She will have no more from this," Magdalene said, facing her maid and speaking as slowly and clearly as she could. "You never saw that man here. We knew nothing of him." When Dulcie nodded, she sighed and added, "Since Sabina had nothing to do with it, I hope she will soon forget." With lips thinned to a hard line, she went to put away the dark lantern, then came back to take the maid's hand. "Thank you, Dulcie. You can go back to bed now."

The old woman bobbed her head. "No need of thanks. You done fer me. I do fer you. This be my house much as anyone else here."

When she had slumped away to her pallet in the kitchen, Magdalene put her arms around Letice. "Thank you, love. I do not know what I would have done without you. Is there anything else you can think of that we have left undone?"

Letice started to shake her head, then made her sign for Ella.

"I do not know what we can do about her." Magdalene sighed. "Pray that she will have forgotten the stranger or not remember what time he was here. To say anything to her will only fix his presence in her mind." She sighed again. "I am almost too tired to breathe. Let's go to bed and pray, that we will have time to think and clean up any loose ends in the morning."

That prayer was not answered. Soon after Prime, the bell by the back door began to ring and ring, and went on ringing until it pierced Dulcie's deafness. She crawled from her pallet, unshuttered a window a crack, and peered out. A tall, lean monk with ascetic hollows in his cheeks and dark circles under his eyes, carrying a staff, was yanking on the rope as if he wished to tear it down. Dulcie opened the shutter all the way.

"It be too early," she cried. "The ladies be asleep."

He shouted something at her, but Dulcie was sleepy and angry and did not try to make sense out of what was a dull cacophony to her. She shook her finger at him. "You should be ashamed 'f yourself, monk that y'

are, t' carry on so. If y' be so hot y' cannot wait till th'
ladies wake, hold it in yer hand or go down th' street
t' th' common stews."

The monk's face turned crimson and his eyes bulged
from his head with fury. He rushed toward the window,
waving his staff as if he would strike Dulcie with it.
She drew back and was about to slam the shutter shut
when Magdalene came into the room.

"Who is—"

By then, the monk was leaning in the window, holding the shutter back with one hand, and screaming that
he had never touched a whore and never would.

"Brother Paulinus!" Magdalene exclaimed. "What is
wrong? Wait. You will hurt yourself. Let me open the
door."

"Don' y' do it, dearie," Dulcie cried, shoving on the
shutter. "He's been locked up too long, he has. He's
gone all horny in th' brain."

"Hush," Magdalene said, barely choking back a laugh
and putting her fingers over Dulcie's lips. Then she
added loudly, "Brother Paulinus is very holy. He does
not wish to use our services."

Dulcie looked at her inquiringly, but since Magdalene
had said what she did to pacify Brother Paulinus, she
made no attempt to explain, only rushed to open the
back door. As soon as she saw the sacristan, she had
remembered what had happened the night before,
which, half asleep as she was, had at first slipped her
mind. It did not happen, she told herself, pretending to
fumble at the lock with the large key. Last night was a
night like any other, quiet. We worked; we talked; we
had no guests. I am frightened only because the brother
is so angry, because I do not understand what could
have brought the sacristan of the priory here at this
hour.

The lock gave. Magdalene pulled at the latch and the
door flew open, almost striking her. She jumped back
with a cry.

"I am so sorry Dulcie misspoke to you," she gasped. "She is deaf and did not understand what you were saying to her. What can I do for you, Brother Paulinus?"

"What can you do for me? Nothing, you filthy whore! To save your own soul, you can confess your crime and prepare to pay for it!"

Magdalene's jaw snapped shut. Despite many encounters with the monk over the years she had lived and worked in the Old Priory Guesthouse, and the fact that he was not alone in insulting her because of her profession, she could not quite come to terms with Brother Paulinus. Good intentions never held in his presence, and she never managed to act properly submissive. She did not know why others who said virtually the same things did not irritate her half as much.

"Crime?" she repeated, raising her brows. "Everything I and my women do, including eat and breathe, is a crime to you, Brother Paulinus." Only, this time there had been a crime, a real, terrible crime, not one of Brother Paulinus's imaginary lewdnesses. Ignoring the sudden, cold hollow that formed under her breast, Magdalene kept her voice calm and indifferent. "Whoring may be a sin, but that is upon my soul; it is not a crime in Southwark."

"Murder is a crime anywhere!" Brother Paulinus roared.

"Murder!" Magdalene did not try to hide the shudder that traveled over her. "Why do you speak of murder?"

"A man has been murdered on the north porch of our church, only feet away from desecrating the holy precinct."

"How dreadful!" Magdalene breathed, tears coming to her eyes as she remembered the pleasant man who was dead. But she could do nothing for him now and quickly found an excuse for the tears. "How sad, that one should come to harm so near God's sanctuary. I am sorry, but why carry this news to us with such urgency that you wake us near dawn?"

"Because it is your doing!"

"No!" Magdalene's lips thinned to a narrow line. "In this house there is no violence. True, we cause the 'little death,' but that brings joy and both man and woman rise from that 'death' refreshed."

"Blasphemy! How dare you speak of rising from death in terms of fornication?"

He waved his staff in rage, and Magdalene backed away down the corridor. He followed, but the staff struck a wall and he set it upright before him with a curse.

Before she could speak, he shouted, "No! I know your tricks. I will not let you distract me. The murdered man came from your house and he died on the porch of mine. We are men of God. We do not kill. You are creatures of the devil, so corrupt that it drove you to madness when the man you had soiled with sin wished to cleanse himself. You crept out and stabbed him— and doubtless stole his purse, too."

Magdalene shook her head. "I do not know what you are talking about, Brother Paulinus. No man who visits this house ever comes to bodily harm through me or my women. We would soon be ruined if those who came here were robbed or died. Nor do we corrupt. A guest comes to us of his own free will. We do not sit by the gate or hang from the windows tempting passersby. I grieve that a man is dead, but it is nothing to do with me or mine."

"The man had to come from your house! The porter did not recognize him. Brother Godwine swears that the dead man never came through the gate, nor his horse, either. So he must have come from the back gate—from your house. Someone from your house followed him and stabbed him to death."

"No one went to the church from this house last night," Magdalene said calmly. "And it is impossible for a horse to pass through the gate. It is too low and narrow. Last night was a night like any other. Sabina sang; Letice, Ella, and I embroidered. No one even went out after dark."

"You forget." Sabina's rich voice came from behind Magdalene. "I went out just around Compline. I sat in the garden and listened to the singing from the church."

Magdalene's heart leapt into her throat and choked any protest. Was Sabina still so shaken that she felt she had to confess? She turned to face her woman and saw that Letice was standing beside Sabina, holding her sister whore's arm.

"You must have seen the man leave the house and go to the church," Paulinus snapped, smiling in triumph. "You must have seen someone follow him. Which of the women was it?"

Sabina gently removed her arm from Letice's grasp and came closer, close enough for Paulinus to see her sealed eyes and that there was nothing behind the closed lids. He gasped and recoiled. Sabina smiled.

"I saw nothing. I am blind. But my ears are very good. No one came out of the house while I sat in the garden, and certainly no horse passed me."

Magdalene let her breath ease out, but carefully. She did not want Paulinus to suspect she had been holding it.

"You are lying," Paulinus thundered, "adding to the black sin that stains your soul. You can still save yourself from damnation, from burning in an eternal fire, by confession."

"I am not lying," Sabina said. "As you said, I would be a fool to lie and add to the burden of sin on my soul. This is the truth, every word. I sat alone in the garden from Compline until after the service was over, and no one came out of the house or passed through the garden with or without a horse while I was there."

This, Magdalene was sure, *was* perfectly true and she decided to add her own true lie. "None of my women had friends who stayed overnight last night," she said.

"I know, because I collect the charges for their lodging."

"If you do not tell the truth, you will all be damned! You!" He pointed at Letice. "Abandon the sinking souls of these other women. Save yourself. Tell me who followed the poor murdered man and slew him."

Letice stared back, shaking her head.

"Contumacious woman, speak! I command you!"

"I wish your command *could* take effect," Magdalene said, struggling to maintain her gravity. "But I am afraid you will have as little success as that king who ordered the tide to stay. Letice is mute from birth and cannot speak."

"Is there no one in this house that is whole? The deaf, the mute, the blind—" His voice checked suddenly and his eyes gleamed. "And the weak-minded," he added softly. "Where is your madwoman, whore? She will tell me the truth."

Magdalene's heart sank. Ella had not responded either to the ringing bell or to the voices in the corridor. She might be asleep; more likely she had heard the monk's angry shouts and was hiding in her bedchamber with the covers over her head.

"Brother Paulinus, you know the prior has given special dispensation to Ella not to be questioned by the priest. However many years since her birth, she is still a child—"

"A child as steeped in sin as any of you!" The sacristan's eyes gleamed and a satisfied smile pulled his lips thinner. "The prior is not here, and the priory is in my charge until he returns. Where is your madwoman kept?"

"Ella is not a madwoman and is not 'kept' anywhere," Magdalene snapped, considering whether she should refuse to allow him to question Ella. She dismissed the idea almost as soon as it came to her. A refusal to let Ella answer questions about matters of simple fact—rather than complex concepts, like the state of her soul—must raise suspicion even in less prejudiced minds than that of Brother Paulinus. She shrugged. "She is asleep in her chamber. I will awaken her and bring her to you."

"Stay!" Brother Paulinus ordered as she started to go to Ella's doorway. "You will not put words in her mouth. I will go within and question her where she cannot see the signs you make to enforce her silence."

Magdalene felt the jaws of a vise closing on her throat. Had she relaxed her will, she would have panted like a terrified beast. Fool, she said to herself, you have been in much worse danger. Even if Ella admits there was still a guest in the house when she went to bed, no one can prove the dead man was that guest. She began a slow gesture toward Ella's doorway, trying to remember whether Ella knew that the guest had intended to stay the night. More frightening was the fact that they would not know what Ella had told him and he could use her words to set traps for them. Unless . . .

She forced her lips into a slow smile. "Alone?" she asked archly. "In a closed bedchamber with a known whore?" She lowered her eyes and found a soft laugh. "Oh, very well." Her smile broadened. "That is her room."

"You would not dare!" Paulinus exclaimed.

"Dare what, Brother Sacristan?" Magdalene asked blandly. "Speak the truth?"

He glared at them. Magdalene managed to look puzzled. She knew that behind her Letice and Sabrina were wearing broad grins.

"I will leave the door open, but none of you are to stand where the madwoman can see you."

"You desire that we stand witness to your questioning?" Magdalene asked.

The sacristan snarled an affirmative and stamped through the doorway, shouting, "Get up at once. You cannot pretend to have been asleep. I know you heard us."

The women heard Ella utter a squeak of alarm, echoed by Brother Paulinus's cry of consternation.

"Cover yourself," he roared.

"You told me to get up at once," Ella protested. "Everyone sleeps naked. Why did you not look away if you did not wish to see me?"

All three women bit their lips. The danger that Ella might expose what they wished to conceal remained, but Brother Paulinus was going to discover that questioning her required a special touch.

"Where were you last night?" he asked sharply.

"Why, here, in bed," Ella replied. "We never go out at night unless it is very hot and Magdalene lets us sit in the garden."

"And who was with you?"

"No one."

Magdalene and her women held their breath, but Ella did not, as she might well have done, go on to explain that she had wanted the last guest but that he had chosen Sabina. Letice took one of Magdalene's hands, Sabina took the other. All prayed that Ella had forgotten.

"You must not lie to a priest," the sacristan said, not shouting but slowly and carefully so that she would understand. "If you lie to me, you will be damned and burn for eternity, your flesh will be torn with nail-studded whips, your limbs will be broken and you will be forced to walk on them. Torments I cannot even name will be applied to you if you do not speak the truth to me."

Magdalene's hands tightened on those of her women and she heard Sabina muttering a litany of curses under her breath. They could hear Ella sobbing. Tears formed in Magdalene's eyes. The poor child would have nightmares.

"I *am* telling the truth. I had no friend with me last night. Earlier—" She stopped abruptly, remembering that she was not supposed to speak about the men who visited them.

"So there *was* a man here." There was a vicious satisfaction in the sacristan's voice.

Magdalene edged to the door frame and peeped in, hoping that Ella would catch a glimpse of her and be less frightened. Poor Ella was trembling, and crystal tears rolled down her cheeks.

"A . . . a friend was with me f-for a little while," she stammered.

"Oh, a friend? A man you do not know, had never seen before in your life, and will never see again? That kind of friend?"

"Oh, no," Ella said, blinking with surprise. "I know him very well. He has been my friend for a long time, several years, I think. And if nothing unusual happens, I will see him again on Friday."

There was a moment of silence, the sacristan being taken aback, but then he asked, "And your friend's name?"

To give a name, Ella knew, was absolutely forbidden, but the question did not trouble her. She would not need to lie. She never could remember the men's names.

"I do not recall his name," she said earnestly. "Magdalene might be able to tell you, or she might not. Some men do not give their names. I—"

"A friend of many years who still will not tell you his name?" He started to say he did not believe her and add to his threats about the results of lying to a priest, but Ella's light laugh stopped him.

"I was just going to tell you. I call him Poppe, and he calls me Little Flower. He brings me pretty things. See, I will show you. He brought me a blue hair ribbon yesterday."

The sacristan ground his teeth. "I suppose you do not know what this friend looks like either?"

"Of course I know what he looks like," Ella said indignantly. She had never been told not to describe the men she lay with. "He has good strong thighs with hard muscles, and a little round belly. But it is not all soft and flabby; it is firm and nice to kiss, with a line of hair growing down from his navel—that is nice, too, a neat little split, not bulging out like some. And the hair around his rod is—"

"Stop!" the sacristan roared, finding his voice, which seemed to have been suspended by shock. "Harlot! Whore!"

Ella said meekly, "Yes?"

Magdalene slid back out of sight, she, Letice, and Sabina pressing their hands against their mouths and grinding their teeth to hold back whoops of laughter. They were safe now. Ella's mind was fixed on Master Buchuinte. The sacristan probably could not get her to think of anything else.

"I meant his face," the sacristan snarled. "What does his face look like?"

"Face?" Ella repeated blankly. "It is a face like any other, not specially pretty nor specially ugly. A nice face; it smiles a lot."

Even the sacristan could see that she was trying to be helpful and describe the man, but it did not really matter what he looked like. The detailed description she had given of his body had already eliminated the possibility that she had slept with the dead man. The corpse, washed and prepared for burial, had been lean and hard.

"A nice smile," Ella continued brightly. "His lips are nice, too. Firm and not wet—"

"Enough. Now tell me what you did last night."

Momentarily, tension again seized Magdalene, and then Ella's little-girl voice, sounding rather doubtful, said, "Poppe was here from about Nones until near Vespers. I am not sure I remember *everything* we did, but first—"

Magdalene breathed again, bit her lip again when Brother Paulinus shouted, "No, not that. I mean, what did you do after your 'friend' left you?"

"Oh, that is easy. I ate my evening meal and then

Magdalene sent me to bed. I fell asleep right away."

There had been one danger point. Ella might have remembered flirting with the dead man, but Magdalene hoped she had put it out of her mind because she had been scolded for it. Apparently she had. Now there was only the possibility that the sacristan would not believe her and would tell her that another man had been there and ask more specific questions. But their luck held. Brother Paulinus had had enough of questioning Ella. She heard him mutter, "Stupid bitch," and then the swish of his staff. Ella cried out, and Magdalene leapt into the room and seized the staff as he raised it again.

"Ella has done nothing to deserve being beaten," she cried. "She answered your questions as well as she could. You cannot beat her because she did not say what you wished to hear."

Paulinus yanked at the staff, but Letice and Sabina had also laid hold of it, and the sacristan's breath drew in sharply at the expressions on their faces. The mute began to twist the staff, the blind woman following her motion. With a gasp of mingled rage and fear, Brother Paulinus let it go before they tore it from his hand. He pushed past them, then past Dulcie, who was about to enter the room carrying a large, heavy pan with a long handle.

"How dare you!" he shrieked, turning to glare at them. "Your bold evil-doing is a result of the prior's leniency. But you cannot threaten me or escape punishment for your crime." He strode on, then stopped at the door and turned, smiling this time. "You have undone yourselves." His voice was replete with satisfaction. "I have a friend close to the Bishop of Winchester, who is here in Southwark. He will tell the bishop what you have done. Threats! Whoring! Murder! You are already damned. Now I will see you all hanged."

Three

As the sacristan went out the door, all five women stood paralyzed, staring after him. When he slammed it behind him, Letice rushed to take Ella in her arms, brushing back her hair and kissing her.

"Why?" Ella sobbed. "Why did he hit me? I did not lie to him. I did not!"

"No, love," Magdalene said. "You told the truth and you did not deserve to be hurt. You are a good girl, and he—despite being in holy orders—is a bad man. Do not cry, love. Come, wash your face and mouth and I will find a sweet for you to break your fast. Forget him."

She went and hugged Ella, too, and the girl blinked away her tears and smiled.

"Are you all right now?" Magdalene asked. Ella nodded. "And can you wash and dress by yourself, or do you want Letice to help you?"

"I can do it."

"Good, love. And when you are ready, go to Dulcie in the kitchen. She will give you a honey cake and milk."

Ella's smile brightened even more and she nodded enthusiastically. They went out, Magdalene stopping

Dulcie, who had turned away, to tell her about the milk and honey cake. Then she drew the other women into the front room.

"You heard him," she said. "He is determined to find us guilty—and I think it is not only because he deplores the whorehouse for being here, but because he wishes to use us to make trouble for the prior."

"I think you are right," Sabina said. "And if he succeeds . . ." She shook her head.

"If he succeeds, we will need to find a new house," Magdalene said grimly. "I wish I knew who that friend is that he spoke of as being close to the bishop. But even if the bishop is not turned against us—where else would he get the rent I pay?—Paulinus would make our lives a misery. We must somehow prove him wrong, or at least prove the dead man did not come from this house."

Letice raised her expressive hands and made a query of her whole face.

Although she had not seen Letice's gesture or expression, Sabina voiced her doubts. "How? How can we prove he was *not* here? Is it possible to prove that a thing did not happen?"

"First we must make sure there is no sign of the man or his horse in the house or the stable. Letice and I cleaned the stable last night, but go and look again, Letice. He was with you, Sabina. Are you sure that he left nothing in your room? Remember, he intended to return, so he might have been careless about leaving, say, gloves or—oh, any small thing—behind."

"There was nothing in the bed or on the chest where I bid him place his clothes. I did feel about last night after he left so I could put everything in one place, but . . . but there was something a little strange. He took a very long time to take off his clothes."

"He was probably just standing and staring at you, admiring you," Magdalene said, knowing Sabina would hear the smile in her voice.

"No." A frown creased Sabina's brow. "I heard him moving about and I asked if he wanted me to help him undress. He laughed and said 'no,' but . . . but his voice . . . he was not facing me when he spoke. Magdalene, I think he had stepped up on the chest. Now I think back, it seems to me I heard it creak. I think . . . I think he was hiding something."

"The pouch," Magdalene breathed. "He never took it off or put it aside, even when he was eating. If he did not trust the man he was to meet, he could have decided to leave it here. He would have thought that you would not see him hide it and thus it would be safe from you and from the rest of us. He stood on the chest, you say?"

"I think so." Sabina's voice was tremulous. "Or maybe he opened it, although that is less likely. I would have heard the latch and the hinges, I think. Still, you and Letice had better come and look through all my things. Who knows what else he might have hidden?"

Magdalene agreed but bid Sabina wait while she looked carefully at the common-room chest and the area around it where she had laid the dead man's cloak the previous afternoon. He must have taken the cloak when he went out to the church, but there was the possibility that something had dropped from it. There was nothing, not even any strands of the fur lining caught on a rough edge or splinter. Magdalene pushed the chest forward, but there was nothing behind it or on the floor. By then, Letice had returned and indicated that the stable was clear of any sign that an animal had been left there.

They went to Sabina's room then, and the worst was over at once. Magdalene, the tallest of the women, set a low stool on the chest there and, steadied by Letice, climbed up. Behind the horizontal beams that supported the floor of the loft, there was a hollow. Stuffed into that, just beyond easy reach, was the supple leather pouch the dead man had carried. It was a good, safe spot; had not Sabina said she heard the man climb on the chest, they probably would not have found it.

Magdalene uttered a small sigh of disappointment as she pulled the pouch from its concealment. "You were right, Sabina," she said, climbing down, the pouch caught in the crook of her arm. "But I could wish you had not been, or had remembered this last night."

"I am sorry," Sabina whispered.

Magdalene sighed. "Oh, no, love, of course you could not. You were half out of your mind." Shrugging, she dropped the pouch onto the bed beside Sabina. "Still, too bad we could not push it into one of the saddlebags. Now one of us will have to go downriver and drop it in." Then she bit her lip and added, "Letice, go and lock the back door. We will need some warning if Brother Paulinus remembers he was too busy demanding a confession to be practical and search for signs of the man's presence. He might get a rush of sense to the head and return to do that."

"What will you do with the pouch?" Sabina breathed.

"Hide it between my legs. Thank God, it is soft. I can wrap it in a rag and say I am bleeding. After the shock Ella gave him and our looks and laughter over his desire to question a known whore 'alone,' I do not think he will demand a search of my flux rags. If he does, I will simply refuse and say he wants to find an excuse for a lewd examination. Now," she said when Letice returned, "let us search carefully. Not even a curly hair should be left behind."

She and Letice were thorough, unfolding and shaking out every garment in the chest, looking behind it and under it, taking the mattress off the bed and examining the frame and straps. Behind the chest they found one Italian silver coin, which Magdalene laid atop the chest. When they were through searching, she picked it up again and sadly rubbed it between her fingers.

"Poor man," she sighed. "He seemed a cheerful, kindly person." Then she looked from the coin in her hand to the pouch, which was lying on the bed. "He was richly dressed and riding a fine horse," she murmured thoughtfully. "And his purse was full of coins, but they were small coins. I saw when he emptied the purse into his hand to pay the fee I named. He had perhaps ten whole pennies, some halfpence, and a handful of farthings. Who will lay odds with me," she went on, looking from one woman to the other, "that there is more coin in this pouch?"

"Not I," Sabina said. "I felt when you put it down on the bed that it was heavy. Coin is heavy."

Letice grinned and shook her head. But then she frowned and touched the intricately tied cord that held the pouch closed. She made a gesture of cutting and shook her head.

"You know, that is a wise thought, Letice," Magdalene said. "If we cut the cord and someone should somehow find the pouch before we can be rid of it, we have hung ourselves." Then she smiled broadly. "No matter. I think I can undo that and even retie it, or make another similar knot. My naughty archdeacon—the one who taught me to read and write—showed me several church knots."

She picked up the pouch, but Sabina said, "We had better dress first. If Brother Paulinus returns, he will want to know what we were doing all this time."

"Clinging to each other and weeping with terror," Magdalene said, her lips twisting.

Letice threw back her head and laughed, making no sound beyond a slight outrush of air; then she tugged at her nightrobe and went to her own chamber. Magdalene did the same, and as soon as she was dressed, went to the kitchen, where Ella was prattling away to Dulcie, who nodded and smiled, although she probably made out about one word in ten. Having sent Ella off to get dressed and told her to work on her embroidery when she was ready, Magdalene showed Dulcie the pouch, made clear that it was the dead man's and that they must be rid of it as soon as she had seen what was inside.

Dulcie nodded. "I be fillin' it wit' rocks and stickin' it in wit' the sheets that need washin'," she said. "On me way to th' laundress, it'll fall in th' river."

"Are you sure, Dulcie? If you were caught—"

"Course I be sure. Who looks at 'n old woman wit' a basket 'f laundry? If you 'r one 'f th' others went out wit' it, there'd be ten pairs eyes on y' every minnit."

When Magdalene came from the kitchen, Dulcie following, the others were waiting, worried frowns alternating with frankly greedy glances. Letice tapped her arm and pointed upward. Magdalene glanced up, too, but then shook her head.

"It is too dusty up in the loft and we have no time to clean. If we were up there when someone came, we would be sure to betray that fact somehow. If someone knocks, I will gather up the pouch and run to my room to tie it between my legs. No one can think it unnatural for me to be in my room. With the shutters still closed, I think we are safe enough here."

She then laid out on the table one of the long, narrow cloths she stuffed with rags to absorb the blood of her flux. In the center, she placed the pouch. If there was any disturbance, she need only roll the cloth around the pouch and run into her room. Then she began to work on the knot. It was not difficult once she found the key loop, and the pouch was soon open. Holding the heavy, round shapes at the bottom, which she was sure were coins, Magdalene tipped it slowly, so it would disgorge the rest of its contents without scattering them all over the table and the floor.

The first thing to slide out was a heavy square packet of parchment, made heavier yet by the large lead seal fastened to the silken cords that bound the document. "Oh, no!" Magdalene started to say when another document, less elaborately sealed, with red wax but bearing the same design, slid out atop the first. Following that was a letter, then another, these also with seals but deliberately left open.

Hoping against hope, Magdalene bent closer to peer at the large lead seal. Around it were words in Latin. She could not read them, but from their position, she guessed they were a motto; within were two stylized faces and above them, the letters S.PE and S.PA. She could not understand the motto, but she knew well enough that S.PE meant Saint Peter and S.PA meant Saint Paul. Biting her lip, she turned the seal over and made out the name—Innocent II.

"Mary have mercy on us," Magdalene said in a failing voice. "That is the pope's seal, and it is lead. This is a papal bull our guest was carrying. Oh, my God, we dare not destroy it."

"A papal bull?" Sabina put out her hand and Magdalene brought it to the seal. The blind woman's fingers touched it delicately. "Are these letters?"

"Yes. On one side is the name of the pope, on the other the faces of Saint Peter and Saint Paul."

Feeling around the parchment packet, Sabina found the second document with its wax seal. "This is the same," she said. "Is it also a bull?"

"No, the seal is not metal. Likely that is a letter." Magdalene's mouth twisted. "Doubtless an important one."

Letice picked up the letter and drew her eating knife. Without actually touching it, she made signs of sliding the knife under the wax.

"It is almost certainly in Latin," Magdalene said. "I will not be able to read it. Let me look at these first." With the words, she took up the open letters. "Ah, this one is in French. It is a letter of credit on the goldsmith Basyngs and those associated with his house, authorizing Baldassare de Firenze to obtain from them a substantial sum of money." She sighed. "His name was Baldassare de Firenze. How sad that I cannot tell anyone who he was."

Letice touched the letter.

"No," Magdalene said, setting it aside and taking up

the second one. "There is no way we could use it, not without being hung for murder." She unfolded the other, read some, nodded, and set that atop the first. "This one is also in French; it is a letter of introduction, asking in the pope's name for any and all to give what help he needs to Baldassare de Firenze. That has been unfolded and used several times. The letter of credit has had less use." She grimaced. "He must have been using the money in the pouch first."

Now she reached in and drew the coins from the pouch and breathed a sigh of relief. They were good English pennies, showing a little wear but no clipping, and mixed in with them, two coins that glinted yellow. She picked them out and stared at them. Gold. No one used gold coin, but no doubt the papal treasury had some hoarded. Small as they were, they were heavy. Meant to be changed for silver by a goldsmith. She sighed and shook her head.

"They are of no use to us," she said and slipped them back into the pouch.

"You be goin' t' drop gold in t' river?" Dulcie asked, eyes round as saucers.

Magdalene looked at her. "No," she said, loudly and clearly. "We cannot throw the pouch in the river. This"—she touched it —"is a bull from the pope. It is *very* important."

"To who?" Dulcie asked. "It'll get us hung if we don' be rid 'f it."

Magdalene bit her lip. Letice drew her knife again and pointed to the red-sealed letter. Magdalene wrung her hands for a moment and then nodded. "Yes, all right. Try to lift the seal, Letice. Maybe I will find a name, a few words that look familiar. . . ."

A nerve-racking period followed while Letice found a thin enough and broad enough knife for her purpose. Then came the task of heating it evenly, bracing the letter, sliding the glowing blade under half the seal, easing the parchment out from under the knife while it still supported the seal. Half the time Magdalene found herself unable to look, but Letice was amazingly skilled. She had done this often before, Magdalene thought, as Letice signed to her to unfold the parchment while she eased the seal off the cooling blade so it would not stick and then slid the knife back to support the fragile wax. Because she is mute, Magdalene thought. Because her previous master had assumed she could never tell what she had done. They had used her to remove seals, and perhaps to affix them on different documents.

With an effort, she brought her mind back to this document. The letter was, as she had guessed, in Latin, but the first few lines told her something. It was from the pope—she recognized the name Innocent II—and it was to King Stephen. Well, she had expected that, too, but it was a disappointment; if it had been to one of the bishops, she would have considered getting rid of it. The Church would easily survive a delayed instruction from the pope. But the king . . . she scanned the letter anxiously, found the name Matilda, and groaned.

"What is it?" Sabina asked anxiously.

"A letter to the king about Empress Matilda, old king Henry's daughter, who was supposed to be queen but the barons would not have it."

"Because she was a woman?" Sabina asked.

"Not only that. There was much talk about her in Oxford—all those students and clerics and churchmen gossip ten times worse than women do—about her pride and stubbornness. Well, she did not oppose Stephen when he first took the crown, and then we moved here, where we have fewer clerks among our clients. But I know that Matilda had set a plea before the pope, claiming that she was the rightful queen because Stephen had violated his oath to the late King Henry to accept her as queen. That clerk of the Bishop of Rochester's who comes to visit us every time he is in London told me that when he was waiting to see Letice."

The mute nodded and made an urgent gesture, followed by several others. Tears rose to her eyes when she saw that neither Magdalene nor Dulcie looked enlightened. She bit her lip and moved a finger as if she were writing.

"The clerk," Magdalene said. "He told you . . ."

Letice made the sign of a peaked hat over her head, held out her hand, pointed to the finger on which a bishop wears his ring.

"About his bishop."

Letice pointed south, moved her hand like waves, then pointed to the pouch and the bull.

"The bishop went to the pope? About Matilda's plea?"

Letice pointed to her ear, then made the sign of writing.

"The clerk and the bishop were going to listen and report about Matilda's plea?"

To that, Letice nodded. Sabina shifted on the bench, reaching out to touch the pile of coins and smiling slightly. "Why should it matter to us whether Stephen is king or Matilda queen?" she asked.

"Because a contest between them might involve London in war." Magdalene had looked back at the letter, then shrugged. "But I think this confirms Stephen. Here are the words *fedei defensor,* which I am sure mean 'defender of the faith.' The pope would not call a man he has just deprived of a throne 'defender of the faith.' So the letter must say that the pope has confirmed Stephen as king. Well, that is important, but not important enough to chance the danger of hanging. It is the bull that worries me."

Magdalene spoke somewhat absently, her eyes fixed on the letter, noticing that some of the words were very like French. And then, toward the end, another name caught her eye: *Henry de Blois, episcopus Winchesteri.* That would be Henry of Blois, Bishop of Winchester. She scanned the lines around the name, word by word, found *felix*, which she was sure meant "happy," and then *legatus*.

"Oh," she exclaimed. "The bull must be to give legatine powers to the Bishop of Winchester." She looked up, met Letice's and Dulcie's eyes. "That *must* be delivered!"

"I suppose so," Sabina agreed, reluctantly lifting her hand away from the money. "I remember how disappointed you were at Christmas when Theobald of Bec was elected archbishop instead of Henry. But I cannot understand why the king would not prefer his own brother, who has done so much for him."

"That would be why, I fear. Few love the bestower of favors." Magdalene sighed. "Or likely, the king's present favorite, Waleran de Meulan, felt that Henry was too powerful already, holding Winchester, the rich abbey of Glastonbury, and administering the diocese of London. William of Ypres said he thought Waleran threatened that Henry, if he should become archbishop, would be a rival king."

Letice, frowning, touched Magdalene, made a gesture that included them all, and then the sign for a question.

"Why should we care?" Magdalene half smiled. "Partly because I like the Bishop of Winchester. He is clever, wise, and quick to act or give a reason why he will not. More important, the more power in the hands of Henry of Winchester, the safer we are. If he had become archbishop, no other priest or bishop would dare complain about us, since he placed us here."

"Well, he already holds Winchester and London," Sabina began, then shook her head sharply. "Oh, I understand. If the new Archbishop of Canterbury should be another such as Brother Paulinus or just wish to impress everyone with his piety, he could call for a cleansing of Southwark."

"Or if he is a creature of Winchester's enemies, he could use us to prove that the bishop is unchaste. But if Winchester is legate, that is even better for us. If he had become archbishop, eventually another man would have been elected Bishop of Winchester. It would be that man who would own this house, and we have no guarantee he would be as understanding as this bishop."

Sabina smiled. "I understand. Even if the bishop does nothing directly, the knowledge that we rent this house from him is a safeguard to us. Protected by the pope's legate! No one will speak against us, not even the new Archbishop of Canterbury."

"Yes, indeed. Which means that the pouch must *not* be cast into the river—it must be found."

Letice gripped Magdalene's wrist, waved at the house, and then shook her head violently.

"No, of course it must not be found here."

"You want the pouch found?" Dulcie asked, seemingly having understood at least part of the conversation.

"Yes. It must be found. The bull"—Magdalene pointed to the document—"makes our bishop legate of the pope. He will be stronger in protecting us."

"Best it be found in th' church, then. Poor man might've hid 't there before he be kilt."

"That's a wonderful idea!" Sabina exclaimed. "But where?"

"There be a place," Dulcie said. "Y' know I clean in th' church. It be me offerin' to God, me own offerin' that don' put no money in th' monks' greedy hands. Y' know that carvin' of Saint Christopher carryin' th' Christ Child? Atween th' saint's neck, th' Babe's leg, 'nd th' wall behind, there's a hollow place. Mebbe th' stone broke 'r was thin there. Cleaned a mouse nest out o' there ony a week since. Be safe there."

"Oh, Dulcie, that's wonderful! Wonderful!" Magdalene jumped up and hugged her. "And if none of the monks finds it on his own, maybe you can get one of the women who cleans with you to 'clean' that statue."

She reached to the pile of pennies on the table and gave five to Dulcie. The old woman pushed three back to her. "Keep 'em for me. Don' want no one t' see too much money in me purse. These two, I be breaking to farthings. That'll be safe. Soon's that be ready"—she nodded at the pouch—"I'll take 't. Church'll be quiet 'til Sext. Monks all busy after eatin'."

While they had been speaking, Letice had refolded the letter, supporting the seal with the blade. Magdalene turned to watch as she laid down the knife and fetched one of the special, fine beeswax candles a client had brought. She carved some thin curls from the bottom onto the spot on the letter from which the seal had been raised. Seeing what she was about, Magdalene fetched a spill, lit it at the fire, then lit the candle. With lips set hard, Letice held the candle so the flame would pass over the wax shavings. Hardly breathing now, she slid the knife free and, most delicately, applied the flame to the bottom of the seal, lowering it back onto the parchment as it warmed. Very carefully, very gently, she pressed down on the edge until the soft seal and the soft wax bonded to the parchment. The pressure also spread the edge of the seal a tiny bit, so that it covered any small smear of wax that might have been made by the original lifting. When the wax had cooled hard, she took a deep breath and held out the letter.

"I can hardly believe we had that open," Magdalene said, examining it carefully. "And I doubt anyone will look as carefully at it as I did. Will it hold?"

Letice raised her hands and then nodded.

"Likely it will, she thinks." Dulcie voiced what Letice would have said if she could. " 'Nd if nothin' else don' look wrong 'nd th' purse be in th' church, not far from where th' poor man be kilt, it don' matter much. Them as finds it'll think stuffin' it in th' hole there did th' damage."

Magdalene took another ten pennies and added them to the gold coins in the bottom of the purse, then replaced the bull, the king's letter, the letter of credit, and on top of the others, the letter of introduction.

"I think that will look right," she said. "The letter he used most is in front, the most precious at the back where he could not pull it out by accident. The fact that the gold and a good sum in silver are there will mean to most that we did not open the pouch. Who would believe that a whore would not take gold, or clean out every scrap of silver?"

She took up the cords that tied the pouch and pulled them until the smooth parts, which had not been part of the knot, matched. Then slowly, carefully, making sure that every bend in the cord folded into the new knot, she wove the knot anew. When it was tied, she examined it front and back, Dulcie and Letice examined it front and back, and Sabina ran her sensitive fingers over the cord and the knot.

"It is smooth," she said. "I cannot feel anyplace where the cord feels crimped, nor any uneven spot on the knot itself."

"I'd swear that were never touched," Dulcie confirmed, and so did Letice with a nod. "I'll go get me cleanin' rags now. Sooner that be out o' here, th' better."

All the woman heaved a sigh of relief when Dulcie had packed the pouch into the basket with her sand and ash and straw and rags. Unfortunately, they had relaxed too soon. In only a few moments, Dulcie was back.

"Can't open the gate," she reported. " 'Tis locked, it is. Latch goes up and down, but th' gate don' move."

"It must be stuck," Magdalene said.

Dulcie shook her head. "I be no weakling, 'nd I pushed hard."

They all stared at her, dumbfound. The gate had been locked when they first moved into the house because the previous renter had run an ordinary stew. There had been noise and brawls, and the women had displayed themselves in unseemly ways, even coupling in the garden, which could be seen from the windows of the second-floor dorter. Henry of Winchester had ordered them out.

On the way to Oxford in company with William of Ypres, an old friend, he had complained about the outrage. When William arrived in Oxford, he had repaired to his favorite house of ease, only to have Magdalene ask her most powerful patron to vouch for her as being honest and discreet so she could rent a larger house. William quickly put two and two together, decided that having Magdalene in London would be more convenient for him, and suggested to Winchester that he offer the now-vacant house to Magdalene la Bâtarde, his favorite whoremistress. She would pay the exorbitant rent, William assured the bishop, and she and her women passed as embroiderers and would not offend.

Within a month of moving into the Old Priory Guesthouse, Magdalene had contrived to meet the prior and convince him that the gate should be opened for the benefit of the souls of her clients and the finances of the church. She had not mentioned that the more secretive of the men who visited her house could thereby reverse the process, that is, enter by the priory gate—a holy and laudable place to visit—enjoy their pleasures, and then go out through the priory so that none would know they had visited a whore. Since the men rarely forgot to leave an offering at the priory, neither Magdalene nor the prior had regretted the arrangement—in spite of the sacristan's displeasure—and the gate had remained open ever since.

"Brother Paulinus!" Magdalene exclaimed bitterly. "Now what can we do?"

"Since the bull names the bishop legate and will be of great benefit to him, could you not bring the pouch directly to him?" Sabina asked slowly. "You would have to admit the man was here, but surely Henry of Winchester is not such an idiot as the sacristan to think we would follow a client to the church to kill him."

"God, no!" Magdalene exclaimed. "Only his worst

enemy would give the bishop this pouch. How could he explain how he came by the pouch of a papal messenger who was murdered so near his London house? And he *must* present to the king the letter that confirms him in power, so he could not just hold his peace until he needed to act as legate. And just now, since the king contrived that election of Theobald, Winchester and his brother are not on the best of terms. William of Ypres told me that really harsh words had been exchanged. That would be a rich broth for the bishop's enemies to find tasty nuggets in. To defend himself, he would have to admit I brought him the pouch. Who would then believe we did not kill the man?"

"Could someone climb the wall?" Sabina asked uncertainly. She had never seen the wall and did not know how high it was.

"Perhaps I could," Magdalene replied, even more uncertainly. "We could put a table against it and I . . . but how would I get down on the other side? And how would I get up again? And we certainly could not be climbing the wall during the day. . . ."

"Meanwhile, what do we do with this?" Dulcie asked, removing the pouch from her cleaning supplies.

Magdalene looked at it with loathing, then drew a deep breath. "For now, I will hide it in the same place the dead man put it, only in the empty room. Then we will have to think of some way to be rid of it."

That was easier said than done, although the urgency of disposing of the pouch diminished throughout the day. By dinnertime, Magdalene was no longer much concerned about Brother Paulinus coming to search. He must have realized, she reasoned, that after his announcement of the murder, they would have looked for and disposed of any evidence they discovered. Nonetheless, the pouch *had* to be found and *must* not be found in their house, so—using obscure terms so that Ella would not understand—they discussed what to do with it, until their clients began to arrive.

Perhaps putting the problem out of their minds while they made merry with their guests did some good, because it was soon after the last client had left them that a solution to the problem was discovered. Letice went to lock the front gate and the front and back doors of the house after Vespers and as she drew the key from the back lock, she looked at it and her mouth opened in a large O. She ran to where Magdalene was lighting torchettes and shook the key in her face.

"Not more trouble." Magdalene sighed. "The door will not lock?"

Letice shook her head, dragged Magdalene to the front door, unlocked and then relocked it, dragged Magdalene to the back door, unlocked and relocked that, and again shook the key in Magdalene's face.

"I see you used the key to lock the doors, but—"

Letice again shook the key, pointed to the back door, pointed down the hall to the front door, shook the key, and finally held up one finger and shook that in Magdalene's face. Magdalene frowned. Letice repeated the process. Magdalene's eyes went wide. Locks were expensive, partly because the locking wards had to be reinvented for each lock. If two locks could be identical and use the same key, the locksmith could charge less, not to mention the convenience of needing fewer keys.

"One key," she breathed. "One key for both doors."

Even as she spoke, Letice held up another, even larger key, her eyes wide with hope.

"The key to the front gate! Oh, hurry, Letice. Unlock the door and we will go and try it."

They were so excited that they nearly stuck in the doorway once the door was opened. Then they rushed down the path, with Dulcie, who had been watching Letice lock and unlock the door, following behind.

"Do it. Do it," Magdalene urged and then held her breath as Letice inserted the front-gate key into the lock.

It turned with only a little difficulty. The latch clicked as Dulcie lifted it. The gate swung open.

four

⸎

20 APRIL 1139
ST. MARY OVERY CHURCH

Although it was not easy, Magdalene waited long enough after Compline for the sky to be completely dark and, she hoped, all the monks to be sound asleep. Then she and Dulcie slipped through the unlocked gate, latching it after them carefully, and around the apse to the north entrance. She shivered as she walked up the stairs, wondering whether the monks had cleaned off the blood. Even if they had not, she told herself, it would be dry now and there would be no danger of carrying a stain if she stepped on it. But it was not that fear that made her shiver, and tears pricked her eyes when she thought of the agreeable man who was now dead.

Before they could even gather in her lids, a new fear sent them back to their source. Had Brother Paulinus ordered that the church itself be locked as well as the gate? She began to think frantically of a new place to hide the pouch concealed under her cloak, perhaps in the graveyard, but Dulcie had lifted the latch and swung the door open a little way before any sensible idea had a chance to form. Apparently the sacristan felt he had shut out the contamination by locking the gate between

the Old Priory Guesthouse and the church and had either not dared or not felt the need to lock the church
itself.

When Dulcie shut the door, it was much blacker inside than outdoors, where even during the dark of the
moon, starlight brightened the sky. Fortunately, once
they had moved out into the chancel, the tiny lamp flick-
ering on the altar gave Dulcie a sense of where she was.
Taking Magdalene's hand, she led her down along the
wall and stopped. Magdalene assumed they were near
the carving of Saint Christopher, but she could not see
it at all and she did not dare ask Dulcie. Deaf as she
was, the old woman often spoke too loudly. Magdalene
reached up and began to feel around.

She soon found the curved stone frame around the
carved image, then the head of the figure. Only a little
way farther to the right was a smaller head. She slid her
hand down, found the Child's shoulder and, below that,
the hollow bordered by His thigh. With her lip tight
between her teeth, she pressed the pouch into the opening. She feared for a moment that it would fall all the
way down, but it stopped and to her delight, it felt as
if a tiny edge protruded from behind the Child's thigh.
If someone looked carefully, it would be found.

The breath Magdalene had been holding eased out
and then caught again as light bloomed suddenly behind
her. Dulcie tugged urgently at her skirt. Without even
turning around, she followed the pull, sidling along the
wall into the nave, where she knelt as if in prayer. Grit-
ting her teeth to keep them from chattering with fear,
she lifted her head.

A robed figure carrying a tallow taper had entered
from the south door, which connected through a chapel
and a short passage to the monastery. Magdalene
clasped her hands and bowed her head, thanking God
that they were well away from the Saint Christopher.
Even so, if they were found and the pouch was also
found in the next day or two, it would not take Brother

Paulinus long to put two and two together and insist they had brought the pouch to the church.

The monk did not bother to look down the nave, however. He hurried from the doorway to the center of the chancel and then walked into the apse. When he was close to the altar, he paused and removed from the breast of his robe an object that glittered faintly, which he lifted, admiring it. Magdalene saw that it was a handsome silver candlestick. Then he walked around to the back of the altar, where he knelt.

Magdalene could see nothing more. Mentally, she groaned. If the monk had come to perform a penance, or even to pray over self-perceived sins, they might be there for hours. But he was not praying. In only a few moments the monk reappeared, no longer carrying the candlestick. Relief nearly brought self-betrayal as Magdalene fought not to giggle. Idiot that she was. Plainly, the monk had come to return the candlestick to its storage place under the altar. Even as she thought it, he made his way toward the door, where the light suddenly went out and she heard the soft click of the latch.

Dulcie jumped to her feet and pulled at Magdalene, who had hesitated, breathing a prayer of thanks to the Mother of God. She smiled as she rose, thinking that perhaps being a whore was less offensive to Mary, the only woman who had ever conceived without carnal union with a man, than to her holier-than-thou disciple. Mary knew the heart, and in this case at least, Magdalene knew her heart was pure.

Not long after, the gate relocked behind them, she and Dulcie were safe inside the house. Magdalene was ready to drop and desired only her bed, but Letice and Sabina, who had been waiting anxiously, had to be told what had happened. Letice only signed that she was glad they got away.

Sabina sniffed. "I thought monks were supposed to keep regular hours," she said, her voice querulous. "It seems to me that they are always walking about, looking for mischief."

At the time, Magdalene was too tired to want to inquire into what Sabina meant, and she only suggested that everyone go to bed. She got no arguments; the fears and tensions of the day had worn on them all. For herself, Magdalene fell asleep the moment her clothing was off and she crawled into bed. She did not sleep peacefully, however; memories of the dead man, of the sacristan's threats, and of Sabina's last remark worked on her.

---

21 APRIL 1139

THE BISHOP OF WINCHESTER'S HOUSE

Magdalene woke the next morning determined to avenge Baldassare de Firenze and prove she and her women were innocent of murder. To take the easiest question first, Magdalene asked Sabina what she had meant by monks wandering about.

"When I went to pray that night," Sabina said, not identifying the time more closely because Ella was sitting at the edge of the bench occupied by Letice, who was cutting up her food for her, "I heard a monk cry out, 'Who is there?' and I had to wait before going into the church. I told you that."

"Likely you did, love, but all I heard was the bad news. Do you mean some monk was near the door of the north porch when you found it?" Magdalene asked.

"Found what?" Ella asked, sidling up close to Letice as soon as she put down the knife she had been using. "Was it nice?"

"No," Sabina said, swallowing. "It was not nice at all, which was why I left it there and did not bring it home."

"Oh. Well, I suppose even if it had been nice, you could not take anything left on the church porch. It would belong to the monks."

"Out of the mouths of babes," Magdalene said. "Perhaps what was on the porch did rightfully belong to the monks. Anyway, I think we should try to find out if it was because it *did* belong to the monks that the sacristan tried to put the blame for it on us. Did you recognize the voice, love?"

"Of course, how could I fail?" Sabina replied. "It is one we hear far too often—just who you said, the sacristan."

"The sacristan was at the door of the north porch that night? But seeing that all are gone is the porter's duty."

"Nonetheless, Brother Paulinus was there. I heard him call out, and something fall, and footsteps running away, and then, a little later, the door close."

Letice tapped her knife hilt on the table. Magdalene turned to look at her. Letice shook her head vigorously, made the signs for hushing and then for forgetting.

"Letice thinks we should stop talking about this and forget the whole thing," Magdalene said so Sabina would know. Then she sighed. "In a way, I wish we could—that is, I wish it had never happened. Certainly we had nothing to do with it, but I do not think we will be *allowed* to forget it."

"Were we supposed to remember something?" Ella asked, putting down the piece of cold meat she had been about to put in her mouth and looking distressed.

"No, dearling," Sabina said. "We are supposed to forget it, so you have done exactly what is right. Pay us no mind."

When something did stick in Ella's mind, however, it niggled at her and she would talk about it, so her comment implied a danger. Ordinarily, like a child, she ignored the talk of the other women, which she found dull and incomprehensible. This time something had caught her attention, possibly Sabina's saying she had found something, and she was listening. With unspoken agreement, talk on the subject of the murder was suspended until breakfast was over. Then, as a treat, Ella was allowed to go with Dulcie to the market.

When she was gone, the other women breathed a sigh of relief. Letice and Magdalene took up their embroidery and Sabina sat beside them, but she did not strike the lute she held in her lap.

"It is wrong!" she said, softly but forcibly. "I liked Messer Baldassare. He was gentle and merry. What happened to him was evil." Tears oozed out at the corners of her sealed eyes and she raised a hand to wipe them away. "It is not fair that he should not be avenged, and if Brother Paulinus has his way, we will suffer and the true evildoer go scot-free."

"That is certainly his intention," Magdalene replied. "Remember he said he would get us hanged. We can swear and swear that Messer Baldassare was never here, but we are whores. Who will believe us? And what if someone in the street saw him ring the bell? Worse, we stood talking for several minutes at the gate before he came in. That could have been noticed, or someone could have seen him leading in his horse. We must do something to save ourselves."

"The horse coming in is a common enough occurrence," Sabina said. "William of Ypres and his men always bring their horses, as do some of the North London merchants. None of our neighbors would think someone leading in a horse to be strange enough to mention."

"Not to mention on their own, but if asked? If Paulinus sends one of the lay brothers to accuse us of murder and to ask if anyone saw the victim with a horse enter our gate?"

Letice sniffed and made an ugly face, poking her finger against her cheeks and forehead.

Magdalene uttered a tired laugh. "A pox on Brother Paulinus." She sighed. "Oh, how I agree. But I doubt that even a pox could take him swiftly enough to stop him from making trouble for us."

"There is another thing," Sabina said softly. "He also said he had a friend close to the Bishop of Winchester. The bishop will not want to listen to what will cost him our rent, but if the sacristan's story is supported by someone who saw Messer Baldassare enter here . . ."

"Oh, heavens," Magdalene breathed. "That would be fatal—" She stopped abruptly and shuddered. The word might turn out to be literally true. "I must tell the bishop. I must tell him everything—"

Letice jumped from her chair and grabbed Magdalene's hand, shaking her head furiously and making signs that Magdalene finally figured out referred to the pouch.

"Oh, no," she agreed. "I will not tell him about the pouch. We must insist that Baldassare took everything with him when he left here and that he did not intend to return." She stood abruptly. "I should have gone as soon as I wakened. I must not waste any more time. I will go now. Letice, come help me to dress."

When Magdalene left the house, she was as soberly and elegantly clad as any rich merchant's wife. A bleached chemise, gathered at the base of the throat with a rolled tie, peeped demurely out of the neck of a soft tan undertunic with long, tight sleeves. Over that she wore a shorter overtunic of warm brown, with bands around the edges of the wide sleeves and down the front exquisitely embroidered in a pattern of climbing roses, golden flowers glinting among the green leaves. To cover her hair she wore a veil, fastened around her forehead with a fillet of the same embroidery as ornamented her gown. The veil was of a thin, delicate fabric but very voluminous, the trailing left edge pulled firmly around her throat and tucked under, the right edge thrown more loosely around the left shoulder so it could be raised to shield her face. She wore no jewelry, and the purse that hung from her embroidered cloth girdle was unadorned and almost flat.

Although it was much shorter to go through the monastery grounds, Magdalene went out the front gate. She bade a grave good-day to the mercer and grocer who had stalls in front of their shops across the road. Both returned her greeting—the mercer, who sometimes sold Letice's or Ella's embroideries, merrily; the grocer with a hasty glance over his shoulder. Magdalene smiled and walked up the road. Likely the grocer's wife was in the shop and watching.

Magdalene had invited both men separately when she first arrived, explaining frankly that she wished them to know her house would cause no riots in the street and make no scandal, that it was no common stew. Then she told them her rate and offered to reduce it once and once only for the sake of good neighborly feeling. The mercer continued to come occasionally, when he had made a special profit on one of the embroideries. The grocer was not as friendly. Still, both greeted her as readily as they ever had, which meant, she hoped, that neither sacristan nor lay brother had gone to them with accusations or questions. Relieved, she stepped out more briskly.

The road from the bridge ran almost due south, but at the end of the monastery grounds, a narrower lane went west and then north, continuing along the priory wall right down to the river, where the monks had a small landing. From the turn north, the side of the lane opposite the priory held four neat houses, then a stone wall, as high and probably stronger than that of the priory. That wall was broken by a large, double-doored gate. This was invitingly open, signaling that the Bishop of Winchester was in residence.

Magdalene walked through the gate and up the path to the heavy door of a stone-built house somewhat larger and taller than her own; this, however, was a private residence, not a place meant to harbor many guests, and was thus impressive. The door of the house was closed, but Magdalene saw that the pull of the bell was hanging outside. She took a deep breath, not sure whether she was relieved or disappointed. The bell cord indicated that the bishop was not only in residence in Southwark, but actually in the house.

Better get it over with, she thought, and pulled the cord. Within, the bell rang. The door was opened with reasonable promptness, and Magdalene stepped inside. For a moment she was swept with nostalgia. The great hall was so much like that of her father's manor. Taking about two-thirds of the length of the building, it was roofed not by rough-hewn beams like her own house, but by handsome stone arches. Between one pair, about midway, was a stone hearth with a good-sized fire burning; two slits in the wall above the hearth drew out most of the smoke. Flanking the hearth were several benches on which were seated a number of men, some of them talking, some idly staring into the flames.

That was better than her father's house, Magdalene thought, where the fire had been in the middle of the floor, with the smoke left to find its own way out under the eaves. Of course the Bishop of Winchester's house had no eaves on this floor. The handsome arches supported another story, where the bishop had his private chambers.

It was more the shape of the hall and the busy people moving about that made her think of her father's manor, she decided. The writing stands near the windows— Magdalene suppressed a smile; no one in her father's manor could write, except the priest who came when asked—would certainly have been foreign to her father's hall. Yet the differences were not so great after all, only those between a knight and a clerk. Near the windows, set between other arches, two lighted and closed with thin, oiled parchment, were busy men taking advantage of the light. In her father's house, men-at-arms would have been caring for armor and weapons;

here there were writing stands at which clerks were working. She shook her head and began to walk toward the far end of the hall, which was partitioned off.

"Mistress? Your purpose, if you will?"

Magdalene started slightly and realized that the servant who had opened the door for her was asking why she had come. There was a note of impatience in his voice that said he must have asked the question more than once, but she delayed one moment more before answering as another difference between the Bishop of Winchester's hall and her father's became clear: Here there were no women, not even one.

"I have news for the bishop, urgent news."

"The bishop sees few women," the servant said doubtfully, but his eyes were measuring the fine cloth of which her sober gown was made, the delicacy of the embroidery, the soft, high-polished shoes that peeped out beneath her long undertunic.

"If you will take my name to him and tell him I have urgent news, I am sure he will see me."

"That is not my duty, mistress. However, you may go to the end of the room. One of his secretaries, Guiscard de Tournai, is there. He will bring your name to the bishop if he thinks your news truly urgent."

Behind the veil she had lifted to shield her face when she pulled the bell, Magdalene grimaced. Because Guiscard already knew her, it was to her advantage that he was on duty, but she had never liked the man. Regardless, she had to tell Henry of Winchester what had really happened. She walked quickly toward the partition that provided the bishop with a private chamber in which to do business.

In front of that partition was an open area, delineated by one of the arches, into which the bustle of the great hall did not intrude. The space held a handsome, heavy table carrying writing materials. On one end of the table perched Sir Bellamy of Itchen, a tall, well-muscled man wearing a short maroon tunic cinched by a heavy sword belt. The tunic exposed, almost to his strong thighs, bright red, long-legged, footed chausses, cross-gartered in the color of the tunic, above calf-high leather boots. He had fair, curly hair, cut unfashionably short to his ears so that it would not get in his way when he was wearing mail and raised the hood of his hauberk.

Sir Bellamy looked down at Guiscard de Tournai, who wore dark but rich clerical robes. The clerk was seated on a stool set about the middle of the table. A brazier burned at his elbow and a sheet of parchment lay before him.

"Where the devil have you been for the last three days, Guiscard?" Sir Bellamy asked.

The clerk lifted his head. Although he was seated and Sir Bellamy loomed over him, he managed to give the impression that he was looking down his nose. "I do not see that it is any of your affair, but I do not mind telling you. I was in St. Albans, visiting my mother."

"Sorry." Bell smiled, one side of his mobile mouth lifting higher than the other. "I forgot. You go to visit her whenever we are in London."

Guiscard, who always pretended to be deep in the bishop's confidence and indispensable, often annoyed him, but Bell swallowed his irritation because he understood; Guiscard was only a physician's son—worse, a butcher's grandson—and he felt the need to be important, to make himself the equal of the better-born secretaries. Still, he visited his "common" mother. Bell now felt guilty, and ashamed.

"You are a good son—" he began and stopped.

A tall woman, holding her veil modestly before her face, approached the table. There was, however, nothing else modest in the woman's manner. She had not lingered on the outer edge of the quiet area, waiting to be gestured forward. After casting him a single glance that dismissed him, she came to face the clerk.

"I have urgent news for the bishop, Master Guiscard," she said. "Would you please tell him I am here and that if he has the time, I would like a few words in private."

Bell blinked, partly at the demand but equally at the assurance in the low, rich voice. It was quite plain that the woman expected Guiscard to recognize her and to accede to her request.

The clerk glanced at her and then away, as if he did know her but did not wish to. However, he spoke in a civil if colorless voice. "The Bishop of Winchester does not receive women in private. If you will leave your name and describe your business, I will see that he is informed of it as soon as he has time."

"Do not be ridiculous," the woman began, then sighed. "Sorry, Master Guiscard. I thought you would recognize me. I am Magdalene la Bâtarde of the Old Priory Guesthouse. You must remember. William of Ypres recommended me to the bishop and you came with an offer to rent the guesthouse. You showed me the house. Really, I *must* speak with the bishop. I assure you I would not intrude on him without good reason."

"I do not care who you are," Guiscard retorted sharply. "Only the king himself could expect so busy a man as the Bishop of Winchester to put aside all his affairs to attend to him on the moment. For such a woman as you—"

"I tell you my news is urgent and the bishop *needs* to hear it," she exclaimed, her voice rising.

"Whore!" Guiscard snarled. "How dare you! Get you out—"

Bell stood up, troubled by Guiscard's reaction and by the woman's urgency. He knew what the Old Priory Guesthouse was; he had been the one sent to clean out the nest of vipers that had gathered there over the years until word of the excesses came to Henry of Winchester. So the woman probably was literally a whore, not merely so named because Guiscard was annoyed with her. But if the woman was William of Ypres's whore, she had a powerful protector, and it was not likely she would have come to Winchester unless her news concerned the bishop himself.

"Guiscard," Bell began just as the door opened and the Bishop of Winchester himself came out.

He was holding a letter in his hand and also said, "Guiscard—" but the woman quickly stepped around the end of the table, passed Bell without a glance and said, "My lord bishop, I am Magdalene la Bâtarde, and I have very urgent news for you about the murder that took place on the north porch of St. Mary Overy church."

"Murder!" Henry of Winchester exclaimed. "What murder? When?"

Bell turned from the woman to face the bishop. Behind him, he heard a wordless exclamation from Guiscard. For a moment, while shock prevented any deeper emotion from taking hold, he wondered whether Guiscard's protest was one of indignation at the whore's boldness or dismay at the news of the murder. They might, Bell thought, be of about equal weight with Guiscard.

"I was told of it yesterday morning, just past Prime," the whore said, "but the sacristan insisted the victim had come from my house and implied that he had been killed Wednesday night."

"God help him—and us," Winchester breathed, not undevoutly, then beckoned to her. "Come, come within and tell me what you know of this."

"Too much," Magdalene said when the door had closed behind them. She dropped her veil. "I . . . I have made trouble for myself—"

"Murder is not just a little trouble," the bishop snapped.

"Oh, no, my lord. I and my women had nothing to do with the man's death. If the dead man is the person I believe him to be, he left the Old Priory Guesthouse with all his belongings, hale and hearty and well pleased with his entertainment, but—" She bit her lip and drew in a deep breath. "But I lied about his being in my house and taking his pleasure with one of my women. I am very sorry, my lord. I was frightened and lost my temper with Brother Paulinus. I knew none of us had harmed Messer Baldassare—"

"Who?" Henry of Winchester cried. "What did you say was the man's name?"

"He told me he was Baldassare de Firenze, my lord, when he first came to the gate. And he is the only one who could have departed my house and come to harm without my knowledge. If any of the others had not reached home safely, you see, someone would have come to ask about them."

"Baldassare," the bishop breathed.

Clearly, the bishop was very distressed. Magdalene abandoned the effort to explain how she knew it was her client who was dead without admitting that Sabina had recognized him.

"You knew him, my lord?" she asked.

"I fear so. Was he . . . was he carrying anything?"

"There were saddlebags on his horse, and he wore a purse and carried a pouch. But he took everything with him. Sabina was careful to remind him to look well. He was not a regular client, you see, so we did not wish to be accused of stealing if he left anything behind. And after Brother Paulinus told us he was dead, we looked again with double care."

"Why did you lie to the brother if you are innocent?"

"Innocent? To Brother Paulinus? He had already decided I had killed Messer Baldassare, and when I asked him why I should do such a dreadful thing, which would ruin my business and my reputation, he said it was because I was so filled with evil that I could not bear that the man should clean my sin from his soul by confessing in the church."

"The sacristan said you committed murder to prevent

the man from confessing?" The bishop's lips twitched.

"Yes. Brother Paulinus said I followed him and killed him so he would remain stained with sin. My lord, I know my trade is sinful; if my clients become uneasy, I would lose them. Thus my women and I have always encouraged those who felt guilty over visiting us to ease their consciences in the church. And the prior was never unduly harsh with them. Although pure himself, he understood that others might be frail, might sin and regret it. We understand, too. We have never committed any outrage——"

"True enough." A very faint smile touched the bishop's lips. "But all this does not explain your lie."

Magdalene sighed. "Well, at first I did not understand the sacristan at all. He kept roaring at me to confess my crime, and kept saying it was the prior's fault for his leniency. First of all, I had committed no crime. Whoring may be a sin, but it is no crime in Southwark. Secondly, I would admit no guilt for anything when he made it so plain that he would accuse the prior of having caused the evil. By then, he had made me very angry and when he said murder, of course I denied it and any knowledge of it. We had done no harm to any man. All our clients were away safe——"

The bishop lifted his hand. "Yes, I see. Once having denied it, you were afraid to admit that the man had been with you."

"Yes, but also how could I be sure the man who was dead had been with us? Brother Paulinus told me nothing except that the porter claimed the man had not come through the front gate of the priory. Thus the sacristan assumed he had come through the gate between our house and the churchyard, but I could not be sure. . . ."

Henry of Winchester shook his head. "But you do seem to be sure. No, do not answer that directly. Begin at the beginning and tell me how it came to pass that Baldassare de Firenze visited your house."

"Because he traveled from Rome to London with a

naughty student of the priory's, Richard de Beaumeis—"

She hesitated slightly as a black frown crossed the bishop's face, but he waved at her to continue, and she told him the entire tale exactly as it happened, except for the caching of the pouch in Sabina's room. In the end, she even told him about the horse and of Sabina's stumbling on the corpse, fearing the smallest chance of a shadow on her veracity.

"And then the sacristan questioned us all separately," she said, coming to the end of the tale, "but he was furious when none of us would admit to murder. He said he would see us all hang and—as I said before— that the evil we did was the fault of the prior. My lord bishop, I beg you not to listen to the evil he speaks of the prior. Father Benin is a good man, truly holy—"

"I am aware," Winchester said. "And I am also aware that he suffers your presence in the Old Priory Guesthouse with more tolerance than would Brother Paulinus, who seeks the prior's place."

Magdalene smiled and shook her head. "I beg pardon, my lord. I should have known that you would understand without my interference." Then she sighed. "But if Brother Paulinus should succeed, I fear I would no longer be able to remain at the Old Priory Guesthouse."

"I know." The bishop grimaced. "The sacristan is a fool. He has no compassion, and no common sense either. Lechery is foul in itself, but when contained in one place, it does not contaminate the whole body of society. This the ancients knew and provided relief for their young men. Horace in his *First Satire* advocates the use of brothels, and since men have not changed, except possibly for the worse, I cannot see that we can do without them." He shook his head. "If such powerful and godless men as William of Ypres had no outlet for their lusts, might they not seize on innocent sisters, wives, and daughters and befoul them as well as themselves?"

Magdalene had heard this argument more than once and would not quarrel with it because it was a strong protector of her way of life, but Henry of Winchester was a very intelligent man and she could not resist giving him something to chew upon. "But whores do not lust, my lord," she said, smiling. "To a whore, coupling is a piece of work for which she is paid as a weaver is paid for a piece of cloth. Just as an anvil accepts the pounding of the blacksmith's hammer so, and with just as little emotion or pleasure, does the whore accept the pounding of the man who uses her."

Winchester flushed slightly. For all his worldliness, he kept the rules: He was abstemious in food and wine; he never touched a woman. Magdalene did not know whether he had ever had a woman, but if he had, it must have been when he was very young and not yet consecrated as a priest.

"That is not according to common knowledge or theological precept," he said.

"No." Magdalene laughed. "That is from a whore's own experience, my lord. I assure you I never lusted after men, and as soon as I could, I ceased from receiving them. I am afraid your authorities rest more on the desire of men to justify themselves than on the perception of reality. We are all sinners, my lord, but whores more than any others are totally free of the sin of lechery."

Henry frowned and glanced away. "They commit the act of lechery."

"Yes, my lord." Magdalene sighed. It was not worthwhile to continue to press her point and perhaps strain the bishop's friendship. He might think about what she said and find some compassion for her poor sisters—or he might not. "And as for what you said of William of Ypres," she said, "you are quite right. William is not a patient or gentle person, although he has always been very kind to me. He does not suffer correction gladly. He would be more likely to burn down the priory than to give up his satisfactions if Brother Paulinus preached at him. Oh, he would be sorry later . . . perhaps. . . ."

Winchester laughed, then sobered. "I am no condoner of sin. I do not like what you do, Magdalene. I do not like my part in it—" He uttered a small self-derisive snort. "Although I like the rent you pay well enough. But it is not for the rent that I look aside from your trade. Worse might follow if great men like William— or others—seized by force what they desired. Feud would follow. War. The destruction of all hope of peace and order in which men can look to God."

"Lesser men need a vent, too, my lord. If they had not the common stews, there would be many more honest maidens seized and raped."

The bishop sighed. "That, too, is true. But body as well as soul is endangered; men die in or near the stews—"

"But not in or near *my* house!" Magdalene said firmly. "That is why my clients pay many times the rate of a common stew, because they know their persons, their purses, and their secrets are safe with us. We are sinners in sins of the flesh, but not in other ways."

"So I have heard from my bailiff, and from the sheriff also. Your house has a good reputation. Not a single complaint has been lodged against you, at least not by men who have used your services. There have been some complaints by those who were not accommodated."

Who? Magdalene wondered, suddenly worried. Who had complained against her? But she dared not spend any time in thought just now. She would keep the matter in mind. Her middle felt hollow. Surely it could not be someone wishing to injure her that had killed Baldassare?

She forced the idea out of her mind. "I promised you, when you offered me the Old Priory Guesthouse, that there would be no noise, no brawling, no scandal of any kind. Those who are refused are men who would beat my women, desire unnatural acts, disturb my other clients with gross drunkenness, or cause a riot in the street."

"I agree it is in your interests to keep a quiet, orderly house. How far would you go—"

"Not as far as murder, my lord!" Magdalene exclaimed indignantly. "And I would not choose such a man as Messer Baldassare to kill. My woman, Sabina, wept when she heard he was dead. She said he was gentle and merry. That means a great deal to such as we. She said it was unfair that the murderer should escape scot-free while the blame was placed on the easiest scapegoat. I swear on my life, on the soul I may yet redeem by contrition, that neither I nor any member of my household is guilty of this abomination."

The bishop stared at her for a long moment, then slowly nodded his head. "I think you speak the truth. I do not believe you guilty. I knew Messer Baldassare, and taking into consideration his character and manners, there is nothing he would have done that could have roused your ire. But others—" He paused and lowered his eyes to his hands, one of which still held the letter he had been carrying. "Others . . . yes. Baldassare may have had with him something for which a few might kill."

Magdalene struggled to keep her face from changing. She suspected the bishop had guessed she knew Baldassare was a papal messenger, and that she knew what he carried. She wished with all her heart that she could tell him about the pouch and where it was. But confessing would be no favor to Henry of Winchester.

Just then her expression did not matter; when he spoke the last sentence, the bishop was still staring at his hands, or the letter, or his ring of office. His eyes then lifted, but not to her; his gaze had moved past her to the door and his face wore an expression of anxiety that changed as she watched to angry determination. Then he looked at her and his lips twisted with a kind of cynical doubt. Magdalene looked back with what she hoped was innocent inquiry, but inside, a cold shiver traveled from her spine to her belly. The bishop knew that William of Ypres used the Old Priory Guesthouse for more than assuaging his lust. Did he wonder if others also used her place for political purposes, purposes that could have led to Baldassare de Firenze's death?

With his eyes steady on her, he added, "No, I do not believe you or any of your women stabbed Messer Baldassare, but it was from your house that he went to his death. From your house, we must seek his killer."

Five

21 APRIL 1139
THE BISHOP'S HOUSE; ST. MARY
OVERY PRIORY

"Oh, *yes,* my lord!" Magdalene exclaimed, clasping her hands together to keep from hugging him. If the bishop would back her search for the murderer, she and her women had a far better chance of succeeding than they would on their own. "We will do everything we can to find the killer."

The Bishop of Winchester's brows rose. "You do not fear retribution? That your clients will not like too much curiosity associated with your house?"

Controlling her impulse to swallow hard, Magdalene smiled faintly. "You think it strange I should be so eager to help? It is not, not at all. If the murderer is not found, will not Brother Paulinus's accusations seem more and more likely? Our only hope of complete vindication is that the true killer will be found and exposed. And as to my clients, some will never know but others may wish to help." Magdalene hesitated for a moment, then looked aside and said, "William of Ypres would not be sorry to see your enemies discomfited."

"Perhaps he would not," the bishop said, "but—" His voice checked as the bells of St. Mary Overy rang for Sext. His lips thinned. "I have no more time to spare for you just now, Magdalene, but if you wish to help, you must have an innocent reason to come here. You may say I have given you a commission to embroider an altar cloth for my private chapel and need my opinion, and . . . yes, a woman is too confined by custom to move about and freely question. Wait here. I will bring in Sir Bellamy of Itchen, who does for me such tasks as are more suitable to a knight than to a clerk."

When the door of the bishop's closet opened, Bell got quickly to his feet. He was interested to see that the letter Winchester had been holding was still in his hand. Either what the bishop had heard in his inner chamber was so absorbing he had forgotten to put it down or the letter itself was important. The bishop raised the hand with the letter toward him; Bell started forward to take it, feeling slightly disappointed, but Winchester shook his head and looked past him, out toward the hall as if he were seeking a new messenger. Bell stood still, thinking with pleasure that the bishop might have more interesting work for him than delivering letters, unless . . . but at that moment, Guiscard stood up. Winchester looked at him.

"Ah, Guiscard," he said. "I was going to send Bell to the Archdeacon of London with this letter and a request that he bring to me all the particulars about the quarrel between St. Matthew's and St. Peter's. But you will serve my purpose better. You can explain to the archdeacon that I will tolerate no more delay. I wish to see that matter settled before I leave for Winchester again."

Guiscard stood up, his mouth turned down in a discontented arch. Bell swallowed a chuckle. Doubtless Guiscard considered it beneath his dignity to be a messenger. "But my lord," he protested, "the murder . . . the whore. She is not to be trusted. The sacristan of St. Mary Overy has often complained of her insolence, her unwillingness to be guided to a better life. Would it not be better if I—"

"No," the bishop said, a certain rigidity about his mouth telling Bell that he probably wanted to laugh. "I have bethought me that you are better fitted than Bell to deal with the archdeacon. Bell would have no idea what was a just objection, which you will surely understand. On the other hand, Bell is just the man to deal with murderers and whores."

Bell bowed slightly, now wanting to laugh himself. He took what the bishop said as a compliment, not an insult, but Guiscard de Tournai, the common physician's son, would probably think the bishop had been denigrating him. He felt a flash of admiration for Winchester's cleverness and then found himself grateful rather than amused. As one of the bishop's secretaries, Guiscard could make a nuisance of himself if he took a person in despite. Bell's messages could get lost or garbled, his stipend delayed. Not that the bishop had been thinking of *him*, Bell reminded himself; he was relatively new to Winchester's service, having been taken into the Household only three years back. By soothing Guiscard with a few words, Winchester was trying to avoid a discord between his servants that might interfere with his business.

"You can send young, Phillipe, to sit here until you return," the bishop continued to Guiscard. "I do not expect any visitor of note until nearly Vespers." He turned to Bell. "You come with me."

Telling Guiscard to set Phillipe to watch the door was another clever move, Bell thought, following his master into the private chamber. Had Henry asked for one of his other secretaries, Guiscard might have thought secrets were being kept from him and he would certainly have been jealous. The young clerk, Phillipe, was no threat. Ahead of him, the bishop stopped and turned. Bell stopped also, looked in the direction of the bishop's gaze—and froze.

Enormous eyes, the color of a slightly misty sky, an infinitely deep, soft gray-blue, met his. Above them arched nut-brown brows, which were almost touched by long, thick, curling lashes. A straight nose, but with a barely tilted tip, which begged to be kissed, perched above a mouth to which lips must go next: full, soft, perfectly arched, with corners that had been curved up to greet the bishop but tucked themselves back at the intensity of his scrutiny.

Bell blinked, looked away from her face to the cloak she had removed and carried now over her arm, but what he saw was a firm and shapely bosom and, falling over her shoulder, tresses of thick, shining, honey-gold hair exposed by the loosening of her veil. The cloak. Bell forced his eyes to look at something that was not part of a seemingly perfect woman. The cloak was a decent, sober brown, modest until one noticed it was of the very best cloth and lined with fur. A whore . . . perhaps, but no common woman for all of that.

"Magdalene," the bishop was saying. "This is Sir Bellamy of Itchen, my . . . I suppose you would call him my man-of-all-work. He hires and trains men-at-arms, he corrects those who will not listen to gentler remonstrances; he was the one who drove out the harpies that were infesting the Old Priory Guesthouse before you came to take it. I want you to tell him your tale—the tale you told me, not the one you told Brother Paulinus. He also knew and liked Baldassare—"

"Baldassare?" Bell echoed. "You do not mean to tell me that he was the one who was killed?"

"I am afraid so, but I am not sure," Magdalene said.

"What do you mean, you are not sure?"

"No, no," the bishop put in. "Do not begin in the middle as you did with me. Remember, the whole story."

The warning, Bell thought, was not only for the woman. He colored faintly—the curse of his fair complexion—knowing that the bishop had seen how hard her beauty had struck him. And her displeasure, Bell thought further and felt his color deepen, was not because of what the bishop had said but because she, too, had seen his admiration, and did not welcome it. Well, beauty or not, she was safe. He was not going to meddle with William of Ypres's woman.

"Very well," Magdalene said.

"Not here, though," the bishop remarked. "I will need this chamber for business. Take him back to the guesthouse with you. Perhaps he can think of things he wishes to ask your women. One of them might have noticed something you did not. And, oh, I just remembered some other business I need to discuss with him. Wait outside."

"Yes, my lord," Magdalene said with a cold look at Bell.

I hope what you tell him is to keep his hands off, she thought as she closed the door behind her. Because Guiscard called me "whore," doubtless that self-satisfied churl will think I will yield my body to ensure a favorable report from him to the bishop.

Within, much the same ideas, only from the opposite point of view, were being voiced. "Have a care," the bishop was saying. "I know she is a woman of almost transcendent beauty and it is hard, even for me, to question what she says. You must. You *must* discover who killed Baldassare and discover what he was carrying and who has it now. You must get the pope's messages back for me or, if they have been destroyed, discover that fact so that I can send to Innocent, tell him what happened, and ask him to send duplicates."

"Can you tell me what you think was in the messages?"

"What I *think* he had was the result of the challenge Matilda made to the king's right to the throne. It is almost impossible that Innocent could deny Stephen's right since his legate already approved it, but the letter will quiet doubts. I can see that Matilda's party might not want the pope's final approval of Stephen to become public if they plan another rebellion. Still, it is hard to believe that would be worth killing over."

"It might be," Bell said slowly. "It might make the difference between a large number of men swearing to Matilda because they once promised the old king to support her. The pope's decision would ease their consciences and keep them faithful to King Stephen."

Winchester sighed and shrugged. "Perhaps. The only other thing he might have been carrying is the answer to Stephen's request that I be made papal legate, and I cannot see how that could be important to anyone but me."

"You think not, my lord? I am not sure the new archbishop would want a legate to overshadow him, nor that Waleran de Meulan would want you to hold the church in your hand while he tries to name his cousins to earldoms and bishoprics."

"Theobald of Bec is no murderer," Winchester said shortly. "Perhaps Waleran would not stop at murder. . . . Oh, Lord be my help. That was what she meant when she said William of Ypres would be glad to see my enemies discomfited."

"She? Magdalene?" Bell asked. "Is she close enough to Ypres to know his mind?"

"He has been her friend and protector for a long time. He was the one who urged me to rent her the Old Priory Guesthouse, and I know he uses her house more for political meetings and other purposes he holds private than he does for satisfaction of his lust. I know it seems an odd place to go to keep secrets, but William is no fool and I have never heard he was disappointed."

"Then she is presumably trustworthy."

"I am sure she is . . . to William of Ypres. Does that warranty that she would be equally trustworthy to us?"

"No," Bell said reluctantly. "His purposes are often not ours, although if it is Waleran de Meulan who ordered Baldassare killed, Ypres's purpose and ours might be the same."

"True, but we cannot be sure that Ypres is involved

in this. I only heard his name from Magdalene, who is a very clever woman and might want us to believe that while she pursued other purposes entirely. She may look like an angel, but a whore lives by selling—her body or anything else that will bring a profit. Not that I think special ill of Magdalene; she does her work and it is necessary, like that of collectors of dung. But you must remember that all whores are for sale—that is their trade."

"You know her to be dishonest and deceitful?" Bell asked, keeping his voice flat. It was awful to think that could be so, to find that such beauty hid utter corruption, like the rainbow sheen on a slice of long-rotted meat.

"No," Winchester said. "Oddly enough, my knowledge of her is just the opposite. In the time I have known Magdalene, I have found her honest and reliable. She has fulfilled every promise she made when she took the Old Priory Guesthouse; she pays her rent on time and in full; no one has made any complaint against her—not the men she serves nor her neighbors. But she *is* a whore. She lives outside the church, so oaths are meaningless to her. I warn you only so you will be cautious. The matter of the pope's messages is too important to be overshadowed by a whore's smile."

"I do not think her likely to smile at me," Bell said, smiling himself. "She was not pleased to see my admiration."

"Perhaps. Nonetheless, have a care."

Bell found Magdalene fully veiled again, looking out into the hall. He picked up his cloak and swung it over his shoulders, feeling her watching from behind the veil. She did not speak, though, only nodded when he asked if she was ready to go, and walked by his side in silence until they were out on the road.

Then she said in an utterly colorless voice, "I hope you remember that I have already told the bishop the whole tale. I doubt you will find any more in it than I have or discover anything new, but if you do, there is nothing I would want kept secret from his lordship."

"If you are telling me not to expect to be bribed, you can save your breath. The bishop pays me very well. I live at his expense. There is nothing you could offer me that would induce me to violate his trust."

"Nothing?" Magdalene asked, and then laughed. "Most men have a price, but be assured I am not seeking yours."

"I suppose I am not better than most other men, but my price, even on matters less dear to my heart, is not so low as a futtering or two. Baldassare was a friend, and neither gold nor kisses and caresses will turn me aside from seeking out the one who harmed him."

"I am glad of that," Magdalene said, her voice suddenly warm and lively. "Until the murderer is exposed, my women and I will be suspect. That is not only dangerous but, in the end, would be very bad for business. I promise you that if you seek earnestly for Messer Baldassare's murderer, you will have all the help that I and my women can give."

She went on then and told him the story she had told the bishop, the exact truth as far as she remembered it, except for finding the pouch and hiding it in the church. She ended with another assurance of her desire to help uncover the killer.

"Good enough," Bell said neutrally. "But I think the first step is for us to make certain that the dead man *is* Baldassare. Why do you think it is? You say you never saw the body."

"Because Sabina recognized him. I told you."

"That seems clear enough. If she recognized him, why should you have any doubts? Because it was night and dark?"

"The darkness would not matter. I must have forgot to say: Sabina is blind. But she was frightened out of her wits—"

"Sabina is blind? If she is blind, how could she recognize anyone?"

"By feel, of course."

"You mean she opened the corpse's braies and felt his—"

"Do not be disgusting!" Magdalene snapped. "She recognized the feel of his clothes. She found the knife in his neck when she was trying to touch his face to be sure. She was terrified. That was why I wondered if it might have worked the other way; that is, Sabina found a dead man and was so frightened that she became sure it was a man with whom she had lain and so she would be blamed."

"I suppose that is possible, but why should she think she would be blamed?"

"Is there anything for which a whore is not blamed? And there she was, kneeling by the body, her hands covered in blood. Who would believe she had not struck the blow?" Remembered terror and bitterness made her voice shrill, and she took a breath and brought it back to its even tenor. "What would it matter that there was no reason for us to harm him? For want of a better reason, Brother Paulinus is convinced we murdered poor Messer Baldassare just to prevent him from ridding himself of sin by confession, and he did not even know that Sabina had been anywhere near the body."

Had she once been accused of murder, Bell wondered, having felt her bitterness. Had William of Ypres saved her? If so, it would be no wonder that she was grateful to him. And then a small frisson ran down his back. Had she committed the murder of which she was accused?

"Be that as it may," Bell said quickly, "I think we had better first make sure the dead man *is* Baldassare."

Since Magdalene could not reveal that they had found Baldassare's pouch, and in it, letters of introduction and credit bearing his name, she simply agreed. She reminded Bell, however, that if she admitted that

Baldassare had been in her house, Brother Paulinus
would immediately have fuel for his fires of accusation,
which would make trouble for the bishop. Thus, the
monks probably would not let her into the chapel to
look at the body. But Bell had the answer for that; when
Brother Godwine, the porter, did object to Magdalene's
entering the priory grounds, Bell said he had been in-
structed by the bishop to bring her to view the dead
man so she could say whether or not the man had been
one of her clients.

Since Henry of Winchester was serving as administrator of the London diocese until a new bishop could
be elected, Brother Godwine could do no more than
make a sour face, but he said to Bell while he led them
to the chapel in which the body was laid out, "That man
did *not* come through the gate into the priory, nor did
his horse. Only three men on horseback came through
the front gate. I know them all, and all three horses were
in the stable when this man's beast was found in the
graveyard. I am not mistaken or derelict in my duty,
and I shall so tell the prior when he returns."

Bell glanced at Magdalene, but she said nothing and
her face was invisible behind the veil. Her mind had
been working frantically, however, since he had insisted
she accompany him, trying to find a compromise between her need to admit she knew Baldassare and her
need to protect herself from Brother Paulinus. Necessity
lends agility to the mind; as soon as the face of the dead
man became visible, the right words came to her lips.

"Oh, my God!" Magdalene exclaimed. "No, he was
not a regular client, but he has indeed been in my house.
He came to my gate yesterday not long before Vespers
and asked for the church of St. Mary Overy. I told him
he must go around, but he protested that the church
looked very near. I had come out without a cloak and
I was cold, so I bade him step into the house, which he
did while I explained that we were no part of the priory.
But I did mention the back gate went to the church. I

did not see where he went when he left the house."

"But you told the sacristan the man had never been with you," Brother Godwine said severely.

"I told the sacristan that all of our clients had left our house safe and sound and that neither I nor any other member of the household followed or harmed any client. I told the truth then, and I have told the truth now."

Bell looked at her sidelong. He knew both tales and suspected that every word she had said was true—and added up to a thumping lie. Clever. Yes, she was clever.

"We will see," Bell said, and then to Brother Godwine. "I know the man. His name was Baldassare de Firenze, and he often served as a papal messenger."

"Papal messenger!" the porter echoed, his eyes filled with horror. "How terrible! What can he have been carrying that he should ask for the church of St. Mary Overy? We have made no recent request of the pope."

Hardly listening to the horrified effusions, Bell bent over the neatly folded pile of clothes and other possessions that were on a small bench by the foot of the bier. The upper part of the shirt, tunic, and cloak were stained, despite washing; the braies were not. On the belt, laid atop the clothing, was a sheathed knife with a horn hilt inlaid with gold wire—a valuable knife, not taken. Beside that was a coiled leather strap about two or three fingers wide.

"Look," Bell said, pointing to a fresh-looking cut in the leather of the belt. "That is where the loop of the purse was cut." Then he lifted the coiled strap. Midway along, it was stained with blood. "He was wearing that when he died, likely to support a pouch. Did you find a pouch?"

"No," Brother Godwine said firmly. "No purse either. You say the purse was stolen? Oh, heaven! What a calamity! Was the pouch stolen, too? Will we ever learn what the Holy Father wished to tell us?"

Bell had examined the strap inch by inch. "No cuts,

and it would be hard to remove the pouch without marks."

"Perhaps he was not wearing it?" Magdalene was dying to say that the pouch could have been hidden, but she dared not.

Sir Bellamy nodded to her remark, then patted Brother Godwine's shoulder. "Yes, of course you will learn what the Holy Father wished to tell. The bishop will send a messenger to inform the pope that Baldassare was slain and the contents of his pouch lost."

"We will be blamed. The Holy Father will call us guilty of great neglect to allow his messenger to be murdered on our doorstep."

"Not if you help me find the killer and we can tell the pope his messenger is avenged."

"Gladly. We will all gladly help. But Messer Baldassare did not enter the priory by the front gate. I swear it! No one knew of his presence until the body was found."

"And when was that?"

"At Prime. We—we heard crows cawing. All through the service, the crows called. The sacristan bade the lay brother who assists him, Brother Knud, to see if some offal had been left in the graveyard. And Knud found . . . found . . . oh, it was terrible!"

"I'm sure it was," Bell said. "Can you show me just where the body was found?"

The porter led the way out of the chapel and across the chancel to the north porch door, Magdalene following silently on Sir Bellamy's heels. As annoyed as she had been with him for forcing her to make a statement about Baldassare, she was now grateful because she realized it was important for her to see where the crime had been committed. Sabina saw much with her fingers, but only what she had touched, and the shock and fear could easily have made her forget things.

The porter opened the door but did not step out. Pointing, he said, "There. You can see where he was found. The lay brothers have not been able to wash away the stain of the blood."

"There was a great deal of blood?"

Brother Godwine shuddered. "A pool of it, and that after his shirt and tunic and cloak were soaked."

"And the blood? Was it red and liquid, or brown and like a jelly or a crust?"

The porter drew a shaky breath. "Oh, I do not know. I could not look." He shuddered again. "And I certainly did not touch it."

Bell wished that the brothers had not been so quick to clean the victim's clothes. He would have liked to see for himself just how hard the bloodstains were and how much blood had been absorbed. To those unaccustomed, blood always seemed a pool or a flood when it might have been only a smear. He stepped past Brother Godwine and knelt to examine the stain. No, the mark was not owing to insufficient washing; the stain had soaked into the rough places in the mortar and stone.

"He was almost certainly killed here, on the porch, and I think some hours before Prime," Bell said. "Let me go look at the body again."

He went in and recrossed the chancel briskly. Brother Godwine hung back, but Magdalene kept pace with him, intensely curious about why he wished to reexamine the body. This time, despite Brother Godwine's anguished exclamation, he pulled down the shroud and turned the corpse so that the cut in the flesh was clear. The body turned like a block, except for one arm and leg that flopped limply. Curious as she was, Magdalene stepped back a bit, and when he bent almost close enough to kiss the wound and pulled and prodded at the flesh, she drew her breath in sharply.

"Yes, as I thought, killed long before Prime. This stiffness takes some hours to form. He was rigid when you found him, was he not?"

"I do not know," the porter said, sounding stifled.

"Brother Infirmarian took charge then. You may speak to him if you must."

Bell nodded, lifting his gaze from the wound for a moment to glance at Magdalene, who had come closer once more now that she knew what he was doing. He nodded and bent to study the cut even more closely. "I will, but later. I will want to know if he agrees with my thoughts. It seems to me that whoever stabbed Baldassare was standing close and that Baldassare made no resistance and did not move until the knife went in."

"How do you know that?" Magdalene asked, voice hushed.

"The wound is not torn, and the way the knife went in makes me think the two were nearly of a height. I would guess they knew each other well, that they walked from somewhere together, perhaps arm in arm, the killer's left arm in or near Baldassare's right. Under cover of their talk, the killer drew his knife in his right hand, turned to face Baldassare—perhaps to make a point, but I do not think they were arguing—and suddenly brought up the knife and thrust it into Baldassare's neck."

Magdalene drew back. "That is a horrible picture. But can it be real? If they knew each other and were not arguing, why should whoever it was kill poor Messer Baldassare?"

"I have no idea," Bell replied, staring sadly down at the man he had known and liked. "But I think I am near right about what happened. If they were close because they were in a nose-to-nose quarrel, Baldassare would never have allowed the other man to bring up his knife hand without raising an arm to protect himself, pushing the man away, pulling his own knife, or trying to dodge. He was well able to defend himself, for he had carried the pope's messages for years and had fought outlaws and others. Perhaps he thought his killer was going to place a hand on his shoulder or make some similar gesture. In the dark, he might not have seen the knife. This could only have been done by someone he knew and had no reason to distrust."

He rearranged the body, pulled up the shroud, and turned toward Brother Godwine. "When he was found, was his knife in its sheath as it is now? Also, do you have the knife that killed him?"

"A friend?" the porter whispered. "A friend did this?"

Bell shrugged. "Someone he did not fear."

"One of the whores did it," Brother Godwine said, his voice stronger. "He would not fear one of them."

"Not impossible," Bell remarked, and then grinned and glanced at Magdalene. "But I generally treat such women with caution, and I suspect Baldassare did, too."

"The pope's messenger?" Brother Godwine's voice rose in horror. "What would he know of such creatures?"

"Whatever any man knows. He was not in holy orders, and I am sure he did not stint himself in common comforts—fine clothes, food, wine. I doubt he stinted himself in women, either, but I also doubt a woman did this. Few are as tall as Magdalene here, and from the bruising, that knife went in with more force than most women could muster. Let me look at the knife, Brother Porter."

"If it is not there on the bench, I do not know where it is," Brother Godwine replied and looked restlessly over his shoulder. "Knud might know. He found the body and helped move it. That is the lay brother who assists Brother Paulinus."

Bell glanced quickly at Magdalene. He really could not find an excuse to take her with him when he questioned the lay brother and the infirmarian, yet he was not willing to send her back to her house where she and her women might prepare answers to questions that would be the same for all. He saw another over-the-shoulder glance.

"Is there somewhere you should be, Brother Porter?" he asked.

Brother Godwine flushed slightly. "It is dinnertime," he said. "I know I should not care for that, and I would not if Father Prior were here, but—"

Relieved, Bell smiled. "Never mind," he said. "Go and have your dinner. Knud and the infirmarian would not be pleased if I should call them away from their meal. I have other questions to ask. I will return later."

"Thank you," Brother Godwine said and turned to lead them out of the church.

When they came to the priory gate, Bell said, "One more word, Brother Porter. You now know who is lying dead and can say proper prayers for his soul. Please do so. Also, please do not bury him until Monday. The body will hold that long, will it not? I need to talk to the bishop about what arrangements he wishes to make if no friend of Baldassare's comes forward to arrange the burial."

The porter nodded brusquely, closed the gate behind them with some finality, barred it, and hurried back to enter the monastery buildings. Bell grinned.

"What will you learn from the knife and the infirmarian?" Magdalene asked as they walked along beside the priory wall. She was developing a marked respect for Sir Bellamy of Itchen and a real hope was growing in her that with his help, the murderer might be exposed.

"From the knife . . . possibly whether it was newly honed, as if it were being made ready for this act. It is no proof. A man—or woman—may hone a knife for many purposes, and I might not be able to tell anyway. With the knife in the wound for so long, the blood might have eaten away at the brightness of new honing. And the infirmarian will know far more about what becomes of a body after death. I know some things from seeing men who died in battle. I know the body stiffens and if it is left long enough, softens again, but the infirmarian may know how long this takes better than I."

"But I told you poor Messer Baldassare was dead

soon after Compline. Sabina found him not long after the service was ended."

"I know when *you* said he was dead. I need to be sure. And speaking of Sabina and what you told me about her experience, why are we walking all around the priory? Did you not say that there was a gate between the back of the church and your back garden?"

"Yes, but the sacristan locked it."

"When did you discover that?"

"Yesterday afternoon when Dulcie—" Magdalene choked slightly as she almost told him they had discovered the locked gate when Dulcie had gone to hide the pouch. "—went to clean in the church," she finished, pretending to cough to clear her throat. "She goes most days."

"So she went around the other way, as we have done?"

His voice was cool and he was smiling slightly.

Magdalene swallowed, grateful that he could not see her appalled expression behind her veil. But he knew, she thought. Even without seeing her face, he knew she was hiding something. And then she realized that Sir Bellamy was not first going to her house and then back to the priory so that Knud and the infirmarian could finish their meal, but so that she, whom he could not have kept by him when he questioned them, should not have the opportunity to go home and speak to her women in private before he did.

She glanced at him above the masking veil. Was he seeking signs of their guilt so she would have to yield her body to him? Behind the veil, her lips thinned. She would not do it—not because she cared about one futtering more or less, but because if he were that kind, he could use her yielding as another proof of her guilt.

If he asked, she thought, she would go to the bishop again—or tell William of Ypres. And then she wondered whether she was making too much of a single look and a quite justifiable desire for confirmation of her statements. Before complaint, she would do her best not to increase his suspicion, and she would explain, most carefully, why it would have been lunacy for her or any of the others to have killed Baldassare.

She swallowed again as she saw he was staring at her and then realized she had not answered him. "No," she said, "Dulcie did not go to the church at all that day, nor today, either. She was furious and said she will not clean again until our gate is opened."

"Was she angry on her own account or out of loyalty to you?"

"I think out of loyalty," Magdalene said, but this time she spoke easily, smiling a little, guessing he would hear the smile in her voice. "And yes, all the women would lie for me if I asked. They are very grateful for an easy employment in comfortable circumstances, which none could expect if I had not taken them into my household. However, I hope you will understand that we have no purpose for lying. None of us harmed Baldassare and none had any cause to do so. Indeed, his death—any client's death so near our establishment—does us the greatest harm."

Bell shrugged. "On the surface, that is true."

"And beneath the surface also. I did not know that Messer Baldassare was a papal messenger, but"—she sighed—"I guessed. His clothes, so rich and yet so sober, the way he spoke his French, which was like a client who came from Italy although he now lives in London, the pouch he carried—"

"You saw the pouch?"

"Yes, Sir Bellamy. Not clearly, he pushed it back under his cloak, and it is never my business to pry into what a client wishes to keep private. But I saw he had a pouch."

"What happened to it?"

"I suppose he took it with him when he went out. He left nothing behind. Well, after the sacristan came and accused us of murder and I had been so stupid as to deny the man had been here, you can lay odds that we searched most carefully for anything that might tie us to him. There was nothing."

"Too bad, Winchester wants that pouch."

"I feared so. The fact that Baldassare was here, so close to the bishop, made me think he carried a message from the pope for Winchester. But then I wondered why he did not simply go to the bishop's house."

"That seems clear enough. Surely he knew his entertainment here would be more lively and . . . ah . . . gratifying."

"But he did not know what kind of guesthouse it was. He stopped because of a joke one of our clients played on him. He told Baldassare that this was the Bishop of Winchester's inn and that it was just behind the church of St. Mary Overy priory. Oh!"

"Oh?"

"Oh, I have been a fool. I was so angry because I thought the intention was to besmirch the bishop with a connection to my house that I did not realize Baldassare asked to stay only after I told him that we had a back gate that led into the churchyard. Earlier he told me he had a meeting in the neighborhood, but I never thought of it being in the church."

"Is not that the most likely place? It is well known, prominent, easy to find, and always open."

"Yes, but—" Magdalene shrugged. "I suppose because he was so much at ease with us, I did not think his next stop would be a church. I thought he might be in minor orders at least, and I suppose I felt he would not stop in a whorehouse just before he planned to enter a church. On the other hand, he did not act as if being with Sabina would weigh on his conscience, or that he would need to confess to ease it, so . . . ah, here we are."

Six

21 APRIL 1139
OLD PRIORY GUESTHOUSE

Magdalene was a little disturbed when Sir Bellamy hardly reacted to the sight of her women, all sitting together near the fire. Letice and Ella were embroidering. Sabina had apparently been singing; her lute was in her lap, her fingers still in position upon it, but she must have stopped as soon as she heard the snick of the latch. Magdalene had hoped that so much beauty of all different types would distract him from her. Not that she planned to allow him access to any of the women without the normal fee—that would be tantamount to admitting they had something to hide—but she would have been more comfortable if he showed more interest and desire.

Ella jumped up as soon as they were in sight, laying aside her embroidery. She did not mind the work and did it reasonably well, if not with the exquisite skill Magdalene had, but she loved her other work much more.

"Have you brought a new friend?" she asked eagerly. "He is very pretty. My name is Ella. I am pretty, too."

Magdalene heard a faint, strangled sound from Sir Bellamy, but did not turn to look at him. "Go back to your seat, love," she said to Ella as the girl started forward. "Sir Bellamy is, indeed, a friend, but he has not come here to lie with any of us. He is on the business of the Bishop of Winchester."

Ella blinked, and her pretty mouth drooped with disappointment, but she obediently went back to her stool and picked up the embroidery. "Does that mean he can *never* come to bed? Surely when his business is done—"

"Hush, love," Magdalene said, smiling. One could not help smiling at Ella's dedication. "That is for Sir Bellamy to decide, and you know we do not urge our friends one way or the other. But I wish to make known to him Letice and Sabina now, so work and be quiet." She turned to him. "Sir Bellamy, the small, dark woman is Letice; she is mute and cannot greet you. And the woman with the lute is Sabina. Please speak so she will know where to direct her conversation; she is, as I mentioned to you, blind."

"Blind, mute, and . . ." Bell swallowed and did not finish his sentence because Ella was looking at him with bright interest and he could not call her an idiot to her face. He turned abruptly to Magdalene. "Why?" he asked. "Do you collect discards?"

"Do my women look like discards?" she snapped angrily. "Each one of them is beautiful, clean, skilled at her work. Discards indeed! I searched long and hard before I found my women."

That was not really true. Ella had been cast out of a house, bruised and bloody, and had fallen almost at Magdalene's feet. She was weeping hysterically, totally unable to understand why she had been so treated, repeating over and over that she had done her work well and carefully, that she had not broken anything or stolen anything. Only after she had got the girl home and clean and calmed did Magdalene learn that Ella had been in both the father's and the son's beds in that house, that she had thought that the greatest fun, was always eager to return, and never once asked to be compensated. It was, of course, the women of the household who had mistreated her and driven her out.

Letice and Sabina had been chosen more deliberately. Letice had come herself, having heard of Magdalene's house through the rumor that flew among such places. Because she was mute, the whoremaster for whom she worked had used her for what she knew was dangerous and dishonest work—like placing genuine seals on false documents. Letice did not mind the dishonesty; she was only fearful that she would be thrown to the wolves when the true guilty parties were suspected. Still, she had been resigned until the whoremaster decided she could be given to men who enjoyed hurting women because she could not scream. Then she had fled.

Sabina had been sold to Magdalene by another whoremistress, who complained that she was altogether too popular because her clients were forever leaving without paying. Since she could not name them nor point them out without touching them, it was almost impossible for the whoremistress to wrench the money out of them. That was unimportant to Magdalene, who collected the fee before the client joined his woman or, from many clients, received a weekly or monthly stipend that permitted reasonable access by appointment.

"Apurpose?" Sir Bellamy asked. "You chose them apurpose?"

"You may be certain I did, and also my cook, who is deaf." She smiled at him. "Have you never heard the tale of 'hear no evil, see no evil, speak no evil'? This is a safe house. Safe. I told you my clients pay very well to be assured that their possessions, their affairs, and their persons will be secret and inviolate. They feel more at ease with women who cannot speak to identify them, cannot see to describe them, and cannot remember when, where, or who. They can say what they like, do what they like—so long as they do no damage to their partners—and feel that no one will be the wiser."

She then laughed aloud. "It is not true, of course. Letice can make herself understood when she wishes; Sabina can see a great deal with her ears and fingers. Ella . . ."

He burst out laughing. "But you see and hear all—"

"Not what goes on in bed, I assure you. And that is where a man likes to feel perfectly free. In the outer chamber, he wears what armor he likes and no one tries to see what is beneath it. Also, most of my clients know me of old and know I will not betray a secret."

He stood shaking his head for a moment, then said, "I hope they realize they must tell *me* the truth."

"I did," Ella said. "I told all the truth, and that cruel man hit me with his staff. Will you hit me if you do not like my answers? They were the truth. They were."

"Certainly not," Bell said. "You see I have no staff, so I could not strike you with it."

"You have a sword."

"Only a madman would strike you with a sword for no reason. I will not, I promise."

Magdalene heard the faint note of impatience in his voice and said, "I think you will accomplish more and feel more comfortable if you question each of my women privately. We have an empty room to which you can take a bench and a stool. I can provide a small table if that will be of help."

"Thank you, that will do very well."

"Shall I ask the women each to go to her own room so that you need not be concerned lest we decide among us what to say?"

He looked at her and smiled slowly, guessing she was making the point because he had not sent her home alone from the priory. In fact, he was amused now to think he had suspected they would concoct answers. They had had a full night and day to do so already. The truth was, he had wanted to walk with her and made a stupid excuse to himself. But he was not about to admit that and spoke his first thought.

"If that had been your intention," he said, "you would have decided among you long since."

She looked surprised. "That is true, but you do not seem sure of it. We *are* innocent. To kill a client of this house would be insane. No matter how much money he was carrying, we would lose more in the long run by having our other clients lose confidence in us."

"Except that this man was a stranger. You indicated to me that you had guessed he came from Italy and that no one knew he was coming to your house. If he disappeared, who would know? If he died on the church porch, who would associate him with you? You could take all that he had—"

"Ridiculous." Magdalene laughed. "This house was the first place the monks thought of. Do you think we are unaware of how they feel? And why should we take such a chance? Would it not be more sensible to have drugged him, then smothered him and dumped him in the river? We may be sinners, but we are not fools."

"What are you saying?" Ella looked up and her eyes were round as saucers. "Did someone fall in the river?"

"No, love. We were talking about dumping offal in the river. You know that Dulcie sometimes does that."

"Does she? No, I did not know. I would never go with her to the river. My mother taught me that, never to go near the river and never to touch a knife."

"Never to touch a knife, Ella?" Bell said. "How do you eat, then?"

"With my fingers, like everyone else who has any sense. I lick them clean and wash my hands after." She shuddered. "I could not put a knife in my mouth. I have to look away when friends do it."

"Letice cuts up her food," Magdalene said, shook her head slightly, and turned away. "If that bench near the hearth on the east wall and the stool by the window will suit you, take them."

Bell picked up the bench and stool and followed her down the corridor to the last room on the right. He had been a little suspicious at first when Magdalene suggested he question the women separately in private, but by now he was reasonably sure it was not to hide anything from him but from Ella, who caught bits and pieces of the talk, did not understand it, and was easily frightened.

It looked less and less likely that these women had had any part in Baldassare's death. The mute was simply too small. Had she used the knife, it would have gone in at a completely different angle. There was a small possibility that the blind woman could have killed him by accident, but the cut would not have been so clean if she had been flailing around. Ella? He shook his head. He tended to believe in her fear of knives; she was plainly several bushels lacking of a full load of corn.

Magdalene could have done it; she was tall enough and strong enough—and he suspected there had been an accusation of murder in her past—but she was the least likely to act out of rage or fear. And if those were not the cause, she had made a telling point about the killing. It would have been infinitely easier for them to drug Baldassare's wine and dispose of him without a drop of blood being shed and, considering how close they were to the river, without much chance of the body's being found anywhere near them. That was more a woman's way, too, than using a knife.

Magdalene opened the door and stepped in. Bell stopped in the doorway, surprised by the chamber. The walls were smoothly plastered, which was pleasant though not unusual, but the size of the room was. It was nearly six long paces wide, four paces deep, and well lit by three small windows right under the ceiling.

"This was a priory guesthouse chamber?" he asked, setting the bench and stool down.

Magdalene laughed. "No, the sisters were not at all given to comforts of the flesh. This was *three* guesthouse cells, as you can see by the three windows. Each cell was just wide enough for a cot for a night's lodging."

"Could you not make more profit by having more women?"

"This is not a common stew," Magdalene said coldly. "And no, I could not make more profit, because no man would pay my price for a filthy cell and a filthy slut. I have told you over and over why I am desperate to find Messer Baldassare's killer. I sell pleasure in comfort and security."

Bell suddenly turned and stared at her, alerted to a fact he had missed by the pride in her voice. He realized that because he had met her in the bishop's presence, he had failed to be surprised as he should have been by her speech and manner. This woman was not common-born. A whore she might be now, but she had been born a lady.

"Besides," she was continuing, "when I came here, the house was in great disorder—" She shuddered. "There was old blood on the walls, and the vermin. . . . There are always fleas and lice, but these were so thick they walked about on each other in layers out in the open. I could not use the place as it was, so it was reasonable to make it suit my purposes. Since the walls did not support anything"—her mouth twisted—"except vermin, I had them taken down and replaced to give more space. I had the bishop's permission."

His lopsided smile acknowledged that he recognized she was unlikely to fail to take that precaution. "I remember now. I remember wondering, when I was driving out the two-legged vermin, whether the bishop should not have the place pulled down."

"A stone-built house with a slate roof pulled down? What a waste. No, after the inner walls were gone and the place stripped to the bare stone—I even had the floors up—we had sulfur burned for three days and shut the place up tight for three more. Then I had the house scrubbed and new walls built and the whole place plastered. An apothecary gave me something to put into the water used for the plaster which, he swore, was a flea bane. We are careful, of course. The bath is across the corridor and if a guest needs one, he gets one—free of charge. So far, we have had no trouble."

He nodded. "Well, it will be a pleasure to work here."

Magdalene said she would get from her chamber the small table on which she sometimes did accounts and left him. When she returned, she set the table down. Sir Bellamy had moved the bench to the wall under the window and placed the stool opposite it, near the middle of the room. He smiled at her, took the table and set it in front of the bench.

"There is another reason why I would not harm a messenger from Italy whom I believed was connected to the Church," she said, "especially one who mentioned the Bishop of Winchester. I am indebted to the Bishop of Winchester, who not only allowed me to rent this house, but gave me personal assurances that—"

"I thought that Guiscard de Tournai carried the offer of the house to you," Bell said, sitting down on the bench. "Did I not hear you say that to him in the bishop's house?"

"Yes, you did." Magdalene sat on the stool and saw that his placement of the bench, table, and stool had been very clever. His face was visible, but not enough light struck it directly to make out small changes in expression, while the light from the windows was full on her face. "However, I did not like or trust Guiscard. He would give me no assurance about how long I could keep the house, the rent was exorbitant, and he spoke as if Lord William had given him grave insult by recommending me. So I refused his offer."

Bell laughed. "Guiscard must have been surprised. But how did you get the house after all?"

"When I told William what had happened, he arranged for me to meet the bishop directly." Magdalene laughed. "I was greatly amused to discover that Henry of Winchester was much less proud than his servant. He offered me a leasehold of the house, under conditions I was delighted to accept—except for the rent—" She sighed. "But his offer was more reasonable than Guiscard's, and the bishop's protection is worth the pennies I could otherwise save."

"Have you needed his protection?"

"Not before this dreadful killing took place. The fact that he is my landlord and I have a leasehold signed and sealed by him has been sufficient against the few pretense churchmen who have tried to exact money . . . or services . . . from us. I hated to trouble him with this matter, but Prior Benin is away and Brother Paulinus only screamed that we had murdered poor Messer Baldassare and would not listen to a word I said." She hesitated, then said, "Is it not strange that no one sent news of the murder to the bishop? Is not St. Mary Overy under his direction?"

"The last I cannot tell you. I am seldom involved in purely Church matters, except for now and again carrying a message from the bishop. It is when Church affairs come head-to-head with those of the laity that I am employed. As to the first . . . I agree that it is very strange. Since the bishop is also acting as administrator of the London diocese, I would assume it would be necessary to inform him when a murder took place near a church just across the road from his dwelling."

The frown on Magdalene's face had grown more pronounced. "I will tell you something else. When I spoke of the murder to the bishop, I thought that Guiscard would spit at me."

Bell grinned. "It was because you passed him by and ignored him. Guiscard does not like to be overlooked, but he can know nothing about the murder. He left Southwark on Tuesday morning and did not return until last night. Each time the bishop comes to stay in London, Guiscard takes a few days leave to visit his mother. In any case, I will attend to that matter and that of whether or not the news was carried to the bishop, and if it was, who received it."

"I will be happy to leave it to you, but . . . I . . . we are very eager to find this killer. Will you not tell me what you discover? Indeed, Sir Bellamy, I know men and their motives. It is possible that I can help."

She rose as she spoke, turned toward the door, turned back. "Which of the women shall I send to you?"

He learned nothing from Ella or Letice. Ella did not even remember Baldassare being in the house, and Letice had seen him only during the evening meal. Sabina had the most to tell and seemed to hold nothing back, but Bell could not see that anything Baldassare said or did while he was with her was pertinent to his murder— except that by Compline the front gate was locked so that Baldassare must have used the gate that led to the church. Finally, he took Sabina through the events after she left the house. She told him of her desire to pray in the church and of how she had to wait because the sacristan would have opposed her entering.

"And you are sure it was the sacristan's voice you heard just before the thud and the running footsteps?"

Her lips thinned. "Yes. I know it well enough; we all do. And I would like to know what Brother Paulinus was doing in the church at that hour. Was he not supposed to be abed? Are not the doors the business of Brother Porter?"

"I do not know, but the sacristan is a high official of the priory, with responsibility for the church plate and vessels. It is not impossible that he came to check on something, make something ready for the next day's service, or perform some other duty. But I will ask him. You may be sure I will ask him. Think again, Sabina. Did you hear anything else?"

She started to shake her head, then frowned. "A door closed. I thought Brother Paulinus closed the door to the porch, which is what I told you. But I never touched the door and cannot be sure whether it was open or closed. Now that I think again, perhaps the air felt as if the door was open? Perhaps the sound of closing was farther away? Oh, I do not know. I am not sure. I have thought so much about this that I fear I am making up things."

Bell rose and came to pat her shoulder gently. She did not start or show any surprise, and her head was turned toward him before he touched her. She did indeed see through her ears, he thought.

"That is enough," he said. "Let us join the others."

His next duty was to search the house, which he did with painstaking thoroughness, examining every hidden corner in the cellar and loft, every shelf, and even the niches between the beams and supports, which made Magdalene catch her breath. Alert, his eyes flicked to her. There was nothing in her expression, but their glances locked and he was surer than ever that Baldassare had hidden the pouch in the house and that the women had found it and hidden it elsewhere.

Aside from that one flicker of unease, the women warmly encouraged the search, which left him torn between feeling that what he was doing was ridiculous and that they wanted him to think it was ridiculous so he would be careless in his examination. Nonetheless, careful as he was, he found nothing and finally returned to the common room.

"I have been thinking," he said to Magdalene, seating himself on Ella's stool, "that what you suggested on the way here is only sensible. We will do better in solving this mystery if we work together and exchange information." He wondered if he was a fool to make such an offer to a whore but he thought, fool or not, he could not lose much; likely they knew more than he did. "You realize, do you not," he added, now intending to frighten them a little, "that the person who killed Baldassare must have been here or in the priory?"

Bell heard the quick, indrawn breath of Letice and Sabina, but Magdalene's expression did not change.

They had not thought it all out, but *she* had. A face like an angel's, a mind like a trap. If he found any reason at all why she should want Baldassare dead. . . . He suppressed a shudder. And a gentlewoman, who could have learned to use a knife, too—a very dangerous lady indeed.

Magdalene nodded slowly. "Yes. I did realize that, which is one of the reasons I have been so frightened. I *know* none of us did this thing, but if our front gate was locked when the last client left, just before dark, and the priory gate was guarded—as it always is by Brother Godwine or his assistants—then the murderer must have been confined to my house and grounds or to the priory."

"That puts more suspicion on you," he said, "but it is not all bad. At least we do not need to suspect the whole city of Southwark and all of London, too. That gives us a better chance to find out who committed the crime."

"Well, of course, someone might have climbed the wall," Magdalene offered, then sighed. "But it is a high wall, and spiked, not easy to climb, and the Watch does keep an eye on this place. So, yes, it is among the people who were within these walls that we are likely to find the guilty one." She sighed again. "I did not mention it before because I hoped you would see some other possibility, but yes, I saw it, too."

You would, Bell thought, but he did not respond to her directly. "Sabina," he said, "would you have been able to tell if someone was hiding in your grounds while you sat in the garden waiting for Baldassare to return?"

The blind girl sat silent, head bowed, hands clasped lightly. Then, slowly, she shook her head. "I am sorry, no. First, if the person was still, I would have felt no movement of air nor heard any crunch of leaves. And even if the person did move about . . . I was listening to the service. I would have heard a loud sound—a sharp crack of a stick or a kicked stone rattling, and I did not hear those. But a soft footfall . . . I fear not."

Bell was more pleased than disappointed by her answer. She knew now that it would be strongly to the advantage of the women of the Old Priory Guesthouse that someone be hiding in the garden, and she still did not pretend to have heard any sign of an intruder.

"That does not mean much," he said, wishing to cheer her up as a reward for her truthfulness. "A person knowing the time of appointment could have slipped in at any time in the afternoon, especially if he knew the gate would be locked at night. He could then have gone into the priory grounds, or even into the church at any time before you came out."

Letice reached out to touch Bell's arm and shook her head vigorously, pointing to the priory and church.

"He did not go to the church or priory," Magdalene interpreted, then asked, "Why?"

Fingers mimed searching, throwing things about.

"The saddlebags and feed!" Magdalene exclaimed. "Of course, he must have been in our grounds—perhaps even hiding in the stable—after Messer Baldassare arrived. How unfortunate that no one needed to look into the stable until after Messer Baldassare was dead!"

"I do not see any connection—" Bell began.

"Yes, yes," Magdalene interrupted impatiently. "If the saddlebags were searched for the pouch—I am assuming it was the pouch the killer was looking for—before Messer Baldassare's death, then the killer had no personal animosity toward Messer Baldassare. Had he found what he wanted, doubtless he would have taken it and disappeared. If he did not look until after he had killed, we know two things. First, that Messer Baldassare did not have the pouch with him when he met the killer, which likely means he was at least a bit suspicious about the meeting, and second, that he had therefore hidden his most precious possession . . . perhaps near where he waited in the church so he could get it quickly if all went well."

"Hid the pouch in the church?" Bell repeated, looking sidelong at Magdalene.

What she said was surely possible, but Bell was more sure than ever that these women, not poor Baldassare, had found and hidden the pouch. Still, there was no sense pressing the point. They would deny it to protect themselves—for which he did not really blame them—and they would be more likely to give themselves away (except Magdalene) if he pretended he believed them.

"But even so," he went on, "why *kill* Baldassare? That wound was not made by someone who crept up from behind and stabbed to steal his purse. The murderer knew Baldassare. He was walking with him, talking to him. Even say he asked for the pouch and Baldassare refused to give it to him, why kill? All he had to do was pretend to leave and watch. Baldassare would have had to retrieve the pouch sooner or later."

"The most obvious reason," Magdalene replied, "is that Baldassare *did* know him and that knowledge was somehow very dangerous. Perhaps the killer should not have asked for the pouch or should not have known about it. Whatever the reason, being known to him, he needed to silence Baldassare. Another reason is that it would not matter to the killer where the pouch was so long as it did not come to light. With the pouch hidden and Baldassare dead and unable to tell where it was, the killer would have accomplished his purpose. And of course there are always personal reasons. It is true that Messer Baldassare was a foreigner, but you did say that he came to England often. Therefore, he could have both friends and enemies here."

She was right, of course, Bell thought, but what had honed her mind to such keenness? A past murder charge she had fled or escaped? That idea took such hold on him that he could not think what to say. Fortunately his silence was covered by the blind woman.

"But would an enemy bother to search through poor

Messer Baldassare's saddlebags, and even the hay and feed?" Sabina asked.

"Hmmm." Magdalene hummed thoughtfully. "Perhaps not, but it would depend on the person. If it was someone within the Church, he might guess what Baldassare was carrying was important and wish to know what it was, or even to use it to gain money or power. Oh, that search is tantalizing. What a shame none of our guests that night rode a horse and we had no cause to go to the stable."

At that moment a bell could be heard pealing briefly and Letice jumped up. "Wait," Magdalene said. "Sir Bellamy, will it be all right for Letice to tell her client about Messer Baldassare's death? I fear it would be unnatural to ignore such an exciting circumstance as a killing next door."

"Why not?" Bell shrugged. "There is no reason not to mention it to your clients. It is no secret. And it can do no hurt also to ask if any of these men knew Baldassare and had any idea of why anyone should want to harm him."

Letice nodded and hurried out the door. Turning to watch through the oiled parchment window, Bell saw her shadow meet another's. He could see some movement, likely Letice gesturing at her client, and then the two shadows moved away around the corner of the house.

"It is time for me to go," he said. "Your clients will be coming now, and I do not wish to cause you trouble."

Magdalene rose, thanked him, smiling, and asked if there was any other way she could help him—and then tucked the corners of her lips back at his expression. Bell was wise enough not to speak the thought that had come in answer to her question. He merely said he would search the stable just to be thorough before he went to report to the bishop, have his dinner, and then speak to the infirmarian and the lay brother who had found the body. If anything new came of those interviews, he would let her know.

She thanked him again, asked if he knew where the stable was, and when he said he did, put aside her embroidery and politely saw him to the door. He had more hopes of the stable, because the women had made such a point of its being searched, but he found no more there than he had found in the house. As he tossed back the last bale he had examined, he heard the bell at the gate peal.

From the shadows by the door of the stable, Bell saw Magdalene come from the house and open the gate for a richly dressed man—a fur-lined cloak thrown back to show a dark tunic embroidered with silver, dark stockings or chausses bound with silver-embroidered cross garters, and silver-buckled red-leather shoes. He had dark hair sprinkled lightly with gray, dark eyes, a prominent nose that in the future might meet his strong chin, and a decided paunch, not quite concealed by the handsome tunic. Bell grimaced; he knew Master Buchuinte, who had only last year been the justiciar of London and still had considerable influence.

Buchuinte stepped through the gate and held out his hands to Magdalene, who took them with a beaming smile and pressed them gently. Suppressing an insane desire to leap out, draw his sword, and smash the smile off that confident face, Bell silently watched them enter the house. He stood glaring at the door after it had closed, cursing the man who was about to have what he could not. And then he took a deep breath and reminded himself that he could, too, have it—for the price of five silver pennies—and had to swallow, and swallow again, as sickness rose in his throat. That was not how he wanted Magdalene.

Seven

❧

21 APRIL 1139

OLD PRIORY GUESTHOUSE

"Oh, Master Buchuinte," Magdalene said as soon as she had closed the door of the house behind her, "the most dreadful thing has happened. There has been a murder, right on the north porch of the church."

"A murder!"

"Yes, and of a papal messenger—"

"What?" Buchuinte roared, making Magdalene gasp and draw back. "A papal messenger? You mean Baldassare?"

"Oh, heavens," Magdalene breathed. "You knew him?"

The man's dark skin had turned a sickly gray. "When?" he asked. "When did this happen?"

Magdalene wondered whether he had deliberately ignored her question, but she answered his. "Wednesday night, we think. We only learned on Thursday morning when—"

"Wednesday night?" Buchuinte echoed, his dark eyes nearly popping from his head. "Wednesday? The day I was here? You mean Baldassare was here, too?"

"No. That is, yes, he did stop here but he did not stay with us." She put a hand on his arm. "Oh, do come and sit down, Master Buchuinte. I can see that you have had a dreadful shock. I had no idea you knew Messer Baldassare, or I would not have spoken so bluntly."

"I cannot believe it," he muttered, following her to the table and dropping down on a bench. He looked up, but his eyes did not see her. "He had told me he had to meet someone that night and could not stay. That was why I did not send a messenger to cancel my appointment here."

"Did he say whom he would meet? And where?" Magdalene tried to keep her voice low and without inflection.

"No. No. He spoke of the meeting only because I said I would change my plans for the afternoon. He told me he could not stay because he was later than he had expected to be in arriving at London and a meeting he had arranged was set for that very night. He said that he would come back to London and visit with me after he had delivered a message to the king." Buchuinte passed a hand over his face and shook his head. "Perhaps he would have told me more but did not wish to speak too freely before his traveling companion."

"Was he on ill terms with the man?" Magdalene asked. Baldassare had seemed more amused by Beaumeis's misdirection than angry. Did Buchuinte, who had been in her house on the night Baldassare was killed, have some reason to make it seem Baldassare and Beaumeis were enemies? That doubt was settled immediately.

"No, not at all," Buchuinte said, still looking dazed and as if he was answering while his mind was elsewhere. "I would say he and Richard de Beaumeis liked one another. But Beaumeis was a churchman, a dean in the Archbishop of Canterbury's service, and what Baldassare was carrying might have been something the pope wished to have kept secret until the person who was to receive it had the news."

"Did they leave together, Beaumeis and Baldassare?"

"Beaumeis left before dinner. He said he needed to ride to Canterbury with all haste on some errand from the new archbishop. Baldassare was not in a hurry and we ate at leisure, but we had begun to talk of old friends and I . . . I never asked again about the meeting." He continued to stare at the table for a moment longer, then suddenly raised his head and asked sharply, "And why are you so curious about Baldassare's movements?"

"Why do you think?" Magdalene replied, allowing her lips to twist with bitterness. "Because we have been accused of killing him, of course. We are whores. We are here. Thus, we are guilty. My only safety, Master Buchuinte, rests in discovering who truly killed Messer Baldassare."

"How can you be guilty if he was killed . . . you said on the porch of the church?"

"Oh, we followed him there to prevent him from confessing a sin he had not committed. After that, we stole his purse and—"

"That is ridiculous," Buchuinte said. "Not a farthing have I ever lost in this house, not even a ribbon I brought apurpose for my Little Flower. Unless I tell her she is to take it, she will untie it from her very body to hand back to me."

Magdalene sighed. "I know it. My livelihood depends on the honesty of my women and the security we provide for our guests. You know it. All my clients know it. But to the monks of the priory, we are whores and thus guilty."

"It is far more likely that some felon saw Baldassare's fat purse." He stopped abruptly and frowned. "Why was he here, south of London, when the king is in Nottingham?"

"For the meeting he spoke of?" Magdalene knew that was true; Baldassare had told her his meeting was close by, but she could not admit that. "He did not tell me. When he rang the bell at the gate, he asked for the Bishop of Winchester's house, which, he had been told—apparently as a joke by that wicked Richard de Beaumeis—was behind the church of St. Mary Overy priory. We spoke for a while. I had to tell him where the bishop's house really was and he mentioned that the church seemed very close to this house. I said there was a gate that led there, but not large enough for a horse to pass. We parted. It was cold. I had run out without my cloak. I did not stay to see which way he went."

He had hardly listened, apparently, for with his eyes fixed on her but not seeing her, he next said, "Yes, I am sure he had a full purse, because after I arranged for the horse he would ride, he said he would go to the goldsmith—Basyngs, it was. He left and I finished up some work, then I came here." His eyes came into focus on her face. "What time did he come to the gate?"

"It was near sunset."

"Then he did not come here from my house," Buchuinte said. "He must have gone to the goldsmith and spent some time there. Near sunset? I suppose I was asleep when he arrived. Ella was very"—a slight smile touched his lips—"very much herself. I woke later than usual. If only I had been awake! If I had heard his voice, I could have gone with him—"

Magdalene laid a hand over his. "Master Buchuinte, he was ahorse, you afoot. You could not have gone together. And the bishop's man, Sir Bellamy of Itchen, says Messer Baldassare was not seized and stabbed from behind as a thief would do. He said Baldassare knew the killer, that he may have walked with him, talked to him . . . trusted him. Are you sure Messer Baldassare gave no hint of whom he was to meet?"

He shook his head. "And now he is dead! Oh, I cannot believe it. He overcame so many dangers in the years he served the pope! How could this happen on the porch of a church, right in the doorway to salvation? I cannot believe it!" He sighed heavily and stood up. "Tell Ella I am sorry, but I cannot . . . I simply cannot . . ."

His hand went to his purse. Magdalene laid hers atop and prevented him from taking out the coins. "We grieve with you. Just send a message and Ella will be waiting whenever you wish to see her."

He sighed again. "Likely at my usual time next week. I do grieve, but mostly from shock. I liked Baldassare. He was a good man. But he was not a friend I saw every day and will miss bitterly. I saw him only twice or thrice a year." He sighed once more. "Nonetheless, we both came from Firenze; our families were acquainted. I must arrange for his burial and for masses for his soul and . . . and I suppose I must write to the pope. . . ."

"No. That will be taken care of by the bishop, I am sure. I brought him the news this morning and he was also shocked and grieved." She hesitated, and then continued. "You know, Master Buchuinte, if you wish to know more than what Sir Bellamy was willing to tell me, you should go and speak to the bishop, or to Sir Bellamy. They will be more open to you, I am sure." And you will think that is how they learned you were here that night and not feel I betrayed you, she thought. "Also, perhaps, because of their knowledge of Church affairs, one of them can guess more from what Messer Baldassare said to you than you or I could."

"Well thought of, Magdalene. Well thought of. Yes, I will do that."

He turned toward the door, but cast a rather longing glance at the corridor that led to Ella's room. Magdalene suppressed a smile. The shock over, she guessed that he was regretting the postponement of his visit with Ella and restrained only by the impropriety of making love so soon after hearing of his friend's death. He knew how Ella would be waiting—sitting up in the bed naked, her hair plaited like that of a little girl, the braids hanging down beside her enchanting breasts, because that was what he found exciting.

Magdalene kept her face placid, although black memories of what she had seen flashed through her mind. She found a smile. Thank God Master Buchuinte was satisfied with Ella's "childishness." There were those men who literally demanded children. Well, not in her house! She rose to see him out. Once more Buchuinte sighed.

"Tell Ella that I will bring her something pretty to make up for missing her company today," he said.

The bell at the gate pealed. Magdalene smiled at him. "Come out the back way, Master Buchuinte. Unfortunately, I cannot take you through the gate to the church. The sacristan locked the gate after Messer Baldassare's death, so you will have to go the long way around."

He was so reluctant to go that he lingered for some time in the garden, talking to her, hoping, she guessed, that she would urge him to change his mind and come back to the house. She did think about it, but decided that although he did not wish to be deprived of his pleasure, that pleasure would turn sour in his mouth when he thought about it later. And, of course, he would blame her for his lust, telling himself that he would have gone to the church to see Baldassare but that she was greedy for the fee and had overpersuaded him so as not to lose it.

Magdalene finally got him out the gate and headed up toward the lane that followed the priory wall. She grinned as she turned back to the house. Likely Master Buchuinte was thoroughly annoyed with her for not permitting him to fry his peas and still use them as seed, but he would never admit that to himself. And it would do her no harm, because his anger would fade in his glow of righteousness at having conquered his lust for the sake of his dead friend. He would be back on Monday with a clear conscience and an even greater taste for the pleasures Ella offered.

As she entered the house Magdalene paused. When she left, Sabina had been sitting by the fire, humming softly to herself. Now she was gone. Apparently she had got Dulcie to go with her to let in the client while Magdalene was in the back garden with Buchuinte. She was surprised not to see Letice yet. Her guest was keeping her later than usual, unless he had left and the late-afternoon client had already come? She had not heard the bell, but several clients liked to walk in without the courtesy of ringing it. And just as the thought formed, the peal sounded. Magdalene laughed at herself for that prick of pride. The last thing a whore needed was pride. Smiling, she went out to the gate again.

"Somer!" she exclaimed when she saw the man who had just dismounted. "Did you send a message for me to expect you?"

"No, because I did not know I was coming until late last night. I have been on the road since first light. Take me in and feed me at least, and give me a bed for the night, even if none of the girls can lie in it with me."

"Ah, I can do better than an empty bed—" She broke off abruptly, remembering why Ella's bed was empty, then grasped his hand and drew him in. "Good Lord," she said as she shut the gate behind him, "you are the man I should have prayed to see if I had a grain of sense. Put your horse in the stable and come in. I will get Dulcie to find something for you to eat. I have news I think William should hear."

Somer de Loo grimaced when Magdalene said she had news for his master, but he nodded and led his horse briskly to the stable. Magdalene understood the expression. Somer was one of William of Ypres's most trusted mercenary captains. He had doubtless come from Rochester to London on some business of William's, since he said he had been on the road since first light; however, business done, he probably had William's permission to spend some time enjoying the delights of the city—including several visits to Magdalene's house at his master's expense. It was a reward William often offered his men for good service that was not dangerous enough or important enough to be rewarded in gold. Now Somer guessed he would have to ride back to Rochester with the news Magdalene had mentioned.

When he came in he was still scowling, but the expression changed to a smile when he saw a place at the table provided with a large wedge of pasty, several slices of fat roast pork on a trencher, a bowl of stewed greens, a tall footed cup filled with wine, and to the side, a substantial piece of tart, spilling a luscious-looking filling into the baking pan—and Ella, sitting on the bench beside his place and dimpling with smiles.

"I am starving," he said, sitting down and kissing her.

She returned the salute with enthusiasm, embracing him with one arm and breaking off a chunk of the pasty with her free hand. As soon as he came up for air, she popped the tidbit into his mouth. Between laughing and trying to chew, he almost choked. Ella patted him on the back and apologized anxiously, so he kissed her again, but after that he gave his attention to the food, and Ella slid away from him when he drew his knife to spear a piece of meat.

"There is plenty more if you want it," Magdalene assured him.

He paused with the meat on the point of his knife and raised his brow at her tone of voice. Magdalene shrugged. Somer bit off a substantial chunk of meat.

"None of us had much appetite for dinner with the bishop's man searching our house while we ate."

Somer's eyes bulged as he struggled to swallow his mouthful of food. "Searching?" he croaked. "Searching for what?"

"The papal messenger's pouch."

"What?"

It was as well he had swallowed the meat, Magdalene thought, or he would have choked in earnest. "Baldassare de Firenze, a papal messenger, was murdered on the north porch of the church of St. Mary Overy priory on Wednesday night."

There was a moment of silence. Somer laid down the knife still holding a bite of the pork. "The damned fool," he said. "Why did he not come—" He cut that remark off and went on hurriedly. "Then the king's matter has been decided and the messenger killed before the pope's decision could be announced. So the bishop's man searched for the pouch and did not find it. Where is it?"

Magdalene shook her head nervously. "I do not know," she said. "When the messenger came here he was carrying a pouch, but he took it with him when he left. I doubt whether it has been destroyed, however. Sir Bellamy of Itchen, the Bishop of Winchester's knight, thought Messer Baldassare was not wearing the pouch when he was killed. Baldassare could have hidden it." Then, as Somer's mouth hardened, she added, "You had better hear the whole tale from the beginning—as much as I know myself—and let William decide for himself what he wants to do."

* * *

21 APRIL 1139,

THE BISHOP'S HOUSE

When Bell left the Old Priory Guesthouse, he was so sick and angry that he was sure he had been trapped, tricked, lied to, and led around by the nose like a newly ringed bull. All that sweetness and light. All that eager cooperation. Now everything the women had said seemed false, and Magdalene's winning smiles and dulcet tones were the falsest of all.

"Whore," he muttered to himself, striding along the street, so blind with rage that he did not realize he had passed the priory gate until he walked into the bishop's house. Then he stood in the midst of the hall, shaking with shame and self-disgust. He was so taken up with jealousy over a common whore that he had forgotten he wanted to speak to the sacristan's assistant and the infirmarian. About to turn on his heel, he heard Guiscard call his name. He took a deep breath and walked to the end of the room.

"So how did you make out with your whore?" Guiscard asked, smiling knowingly. "You do not have to tell me. You are now sure she is innocent." He chuckled. "Do not let it trouble you. She can even convince the bishop that the sun is shining when it rains."

Bell struggled to keep his lips from thinning with fury; he would not give Guiscard the satisfaction of knowing his shaft had struck home. He raised his brows. "You are wrong about the bishop," he remarked, pleased by the indifference in his voice. "He warned me against Magdalene's charms."

Guiscard frowned, his hand stroking the rich, shining velvet of his gown. "But he himself is not invulnerable to them. She diddled him out of nearly half the rent I could have got for the house. And cheated me out of my fee as agent, too."

"Oh-ho." Bell grinned, feeling better. What Magdalene told him about renting the house was true. "She told me she rented direct from the bishop, but she did not admit that any agent's fee was involved. She said you did not offer her a leasehold."

"Who offers a whore a leasehold—except a man befuddled by her beauty? You let a whore rent from week to week. If she does well, you raise the rent." Guiscard sniffed. "The bishop is too indulgent toward sin."

Bell watched the clerk's hand stroke his velvet gown. There were sins and sins, he thought. "I worry more about guilt than sin," he said. "And despite her trade, I cannot find any reason to think Magdalene guilty of murder."

Guiscard sniffed again. "Well, I do not like her, but I agree she would not be likely to murder unless Baldassare was carrying so rich a purse that she could not resist killing him for it, or"—his lips turned down with distaste—"her great patron paid her well to kill."

"Baldassare—" Bell began, and then the last thing Guiscard said struck him. "You mean William of Ypres? But why under heaven should William of Ypres want the papal messenger killed? And how could he know Baldassare would go to Magdalene's house?"

"Because he had arranged to meet him there? It is a common place of resort to those who wish to talk to William of Ypres. And murder is the first thing Ypres would think of to make trouble, coarse and brutal as he is."

"Coarse and brutal I will allow, but not stupid," Bell said. "William of Ypres does not need more trouble."

The bishop had commented, however, that Ypres used the Old Priory Guesthouse for purposes other than lechery. Could one of Ypres's men have met Baldassare there and killed him? For what? The pouch? But if the pouch held a decision in favor of the king and a bull granting legatine power to Winchester, William of Ypres should want it delivered.

Guiscard shrugged. "You were the one who needed reasons. If you were not bedazzled by her, you would know the whore was guilty and not look further."

It was too common a sentiment for Bell to allow his anger to show. "Unfortunately, until I know who is truly guilty," he said, "I will not know what happened to Baldassare's pouch, and the bishop wants that pouch."

"Pouch!" Guiscard exclaimed, paling. "What pouch?"

"A papal messenger carries a pouch—and it was not with the body."

"My God," Guiscard breathed, eyes wide. "Could he have been carying the bull making our bishop legate?"

"It could be," Bell said. "I think Winchester has that suspicion also and is greatly concerned that one of his enemies might have attacked Baldassare."

Guiscard nodded. "The bishop is much overset by Baldassare's death, and in such a way. I hope the pouch was not stolen and the bull destroyed." He sighed. "He asked to see you as soon as you came in, but he is eating now."

The word "eating" made Bell's mouth water. He suddenly remembered that he had had no dinner and that the bishop was not above inviting him to join him in a meal if he had no other guests.

"Good," he said. "I am starving. I will go in right now." He suited the action to the words before Guiscard could rise or protest.

"My lord?"

Henry of Winchester lifted his head. "Bell. Do you have news for me?"

"Nothing definite about the pouch, my lord, except I can assure you that it is not in the Old Priory Guesthouse or the stable, and I have some hope that Baldassare was not wearing it when he was killed."

"Then where is it?"

"That is what I do not know . . . yet."

He should have said that he had a strong suspicion that Magdalene had found it and hidden it again elsewhere, perhaps in the church, but he could not get the words out. Because he dared not meet his master's eyes, he looked fixedly at the tureen of stew standing before the bishop. Then the smell hit him, and he swallowed.

"Are you hungry? Would Magdalene not even feed you?" Winchester asked, laughing. "I thought she would do that."

"She did offer me dinner, but I wished to search the house and stable while she and her women were fixed in one place."

"Then sit down and eat, man. You must be starved."

"Thank you, my lord."

Bell fetched a stool from against the wall and set it near the bishop's chair. Henry pushed a loaf of bread and several dishes toward him. Bell pulled his knife from his belt and carved some slices off a roast haunch, which he laid on one piece of bread, then tore off another piece to scoop chunks of fish and vegetables from the bowl of stew.

The bishop frowned. "But if Baldassare died Wednesday night, Magdalene and her women had all day Thursday and all Friday morning to be rid of the pouch. Why did you search?"

Bell swallowed hastily but did not speak at once, trying to separate his angry jealousy from the information he had gained from questioning Magdalene's women. "I think they are hiding something," he said slowly, "but I do not believe it is knowledge of Baldassare's death. For the other question . . . I searched because they kept telling me over and over that they would not be such fools as to leave anything of Baldassare's in the house—"

"Ah, I see." The bishop laughed again. "A wise move."

"But I found nothing. And that brought to mind another important question. Why did Magdalene have nearly two days to search her own house and grounds before the news of Baldassare's death came to you? The fault was not Magdalene's. She did not find the body. Why is it that the monks did not send you word of a dead man on the porch of their church?"

Winchester watched Bell bend a slice of meat in half with his knife, push the point through it, and raise it to his mouth. "That *is* strange," he said slowly. "I think you will have to ask Prior Benin—no, he is away at the mother house of his order and will not be back until tomorrow, so he cannot be faulted for this. It is Brother Paulinus, the sacristan, who is in charge." Winchester smiled thinly. "Yes. Ask Brother Paulinus why I needed to hear this news a day late from a whore. And what else?"

Bell smiled also. Then, between chewing and swallowing, he told Winchester everything he had seen and learned, including the position and shape of the wound, which implied Baldassare had known and trusted his killer, and the fact that with the guesthouse gate locked at dark and the porter on duty at the priory gate, it must be one of those within the walls who was guilty.

"Or someone who came in before the gates were locked," Winchester said. "But let us deal first with those known to us. You have questioned the women and do not believe them guilty?"

Bell shrugged. "No, not of murder." Except Magdalene, he thought. She knows too much of murder. But he went on smoothly. "The mute is too small. Baldassare slept with the blind woman, Sabina, but I cannot see how she could have placed the knife so cleanly. And the idiot . . . no. One must experience Ella to believe her, but murder with a knife is not possible."

"Mute? Blind? Idiot?" Winchester said, shaking his head doubtfully.

Bell laughed. "I had forgotten you have never been there and know none except Magdalene. She says she chose her women on the 'hear no evil, speak no evil, see no evil' principle and that her wealthy and powerful clients are more comfortable with women they believe cannot identify them."

"Very well. I never thought Magdalene or anyone she controlled guilty. She is too clever to get caught with a dead body so near her as the church porch or to permit so bloody a death. If she were guilty, her victim would be clean and neat and no one would ever know how, when, or where he had died. So, the monks and their guests?"

"I will have no trouble questioning the monks. I have already told Brother Godwine, the porter, that the way to escape the pope's blame for allowing his messenger to be slaughtered on their doorstep is to find the killer and see that Baldassare is avenged."

"Very good. Very good indeed." Winchester hesitated, surprised by Bell's expression, and then asked, "Why do you look so black?"

"Guests," Bell snarled through set teeth. "Those

women so befuddled me that I forgot to ask the names of the men who were with them the night Baldassare died."

"Ah, well," Winchester said indulgently, "that is not something that a few hours will change. Nor will the men disappear. Mostly the same men come there, and all her clients are recommended by others."

"But she took Baldassare—"

"No, he had a recommendation of sorts," Winchester said, his voice cold and his lips stiff. "Richard de Beaumeis told Baldassare to go to the Old Priory Guesthouse—only, he called it the Bishop of Winchester's inn."

Bell was surprised by the bishop's controlled rage when he mentioned Beaumeis, for the name meant nothing to him, but the last phrase explained it. "I think that pup needs a lessoning," he remarked, his hand dropping to his sword hilt.

"Not from you," Winchester said quickly. "He knows you as my man. It will only give him another cause to complain of my persecution to his new master"—the bishop's mouth pursed and twisted as if he had swallowed a bitter draught —"the Archbishop of Canterbury."

Eight

Meal finished, Bell set off for the priory again. He had wanted to go directly to the Old Priory Guesthouse, but had curbed that impulse because he knew it was bred more of his desire to see Magdalene once more than of any immediate need to learn the names of her clients. Having suppressed personal desire, he considered those he needed to speak to in the priory. Of the two who had dealt with the body—the sacristan's assistant, Knud, and the infirmarian—he decided to deal with Knud first so he could confirm the lay brother's observations of the body with those made by the infirmarian.

That intention, he thought as he rang the bell at the priory gate, might be more readily sought than accomplished. He had had some experience with Brother Paulinus and suspected he would not be allowed to question any of the monks without the sacristan's interference. Bell grimaced, then hurriedly straightened his face as he heard the bar of the gate lifted. Anyone questioned in Paulinus's presence was unlikely to say more than "yes" or "no." But how to rid himself . . . of course! So beatific a smile bloomed on Bell's face that Brother

Godwine, who had opened the gate, was startled.

"Yes?" he asked, stepping back.

Bell promptly walked in. Still smiling, he said, "I must speak to Brother Paulinus."

The porter blinked; few smiled so happily at the prospect of speaking to Brother Paulinus. That tempted Bell to grin more broadly, but he controlled himself. He was not, after all, certain of the outcome, but the questions he had to ask Paulinus could be highly embarrassing, and he hoped that the sacristan would not be inclined for more of his company after answering them. Thus Bell might be able to speak to Knud and the infirmarian alone.

After a longer wait than he thought necessary, he was ushered into a small visitor's cell adjoining the lay brothers' building. He had thought those cells had fallen out of use when the nuns gave up St. Mary Overy, but then he realized that a cell would be kept in case one of the novices or postulants had a female visitor. Shaking his head, he sat down on the stone ledge provided, undecided as to whether to laugh or be annoyed. He was amusing himself by wondering what sort of contamination Brother Paulinus thought he carried, when the monk entered through the opposite door and sat down behind the grille that separated the cell into two parts.

Bell immediately lost all sense of amusement; he would be able to hear well enough through the stone fretwork, but not be able to make out the sacristan's expressions. To save an aspiring brother from the unhealthy excitement that might be engendered by seeing a woman's face, the pierced stone was perfect. For examining the expression of someone answering questions about a murder, it was highly inappropriate. Bell stood up.

"I have been sent by the Bishop of Winchester to ask some questions about the death of the papal messenger, Baldassare de Firenze," he said. "It is necessary that I speak to you face-to-face, Brother Sacristan."

"Since I know nothing whatever about the death of Messer Baldassare, and I prefer not to come into contact with men of such worldly—"

"Worldly? But you thought nothing of visiting a whorehouse on Thursday morning," Bell snapped.

"Whorehouse!" Paulinus gasped, jumping up. "Never! I have never in my life visited a whorehouse."

"I did not say you sought carnal satisfaction there, but I offer less threat of corruption by speaking to you in your own monastery than you suffered from your visit to a whorehouse on the morning after Baldassare was killed. You seemed then to be very certain how he came to die, so you must have some knowledge of his death. Now will you tell me where to meet you so I can see to whom I am speaking—or do I need to tell the bishop that you refused to answer questions about the death of the pope's messenger?"

There was a long moment of utter silence. Then Paulinus said, "You are godless and damned and without proper respect for your betters, but you are the bishop's messenger. Whom God loveth, He chastiseth. Very well, I will accede to your demand. Go around the end of the lay brothers' building. Between that and the kitchen, you will find an entrance to the cloister. I will speak with you there."

Bell was not overjoyed at the choice because the cloister, at the very center of the monastic buildings, was well traveled, which might lead to interruptions; however, he thought he knew how to obtain greater privacy if he needed it, so he simply did as he was told. He was the first to arrive, but before he began to grow impatient, he saw the tall, cadaverous form of the sacristan coming toward him.

"I have only the knowledge of Messer Baldassare's death granted by God to a pure heart," Brother Paulinus said before Bell could open his mouth. "It came to me as soon as I heard of the murder that we in this monastery are pure and holy; we do not kill. In the pesthole beyond our wall are foul, corrupt creatures who engage in every vile practice. Clearly then, they must be guilty of murder. That is what I know."

"In other words, you had no reason—beyond your dislike of them and what they do—to accuse the women of the Old Priory Guesthouse?"

"The man did not come through the front gate. Brother Porter will swear to that. Thus, he came from the whores. No one else could have known he was coming to the church. They must have killed him."

Bell was tempted to ask "Why?" but he already knew the answer he would get. He was sure the sacristan would have told him had he had any better evidence against Magdalene or her women, and he decided not to waste time going through arguments that proved nothing.

"I do not think so," he said instead. "Had they wished to kill Baldassare, he would have died by poison or strangulation and his body would have been disposed of in the nearby river. No one would have known of his death. Such women might be willing to kill, but not in any way as to endanger themselves."

"You are as corrupt as they. How can you be a servant of a bishop and defend them? Clearly, they spilled blood to desecrate the church, to bring shame on this holy place. You are only trying to protect your paramours."

Bell laughed. "I cannot afford such women. I assure you, I have never lain with any of them. And if the intention was to desecrate the church, why kill the man on the porch outside?"

"Because they knew no better, of course. They are blinded, deafened, and made mute by sin. God protected His church. It is through His will I learned of their guilt."

"And also by His will that you did not inform the bishop that the pope's messenger had been slain?"

The sacristan blinked as if Bell had slapped him. "Did not inform the bishop? Why should I inform the bishop? I told Knud, the lay brother who assists me, to send a messenger to the abbot of our order."

"You sent a messenger to the abbot of your order twenty miles away but not to the bishop's house across the road? But Lord Winchester is the administrator of the diocese of London as well as bishop of the see of Winchester. How could you withhold the news of Baldassare's death from him?"

Paulinus drew himself up, but a faint color stained his grayish cheeks. "Our order is autonomous," he said stubbornly. "We need no direction from a worldly bishop. Our holy abbot will tell us what to do."

"But the man was a papal messenger," Bell protested.

"Perhaps carrying a bull to make Winchester legate," Paulinus said, his eyes fixed on a decorative crucifix carved into a pillar. "Too worldly. Too worldly. God works in His own mysterious ways to keep the Church pure."

"A murder cannot be pleasing to God, no matter what the cause," Bell said, wondering if the sacristan was mad.

"That is true," Brother Paulinus said. "Yes, quite true." He shuddered suddenly and his eyes came away from the crucifix and fixed on the ground. "It was horrible. Horrible to find a dead man covered with blood on the church porch. I had sent Knud to discover why the crows were making so much noise. He found the body and cried for the infirmarian, who looked at it and told us the man was dead. The infirmarian called his assistants to take the body away."

"Did you know who the man was?" Bell asked, frowning.

"No, I did not. I had never seen him before in my life. But I knew at once who had stabbed him, and I knew even the bishop could not shield those whores from punishment for such a crime. Maybe a papal legate. . . . No, not even a legate. So I went to demand a confession from the whores." His eyes narrowed and he shook his head. "Foul beasts, they are further lost in sin than even I believed, and they resisted me. They would not acknowledge my God-granted knowledge of their evil and abase themselves; they even threatened me when I tried to chastise the idiot for mocking me."

Bell's teeth set hard at the thought of Paulinus hurting Ella for mocking him—as if Ella would know how—but that was not important. Could Paulinus have killed Baldassare to steal the pouch and destroy the bull that would make a man he considered unworthy a legate?

It was too soon, Bell thought, to come to such a conclusion. Sabina had heard the sacristan's voice just before she found the body, so he was in the church when Baldassare was killed. But it seemed impossible that Baldassare had come to meet Brother Paulinus or that Paulinus could have known he was a papal messenger.

"Those whores—" Brother Paulinus began angrily.

Bell watched the sacristan's face. The insistence on Magdalene's guilt might be a result of Paulinus's prejudice against carnal sin, but it could also be an effort to protect himself. If the whores were adjudged guilty, no one would look further for a murderer.

"It would be best," Bell said, "to leave the whores to me. Since they are already excommunicate, there is little with which *you* can threaten them." The implication that he could and would use other threats would save a lot of argument, Bell thought. "Now," he continued, "I need to speak to Knud to learn exactly what he saw when he found the body."

"Is that really necessary?" Paulinus asked. "The man was greatly disturbed. He did not touch Messer Baldassare—"

"Did you see that?"

The sacristan frowned. "No, but why should he—"

"I wish to speak to him. I need to know if the blood was red or brown, dry all through or jellylike, how the knife stood, whether erect or fallen out. Such things Knud would not speak of in the first excitement, but he is likely to remember under careful questioning."

"You will give him nightmares."

"I am sorry for it if I do, but it is more important that the killer be caught than that one man sleep easily. He can pray for peaceful slumbers."

"I do not see how the horrible details you will bring back to his mind can help find a murderer," Brother Paulinus protested.

Bell did not think they would help much, either, because he was convinced that Baldassare had been killed only moments before Sabina found him, just after Compline. However, he could scarcely admit to Paulinus that he wished to ask Knud whether he was with the sacristan when Sabina had heard his voice calling, "Who is there?"

"Your labor is interceding with God," Bell replied. "Mine, by the bishop's order, is dealing with the evil men do. I will leave you to your labor. Do leave me to mine. Fetch Knud to me now."

"I do not run the errands of lackeys, even the bishop's lackeys," Brother Paulinus said, drawing himself up and stalking off across the cloister to enter the monks' chapter house.

Since that was exactly the reaction for which Bell had been hoping, he made no protest but hurried back to the gate. He was about to ring the bell lustily when Brother Godwine stepped out of the small shelter the gatekeepers used at such times as they expected to need to open the gate frequently.

"I have spoken with Brother Paulinus," Bell said. "Now I must question Knud, who found the body, and when I am done with him, the infirmarian."

"Come with me," the porter said, leading him along the west wall of the building and into the lay brothers' hall.

He bade Bell wait near the entrance, looked around,

nodded with satisfaction, and went toward a group of men who were working at some task Bell could not distinguish. One looked up when the porter spoke to him, seemed to make some protest, and then began to fold something into a cloth. The porter returned, told Bell his man was coming, and went out. Bell waited without impatience, well satisfied that Paulinus had no chance to talk to his servant.

Knud was a middle-aged man, thin and wiry, with sparse brown hair, who approached with his head down, his hands concealed inside his sleeves. Midway he stopped uncertainly, and Bell gestured for him to come nearer. He resumed his approach, but with apparent reluctance.

"Yes, my lord?" he whispered when he was near enough.

"I have been sent by the bishop to—" Bell stopped abruptly and reached out to steady the man, who had uttered a gasp and listed to the side. "What is wrong?" he asked, feeling Knud shudder. "We do not blame you for Messer Baldassare's death. I only want to know what you saw when you found the body, and where you and others were on the night of the murder."

Bright brown eyes flashed up at Bell and away, and Bell thought of a small trapped animal. Almost fearing Knud would bolt, he kept his grip on the man's arm and drew him to a spot farther away from the group among whom he had been working.

"The crows were cawing," he said to start Knud off, "and Brother Paulinus sent you to see why."

"Brother Sacristan is responsible for the building and the grounds. He thought someone might have left offal on the porch. Sometimes sinners seek shelter there to make merry . . . or worse."

"I know that. So you went to look, and you found?"

Knud shuddered and his eyes flickered up toward Bell again. "You know what I found. A dead man. I had nothing to do with that. I did not know him. I had never seen him before."

Despite the defensive words, Bell had the feeling that the lay brother was now more at ease. "Never?" he asked, seeking for what could have frightened the man so much when he first mentioned the bishop. "Not in the church attending the Compline service?"

For a moment the man did not answer, frowning slightly and obviously thinking back. Then he shook his head slowly. "I do not think so," he said, even more at ease and seemingly trying to answer truthfully. "But he might have been there. It was quite dark in the nave. There were some others besides the lay brothers there, visitors to the priory and a few folk from the neighborhood. He might have been among them, but I cannot remember seeing him."

"Very well. It is true he might never have entered the church. Now, tell me what you saw when you opened the door to the porch, exactly what you saw."

"Blood," Knud said. "At first all I saw was blood—blood all over, all over the man, all over the porch. I cried out and jumped back. I do not remember what I said, but it must have been that someone was hurt, or dead, because the infirmarian came running."

"Was the blood red?"

"No. It was black." He glanced up again, not so fleetingly this time. "I suppose it could have been red, but it is the north porch. The sun does not touch there, and it was dark."

"But you were sure it was blood?"

"The knife was there, in his neck."

"Who took it out?"

"I do not know. The infirmarian, I suppose, or the lay brothers who are healers. I did not touch it. I did not even look at the body again."

"Very well. Now, after the body was carried away by the infirmarian, Brother Paulinus told you to send a messenger to the abbot. After that what did you do?"

He expected the man to say he went back to his work or his prayers; instead, the quick glance flicked at him again before the eyes were humbly lowered.

"I . . . I did not know what to do, and in the end, I did nothing because I am bound to obey the sacristan." Knud's voice was scarcely above a whisper and he leaned a little closer to Bell, his body tense. "*I* thought the bishop should be told, but Brother Sacristan does not trust the bishop."

Bound to obey the sacristan but eager to tell tales about him, Bell thought. Was that because Knud disliked his master, or because he feared the bishop and wished to curry favor by placing the blame on the sacristan—Bell had not forgotten Knud's initial reaction when he said he was the bishop's man—or simply because he was a sneaking little rat who liked to make trouble? However, Bell only asked mildly, "Why does Brother Paulinus not trust the bishop?"

"He says Lord Winchester is worldly and that he prefers the secular clergy."

"That cannot be surprising, since your order is autonomous," Bell said. "Lord Winchester must necessarily give most of his attention to the churches and parishes under his management."

"Brother Paulinus says that we live by harsher rules and are more pure and closer to God. Thus, the needs of our orders should come first. He told me once that the Bishop of London used to contribute a substantial sum to our priory for the maintenance of our buildings, but when London died and Winchester was appointed as administrator, he refused to continue the donation. Brother Paulinus was furious."

Knud hunched his shoulders and Bell saw a slight movement within the sleeves of the gown, as if he had clutched his hands tighter around his forearms. Bell could not help wondering whether Brother Paulinus had beaten his assistant because he could not take out his fury on the Bishop of Winchester. If so, Bell hardly blamed Knud for making clear that he was not at fault for failing to inform Winchester of the murder. No doubt he guessed that the bishop would not be pleased to be left in ignorance.

"I will remember that you wished to inform the bishop about Baldassare's death but had no instruction and no permission to do so," Bell said. Knud raised his head a bit and allowed a small smile—of complicity?— to curve his lips; then he dropped his head again. He seemed to think he had made a favorable impression, implying they were in league together against the sacristan. Bell returned the smile and said, "Now, tell me where you were during the Compline service and who can say you were there?"

Knud looked up fully, mouth agape. "Where *I* was? Why do you ask me that?"

"I need to know where everyone was, especially at the end of Compline," Bell said blandly.

Once again with bent head, Knud said, "I was with the other lay brothers. We all stood together."

When Bell asked him to name them, he did, again growing calmer until Bell added, "And when the service was over, did you leave the church with the other lay brothers?"

"No, of course not," Knud said, trying to sound indifferent but with his voice gone thin and breathless again. "I went to the altar to replace the vessels used during the service in the safe box. Brother Sacristan unlocked the box and handed me each piece. When they were all replaced, he relocked the box and left. I stayed a moment longer because someone had spilled water on the floor. I wiped it up before it could run along the safe box and wet the wood."

"Were you alone in the church then?"

"No. Some of the older folk who had been in the nave walk slowly. I think I went out by the monks' door before all of them left the church."

"The sacristan had left before you? Do you know where he went? And where did you go?"

Knud shook his head, then said slowly, "He often went to walk in the cloister after services. Perhaps he went there. I went up to bed." His voice was easy, although he did not look up to meet Bell's eyes. "The other lay brothers will tell you. We do not have separate cells but sleep like the novices"—his voice checked suddenly and Bell saw him bite his lower lip—"in a dormitory."

"Was anyone missing from the dormitory?"

"No." The man's eyes flicked up and away again. "My lord, is it true that the murdered man was a papal messenger carrying a bull that would have made the Bishop of Winchester a papal legate?"

"The man was a papal messenger," Bell replied. "We do not know what he was carrying. His pouch was missing, as was his purse. Why do you ask?"

"His pouch was missing?" Knud's voice drifted into silence and his eyes flicked up and away once more.

"That has significance to you," Bell said harshly. "Have you seen a pouch somewhere?"

"No. No."

Knud backed away a step. Bell caught his arm. "Then why did you ask about the pouch? Are you implying that this killing was a Church affair?"

Knud flinched. "The man was a papal messenger, so I thought . . ."

For the second time, his voice faded away as if he had spoken before he realized what the end of the sentence must be. "So you thought that a churchman—but none were here except the members of this priory—had committed the crime?"

"No. No. Of course not. Brother Paulinus said it was the whores who killed the man, that Satan had possessed them to make them desecrate the church."

"Satan may possess them, but I doubt for that purpose." Bell could not help grinning. "If the devil is trolling for souls, he will catch more by leaving the whores to their usual work. Now, why was the first thought that came to your mind that one of the brethren was guilty when you heard Baldassare was a papal messenger?"

"No, I did not. I . . ." Knud looked fearfully over his shoulder and then whispered, "A papal legate has authority over the monastic orders as well as over the secular clergy."

The swift glance touched Bell again, this time with a spark of satisfaction in it. Despite the fearful looks and the whisper, this was what Knud had wanted him to know, what he had been leading up to when he first spoke of Brother Paulinus's distrust of the bishop. Likely Knud had known all along that Baldassare was a papal messenger—not surprising that what one knew, all knew in a small, tight community like the priory. But the idea that a man would kill to keep papal authority out of the hands of another was fantastic. Only, Brother Paulinus was a fanatic, and men did strange things when driven by what they believed was religious righteousness.

Bell nodded acknowledgment and released Knud's arm, but said only, "I need to speak to the infirmarian now."

Knud bowed slightly and gestured toward the south end of the hall, where a sturdy partition was broken by a solid door. "You will find him within."

With a hand on the infirmary door, Bell watched Knud walk away. Then he opened the door and stepped inside. His first impression was one of pleasure. The room was full of light from three windows, east, west, and south, open to the spring air. It was also warm from fires blazing in two hearths, which were obviously new additions as the stone was different from that of the walls. The air was redolent of spices; Bell took a deep breath and then coughed. Beneath that pleasant scent was a musk of sickness. An elderly monk with kind eyes and a worried expression hurried up to him.

"Are you ill, my son?"

"No, Brother," Bell replied. "I am the bishop's knight, and he has asked me to look into this dreadful murder. I understand that you examined the body and cared for it. Can you tell me when you think Messer Baldassare died and what killed him?"

The infirmarian looked over his shoulder at the four occupied cots. In two, near the hearth on the west wall, a pair of very old men were sleeping. In one near the window on the south wall, a young monk was sitting propped up praying, sliding the beads of his rosary through his fingers. The last cot was on the east wall, and another young monk was tossing to and fro on it, a lay brother seated beside him on a stool. The infirmarian sighed and shook his head.

"Come, we can walk in the cloister while I tell you what little I learned of Messer Baldassare's death."

Here, Bell thought, listening to Brother Infirmarian, was no withholding and little doubt. He was glad to learn that the infirmarian's observations tallied exactly with his own, although the monk had drawn no conclusions from the condition of the wound or the body's stiffness. Bell put forward his ideas about the killing. The infirmarian's eyes widened with surprise and recognition.

"Yes, I agree. I would never have thought of it, but so clean a cut and so deep a wound must mean that the murderer took deliberate aim and meant to kill, and poor Messer Baldassare did not expect the blow or try to defend himself against it. Oh, dear! How dreadful! Why?"

"When I know why, I may also know who," Bell said. He thought for a moment, but could find nothing more he wanted to ask. The infirmarian, he believed, was hiding nothing and was likely unaware of any undercurrents flowing through the priory. "Thank you, Brother Infirmarian," he said. "I am very glad to have your confirmation of my conclusions."

"I do not understand men who do such things," the old monk said sadly, and then smiled. "I suppose that is why I am here and not out in the world." Then his eyes grew shadowed. "But there is no escape from evil. It has followed us right to the door of our church, has it not? It must be fought."

"That is my work, Brother," Bell said. "I hope I can root it out for you. That is the bishop's order."

"A good man." The smile was back. "Not perhaps totally patient and submissive to God's will, but of good heart and great wisdom."

When the infirmarian had nodded at him and returned to his duties, Bell stood irresolute. What he wanted to do was go to the Old Priory Guesthouse, and because he recognized the strength of the desire as being unhealthy, he sought to curb it, but there really was nothing else he could think of to ask, except . . . yes, ask for a list of the visitors who had stayed at the priory on Wednesday night. At the gate, he communicated this need to the porter.

"But it was the whores," Brother Godwine protested. "I told you that Messer Baldassare did not come through the front gate. He came through the back, from the whorehouse, and Brother Sacristan says the whores followed him and killed him."

"So Brother Sacristan says," Bell replied, "but as I told Brother Paulinus, I think it highly unlikely. Why should a whore take such a risk when she could poison Baldassare's wine in the comfort and privacy of her own house and be rid of the evidence of her crime by throwing his body in the river? A knife, used so precisely, is more likely a man's weapon. Moreover, it seems that Messer Baldassare had planned a meeting with someone that night, so it is not impossible that one of the guests came for that purpose—"

"And committed murder? Oh, I do not believe it."

"Perhaps your faith will be justified," Bell said, "but I still need to know who guested here that night."

"I am not sure I know all the names. I did not open the gate for every single guest—"

"But you *know* Baldassare did not enter by this gate?"

"Because Brother Patric and Brother Elwin watched the gate when I was not by. I asked them. They swore that only three mounted men came in by the gate and that only three horses were ever in the stable at any time that afternoon and night."

"Very good. Make sure the names of the three mounted men are included among the guests."

Brother Godwine shook his head. "I do not know their names, not two of them, at least. But they are all known to Brother Paulinus. They have done work for the mother house and were sent to examine what, if anything, needs to be done here. But I cannot go about finding out all the names right now. I will send you a list of them after Vespers."

"That will do. Send it superscribed with my name— Sir Bellamy of Itchen—to the bishop's house. I will then want to question the brothers at large as to whether and when and where they saw the guests."

"It is almost time for evening prayers, a little supper, and then for bed."

The last two phrases set off an urgent desire. The sun was low in the west and Bell could just imagine a small table in Magdalene's chamber set with a cozy supper for two, the good bed with its coverlet turned down in the background. He nodded brusquely to the porter, and as he signaled for the gate to be opened, said over his shoulder that he could ask his questions the next day, but desired to have the list this night to discover if any in the bishop's Household knew those on it.

Nine

21 APRIL 1139
OLD PRIORY GUESTHOUSE

The image of warm food, comfort, and hospitality was still vivid in Bell's mind when he rang the bell at the gate. When there was no quick answer, he ground his teeth and rang again, louder. Doubtless she was plying her trade and did not wish to be disturbed, but that was nothing to him. He was about to peal the bell for the third time when he saw the door of the house open. Magdalene came forward slowly, but she was fully dressed, not covered in a hastily donned bedrobe.

"Sir Bellamy!" she exclaimed as soon as she could see his face. "I did not expect you again today, but I am very glad you came. I have some interesting news for you."

"I am sorry to disturb you when you are busy," he said stiffly.

"I was only embroidering, but since Messer Baldassare's death, I find myself reluctant to answer the bell if everyone I expect is already in the house. Come in, Sir Bellamy."

He followed her, speechless for a moment—he had forgotten how beautiful she was. Then he said, "Since we are to work together to solve this murder, why do you not call me Bell, to which I am more accustomed."

She glanced back over her shoulder with an enchanting smile. "Very well. I like it."

"Even though you do not like to answer the ring? Have you ever thought of pulling the bell cord within so that the bell cannot be rung?"

She laughed. "Many times, I assure you, but I am running a business, not playing games when I choose. I cannot afford to turn away custom or to annoy clients who wish to be entertained at times other than their set appointments. The bishop favors my tenancy, but only while I pay my rent."

When they were in the house, she gestured him toward the empty stools near the fire as she took her own place. Bell was aware of the weight of his purse against his thigh and he felt uncomfortable remembering how, after he promised himself he would not, he had gone to his chamber to get more money from his chest. He glanced at her, but she was looking intently at the strip of ribbon she was embroidering. He had the money. He could have her if he wanted her.

"You said you had news?" he asked hurriedly.

"Yes." She looked up, seemed to make a decision and put aside the embroidery, clasping her hands in her lap. "Did you see the man who came in while you were in the stable?"

"Yes. I hope I was not supposed to look away. In fact, I know him."

"I thought you might because Master Andrew Buchuinte was justiciar of London until last year. More significant to our purpose, he was a friend of Messer Baldassare. He said they came from the same city in Italy and that it was to his house that Messer Baldassare went from his ship."

"Baldassare only arrived on Wednesday, then?"

Magdalene nodded and repeated what Buchuinte had told her about Baldassare's arriving late and having an appointment that very night. Bell listened quietly, stopping her only when she mentioned Baldassare's traveling companion.

"Beaumeis. Yes. You mentioned him before. He is the one who sent Baldassare here, is he not?"

"As a joke. I am sure Baldassare did not come to visit a whorehouse. Beaumeis told him this was the Bishop of Winchester's inn. I was very angry. It was as if Beaumeis wished to besmirch Winchester's reputation. But I believe Baldassare came here because his meeting was set in the church. He did not say so, but he asked if there was a short way from this house to the church, and when I said there was, then he asked to stay the night."

"Even if he had a meeting there, he would not be likely to tell a whore."

Bell was sorry as soon as the words were out. He was angry at himself because his desire for Magdalene would not be stilled, but that was no reason to insult her when she had not invited insult. However, Magdalene did not flinch. Her brows drew together very slightly, but then she smiled.

"You might be surprised what men tell whores, especially those they trust—but you are right insofar as Messer Baldassare had no reason to trust me. And, if you remember, he did not even tell Buchuinte, a longtime friend, whom he was to meet or what he was carrying. No, he did tell Buchuinte he was going to the king."

Bell nodded. "The pope must have sent a letter stating his decision about whether Stephen was rightfully king."

"That was what Somer said."

"Somer?"

"Somer de Loo. He is a captain under William of Ypres. He came unexpectedly, which was a piece of luck because Master Buchuinte was too upset after hearing of Baldassare's death to wish to go to Ella. And you know Ella." Magdalene grimaced and Bell could not help laughing.

All he said, however, was, "The bishop thought news of that decision might have been in Baldassare's pouch, but I cannot believe it was worth killing over. There can be little doubt that the pope decided in Stephen's favor. After all, the papal legate approved when Stephen first claimed the throne."

"Mayhap the bishop is thinking like a churchman, not a soldier? Somer just wondered whether those who killed Baldassare were the king's so-called friends or his enemies."

"If he is Ypres's man, 'so-called friends' means Waleran, but I think like a soldier, too, and I cannot see any reason why Waleran should wish to keep the pope's decision secret. And if, for some unthinkable reason, the pope decided against Stephen, Waleran could not know that; I cannot believe anyone came from Rome more swiftly than Baldassare."

Since Magdalene knew that the pope's decision was favorable, she saw no point in continuing the conversation along those lines. "There is a thing that puzzles me," she said. "Beaumeis told Baldassare that this was the Bishop of Winchester's inn and that was what Baldassare asked for when he rang my bell. Yet when I told him my servant would take him to the bishop's house, he said he had no business with the bishop."

Magdalene now knew that was a lie. He had had the bull to deliver to Winchester, unless . . . she bit her lips to stop herself from asking Bell why Baldassare would say that. Was it possible that he was going to deliver the bull to someone else? To hide? To destroy? That made no sense. . . . Yes, it did. There was one way it did make sense. Possibly he was going to deliver the bull to King Stephen so that the king himself could give it to Henry of Winchester to soothe his anger over being passed over for Archbishop of Canterbury. And if Stephen knew that Baldassare was coming with a legatine commission for Winchester, Waleran would know also.

"But I think he did have business with the bishop,"

Bell said, startling her, because her mind had wandered. Magdalene could have kissed him; she knew her surprised expression made her look more innocent. "Did you not know that the king had asked the pope to make Winchester legate?"

"Yes, I did," Magdalene said. "William told me. He knew I was interested because I had told him how disappointed I was when Theobald of Bec was made archbishop instead of Winchester."

Bell looked astonished. "Why should you care who was archbishop?"

"Do not be a fool. If Winchester became archbishop, who would dare speak against whores who were his tenants? Contrariwise, if we got a man like Brother Paulinus for archbishop, would he not be likely to order the bishops and deans to 'cleanse their houses of corruption'? Even the Bishop of Winchester could not ignore an order from the archbishop."

"I see." Bell nodded. "It would make a difference to you."

"Yes, it was on my mind, and when William stopped in a few days after Christmas last year, I mentioned it to him. He was strange. When I said I wished Winchester had been elected archbishop, he shouted at me because he did not know what he wanted. I cannot remember ever seeing William so undecided. He said that if Henry of Winchester were archbishop, there would be two kings and the Church would have the more powerful ruler."

Bell whistled between his teeth over that statement. "I had heard that was the argument Waleran used to convince Stephen not to urge the election of his brother. I had also heard he did not need to argue very hard, that Stephen had realized that without help. So, Ypres agreed with Waleran about keeping Winchester out of the archbishopric?"

"I would not say he ever agreed completely, but later he came to believe that rejecting Winchester was a mistake. He was greatly disturbed at how bitter Winchester was over what he saw as his brother's treachery and ingratitude."

Bell shrugged. "That was how it looked to me."

"But can it do any good to have the king and his brother at odds? I think William tried to blame Waleran—he did not actually admit that, of course—but this time Winchester would accept no excuses for Stephen's action. In fact, William remarked that the excuse seemed to make Winchester more bitter, as if it were proof that the king preferred Waleran to himself. I think William was actually worried about an open break between them, and it may have been he who suggested the king ask for the appointment as legate as compensation."

"Interesting, but nothing to do with us. To get back to Baldassare. The bishop thought the bull appointing him legate might also have been in the pouch."

"You must be right!" Magdalene exclaimed, barely preventing herself from shouting in her relief. Now, at last, she could ask questions and speculate about why anyone would want to seize the bull she knew was in the pouch. "But why and to whom could that be important enough to cost a man's life?"

Bell shook his head. "I have never understood that from the beginning," he replied. "As to 'to whom,' there are only two I can think of: Waleran and Theobald of Bec."

"The archbishop?" Magdalene asked faintly. "But he is not even here in England."

Bell laughed shortly. "Winchester did not like the idea any better than you. He cut me off when I suggested it, but I was not suggesting that even if he were in England, Theobald would have used the knife himself." He shrugged. "I know nothing of the man; he might be a saint and not care, but you know having a legate above him before he can establish his authority over his suffragan bishops must undermine that authority. And, after all, the archbishop does not even have to be directly involved. When he learned of the bull, could he not have lamented to those in his Household that it should be issued—not with any intent to arouse violence or disobedience against the pope's will, but just as an expression of his disappointment?"

"And someone took him literally and decided to intercept and destroy it?" It was Magdalene's turn to shrug. "But any in the Household who could have heard him are *with* him in Rome. You yourself said you did not believe anyone else could have outstripped Baldassare in traveling from Rome to London."

"Have you forgotten that there was someone from the archbishop's Household who traveled *with* Baldassare?"

"Beaumeis?" Magdalene smiled. "Richard de Beaumeis is far too selfish and self-indulgent to kill anyone for a cause not his own. I could imagine him stealing the bull if he thought it would bring the archbishop's favor, but I am not sure he has the courage to engage in violence. Besides, did I not tell you that Buchuinte says Beaumeis left his house long before Baldassare did, before dinnertime, to ride to Canterbury on some errand for the archbishop?"

"Could Beaumeis have sent a message to someone before he left the city?"

"You mean hired someone to kill Baldassare for him?" Magdalene frowned. "He might be stupid enough to have done that, but I do not think he would have money enough."

"The archbishop—" He saw her expression and smiled. "It does not matter. A stranger could not have done it. Remember that the killer would have had to be within the gates of the priory or this house before those gates were locked."

"I had almost forgot that." Magdalene sighed.

Bell frowned. "Your wall and gate look formidable. How many would know the gate is not locked until dark?"

"I am not sure." Magdalene looked down thought-fully. "Someone goes to open the gate whenever the bell is rung, so anyone might assume the gate was locked or barred, but some would surely notice there was no sound of a lock being opened or bars withdrawn. I imagine all my clients know." She shrugged and sighed. "I can see you *will* need a list of their names. I have written it out for you, but for most of them, it is ridic-ulous. It could not matter a pin to them if the bishop was made legate. And it does not change the fact that neither of the two you mentioned who *could* profit by preventing the bull from being delivered are close enough. Those who elected Theobald are in Canterbury, and Waleran de Meulan is with the king at Notting-ham."

"Hugh le Poer, Waleran's youngest brother, is no far-ther away than the Tower of Montfichet. He came from Bedford soon after Easter."

"Do you know why?"

Bell shook his head. "I only know by accident that he is here. I went to speak to the Archdeacon of St. Paul's and was nearly swallowed up into Hugh's party as it was coming out the gate of Montfichet. The arch-deacon told me when he arrived. I asked because Hugh le Poer is no friend to Winchester. He does not like or trust the bishop, even though it was Winchester who finally persuaded Miles de Beauchamp to yield Bedford Castle so Stephen could bestow it on Hugh. Hugh be-lieves that before he arranged the truce, Winchester made Stephen swear that if Miles yielded, he would not give the barony or the greater part of the estate to Hugh."

"The king must have known a messenger from the pope was on his way, and if he knew, Waleran de Meu-lan knew. Do you think Hugh came to watch for the pope's messenger?"

"It is possible," Bell said, "but why? I cannot believe Waleran can feel any strong desire to strengthen Theobald, and if Waleran does not, neither would Hugh. In fact, I am sure they would prefer a weak archbishop. Theobald's election was surely more because he was *not* Henry of Winchester than because he *was* Theobald of Bec."

"That was how it seemed to William," Magdalene agreed. She saw a flare of Bell's nostrils, a tightening of his lips. Something had made him angry. Possibly just the reminder that his master had been passed over; well, he had mentioned it, not she, and he would not be angry with her over that. "And I can understand," she continued, "that Waleran and his party would not want Winchester to be made legate, but surely delaying delivery of the bull for a few months could not be reason enough to kill a papal messenger."

"We always come back to that sticking point," Bell said. "Why *kill* Baldassare? I suppose what you said this morning—that he was killed because he knew his murderer—must be the answer, but—"

He stopped speaking abruptly as a door opened and a man's shout of laughter mingled with a high female giggle. Then the door shut again and footsteps went down the corridor toward the kitchen.

"That will be Ella getting an evening meal for herself and Somer. He is spending the night and will ride back to Rochester tomorrow to bring news of Messer Baldassare's death to William." She hesitated, then went on. "I will tell William everything I know, but I hope you will agree that I should also tell him what we have been talking about."

She went on, explaining why she thought it important for William of Ypres to know everything, but Bell did not hear her. He was consumed with a rage of jealousy. Whore! She had acted while they talked as if he were the only man in the world, the only man of importance to her, and all the while she was collecting information for another. Ella's footsteps came back; her door opened and closed. His hand went to his purse.

"How much?" he asked.

Having been intent on what she was explaining—even more intent as the frown on Bell's face darkened, because she felt she had to convince him that William of Ypres would be a valuable ally in discovering who killed Baldassare—Magdalene hadn't the faintest idea what his question meant.

"How much what?" she asked, bewildered.

"How much to spend a night in your bed?"

Magdalene's mouth fell open inelegantly. She was stunned. After her first suspicions that Bell would demand use of her as a bribe were put to rest, she had dismissed from her mind the problem of her trade when talking to him and concentrated on Baldassare's death.

"That is impossible," she said. "You cannot seek the solution to a murder of which I have been accused at the same time that you are playing games in my bed. Everyone would laugh at any solution you presented and say you were merely accusing another to cover my guilt."

"They are saying it already," he snapped, "and will say it no matter how pure I am, so why should I not have what I desire?"

She shook her head numbly. She had liked and trusted Bell, welcomed what seemed like a friendly alliance. She had believed he was fair and honest; instead, he was worse than the others. Mostly they made their demands at once, openly; he had offered a partnership and then used her confidence to demand she bribe him with her body to . . . and then she realized he had asked her price. He had not demanded her service as a bribe. He had asked her price.

Shame brought a flood of color to her face. Shame? Of what had she to be ashamed? She *was* a whore. And being a whore had brought her freedom—now that she had won her way up to a place where she could say "no" when she wished. What was wrong with her? Having a man ask her price had not wakened shame in her for nearly ten years; mostly it had amused her, since she had women to do the actual work.

"Oh, do forgive me," she said. "How thoughtless of me to assume that you came here on the bishop's business rather than your own." She curved her lips into a smile. "How obtuse you must have found me, talking about the murder and William and never giving you a chance—"

"How much?"

The voice was a low, rough snarl, the eyes fixed, furious, and his face redder than she thought hers had been. Magdalene could feel her blush fade to pallor. She dropped her hand to the basket that sat beside her stool and grasped the small knife she used for cutting thread. It was not a real weapon, but the sting of being cut or stabbed by it nearly always startled an attacker enough for her to scream and break free. In the kitchen there were weapons enough, and Dulcie to help her, and a scream would likely bring Somer de Loo, and possibly the other clients, to her rescue.

"At this hour the price is five pennies," she said, struggling to keep her voice steady, "but that includes the evening meal, breakfast, and entertainment for the whole night. However"—Magdalene took a firm grip on the knife and made sure it was not tangled in any hank of yarn—"you would have to wait until Letice or Sabina were free. I am sorry to disappoint you, but I no longer take clients."

He blinked as if she had slapped him, and cleared his throat. "You no longer take clients?"

To Magdalene's amazement, the question did not explode in a shout of fury over her refusal. His voice was calm, maybe a trifle flatter than usual, and the high color was fading from his face.

"Not for many years," Magdalene assured him. The last thing she wanted was for him to fly into a rage again because he thought she found him unattractive or was rejecting him for some other personal reason. "Not since Ella and the other women came to work for me. I . . . I have no real taste for making the beast with two backs, although I enjoy managing this place. And I have taken care to choose women who do have a taste for their work. Letice or Sabina will provide you with far greater pleasure than I would."

He smiled slowly, a real smile, not a stiff rictus of the lips. "I thank you, but I have no desire whatsoever to lie with any of your women. It is not carnal relief I desire, but you."

Magdalene, who had started to relax when he seemed so calm, tensed again. Nervously, she shook her head. "It is useless to desire me. I no longer sell my body to any man who has my price, and I have no other reason to lie with you."

Still smiling, he asked, "Are you sure I could not give you a reason?"

The sensuous quality in smile and voice assured Magdalene that his question was not a threat, but a promise. She could not help smiling in reply and letting go of her little knife, surprised by a stirring of interest. He was a fine, strong man and not so old or brutal as William of Ypres. He would make a pleasant lover, possibly even a satisfying one, if his easy assurance of his own ability was not self-delusion. She was tempted to discover whether that was true, but as the thought came to her, a freezing fear followed. He wanted *her*, not a whore. Down that road lay the deaths of two men. She shook her head.

"Yes, I am certain." The look that replaced his smile made her raise a hand placatingly. "Please do not be offended. I have no fault to find with you as a man; indeed, you are most appealing. You are clean and good to look at, with a sharp mind and a beautiful body. You desire me as a person rather than simply for your own body's satisfaction with any whore, which is flattering, but for all of that, you cannot wake any answering desire in me."

"I do not believe you." He was smiling again.

Magdalene sternly resisted the impulse to look away and wondered if he had read something in her face. She thought she had controlled her expression, but at this moment, despite reminding herself of danger, her last statement *was* a flat lie. She did not want to lie to Bell, but it was all the safety she could offer him and herself.

"Believe me or not," she insisted, "what I say is true. As I told the bishop this morning, one sin that hardly ever touches any whore is the sin of lust. Some begin because they enjoy the work and then lose their taste for it. But whoring was never my choice. I assure you, now that I do not need to spread my legs or starve, I cannot be tempted."

The smile disappeared. That last crudity disgusted him, as she intended.

"You must have given poor recompense for what you were paid when you did practice your trade," Bell said nastily.

"Certainly I could never offer what Ella does." Magdalene could not help laughing. "That is why so many men come back to her again and again, even though her conversation must leave much to be desired." Then pride pricked her and before she thought, she added, "I had clients enough, however, so I suppose if my enthusiasm for futtering was less, I offered pleasures of other kinds."

"But you will not offer them to me?"

"No." A flat, unadorned statement.

Magdalene braced herself, but Bell was smiling again. He should have been more furious over that flat refusal than he had been when she first misunderstood his question about how much she charged, but he looked pleased. Magdalene did not understand his attitude at all. It was as if he wanted her to refuse him. But if that were so . . . no, she had no time to think out so complicated a notion. He had begun to laugh and she decided to temporize.

"Not now, anyway. You may say that you are already being accused of lying to protect us, but I have the feeling that you are a very poor liar. Now if you are asked whether you have enjoyed any of our favors and you say 'no,' there will be no shift of your eyes, no color in your face, no twitch of hand or shoulder to betray unease."

"Nonsense," he replied, grinning. "I will show even more signs of distress because of my unfulfilled desire whereas, having sated myself, I would show only disgust—"

Magdalene raised her brows. "You offer disgust of me as a temptation to satisfy your desire?"

"Not disgust of you. Of myself for having yielded to weakness." He chuckled softly. "But I do not believe I would feel that. I am not at all sure it is a weakness to desire you. In fact, I think that takes a courage near to foolhardiness."

Before she could control her reaction, Magdalene's eyes had dropped. Furious with herself, she raised them at once, but she knew Bell had seen her response to his flattery. She stared at him defiantly.

"Do not dignify it with such a description. To desire me is simply stupid, not bravely foolhardy."

As he was about to reply, another door opened. This time two pairs of footsteps went down the corridor toward the back door. Bell glanced over his shoulder and saw that the light beyond the oiled parchment covering the window was dimmer. He frowned, considering whether he wanted to ask to share their evening meal and decided not to provide more fuel to any burning suspicions about his relationship with Magdalene and her women. He got to his feet, then leaned forward and touched her face.

"I will yield to you insofar as to go now—taking, as an excuse for coming, that list of clients you said you had written out for me, but do not believe I have yielded altogether."

Ten

22 APRIL 1139
PRIOR'S HOUSE, ST. MARY OVERY
PRIORY

Magdalene woke smiling on Saturday morning. She lay abed for a few moments considering her good spirits. There were some reasons. Both Sabina's and Letice's clients had not only been their usual pleasant selves, but had innocently cleared themselves of being involved in Baldassare's death. The master leather-worker had been at a guild function on Wednesday night until nearly midnight, and the mercer had arrived in London only on Thursday with a cartload of fleeces for his factor. And neither man knew Baldassare. Magdalene had taken pleasure in noting these facts and drawing a line through their names on a copy of the list she had given Bell.

The name first brought a smile back to her lips and then made her bite them. She could not deny that she was sorry she had to refuse him. She had been celibate for a long time and was not really as indifferent to the delights of a good futtering as she pretended. No, she could not, she must not, accept him. But to turn him away . . .

She did not need to do that yet, Magdalene told herself. He had already accepted the fact that she could afford no relationship with the man investigating the murder. Until she and her women were cleared of Baldassare's death, she could put him off. Later, if she could convince him that he could not own her, that she could and would take other men . . . he would not need to know that he was the only one.

She sighed. No matter what she said, Bell might grow jealous. Magdalene sat up abruptly, recalling that she had been talking about William when Bell suddenly asked her price—and she had mentioned William again when Bell became enraged. Was he jealous already? Of William?

Ridiculous! Bell knew what William had done for her, what she owed him. God knew to what depths she might have fallen if not for William's support. If Bell was jealous of William, she must have nothing to do with him, not even as a one-time client. Then Magdalene bit her lip again. It was not so simple; if she drove the bishop's knight to hatred, he could do her infinite harm.

Throwing back the covers and swinging her legs down, Magdalene uttered an exasperated sigh. It was useless to think about this. For now, she had a good excuse to refuse to take him as a client. As she got out of bed, she resolved firmly to put Bell out of her mind.

That was easier to resolve than to accomplish, Magdalene found. Somehow, the mechanics of preparing for the day—chewing a green twig into a brush to clean her teeth, washing her face, neck, and hands, pulling on clothing—kept bringing Bell to her mind. However, emptying her inner pocket of coins to be transferred to the strongbox locked in the bottom of her chest turned her thoughts into more profitable paths.

Business, she now thought, would not be affected adversely by the murder. The mercer had already made an appointment for the next week and paid in advance for it to be sure no older or better-favored client would oust him. Far from turning away from the Old Priory Guesthouse, he and the leatherworker had been titillated by hearing about the messenger's death.

As soon as she opened her door, Magdalene heard the voices of her women and went out to join them. The table was laden with cheese, bread, the remains of a rabbit pasty, a bowl of cold stew, ale, and wine. As Magdalene helped herself to a substantial breakfast, Ella told her that she had fed Somer de Loo cold meat and pasty and served him wine from William of Ypres's casks so he could break his fast at first light. He had been off to Rochester as soon as he finished. He would have liked to stay, Ella said, smiling; he told her he had enjoyed himself, but this time it was only for one night. He would try to return soon.

Magdalene praised her for contenting her client, and for remembering to provide him with food and drink. She was about to ask Ella whether she had tried to persuade Somer to stay, and if she confessed she had, explain again that she should not importune a guest who wanted to leave. As she sought the simplest words, the bell at the gate began to peal.

Ella might lack understanding, but she had a remarkable sense of self-preservation. Sensing a coming lecture, she rose from her seat at once. "I'll get Dulcie," she said. "I don't think it can be a visitor at this time."

Although Magdalene had a sinking feeling that anyone who rang her bell so early in the morning was carrying trouble, she went on with her meal with determination. Trouble might curtail either time or appetite. Her decision was correct. She was just washing down the last bit of pasty with several swallows of ale when Dulcie ushered in a robed monk. Ella, sensitized to monks' robes, had disappeared

Keeping her face as expressionless as possible, Magdalene looked up at the intruder and said, "Yes?" Then she caught sight of the face half hidden in the hood, set down her cup hastily, and got to her feet. "Brother

Fareman!" she exclaimed. "Please forgive my rudeness. Is the Father Prior returned?"

"Yes, we arrived last night. What a terrible homecoming! Poor Father Benin, he was much overset at hearing of the dreadful events of Wednesday night, but was too fatigued to do anything then. However, this morning he wishes you to come to his chambers and explain to him how you are involved in this horrible murder."

"I will gladly come, Brother Fareman, and I will tell Father Benin all I know, but I must assure you that neither I nor my women are involved in any way."

"Brother Paulinus insists you are." A very small, pinched smile moved Brother Fareman's lips. "And it is no use protesting to me. You must come and speak to Father Benin."

"Most willingly," Magdalene said. "Letice, bring me my veil."

While Letice fetched the veil, Magdalene swung her cloak over her shoulders. Having swathed her hair and most of her face in the veil Letice brought, she started for the back door. After a step or two, she corrected herself with a low exclamation of irritation.

"The gate between the church and this house was locked by Brother Paulinus on Thursday," she explained.

"Yes, I know," the prior's secretary said. "Nonetheless, we can go that way." He showed her a key. "I rang your bell to give warning," he added as he waved her toward the back, "but I could see no reason to walk near a mile if it was not necessary." The plump secretary smiled. "I thought to myself that it was rather like locking the barn after the horses were stolen. After all, even if you *had* killed poor Messer Baldassare, surely Brother Paulinus could not expect that you intended to murder a whole series of clients on the church porch—"

Magdalene choked and then said, "Was ever an accusation so ridiculous? This is not a common stew where men who will never be seen again are beckoned in off the street by women who will be in another house the next day. The last thing I desire is harm to any client. But, Brother Fareman, it is really not funny. My women and I *are* whores. If the sacristan's accusations become public, we might be judged guilty no matter how innocent we are of actually doing murder."

"I think that is why Father Benin sent for you. Brother Paulinus has no evidence against you beyond the fact that you and your women are likely to do murder because you are evil and corrupt—"

"Evil and corrupt we may be, but that does not make us idiots!" Magdalene protested.

Brother Fareman shrugged. "And that Messer Baldassare probably came through the back gate. If you can convince Father Benin that there is little likelihood of your guilt, I believe that he will forbid Brother Paulinus to make any further accusations, or even speak of the murder in public, unless he finds proof."

That was a comforting notion and Magdalene set such a pace that the short, rotund secretary had to beg her to slow down. They went through the gate, which the secretary relocked, to Magdalene's disappointment. A short way down the path to the church, Brother Fareman turned left and walked past the wall of the south transept and to the prior's house, just opposite the chapter house.

Magdalene could see that the prior's house was much smaller than the bishop's house; she thought there would be space tor only a comfortable room for business on the ground floor and possibly a solar and bedchamber above. An outside flight of stairs beside the door to the lower floor led directly to the solar, and to Magdalene's surprise, it was to this that the secretary led her.

She was surprised again by a feeling of acute discomfort wakened by the large, curtained bed that stood with its head against the wall to the far right. She turned away and saw with some relief that this was not only a bedchamber. To the left was a beautifully carved, cushioned chair with a high back and arms, set beside a hearth under a stone overhang. To the right of the hearth was a heavy, polished table; behind it, the prior sat in a second chair with a back and arms, although not so large or high. The table was lit by a window in the wall. Another window on the same wall as the door made the room bright.

"Magdalene the whore, my lord," the secretary said, gesturing Magdalene forward.

She walked to the table and bowed. "Father Prior, I am glad you are come home again. May I hope that your business prospered?"

The prior waved a hand in dismissal and the secretary stepped out, closing the door behind him.

"Well enough," the prior said, "but now I wish I had not gone. What a dreadful thing! A murder at the church door. And Brother Sacristan saying that the dead man came from your house—"

"Father Prior, the man may have gone to the church through the back gate, but not with my knowledge or by my contrivance. And I swear to you that neither I nor any in my household did him harm or wished him harm. Nor was Messer Baldassare one of my regular clients."

"Then how did he come to use your back gate?"

"I believe he was to meet someone in the church," she replied, and launched into the tale of Baldassare's coming to her gate, just as she had told it to Brother Paulinus.

She had just begun to explain—for the thousandth time, it seemed to her—why it was ridiculous to suspect her or her women of the crime, when the door burst open and Brother Paulinus stalked in. When he saw Magdalene, his eyes widened and he stopped dead, then rushed forward.

"Did you know what she had done?" he asked, his

eyes wide. "How did you know? I only discovered the theft less than a quarter candlemark ago." He turned on Magdalene, shouting, "Whore! Thief! How dare you touch a holy vessel of the church?"

"But I am not touching Father Benin," Magdalene said, completely bewildered by the accusation and trying to make some sense of it. "I might kiss his hand in gratitude for his kindness, but I have not—"

"Liar!" Paulinus bellowed. "What have you done with the small golden pyx? Give it back! I will—"

"Brother Paulinus," Father Benin said, "calm yourself. What are you talking about? I know nothing of the small golden pyx. What small golden pyx?"

"The one that was left here by the sisters. It is gone. Stolen. By this whore! You knew it. You summoned her to answer for her crime."

"She is here to tell me what she knows about the death of Messer Baldassare."

"I explained all that to you," the sacristan said; then, turning on Magdalene again, he shouted, "You filthy whore, how dare you come here and spew your lies into the holy father's ear?"

"I told him no lies." That was true enough, Magdalene reassured herself. She had been very careful what she said to Father Benin. She had left out quite a bit, but told no lies. She met the sacristan's furious gaze steadily and added, "You are correct in one thing at least, that I would never dare lie to Father Prior. Even a whore can tell the truth when it is to her advantage, and the more truth that is known about Messer Baldassare's death, the safer I will be. I deal in the joys of life, never in death."

"The death of the soul is the fruit of your joy!" He turned from her to the prior and said, "How can you allow that whore to contaminate your private chamber—"

From the mingled expressions of chagrin and impatience, just tinged with shame, that Magdalene saw flit across the prior's face, she suddenly realized why she had been taken to his private chamber instead of being interviewed in the room devoted to business below. Father Benin had hoped Brother Paulinus would not know she had been invited to explain.

Magdalene laughed, knowing it would infuriate the sacristan and hoping to draw his attention to give the prior time to gather his forces. "Rest at ease, Brother Paulinus," she said. "Whoredom is not something you can breathe in and catch like a fever from the night air. Unless you desire it and seek it out, it will not touch you."

"Me?" Brother Paulinus bellowed, raising his hand.

"Nay, Brother Paulinus," the prior said sharply. "Even with such as she, we do not practice violence." His countenance once more placid, Father Benin shook his head at her and she bowed hers in response. He turned to the sacristan again. "Magdalene is in my solar to keep her out of the way of the younger brothers, who often come to my secretary with problems." He smiled slightly. "At my age, I hope I am safe from her no matter where I choose to speak with her. Now, what is this about the small golden pyx being stolen? Are you sure it is missing, Brother Sacristan? It was very small and never used. Could it not have slipped back into the dark, or even into another of the vessels?"

"Of course I am sure. As you know, usually we clean the church plate on Friday so that it will be perfect for Sunday, but we have been all turned around by Brother Knud being questioned, so the work was not completed Friday. Today, when Brother Knud was about to finish that task, something moved me to examine the safe box, and I counted over every piece. The pyx was gone." His face contorted as if he were about to burst into tears. "I have failed my trust. And"—he whirled about and glared at Magdalene—"it is her fault. She stole it!"

"Paulinus!" The prior got to his feet. "How can that

be true? How could she steal the pyx out of a locked chest?"

"Who else could do it? Is she not a whore? Does not the foul sin she commits corrupt the whole being of those who engage in its evil practices? Is this not proof that the whores murdered the pope's messenger?"

"Proof?" Magdalene cried. "What has a stolen pyx to do with Messer Baldassare's death?"

"Who else but a whore and a murderess would dare steal from the church, from the storage closet beneath the very altar itself? Indeed that must be why you killed him. He must have seen you stealing the pyx."

"Father Benin," Magdalene protested, "this is madness. I never left my house the night Messer Baldassare was killed. My women and I were together after Vespers. My maid, who is not a whore, not excommunicate, and a faithful daughter of the church, will attest to that."

Dulcie would not have to lie, she told herself. They *had* all been together after Vespers, and *had* remained so until Sabina went to bed with Baldassare, but he was certainly lively enough then. And she had not left the house after he did.

"And after Thursday morning," Magdalene continued before either the sacristan or the prior could speak, "the gate between the church and the Old Guesthouse was locked, so I could not come into the priory grounds unseen. You may ask your porter if I passed the gate since then—"

"You did, you lying whore. You were here yesterday."

Magdalene blinked, for a moment terrified by the notion that Brother Paulinus had suborned the porter or one of his assistants to say she had entered the monastery—and then she remembered and smiled. "Yes, I was. I came with Sir Bellamy of Itchen, the bishop's knight, to look at the dead man to see if I recognized him, which I did, and so did Sir Bellamy. But Brother Paulinus, I was in his presence and that of Brother

Porter the whole time. Are you trying to say that Sir
Bellamy and Brother Godwine either ignored me or
watched me break open the safe box and take out the
pyx?"

"You bemused them. You cast an evil glamour—"

"Hush, Brother Paulinus," the prior said, coming
around his desk and putting his hand on the distraught
sacristan's arm. "You are beside yourself with worry. I
am sure it is not through any neglect of yours that the
pyx is missing. Just calm yourself." Then he turned to
Magdalene. "Did you say you were with Sir Bellamy?
How is he involved in this?"

"He was bidden by the bishop to discover, if he
could, who had killed Messer Baldassare and what had
happened to the pouch Messer Baldassare was carrying."

"I was blamed for that, too," the sacristan burst out.
"Sir Bellamy accused me of not sending word to the
bishop about the murder, but this priory owes no obe-
dience to the bishop. I sent word to the abbot. Now the
pyx is gone—"

The prior was looking desperately confused, and
Magdalene said, "*I* told the bishop a man had been
killed on the church porch when I went to speak to him
on Friday morning. He was distressed by the news and
by the fact that he had to hear it from me, particularly
when he learned that the victim was Messer Baldassare,
a papal messenger. He then ordered his knight, Sir Bellamy, to discover the identity of the killer."

"He need not look very far if he will only look honestly," the sacristan spat. "And I will insist a search for
the pyx be made in your premises."

"You may search and welcome," Magdalene said,
laughing. "Sir Bellamy all but scratched the dirt out
between the boards of the floors when he searched on
Friday."

"He searched your house? Why?" Father Benin
asked.

"He was looking for Master Baldassare's pouch. I had seen it under his cloak, although I had not seen it clearly because he had thrust it to the back. But the pouch was not found with the body. The bishop wondered if Messer Baldassare had hidden the pouch in my house because he did not trust the person he was supposed to meet. And since the bishop is sure that Messer Baldassare had come with important documents from the pope, he is eager that Sir Bellamy find the pouch if he can."

"I see. Well, I must say I am greatly relieved to learn that Sir Bellamy has been ordered to discover who committed this crime. I have found him to be honest and clever when he did the bishop's work in the past."

"He is not so honest now," Brother Paulinus hissed. "He is bedazzled by this whore and his sole purpose is to remove any stigma from her. I tell you, she stole the pyx."

The last idea Magdalene wanted fixed in the prior's mind was that Bell was enamored of her. Better let him think about the missing pyx. "How did I steal it?" Magdalene cried. "Do I look strong enough to break open a safe box?"

"Your strength does not matter—the box was not *broken* open."

Both Magdalene and Father Benin drew a sharp breath and turned to stare at the sacristan. Now Magdalene knew why he was acting like a madman. He had always been strongly opposed to having even so discreet a house of pleasure as hers adjoining the monastery and had always been more rigid about carnal sin than most. His effort to involve her and her women in the murder, once he learned that Baldassare had come through the back gate, was not really unreasonable; however, his insistence that she had stolen the pyx, which was impossible, was mad. But if the safe box had not been broken, someone who had the key must have stolen the pyx . . . and the person who held the key to the safe box was the sacristan.

"Oh, dear," Magdalene whispered.

She did not like the sacristan. In his passionate desire for purity, Brother Paulinus could be cruel and, as she had seen when he struck Ella, violent. She could easily imagine him murdering Baldassare in some mistaken fit of righteousness; she could even imagine him blotting out the memory, or convincing himself that God had directed his act for the purpose of driving out the whores and their corruption. But what reason could Brother Paulinus possibly have for stealing the church plate? And she learned the answer in the next breath.

"It is not possible," Father Benin had murmured simultaneously, and then, smiling wryly, said, "No, not even to repair the belfry roof. Even if you hold the key, Brother Paulinus, there must be another answer."

"It cannot be the only key," Magdalene said.

"Do not you dare defend me!" Brother Paulinus shouted. "Your evil purpose lies like a putrid glow over you. You—"

"Hush, Brother Sacristan," Father Benin said. "The woman may be a sinner, but she means well in this. Why do you not go to my prie-dieu and say a prayer to calm yourself."

That was not really a suggestion; no matter how gentle the voice, it was an order. And when the gaunt monk had walked to where the prior's crucifix hung on the wall near his bed and knelt before it, the prior turned to Magdalene.

"I think you should leave us now, daughter. Go down to the chamber below and Brother Fareman will see you home."

"Thank you, Father Prior," she said, and then, struck by a notion, added softly, "Is it possible that because the little pyx is so small, it was left out when the other vessels were cleaned and returned? Could it be that after the box was locked, the person who forgot it was afraid to admit his fault and hid it somewhere in the church, intending to return it today when the box was opened to make the vessels ready for Sunday? If the church were searched—"

"You are a good-hearted, forgiving creature," Father Benin said, smiling. "I am supposed to be humble and submissive to God's will, but I do not know whether I could try so hard to help someone so eager to harm me. I will certainly ask the sacristan's assistant if the pyx could have been mislaid, and I will also speak to Sir Bellamy about the murder to learn what he knows and to offer what help I can. Go with God, my daughter."

Feeling somewhat guilty for gaining Father Benin's good opinion on completely false premises, Magdalene bowed, kissed the hand he held out to her, and left the room. Her purpose in suggesting the pyx had been mislaid with good intentions had been to get the church searched and Baldassare's pouch found, not to protect Brother Paulinus, of course. Unfortunately, Father Benin had not taken the notion seriously. She could not decide whether she was more annoyed with him for being so good-hearted himself that he saw her suggestion in that light, or pleased at being called "daughter" just as if she were not an excommunicated whore.

She went down the inner stair into the chamber below and almost ran into Brother Fareman, who was staring up at her with a troubled expression. He said he was sorry her interview with the prior had been interrupted and exclaimed over the sacristan's behavior in thrusting him aside and intruding on the prior without leave or announcement. Magdalene promptly told him about the lost pyx.

Brother Fareman was shocked, but now he understood why the sacristan had been so distraught. He *tched* and clucked, wondering how anyone could have broken open the safe box, it being so strong and bound in iron. But when he took out the huge ring of keys he was carrying to open the gate for her, Magdalene suddenly remembered her own question to the prior.

"But the box was not broken," she said. "It must have been unlocked."

"Nonsense!" the secretary said. "I do not like Brother Paulinus—I cannot deny it; he makes Father Prior very unhappy from time to time—but steal from the church? Nonsense."

Magdalene laughed. "Well, the prior said something about money for the leaking belfry, but the first question that came to my mind was, who had another key?"

"Who? I. Father Prior has duplicates of all the keys to the church and the monastery, and those keys are in my charge. Are you suggesting—"

"Of course not. That is even more ridiculous. It is barely possible that Brother Paulinus could blind himself to the impropriety of taking the pyx for some purpose like repairing the belfry and call what he did God's will; he is not a reasonable or clear-sighted person. You could never be so self-deluded. But you and Father Benin were away last week. Is it not possible that someone found your keys—"

"I took them with me." Brother Fareman grimaced and then sighed. "I did not intend to take the keys to the church and the monastery, just those to Father Prior's house and personal chests, but I was in a hurry and instead of taking the time to separate them, I took them all."

"That does seem to fix the blame more surely on Brother Paulinus." But her doubt still sounded in her voice.

"Who could imagine that such things would happen? A murder on our very doorstep! And now a theft. We have never had anything stolen. Oh, a little food now and again when the novices find themselves still hungry on a fast day, and once—yes, I remember, it was soon after the Bishop of Winchester was appointed to administer the London diocese—a monk's robe was stolen. Brother Almoner was annoyed. He does not like carelessness. But nothing came of his seeking and questioning. Likely it was taken by some poor soul in need of a warm cloak." He sighed and pulled open the gate for her. "Poor Father Benin. He will blame himself for all of this."

Magdalene stepped through, but put out her hand to stop the secretary from closing the gate for a moment. "The murder at least is nothing to do with Father Benin, Brother Fareman. Send for Sir Bellamy of Itchen, the bishop's knight. He will explain what happened to Messer Baldassare, and Father Benin will understand at once that there would have been nothing he could have done even if he had been here."

"Sir Bellamy?" The secretary looked relieved. "Then the bishop is seeking the killer?"

"Yes, and not in my house, thank God."

She let go of the gate, and the secretary closed and locked it. Magdalene sighed and then thought perhaps it was just as well. If more mayhem took place in the priory, she and her women would be safer with the gate locked. She thought Father Benin had been joking about stealing the pyx to obtain money to repair the leaking belfry, but a chill went down her back. Was Brother Paulinus insisting that she was guilty to cover his own crime?

She did not voice that doubt to her women, who rushed to greet her and discover what the prior had wanted. She did tell them about the missing pyx and Paulinus's accusation, which drew gasps of alarm until she pointed out that the fact the safe box was kept locked had absolved her completely. Reassured, Ella and Letice picked up their embroidery and Sabina began to practice a new song. Magdalene went to her chamber and pored over a copy of the list she had given Bell, putting a check here and there.

"Magdalene?" It was Sabina at the door. "The bell at the gate is ringing."

Eleven

22 APRIL 1139

OLD PRIORY GUESTHOUSE

"Master Hugo Basyngs," Magdalene said as she opened the gate to a familiar but not frequent visitor. "You are very early, but do come in."

Basyngs smiled and apologized for his untimely arrival. He said he knew that Saturday was a busy day for the women of the Old Priory Guesthouse and that he wanted to catch them when they still had time for him. Magdalene led him in, offered Sabina's company, which he accepted and paid for graciously, but it soon became apparent that he was in no hurry to go off with her. What he wanted was to talk about the murder, particularly to ask if a letter of credit had been found and to bewail the fact that he had not offered Baldassare lodging for the night.

"He was with me that very afternoon," Basyngs said, shaking his head slowly. "He came from Messer Buchuinte's house after dinner to change Italian money for English and to draw some silver against his letter of credit. I should have bade him lodge with us, but I was promised to spend the night at my son's house in Walthamstow, his wife having delivered a third son the day before. I only came back on Friday."

Walthamstow was north of London, and Basyngs's son would be easy to find. Another to cross off her list, except . . . "How did you hear of Messer Baldassare's death?" she asked.

"From Buchuinte."

She should have guessed that, she thought. Likely Basyngs was Buchuinte's banker, and Buchuinte might even have recommended him to Baldassare. She told him then what she had told almost everyone, but Basyngs had no new information. Baldassare had not mentioned any meeting to him. And, since Sabina had been standing beside him and tickling his ear, he rose and went off with her a few moments later.

He was not the only one who came to ask about Baldassare's death. About half a candlemark later, a cordwainer, Bennet Seynturer, arrived. He pushed roughly past Magdalene as soon as she opened the gate. Slamming it closed behind him, he hurried her back to the house, where he also slammed the door. He told her, in a voice choked with fury, that he had heard of the murder from the sacristan, whom he had come to see on business. Was it true, he asked, that Messer Baldassare had come from her house?

Seynturer, married to a frigid, fanatically religious wife who had taken all too seriously the Church pronouncement that one should eschew any sexual congress except for the purpose of procreation, was one of those regular clients who came through the priory gate to conceal his visits. Having been told, with significantly raised brows, that the gate between the Old Priory Guesthouse and the priory was now was locked, he had leapt to the conclusion Brother Paulinus desired and assumed the whores were guilty.

Desperate to assure himself his secret would be kept, Seynturer had come to the front gate, hooded to hide his face. He was livid with fury, excoriating Magdalene for "her crime"—less, it seemed to her, because he minded the murder than because it might lead to his exposure—and demanding that she keep his use of her establishment a secret. Although she felt like bursting into tears and shrieking curses at the sacristan, Magdalene dared not make a counteraccusation. She made herself laugh lightly.

"If you can prove to me that *you* are innocent of murder," she said, "you need not fear that any of my women will spread the news that you are our client. Silence is part of our service."

He gobbled at her, incoherent with anger for a moment, then gasped, "You are mad!"

"Why? After all, it is as likely that you are guilty as that we are. More likely, perhaps. For all I know, you and Messer Baldassare were deadly enemies. As for us, it is in our interest to protect any who come to our house from harm. Your own reaction should be proof that I speak the truth. If one client is hurt, the others abandon us."

He stared at her, hesitating because he recognized the good sense in what she said, yet he still protested, "But—but you are whores! And you were here, where the murder was committed. *I* was at a guild dinner on Wednesday. Many guilds have their dinners on Wednesdays."

That was an interesting piece of information, Magdalene thought—and true, too, she believed. She realized, now that the fact had been brought clearly to her mind, that few craftsmasters visited the Old Priory Guesthouse on Wednesdays. She nodded slowly.

"We were here, but all of us were together, all of us behind locked doors. I cannot make you take my word, but I will take yours that you are innocent, and I will protect you to the best of my ability."

That was not a lie. She had already given Bell his name, but she would certainly urge Bell to be discreet. Nonetheless, it would do no harm to lay a base to push blame elsewhere.

Before he could speak again, she went on. "But you

must know that if you gave yourself away to the sacristan, there is no way I can silence him. It is he who is mad, driven not by any evidence against us, but by his own hatred of carnal weakness. If he guessed—" She shrugged.

She explained yet again how ridiculous it was that she or her women should choose so stupid a way to kill—making a great mess and scandal by stabbing Baldassare on the church porch instead of protecting themselves by quietly poisoning him or strangling him in bed and dumping the body in the river. By the time she was finished, Seynturer looked rather shamefaced, his conviction that he had leapt to the wrong conclusion strongly reinforced by the knowledge that if those of the Old Priory Guesthouse were innocent, his relationship with them would be less likely to be uncovered. Magdalene then assured him that the killing was being dealt with by the bishop's knight, Sir Bellamy of Itchen. That seemed to be a clinching argument, and their innocence was assumed since the bishop's man had not delivered them to the sheriff.

He told her that though he believed her, he could not come again until the gate was reopened. But then Sabina entered, having taken Basyngs out the back and washed and tidied herself, and Seynturer laughed uneasily and said, since he was already in the house, he might as well be hanged for a sheep as for a lamb, paid his three pence, and followed the smiling Sabina to her chamber.

Not another half-candlemark had passed before the bell was ringing again and the whole scene was repeated with another goldsmith, who also had had business with the sacristan. Fortunately, Ella was quite ready to receive the second man. He said that since anyone who had noticed him at the front gate would say there was no smoke without fire, he might as well enjoy the fire instead of being blamed and missing the warmth.

Both clients were ill at ease, however, and because

they did not linger, Ella and Sabina were able to join
Magdalene and Letice for dinner. They were aware of
being late and ate quickly, but Dulcie had hardly cleared
the wine cups from the table when the bell was pealing
again. Ella jumped to her feet; the other three women
sighed and then found smiles. Saturday, before the con-
fessions and Masses of Sunday, was always very busy.

On that day, Magdalene worked no less hard than her
women. Although she never left the common room, she
was responsible for keeping those guests who came
ahead of their time—or those who followed clients who
were slow to find arousal and release—busy, amused,
and just titillated enough to be unwilling to leave but
not excited enough to demand immediate service.
Everyone, even Ella, was exhausted by dusk, and when
Magdalene went out to lock the gate, she was actually
looking at the bell rope and thinking of pulling it in
when a man strode up.

"I am very sorry," she began, then stopped and
laughed. "Bell! Come in. I thought you were another
client and was about to turn you away. For once, I and
my women need rest more than custom."

He seemed to stiffen and hesitate, but she gestured
him in and added as she closed and locked the gate,
"Between those who came to blame us for murder—
and stayed to enjoy what they fear they must deny
themselves in the future—and those who knew nothing
of the crime, I have had my fill of pacifying impatient
men. And my women are tired. Still, I am glad to see
you. I have learned where a round dozen of my clients
were on Wednesday night."

"And you believe what they told you?"

"Mostly yes, and if what I learned is true, you will find
it very easy to prove, most discreetly, the whereabouts of
more than half those on my list. Did you know that many
guilds have their meetings on Wednesday?"

"Yes, I knew—oh! Your clients are mostly craftmasters. I understand."

"So, if the craftmasters were at their guild meetings, they are innocent. No one need question them directly, and my reputation for keeping their secrets will remain intact."

He laughed as he walked into the torch- and taper-lit house with her, and accepted gladly when she asked whether he wished to share their evening meal. As they ate, he told her that all the guests who had stayed at the priory guesthouse the night Baldassare was killed had been cleared also.

Three were still at the priory and would be there for at least another week. Those were the men who had been on horseback. They were stoneworkers, employed for many years by the abbot of the mother house of the priory, and they had readily answered his questions. None knew Baldassare, none had any interest in whether the king held the throne or the empress took it, none cared who was archbishop or whether or not a legate was appointed. They had all attended Compline service together, left the church with several monks who knew them, and gone to bed, sharing blankets and a pallet, so none could have left without waking the others.

Four other guests had annoyed a fifth enough for him to complain to Brother Elwin, one of Brother Godwine's assistants. The four had brought along wine flasks and bread and sat talking and, the fifth guest thought, rolling knucklebones until nearly midnight. They had invited him to join them, which he had refused because he was tired and wished to sleep. But he had not slept, he said bitterly; they made so much noise that he never closed his eyes.

"Well . . ." Magdalene said hesitantly. "He could have dozed from time to time and not realized it, but I tend to believe him."

Bell nodded. "Moreover, Brother Patric, another of Godwine's assistants, confirmed that they were together at midnight. He saw the lights in the guesthouse when he went to relieve Brother Elwin at the gate, and stepped in to tell them to go to bed. And those were all the guests that stayed the night."

"All that stayed the night?" Magdalene repeated. "Is that what Brother Godwine actually said?"

Bell stopped with his knife extended toward the platter of sliced cold meat. He grimaced and banged his hand down on the table so that the hilt of his knife cracked against it. Ella jumped and cried out. Bell said, "I am sorry," frowning so horribly that Ella whimpered and shrank against Letice.

"What is wrong?" Sabina cried, turning her head toward him anxiously.

"Nothing," Bell said. "Forgive me. I have just realized that I have done something stupid, and I do not enjoy it. I did ask Brother Porter for the names of those who had stayed in the guesthouse, but there may have been many others who attended the Compline service and could have lingered behind and killed Baldassare."

"Not many," Magdalene said. "I occasionally attend that service with Sabina. If we do not expect any other guests, and after the gate is locked, we can slip into the church in the dark. Few others ever came—five or six pious women from the neighborhood, perhaps a husband or two accompanying them, a few men from the bishop's Household when Winchester is in Southwark— perhaps nine or ten in all, not counting Sabina and myself. I cannot imagine there could have been more this time."

"But I cannot see how I can trace those. The porter might have asked their purpose for entering the priory, but if they said it was to attend the service, I doubt he would have asked their names."

"True enough, but most of them come regularly and he probably knows who they are. Besides, it seems unlikely that any of those would have murdered Baldassare."

"I am not so sure. The church might have been named as a meeting place because the killer was familiar with it."

"Killer?" Ella asked, eyes wide.

"They are talking of a long-ago tale, love," Sabina said, reaching across the table to pat Ella's hand. "You know you do not like those stories where men are forever being stabbed. Do not listen to them."

Both Magdalene and Bell sighed. "Eat your supper, my love," Magdalene said, "and then you can go to bed. You look very tired."

"Will not our guest want company?" Ella asked, but her voice lacked its usual bright welcoming.

"No, love. This is not a guest, remember? He is the bishop's knight. He is here on business for the bishop."

Ella smiled and turned her attention to the food that Letice had cut up for her, and Magdalene said, "Well, of those who attended the service often, three of the women and two of the men are frail and bent with age. The other three or four you can find and question. More significant, I think, is that the porter will be able to tell you if there were any who came that he did *not* know."

Bell groaned. "And if there were, that person might have come from anywhere in London or Southwark"— he sighed—"actually, from anywhere in England, for it would take longer for Baldassare to reach this country from Italy than for anyone to come from any part of it to Southwark."

---

23 APRIL, 1139

ST. MARY OVERY PRIORY

They were at least spared that possibility. The next morning, after attending Sunday Mass, celebrated by the bishop at St. Paul's, Bell returned to the priory to question the porter again. He found him sitting in the small gatehouse reading a breviary. The porter closed his book and civilly enough offered Bell a stool to sit on. There had been no strangers at the Compline service on that Wednesday night, Brother Godwine said with brisk certainty. So swift a response of exactly what he wanted to hear made Bell suspicious of his willingness to accept the answer.

"How can you be so sure?" he asked.

"Because when a stranger comes through the gate after Vespers, we ask if he wishes to stay the night in the guesthouse, of course," Brother Godwine said sharply. "I know I did not need to ask that question at any time last week, so I know no stranger, except those who did stay in the guesthouse, came through the gate after Vespers on Wednesday."

"Thank God," Bell sighed, but shook his head before the words were really out. "Wait, what about Brother Patric and Brother Elwin? Could one of them have opened the gate for a stranger that night?"

"Not between Vespers and Compline. I was on duty then."

"What about during the Compline service? Who watches the gate then?"

"No one. During the services, the gate is locked. Any visitor must wait until our religious duties are performed. This is not an inn, Sir Bellamy. Though we maintain a guesthouse out of charity, to shelter travelers from the dangers of the night, our religious duties come first."

"Of course," Bell said, but he recalled the fees he had paid to various religious houses for bed and food when he did not travel in the bishop's train, and he thought that the abbeys and priories probably made a nice profit on their charitable enterprise. "I must say, I am very glad there were no strangers. If there had been, it would have increased the difficulty of finding the killer of Messer Baldassare."

"The whores must have killed him," Brother God-wine said. "I do not wish to be uncharitable, but they are steeped in sin already. Besides, we were all to-gether—we always are after Compline—"

"Not all, and not every moment," Bell said. "Remem-ber that Brother Sacristan had to go back into the church because he thought he saw a light."

"Are you accusing Brother Sacristan?" the porter asked, his voice scaling upward.

"I am not accusing anyone, only pointing out that you are vouching for each other out of faith rather than fact."

"Faith is no bad thing," Brother Godwine snapped.

"In a general way, but not when I need facts. The facts say that after Compline service, you all went to your beds and each was alone in his own bed."

"Of course!" Brother Godwine exclaimed.

"And you can prove that no monk left his bed at any time during the night?" Bell asked pointedly, then felt stupid.

He had been annoyed and had asked without really thinking. He knew it did not matter if a monk left his bed. Baldassare had been killed before or just after Compline; Sabina had found the body then.

To his further chagrin, Brother Godwine said, "In fact, I can. There is always a brother at the foot of the stair into the warming room to make sure the novices do not try to sneak into the kitchen or create any other mischief. Since the dormitory of the novices is beyond the monks' cell, the brother knows by coincidence when one of the monks leaves his cell."

"Thank God for that," Bell said, smiling, very willing now to drop the subject.

Brother Godwine insisted on vindication. "No one moved about . . . well, except Brother Patric, who went to relieve Brother Elwin at the gate, and I used the privy just before Lauds, and Brother Aethelwold, the infir-marian—"

"They are innocent, I am sure," Bell said hastily.

"Of course. I tell you it was the whores."

"And I say to you that the facts I have gathered so far tell me it is most unlikely that the whores are guilty. They also tell me that whoever killed Messer Baldassare had to be inside the priory grounds or the Old Guesthouse grounds before dusk, or had to come through your gate, since the gate of the Old Priory Guesthouse was locked at dark."

"And the whores could not have unlocked the gate and lied about it?" Brother Godwine asked angrily.

"Of course they could have, but it would be greatly to their benefit if the murderer were caught and proven guilty. There is no reason for the whores to shield anyone—they are all likely to hang for this killing if no other murderer is found." As Bell said the words, a chill chased itself up and down his back; he did not want Magdalene to be executed for murder. He stared at Brother Godwine, his mouth hard, then curved his lips in what was not really a smile and said, "Now, since I cannot believe a monk vowed to faith and *caritas* could wish even a sinner who was innocent of the crime to be punished and the guilty to go free—"

"They are guilty of sin!"

"Yes, indeed, but not of murder. If they burn in hell for the sin of lust, I have no objection; they are guilty. The punishment will be God's, and just. So far, I have no reason to think them guilty of murder—and I want to know who is. Thus, I still need the names of those who came to Compline service and did not stay the night."

"None of those at Compline service could have done murder."

"Perhaps not, but I must know who they are."

"Oh, very well. There were only six . . . ah, no, seven. The servants who keep the small guesthouses that flank the bishop's house, old Nicholas and Martha and Bernard and Elsa. They can barely walk, let alone strike down a man in his prime. That is four. Then two clerks from the bishop's Household, Robert and Phillipe, which makes six."

"Robert and Phillipe?"

Bell was momentarily distracted from the murder by a naughty notion. Phillipe was a very pretty, delicate young man. Robert was Guiscard's chief rival for principal secretary. Was Phillipe far less innocent than he seemed? Did he hope to win promotion through Robert's support by offering him friendship . . . or more than friendship? The porter's voice jerked Bell's mind back to murder.

"Yes." Brother Porter nodded approvingly. "They come quite often, perhaps twice a week for the last half year whenever the bishop is in residence. And the seventh . . . I cannot bethink me of his name, but it will come back to me. I know him well. He was a student at the priory until a year ago and used to return every week or two. I had not seen him for several months and thought he must have obtained the preferment he was seeking when . . ."

Brother Godwine's voice faded and a frown creased his brow as if some unpleasant thought had occurred to him, but when Bell asked what was troubling him, he shook his head and said he was not sure. Something was niggling his mind about that student, he admitted, but he could not make a clear memory.

"It will come back to me," he assured Bell. "When I remember the boy's name, I will remember what else is teasing my memory, too."

Then Bell remembered something Magdalene had told him that pushed the relationship between Robert and Phillipe—if there was one—right out of his mind. "The name, it would not be Beaumeis, Richard de Beaumeis, would it?"

Brother Godwine's eyes opened wide. "Yes, yes, that

is who it was. However did you know? But now I remember, he came to the service at Vespers, not at Compline. Now why did I think he was at Compline? Did I
see him there? No, no I did not. And I did not see seven
in the nave, only six. Of course the nave is so dark, if
he had been at the back . . ."

"Did you see him leave the priory after Vespers?"

Bell kept his voice flat, fighting against displaying
any excitement. Beaumeis had traveled from Rome to
England with Baldassare. He probably knew what Baldassare was carrying. He was part of the archbishop's
Household and might well wish to keep hidden or destroy the bull naming the Bishop of Winchester legate.

"No, I did not, but then I did not see anyone leave
after Vespers. They were all gone by the time I was
able to return to the gate. Brother Sacristan stopped me
for a few words." Brother Godwine's lips thinned and
pressed together. Then, as if he wished to divert Bell
from whatever Brother Paulinus had said, the porter
feigned interest and asked again, "How did you know
that it was Beaumeis?"

Bell would have preferred that he had forgotten about
the question, he did not want the porter to connect
Beaumeis with the murder yet. For one thing, he was
by no means sure that the coincidence meant anything;
for another, he suspected that Brother Godwine would
be far too likely to expose his suspicions if any were
aroused.

"I knew he had been a student at the priory and that
he had recently returned to England," Bell said, skirting
the truth, "so I thought he might come to visit his old
school."

"Yes, that was what he said, that he had been quite
homesick for the old school."

Brother Godwine frowned, and Bell, again suppressing a rising excitement, asked why.

The porter shrugged. "He did say that, I remember
very well, but it seems to me that it was at another time.

I told you, did I not, that he used to come every week or two. Perhaps it was one of the other times I spoke to him, because I know he came at Vespers, but it seems—"

Brother Godwine stopped speaking as a shadow darkened the open door of the little gatehouse. Both he and Bell looked up to see the prior's secretary, who was staring at them with an expression of extreme surprise.

"Sir Bellamy," Brother Fareman said, "I just came to ask Brother Godwine to watch for you and ask you to come and speak to Father Prior and here you are."

Although he would have liked to hear the end of the porter's sentence, Bell knew it was too late and rose without any reluctance. He hoped that Brother Godwine would continue to think about his meeting with Beaumeis and might have more to tell him later. Thus, he merely thanked Brother Godwine for his help and said he would be glad to see the prior.

Bell assumed that the prior wished to ask what progress he was making in finding the killer of the pope's messenger. Since he felt he had at last discovered a likely suspect, he was eager to recapitulate the evidence to an intelligent and impartial listener. He hoped that the prior would find as significant as he did the question of why Beaumeis was in the priory at Vespers when he had told Buchuinte that he was leaving for Canterbury immediately and could not stay for dinner. He also hoped the prior would be able to tell him something of Beaumeis's character. Surely he would know the man better than Magdalene, who seemed to doubt that Beaumeis could be the killer.

He was considerably disappointed when Father Benin listened to him with a rather distracted air and said no more than, "You must find young Beaumeis and make him explain. I suspect he will have a good reason for being here and be able to clear himself. As to his character"—he sighed—"it was not what I would have wished for a churchman. He was clever enough, but also shallow, selfish, and lazy. It was shocking to me because he was nephew—sister's son—to the abbot of St. Albans, who recommended him to our school and paid his fees." He shook his head. "I would not like to think so ill of Richard. More likely the guilty one is among those of Magdalene's clients who bear arms. How would Beaumeis know where to stab a man?"

The fatal knife wound could have been an accident, Bell thought, but many of Magdalene's clients *were* knights and some could be attached to the Empress Matilda's party. Still, he would expect an accounting of every minute of Beaumeis's time before forgetting that the man had traveled all the way from Rome with Baldassare. All the way from Rome? And never found an opportunity to steal the bull or murder his companion? The journey together was something Bell had not considered.

"It *is* most worrisome," Father Benin said, and Bell realized the prior had been telling him something he had not taken in.

"I am sorry—" he began.

"Oh, please do not say that Brother Paulinus must be the thief because he was the only one who had a key to the safe box. Sometimes Brother Paulinus can be difficult—even violent—because of his strong convictions, but I cannot believe he would steal from the church."

Bell blinked. "Steal from the church? For what purpose? Not for luxurious living. What did you say was stolen? I am afraid I was still thinking about the murder."

Father Benin, who was as much troubled by the theft of the pyx because of the shadow it cast on Brother Paulinus as by the death of Baldassare, told the story again willingly, repeating in a voice that now trembled with doubt how impossible it was for the sacristan, even to repair his beloved buildings, to be guilty.

"And when did this theft take place?" Bell asked.

Father Benin sighed. "We do not really know. It would have to be after the plate was cleaned and inspected for the Sunday service last week and before it was again removed from the safe box yesterday."

"It could have been stolen Wednesday night, then?"

"The same night as the murder? Would that not be too much of a coincidence?"

"If it was a coincidence at all," Bell said.

Twelve

That Brother Patric be a nice boy," Dulcie said as she brought in a large bowl of porridge and began to serve it into smaller bowls. "He said he be sorry I had t' walk so far t' attend th' service this mornin' 'stead o' just coming across th' back like I did before."

Magdalene waited until Dulcie's eyes came to her face and said slowly and loudly, "Most of the monks do not blame you for our sins. They know one must work to eat." She saw Dulcie nod, to indicate that she had understood, and went on. "That was why I said you must go to Mass. You are still a good daughter of the Church, not excommunicate. If you swear under oath we were all here when Baldassare was murdered, they must accept your word."

Dulcie laughed at that. "It even be true—not that it matters," she said. "I be dead in th' street if you didn' take me in. Yair, I be a good daughter o' th' Church. An' don' I know how easy it be t' get absolution fer a lie—a lie tol' t' help a friend. No need t' say what lie. Priest never asks. If penance be in silver—you pay. I know that. 'Nd I don' mind extra aves. Like to pray, I do. Sounds pretty in me head."

Finished serving out the porridge, she brought a platter of thin-sliced ham from the kitchen and a tray of
yesterday's bread fried in lard. Then she went back to
fetch pitchers of milk and ale before sitting down at the
end of the table, as she often did when there were no
clients and none were expected. Sunday breakfast was
a big, leisurely meal. The morning was always free because nearly everyone was in church, and those hardened sinners who did not attend Mass were not the kind
of men that Magdalene accepted as clients.

All of Sunday was usually quiet; Magdalene took no
regular appointments. That made a good impression on
clients with uneasy consciences, and actually, she lost
very little. Between the time taken by attending religious observances and that given to family obligations,
and the reluctance of most men to stain a soul newly
cleansed by going to confession and hearing several
Masses, few clients wished to visit a whorehouse on
Sunday.

The women, even Ella, were glad of a day free of
men. They had time for long, lingering baths, for mending garments damaged by too-eager clients, for examining their clothing and underclothing, their ribbons and
laces, and deciding whether they wished to go to the
East Chepe market the coming week. All had money in
plenty, since Magdalene paid them the very generous
fee of ten pence a week each, all found; the brothel
absorbed the cost of rent and food.

To Magdalene's relief, this Sunday was no exception.
The women cleaned and mended, talked about their
clothing, told each other tidbits of news and gossip suppressed during the week by the press of work or fatigue.
This Sunday, as she sometimes did, Letice spent the
afternoon with her countryfolk. Magdalene did not think
she plied her trade among them, but she never asked.
The farthings those poor folk could pay meant nothing
to her—and likely nothing to Letice, if she took money

from them at all. She came back in good time for the evening meal.

Ella and Letice had already gone to bed, and Sabina had just handed her emptied wine cup to Dulcie when the sounds of horses' hooves and men's shouting came over the wall and through the shuttered windows. Although Sabina and Magdalene turned their heads toward the noise, neither was troubled. Parties of men did come over the bridge, even at night. But this time the sounds did not rise to a crescendo and die away. They rose and increased, as if the men were milling around near the Old Priory Guesthouse gate. Sabina rose slowly to her feet, her face white.

"They are not going away," she whispered, stretching a hand to feel for her staff.

Magdalene also got to her feet. She caught Sabina's hand and held it tight. "Perhaps they only—"

"There are too many," Sabina breathed. "They cannot have come for our services. It is my fault. Because I found the dead man!"

The bell rang. "Do not be silly, Sabina," Magdalene managed to say between stiff lips. "No one knows of that but the bishop and his knight. And they believe us innocent."

The bell rang again. Sabina clutched at Magdalene. "Do not go out," she whispered. "We can bar the door."

The bell rang yet again, more insistently. Several men shouted. Dulcie, now aware of the fear Magdalene and Sabina were displaying, asked, "What's wrong?"

"A large party of mounted men are at the gate. Far too many for us to serve. Could the sacristan have . . ."

Magdalene stopped and took a deep breath. It was useless to add to Sabina's terror, but she could not forget how near madness the sacristan seemed to be the previous day. Could the prior's order that he not accuse her and her women without proof have driven him over the edge? Could he deliberately have spread the tale that they were guilty of murder and being protected because of what they paid in silver and service? Could he have urged some too-righteous folk to exact justice on their own?

Peal after peal now came from the bell, as if whoever was pulling the cord was determined to continue until someone answered. Magdalene swallowed hard.

"Oh, Lord. They will waken everyone on the street," she murmured. "The bishop will get complaints about us." Then she bit her lip and took a deep breath and said loudly, "Dulcie, get me the key and come with me. Let us put the bar across the gate. I will unlock it. Then you take the key and go with Sabina, Letice, and Ella to the back gate. Unlock it and go into the priory grounds. I will see if I can calm—"

"No!" Sabina cried, clinging to her. "God knows what they will do to you."

Dulcie had grabbed up a candle and scuttled toward the kitchen, where the keys were hung.

"If you hear blows against the gate," Magdalene said to Sabina, "run to the prior's house and call for help. Father Benin does not believe us guilty and will send help, I am sure."

"Quick enough to save you?"

Magdalene did not answer that, but unwound Sabina's arms from her. Dulcie came running back. Sabina was weeping and shaking. Magdalene was shaking, too, but actually she was already less frightened as she pushed Sabina toward Dulcie. If so large a group of men had come to wreak violence, surely they would have forced the gate by now. But, aside from the continued pealing of the bell, there seemed to be less noise from the street. Then a single stentorian voice called out. With a quick, indrawn breath, Magdalene snatched the key from Dulcie and ran out the door.

"William?" she cried as she reached the gate. "William? Is that you?"

"Of course it is, you stupid slut! Who else would arrive at this time of night with twenty men-at-arms?

Let me in! I have been ahorse since Prime."

Magdalene already had the gate unlocked. As she swung it open, two of the mounted men came down from their horses. One strode through the gate. The other caught the rein of the loose horse and followed, leading the horses behind him. While William of Ypres strode toward the house, the second man led the horses toward the stable. Magdalene saw a third man gesture, and the troop turned their mounts to ride back up the street to the bridge. She closed the gate, relocked it, and ran to catch up to Lord William.

"I am so sorry," Magdalene gasped as she reached his side. "I was afraid because of the murder."

"What the shit has that to do with you?" he growled.

"The sacristan of the priory has been accusing us of killing Messer Baldassare. He says because we are whores, we must be murderers, too. I thought he had preached against us before the prior told him not to— or that because the prior had silenced him, he bade someone punish us for our crime."

His step checked and he put an arm around her, pulling her roughly against him. "Forgot about that, chick. Nothing to fear now. I'm here. I'll send word to the sheriff and the Watch that the Old Guesthouse is under my protection and I'll have the ears and skin off anyone who hurts you."

His mail was biting painfully into Magdalene's arm and side, but she did not pull away. "Thank you, William," she said.

He reached out and opened the house door, stepping to the side and shoving her through in front of him. Magdalene could not help smiling. He had just offered her protection but instinctively used her as a shield in case an ambush had been laid for him in her house. Not that he really expected an ambush in her house, but caution was a habit long ingrained in William of Ypres.

"Hello, girls," he bellowed as he came in behind her, and then, taking in Ella's and Letice's half-open gowns over naked bodies, added, "All ready for work, I see."

Letice wriggled and Ella put her thumb in her mouth. She was overawed by Lord William and never aggressive toward him. Sabina smiled and set her staff against the wall.

"We are very glad to know you are our visitor, Lord William," she said, having easily recognized his voice and manner. "We were afraid it was someone who did not appreciate our art. Each and all of us are more than willing to entertain you, separately or all together."

He laughed loudly. "Each and all, separately and together, eh? Well, once I might have been able to take you all, but a hard life has tamed me a little, especially after being in the saddle since dawn. Tonight I will be content with Magdalene. You girls can play with Somer"—he laughed again, even louder—"if he can get it up after riding almost without stopping for four days."

"Those three can get it up on a dead man," Somer de Loo said from the doorway, coming in from the stable. And then, into the tense silence that followed his words, "Oops! Didn't think."

"The dead man is nothing to do with us," Magdalene said, shaking her head at the younger man. And then, turning back to her patron, "Are you hungry, William?"

"In your room," he said. "I don't want a lot of chatter and giggling distracting me. Bread and cheese and my wine will do, if you've nothing else."

Dulcie, who heard his bellow well enough to understand that he wanted food, dropped a curtsy and scuttled toward the kitchen. Magdalene smiled, knowing that Dulcie would bring the best of everything they had, and preceded her guest into her chamber. She was aware that William of Ypres was watching her as she closed the door, and turned to smile at him, her hand going to the veil that covered her hair. His face had no expression at all as she asked, "Shall I help you to undress now, or would you like to unlace me first?"

He did not move and one brow lifted. "You are the

most beautiful woman I have ever seen," he said. "One would think that God had designed you specially for the purpose of rousing and futtering a man. Yet you take little pleasure in the congress between men and women."

"I take pleasure in serving you, William, because you have done so much for me."

He came forward then, smiling, and gave her a rough hug, which made her bite the inside of her lip as his mail cut into her flesh again. "Whore you are," he said, "but only with your body. Your heart is steadier than most of the men sworn to me, some of them with more reason to be grateful to me than you."

"I suppose it is because the selling of their bodies is not considered a sin and a shame," she said, laughing up at him.

He relaxed his grip suddenly and stared down into her face. "Is that why you are so faithful?" he asked, grinning. "You believe in a special bond between us? That we are two sides of the same coin? That I am a whore, like you, because I sold my body to the king?"

Magdalene lifted her head, eyes wide. She had forgotten again that William might be coarse and brutal but his mind was quick, as quick as Winchester's. He had understood more than she meant him to. Fortunately he had a wry sense of humor, but, she thought, he was tired, and under his surface good spirits, irritable. She did not want him thinking of the comparison she had made. She shook her head.

"Not that. Only that because a mercenary's trade is not condemned like a whore's, a mercenary can afford a slip or two in honor and honesty and expect it to be overlooked. A whore, who is thought to be evil by nature, must take care *never* to be dishonest with those whose trust she desires."

"Yet there *is* that bond between us, that we both sell our bodies." His lips tightened. "And if Waleran de Meulan has his way, I may be forced into true whoredom, selling myself to others than the king."

"I do not believe that," Magdalene said.

"No." He shook his head. "I have given my faith and I will hold by it." His mouth twisted. "Perhaps for the same reason as you. Waleran, who exacts lands and honors from the king for 'love' rather than for service, can afford a little betrayal here and there. I, who have been granted lands and honor for service, cannot."

"Nor would you wish to," Magdalene exclaimed. He stared at her, then snorted with wry laughter and tightened his grip in appreciation of her defense of his honor. She gasped with pain but smiled up at him. "William, love," she said, "do let me help you undress. My skin is going to look like fishnet tomorrow from being bruised by your armor."

For the answer, he gave her an even tighter squeeze, making her squeal. Then he let her go, allowing her to untie the laces that held his hood. When that hung loose, he bent double at the waist; Magdalene pulled the hood over his head as he lifted his arms even with his ears. She transferred her grip to the sleeves and hauled them forward. The whole mail shirt followed as William backed away, and Magdalene gathered it to her, staggering a little under the weight but holding it firmly until she could lay it out on top of her chest. Free of the armor, he sighed deeply and went to sit on her bed.

As if the relative silence was a signal, there was a scratch on the door. Magdalene let Dulcie in with a laden tray. She hurried to bring the small table from against the wall and set it beside Lord William. Dulcie deposited the tray and went out. William looked at the food blankly.

"You really are tired, love," Magdalene said. "Why not sleep for a while. I will be here whenever you want me."

He did not seem to hear her. "I hardly believed it when Somer told me the pope's messenger was dead," he said, his mouth hard. "I thought I had a way to remind Stephen how ill Waleran had advised him." He ran a hand through his matted hair. "Ernulf, Bishop of Rochester, agreed it would be wise for Winchester to be legate. He promised to speak to the pope in Winchester's favor. Well, all of them would, even the Bishop of Worcester, despite Waleran's order that he should not."

"Perhaps *because* of Waleran's order?" Magdalene suggested, not because she cared, but because any hint of opposition to Waleran de Meulan would please William.

"That did not matter. They all trust Henry and were glad Stephen asked for legatine powers for him. But I wanted to put the bull into *Stephen's* hands so that *he* could give it to Winchester himself and smooth over the breach between them. Ernulf agreed that that would be better than having the bull delivered to Winchester by the papal messenger. He said he would suggest it to the pope if he could, or try to convince the messenger to stop at Rochester—"

"Oh, my God," Magdalene interrupted, "was it your man the messenger was supposed to meet? Winchester's knight is convinced that the man Baldassare met killed him."

"Meet? How could I arrange for anyone to meet him? I had no idea when he would set out or arrive. I hoped Ernulf would get the pope to instruct him or convince him—you say his name was Baldassare?—to have himself set ashore at Rochester instead of London. I would have provided him with a safe escort to Nottingham, gone with him myself directly to the king, been with him when he gave Stephen news of . . . Magdalene, what was in his pouch?"

"I do not know," she said, sighing with regret over the lie, but knowing that if she told William the truth, he would insist that the pouch be unearthed from its hiding place so that he could deliver the contents to the king. The exposure would be her death warrant. "I know he was carrying a pouch; I saw it. But he took it with him when he went out." She uttered a frustrated sob. "How could I know he was going to his death? He told us he had to meet someone, but he was not in the least apprehensive. He joked and laughed with me and with Sabina, who liked him so well that she has been weeping every time she is reminded of his death."

William let out an explosive, exasperated breath and said, "Now see where all your honor and honesty gets us? If you were like other whores, you would have been in his pouch and his purse—"

Magdalene poured a cup of wine and put it into his hand. "And you would be none the wiser for it, even if, like a common whore, I decided to extract a few more pence from your purse by selling you information. If I were like other whores, I would not have been able to make head nor tail of any writings he carried."

He downed the wine in three long swallows. "And now the pouch is gone, likely destroyed."

"No, not that. Winchester's knight—his name is Sir Bellamy of Itchen—believes Baldassare was not carrying the pouch because there was no mark of cutting it loose from the strap, which also was spotted with Baldassare's blood where the pouch should have covered it. Bell—"

"Another benefactor that you oblige with your favors?" William interrupted sharply.

Magdalene laughed around the spot of ice that had suddenly appeared in her belly. If William turned jealous, she would have another dead man on her conscience. Bell dead? No! Because she did not dare look up, she took the cup from where William had set it and refilled it. He took it from her and she reminded herself that William had never been jealous. He had always accepted that she was truly a whore. And then the curve of her lips grew more natural.

It was not the favors of her body of which William was jealous but his place as her benefactor—which was silly. No one could ever take that. William had taken her out of a house where she had to spread her legs for any man who came, set her up in her own place where she could choose her clients, let it be known that he was her protector so that she would not be persecuted, recommended her to the Bishop of Winchester as a good tenant for the Old Priory Guesthouse, where she would—if she could find Baldassare's murderer and free herself of suspicion—end up rich enough to retire. . . . No, William would always come first.

She put her hand on his and squeezed it gently, then drew her eating knife and cut some strips of meat which she rolled into bite-sized pieces. Piercing one, she handed the knife to William.

"Bell is Winchester's knight, not his own man," she said, "and must do as he is told. As to my favors—he would wish it, but I would be an idiot to take his coin. He is supposed to be investigating a murder in which I am suspect. How much would anyone believe a solution that cleared me if he were sporting about in my bed?"

Around the mouthful he was chewing, William said, "Cold as yesterday's roast, are you?"

"Until this murder is solved. I am like to be gutted and hanged if it is not."

"Not while I hold some power," William said calmly, taking another drink of his wine and using Magdalene's knife to spear another piece of meat. "But you had better tell me this whole tale from the beginning. Then maybe I will be able to make some sense out of it."

So Magdalene began with the arrival of Baldassare at her gate, recounting everything he had said as closely as she could remember. She did not get very far, however. As soon as she mentioned Richard de Beaumeis, William said, "Who? Say again."

"Richard de Beaumeis. He had been a student at the priory and came here to lie with Ella whenever he could scrape together the price. A nuisance he was, always whining about the expense but not willing to go where the price was cheaper."

William was staring at her and apparently had not listened to her complaint, because he said, "Are you telling me that Richard de Beaumeis was in the archbishop's Household and traveled from Rome in the company of this messenger . . . ah . . . Baldassare? And that Beaumeis was the man who recommended that Baldassare come to the Old Priory Guesthouse?"

"Yes, love. Why do you think it so strange? I did not realize that Richard had a mischievous streak, but he was just playing a joke on a foreigner . . . was he not?"

"Like hell he was!" William roared, banging his hand down on the table so hard that everything on it jumped and Magdalene just managed to catch the pitcher of wine before it tipped over. "Beaumeis is the man whose ordination was arranged so that Winchester would be away from the ecclesiastical conference when Theobald was elected archbishop."

"Oh, dear heaven," Magdalene gasped. "I knew what had happened, of course. You told me yourself. But if you gave Richard's name, I did not remember it. But even so, William, I cannot see—"

"If Beaumeis was in the archbishop's Household, Theobald must have been told how his ordination was interrupted. Perhaps Theobald was even told that Winchester believed Beaumeis knew why his ordination had been set for that day and refused to complete the ordination later. Likely as not, Theobald himself then completed the ordination. He must have felt some guilt over Beaumeis's state, even if he was not party to the arrangement to gull Winchester."

"We will never know the answer to what Theobald knew," Magdalene said slowly, "but it should not be difficult to discover who completed Beaumeis's ordination. I am sure someone at St. Paul's will know that, and Sir Bellamy has the Bishop of Winchester's authority to ask questions."

William's brows rose, marking his notice of Magdalene's use of "Sir Bellamy" instead of "Bell," but he did not allow himself to be distracted from the main point. He said only, "So Beaumeis would no doubt feel himself obliged to Theobald—and probably hate Winchester for his own reasons. Now, I do not know Theobald of Bec, but I doubt he is an idiot. He must have realized how he would be overshadowed if Winchester received legatine power before he could even return to England and show himself in the pallium bestowed by the pope."

"Yes, Theobald was aware of that. I assume that was why he sent Beaumeis back to England with Baldassare. Beaumeis told Buchuinte that Theobald wanted news of his receipt of the pallium and the pope's honorable reception of him to come to Canterbury before Winchester was announced as legate."

"He could have asked Beaumeis to destroy the bull— or bewailed the pope's making Winchester legate in such a way that Beaumeis was bound to understand his desire. . . ."

"But would Beaumeis perform so dangerous an act? He is not very strong or brave, and he is very selfish."

"And ambitious, too? Can you imagine what preferment he might be able to wring from Theobald if he threatened to spill the tale of the stolen bull?"

"And he probably hated Winchester." Magdalene sighed and nodded. "Yes, to assuage his spite and gain a lifelong hold over the archbishop, he would have dared. And he could have estimated the time they were to arrive and told Baldassare he had been asked to arrange a meeting with the papal messenger." As she said that, she frowned. "But is that not nonsense? He was in Baldassare's company on the whole voyage from Italy. Could he not have stolen the bull then?"

"Not if he had a brain in his head. That would make him the only person for hundreds of miles who could want the bull. Here in England, there might be many who would wish to seize it, either to hold it for ransom from Winchester or to destroy it. Who in Italy or France could care about a legate in England?"

"But would not Baldassare know him?"

"Maybe that was why Baldassare died. Perhaps he was not supposed to recognize the man he met, but knew Beaumeis too well for a disguise to work."

That was when Magdalene shuddered and rubbed her arms to warm them against an inner chill. She had not really believed Richard de Beaumeis could gather the will to murder in cold blood, but if Baldassare had recognized him, Beaumeis could have drawn his knife and struck once in an hysterical panic. They would have been standing close, talking—as Bell said.

"Horrible," she whispered, and then, "No. Buchuinte says that Beaumeis left his house long before Baldassare did."

William, who had been staring down into his wine cup, looked up. "Well, I can discover when he arrived in Canterbury, and I can have my men ask along the way about his passing. Now tell me the rest of the tale."

So she did, from Baldassare's decision to stay in the whorehouse once he heard there was a short way to the church, to Sabina's finding his body on the north porch. Then she described Bell's investigation and conclusions and was relieved when William only grinned at her. He stopped her a few times to ask questions, like why she and Sir Bellamy were so certain the killer had to be inside the walls, but in general, he just listened intently until she suggested that there might have been another piece of news that Baldassare was carrying that was important and asked whether the pope could not have included a letter to the king stating his decision about Stephen's right to the throne.

"If the decision had been made," William replied, yawning, "and it may have been, because I doubt the pope would waste much time over it. I expect he did send a letter. It makes sense to send one messenger with both documents. But there has never been any doubt what that decision would be. William de Corbeil, who was then the pope's legate as well as Archbishop of Canterbury, had accepted Stephen as the rightful king. The pope is not likely to reverse that decision."

"No, but one of my clients felt that there was a great difference between that old approval by a legate and the pope's personal decision recorded and sealed by the curia. He seemed to fear that an attack by the empress was planned and that her partisans would feel that news of the pope's decision would discourage men from flocking to her banner. If so, it would certainly be worthwhile to destroy the document and, perhaps, the messenger, who might know what he carried and cry aloud of the theft."

"One of your clients—"

William's stare challenged, but Magdalene ignored it. He knew she would not reveal the name of a client unless the need was acute. She said, "This client could not have been involved with the murder. He was in Berkhampstead on Wednesday night, fetching his son home from fostering. However, he might well fear invasion. He comes from the south, although he never told me exactly where his lands lie."

"Fear of invasion, or hope for it?"

"If he hoped the empress were coming, would he have mentioned the idea of someone killing Messer Baldassare to keep the pope's decision secret?"

"Likely not."

William sighed and pushed away the platter from which he had been eating, took a last drink of wine, and allowed himself to fall sideways onto the bed so that his head was on the pillow. Magdalene jumped forward to get the table out of his way before he kicked it over as he lifted his feet onto the bed. Setting the table aside, she went to remove his shoes and undo his cross garters. When she looked at his face, his eyes were barely open.

"Tired," he mumbled, and then, "When I wake, remind me of the names of my men who are allowed to come to you and know the ways of your house and about the back gate. I will be able to clear most or all of them, which will save your Bell from needing to pry into my affairs."

Thirteen

By midmorning on Monday, William was gone, having cleared all but two of the men sworn to him who frequented the Old Priory Guesthouse. Those two had been away from Rochester on his business, and it would be easy enough for him to discover where they were on Wednesday night and let Magdalene know.

By accident, while talking about who was with the king in Nottingham, William had also cleared five other noble clients. Although he had chosen not to join the court himself—mostly, he said sourly, because he had been hoping to bring the papal messenger with him when he next approached the king—William knew who was there and what was going forward almost day by day. A stream of messengers—sent by this man and that who owed him favors (or wanted one), or who simply hated Waleran de Meulan—flowed out of Nottingham to Rochester and would follow him to London.

Magdalene was tempted to ask him about the rest of the noblemen on her list, partly because she felt very fond of him that morning and she knew her confidence would please him, but she resisted. William could not really be trusted with information that might conceivably be exploited to apply pressure to a person he could use. He would apply that pressure, without regard to anyone else, if it would forward his own plans and ambitions.

Fortunately, he never guessed her temptation or her resistance to it, and they parted quite tenderly. Although he had been too fast asleep to take her when she came to bed, he had wakened very amorous, and had loved her—a little to the surprise of each—very successfully, so that both had risen from her bed sated and pleased with themselves. That, Magdalene told herself, should diminish any interest she felt in the less predictable and possibly dangerous Bell.

William was very merry at breakfast, teasing Somer, who did look rather heavy-eyed, and the women until the room rang with laughter. He grew serious, however, while Somer went to saddle the horses, assuring Magdalene as she walked with him to the gate that he would stay in London to be certain no harm came to her until the murderer was found or she was cleared in some other way. She flung her arms around him and kissed him, but she laughed, aware that the offer was not completely altruistic, and promised, without prompting, to let him know if she possibly could, if the pouch was found.

"Good girl," he said, flicking the tip of her nose with a finger. "And I promise that Winchester and your Bell won't lose by it."

Her Bell? No, Magdalene thought, he was not, and would not be, *her* Bell, even though William seemed to have gotten over the resentment he had first shown. Fond as she was of William, it was as great a pleasure to see him go as to see him come. She resolved anew not to allow any man ever to think of her as his, waving to William as he set off and then closing the gate behind him.

It would be to her benefit as well as William's if Winchester's relationship with his brother improved, but she was not sure having Stephen hand the bull to him would work. Magdalene suspected a better feeling between the brothers was not really William's prime purpose. He liked Winchester well enough, but he wished to please Stephen, and it might please Stephen just as well to use the bull to demonstrate his power to Winchester as to be reconciled to him.

She reentered the house, shook her head when Dulcie asked if she wished to finish her ale, and the maid continued clearing the table. Her women were gone. Vaguely, she heard sounds through the open doors to the corridor and knew they were cleaning their rooms. Automatically, she walked to the hearth, sat down on her stool, and picked up her embroidery.

One by one, the other women joined Magdalene. Letice and Ella also took up their embroidery and after some desultory talk about the clients, Sabina struck the first notes of a lively and rather bawdy tune about a soldier. Magdalene looked up and smiled. William's visit had done them all good. This was the first time since Wednesday night that no one made a reference to the murder.

Listening to the song, Magdalene laughed aloud. With his rough good humor and his rough-and-ready ways, the hero was a bit like William; his inventiveness reminded her of William. She shook off her concern about political problems. They did not really matter to her. Her protectors might suffer small setbacks that displeased them, but both the bishop and William of Ypres were too important and too powerful to have more than their pride hurt by Waleran de Meulan.

The morning was quiet, except for a minor and very delightful flurry caused by Magdalene's finding a heavy purse on her pillow when she finally went to make her bed—an extra token of William's affection (or satisfaction with her response to him). The day proceeded pleasantly; dinner was uninterrupted and the right clients arrived at the right time. Three more men were crossed off the list of possible suspects when that set of clients left.

Two more arrived without overlapping or colliding with each other, and Buchuinte, the third, came at his regular time. He was still saddened by Baldassare's death—he told them he had arranged the burial for Tuesday—but he was not so sad as to give up his appointment with Ella. An easy day.

Magdalene had settled to her embroidery again after hearing Ella's squeal of pleasure, cut off by the closing of her door. She was enjoying her solitude and looking forward to the completion of a complex pattern and the delivery of a piece already ordered, when the bell at the gate rang. She gave a quick thought to the men being entertained behind closed doors. Sabina's second client, an elderly widower whose children were established in their own homes and was more lonely than lustful, was staying the night, but Ella's and Letice's guests would be gone in time for this new man to be accommodated.

Sighing, Magdalene fixed her needle into her work and rose to answer. She would have preferred not to need to entertain anyone until one of the women was free, and William's extra purse would have made it possible to indulge herself, but she had left the bell cord out. That was an invitation that could not be withdrawn without offense. She would let this man in, she told herself, and then pull in the bell cord. Fixing a pleasant smile on her face, Magdalene started toward the gate, only to stop dead a few steps along the path.

The man had let himself in, which always annoyed her, but the face she saw rendered her too speechless to protest.

"Delighted to see me, are you?" Richard de Beaumeis said, grinning broadly. "How did you like the client I sent you?" And when Magdalene still just stared at him, gaping, he laughed and went on. "Baldassare did mention my name, did he not? I told him he should." He laughed again. "I would wager he was surprised at what he found here. I would have loved to be invisible and have seen his face."

"I thought you were in Canterbury," Magdalene got out, still too stunned to say anything sensible.

Beaumeis certainly sounded as if he thought Baldassare was alive. Could he have struck with the knife and then run away without realizing he might have killed the man? There was a kind of self-satisfied spitefulness under his final words that simply did not fit with having already taken the ultimate revenge.

"Canterbury?" Beaumeis repeated. "I brought the archbishop's news on Friday. The cannons celebrated fittingly on Saturday, and I returned to my duty in St. Paul's. . . . Why should I remain in Canterbury? It is a nothing place after London and Rome."

He started to step around her, and Magdalene was suddenly enraged. "Oh, no," she said, catching his arm. "You are not welcome here. You do not know the ill you did us with your nasty little jest. Baldassare de Firenze is dead, and I have been accused of killing him."

"Dead?" Beaumeis's voice came out as a squawk and his face had gone parchment yellow. "No! No! He cannot be dead. I saw him. . . . No! He cannot be dead."

He sounded genuinely shocked, but so he might be if he did not know his blow had struck home. Magdalene said, "He *is* dead. He was killed on the north porch of the church—"

"No! I do not believe you! I cannot believe you! You are a lying whore."

Beaumeis's eyes bulged, looked ready to fall out of his head, and he swayed on his feet. Magdalene would have felt sorry for him if not for that last sentence.

"Then go look at his body yourself," she said coldly. "It is laid out in the small chapel between the monks' entrance and the church."

He pushed past her roughly, running toward the back gate. Magdalene called after him, but he did not stop or even turn to look at her, and she shrugged and went into the house, walking quickly through it toward the back door. As she expected, it burst open a few moments later and Beaumeis stood in it, panting. Magdalene blocked his entrance; Dulcie waited in the kitchen doorway, the long-handled pan in her hand. But Beaumeis did not try to push his way in this time.

"The gate is locked," he shouted. "Give me the key."

"I do not have a key," Magdalene said mendaciously. "And keep your voice down. I do not want my clients disturbed."

"It is never locked," he said angrily but in a lower voice. "It was open when . . . when I was last here."

"When was that?" Magdalene asked. "I do not remember."

There was more color in Beaumeis's face now, but he did not meet her eyes when he said, "I do not remember, either, but it must have been before I left the country in January." He hesitated, then drew a deep, almost sobbing, breath. "Is Baldassare truly dead?"

"Truly. He was murdered on Wednesday night—according to Brother Paulinus, who came to accuse us of the crime on Thursday morning. Where were you on Wednesday night?"

"I do not know," he muttered. "On the road. Somewhere on the road." And then, as if the words reminded him, he asked, "What did you do with his horse?"

"I? I did nothing with his horse. He took it with him when he left, I assume."

"Took it with him? Did he not—" He stopped abruptly, but now he was watching her avidly, appearing more interested than distressed, his color back to normal and a slight supercilious droop to his lips. "When did he die?"

"How would I know that?" Magdalene snapped. "If you are so curious, go ask Sir Bellamy of Itchen, who is trying to discover the facts on the bishop's behalf."

"Bishop? Winchester?"

"Yes, Winchester. Since Baldassare had come here to Southwark, it is possible he came to see the bishop."

The remark did not have the effect Magdalene expected. She had hoped to surprise a look or a word confirming that Beaumeis knew about the bull, but he said nothing. He had paled again and looked away as Magdalene spoke, but not quickly enough. She was sure it was rage that thinned his lips, and the concentrated venom of his expression surprised her. She was certain now that Beaumeis was more than a selfish nodcock. He could have arranged to meet Baldassare. He hated Henry of Winchester enough to take some chances to spite him.

In another moment Beaumeis's face was smooth and indifferent once more, although still rather pale. Magdalene again revised an opinion. He was well able, it seemed, to hide what he was thinking. She was annoyed with herself for her lack of comprehension. Of course he had never tried to hide his honest feelings from her or her women in the past; they were not important enough for him to bother.

Suddenly he seemed to notice that she was blocking his entrance into the house. "You do not need to try to keep me out," he said, first glancing over her shoulder at Dulcie and then looking down his nose at her. "I am rich enough now to keep my own woman, who will not drip on me the leavings of other men."

To that, Magdalene made no reply other than stepping back and slamming the door in his face. She did not waste time fuming over so silly an insult, knowing her women were trained to wash carefully between clients and remove any signs of previous use. She peered out the kitchen window in time to catch a flicker of his cloak as he rounded the corner of the house, heading for the front gate.

"I must go out," she said to Dulcie, who nodded understanding and replaced her pan on a hook by the door. Magdalene then took the key to the front gate and hurried to her own chamber, where she wound her out-door veil around her head and face. Taking her cloak, she peered out the door to make sure Beaumeis was gone, then ran to the front gate and pulled in the bell cord. Until she could return, they would do without extra custom. It was more important to tell Bell that Beaumeis was back.

As she walked to the rear gate, unlocked it surreptitiously, and slid through, she tried to decide whether to tell Bell that William had been with her and had remembered that it was Beaumeis whose ordination had been interrupted. She could say she had remembered the name herself, she thought, and then bit her lip. Fool that she was. Of course she must tell Bell—perhaps she had better begin to call him Sir Bellamy again—about William's visit. She needed to remind him of what she was.

Magdalene slipped by the monk at the gate by pulling the hood of her cloak down so far that her veiled face could not be seen. When she came near the gate, she bent forward and uttered hoarse sobs. Young Brother Patric, as Magdalene had hoped, allowed his soft heart to overcome his strict duty. Although he could not actually remember the arrival of the sad lady, he was sure she must have come in if she was now going out. There was no need to stop her and add to her distress by demanding to know who she was.

Very shortly afterward, breathing prayers of thanks to the Merciful Mother for her help and indulgence, Magdalene walked through the open gate of the bishop's house. He was not personally in the house, Magdalene noted, rather relieved than disappointed. Winchester had looked strange when she mentioned Beaumeis and she had no inclination to say that name to him again, particularly knowing what she now did.

A few blows on the door brought a servant, who looked shocked at seeing a woman, but Magdalene gave him no time to react. She pushed firmly against the door, stepped in, and said, "I wish to speak to Sir Bellamy of Itchen."

"He is attending on the bishop. He is not within," the servant said, looking faintly pleased.

Magdalene was sharply disappointed. She had told herself that she was hurrying to the bishop's house to give Bell the opportunity to question Beaumeis while he was still shocked by the news of Baldassare's death. Now she realized that she had used that purpose as an excuse for another meeting. Furious with herself, she determined to give her information to anyone responsible and intelligent enough to repeat it adequately.

"Then I must leave a message for him with one of the bishop's clerks," she said.

The servant was not pleased with her persistence, but either he remembered that the bishop had been willing to speak to her a few days earlier or he was impressed by her rich cloak and veil, and he directed her to the back of the room. When Magdalene saw that it was Guiscard sitting at the table, she was tempted to turn around and walk out. She resisted the temptation, telling herself that explaining to Guiscard was her penance for not waiting for Bell to stop by the Old Guesthouse.

To her surprise, Guiscard did not shout "Out, whore!" as she approached the table. She felt a flush of gratitude, guessing that the bishop had reprimanded him—or perhaps Bell had. Not that Guiscard had altered his manner as far as cordiality or even civility.

"What do you here?" he asked, barely glancing at her when she stood before the table, and then determinedly looking down at a parchment spread before him.

"I have a message for Sir Bellamy," she replied.

"Neither Sir Bellamy nor the bishop are here," Guiscard said without looking up.

"So the servant told me." Magdalene kept her voice level. "However, I think it important that Sir Bellamy be told that Richard de Beaumeis is back in London. He—"

"Beaumeis?" Guiscard raised his head abruptly. "That is the man who caused the bishop so much grief. Why should Sir Bellamy be interested in him?"

"Because Beaumeis traveled from Rome with Messer Baldassare."

"He did?" Guiscard stared at her. "Are you sure?"

There was so much interest in Guiscard's voice and manner, an intentness that contrasted with his normal studied indifference, that Magdalene was rather startled.

"Yes, I am sure," she said. "Baldassare mentioned him when he stopped at my gate. He said Beaumeis had told him my house was the Bishop of Winchester's inn."

"How dared he!" Guiscard snarled, half rising and then forcing himself to sit down again. "Had he not done harm enough? Had Winchester been there when Theobald of Bec was proposed for archbishop, I am sure he could have done something to stop that stupid election. Beaumeis! The presumption of him, demanding that the bishop finish his ordination, after selling himself to Winchester's enemies."

"Selling himself?" Magdalene repeated. "To whom?"

Guiscard drew an indignant breath, and then, as if he had not heard her, asked suspiciously, "How did a nothing and no one like Richard de Beaumeis come to be in Rome?"

"He did not tell me, but from what he said, I can guess. I think it possible that Theobald heard about Beaumeis's ordination being interrupted and felt responsible for it. He may have completed the ordination, and even taken Beaumeis into his Household . . . no, Beaumeis said he was still tied to St. Paul's. But I must assume that out of guilt or sympathy, Theobald invited Beaumeis to accompany him to Rome."

"Guilt or sympathy? Ridiculous. Doubtless it was a reward for ensnaring Winchester and preventing him from protesting the proposal of Theobald for archbishop."

Magdalene thought about that for a moment. It seemed logical, yet it would mean Theobald knew and was in contact with Beaumeis, which really did not seem likely. She shrugged.

"Whatever the reason, Beaumeis must have traveled in the archbishop's Household. I cannot believe he is rich enough to make such a journey on his own. He certainly complained bitterly about my prices."

She was amused to note that Guiscard, who habitually sneered when she mentioned her trade, was too intent this time to react. He was looking at her, but with eyes that did not see, one hand idly smoothing the fur band that bordered the wide sleeve of his fine black gown. As he moved his hand, a ring with a bright stone flashed on one finger. Well found, Magdalene thought. He must be from a family with enough wealth to allow the second or third son they had educated for the church to indulge in fine clothing and jewels. And then she remembered that Bell, too, had been well dressed. The bishop apparently paid well.

"So Beaumeis was in Rome with the new archbishop," Guiscard murmured.

"That much is sure," Magdalene agreed, "and that he traveled to England with Messer Baldassare. Perhaps it would be useful for Sir Bellamy to try to discover whether there was some connection between Beaumeis and the archbishop before his election, but what is even more important is what Beaumeis did after he parted from Baldassare."

For a moment Guiscard's focus on her sharpened and his mouth twisted, but the look of disgust did not last. Oddly, an expression of satisfaction followed.

"He must have known what Baldassare was carrying in that pouch Sir Bellamy mentioned yesterday," Guiscard said thoughtfully. "Perhaps Baldassare had with him the papal bull granting the bishop legatine authority. Yes, yes, of course he did. I am sure the pope would be glad to have Winchester as his legate; Innocent's letters have always been full of praise for the bishop."

"All that may well be so," Magdalene said, "but—"

"Listen, you fool. Beaumeis hates the bishop because all those assembled to see him ordained now wonder what evil he did that caused the bishop not only to break off the ordination but refuse to complete it later. Is it impossible to believe that Beaumeis wished to steal the bull or destroy it and thus withhold from Winchester the honor and power it would grant him?"

"Not impossible at all, but when I told him of the murder, I will swear he was much overset."

"Pooh, pooh." Guiscard made a brushing gesture. "That Beaumeis is a sneaking, sly creature given to pretense. You should have heard him whining and pleading for the bishop to ordain him before Christmas so that he could be in orders before the holy day. You would have believed him of the most ardent faith."

"I do not think him very religious, but—"

"Clearly not if he was a common frequenter of your house," Guiscard said, this time not forgetting his moue of distaste.

"But," Magdalene continued, ignoring the clerk's remark, "if he is so fine a pretender as you say, he may well be able to convince others of his innocence. It will not be enough simply to accuse him. Moreover, those who know of the interrupted ordination may well know the true cause. Might they not think this accusation against Beaumeis was bred by spite on the bishop's part?"

"I would not be so quick to defend Richard de Beaumeis or to accuse the bishop of spite if I were you," Guiscard snapped. "The Bishop of Winchester does not love Beaumeis, and you would be gutted and hung already if the bishop were not protecting you."

The threat to tell Winchester that Beaumeis was a client she was trying to protect was implicit behind the angry statement. "I was not defending Beaumeis," Magdalene protested. "He may well be guilty. And I am well aware of my debt to the Bishop of Winchester. What I do not want to see is Beaumeis escape and the bishop's name be besmirched because of an accusation without proof."

"What more proof is needed than the harm he has already done?" Guiscard asked bitterly. "That ungrateful little cur conspired with Lord Winchester's enemies to keep him from being archbishop. Who can say Beaumeis would not kill to prevent the bishop from receiving an even greater honor?"

Magdalene was surprised by Guiscard's sincere anger and regret over the loss of the archbishopric and the possibility that Beaumeis had taken the papal bull. She had not thought Guiscard so attached to his master.

"Unless you wish this to come to empty counter-accusations," she pointed out, "there must be real proof. Beaumeis claims he was on the road to Canterbury on Wednesday night. If he can bring witnesses, would not that make the bishop look a fool or worse?"

Guiscard stared at her, rage and disappointment mingling in his expression. "It is not possible! He must have lied!" he exclaimed.

"Perhaps he did, but if so, witnesses must be found to say he was still in Southwark, or he must be brought to confess his crime. It is not enough to say he is guilty. That is why I came to tell Sir Bellamy that Beaumeis had been at my house, that he was sore overset by the news of Messer Baldassare's death, and that if he were straitly questioned soon, he might speak more truth than he intended. Will you not pass that message to Sir Bellamy as soon as possible?"

The secretary's expression grew eager and hopeful as she spoke, and he even unbent so far as to nod agreement. Plainly, he was looking forward to offering up Beaumeis to the bishop as the man who killed Baldassare.

"And where is Sir Bellamy to seek for Beaumeis, since you say he is no longer in your house?"

"He might still be at the church of St. Mary Overy. He kept saying he could not believe that Messer Baldassare was dead and rushed off to see the body when I told him it was laid out in the chapel of St. Mary Overy church. If he is gone from there, I do not know, unless . . . of course, someone at St. Paul's will have the directions of their deacons, but I am not sure Sir Bellamy knows Beaumeis is tied to St. Paul's. You will tell him that, too, will you not?"

"Yes, I will tell Sir Bellamy *and* the bishop. You may be sure I will," Guiscard said.

Magdalene left the bishop's house better satisfied than she expected to be after she heard the servant say that Bell was out. Ordinarily she did not trust Guiscard de Tournai. When she had been in the process of restoring the Old Priory Guesthouse and had needed Winchester's approval for changes she wished to make, messages she had sent by Guiscard to the bishop had never reached him, or had been long delayed.

This time she believed what she wanted fit so well with what Guiscard thought was his own advantage that she was sure her message would be transmitted—and as soon as possible. Of course it might be garbled into something she had never said, but since Bell would surely come to find out what she had learned from Beaumeis, she could untangle any knots Guiscard had tied in the truth.

She took the long way home, knowing it would be impossible for a woman to enter the priory without identifying herself. She would not be welcome, and even if the porter admitted her, she could not get home through the back gate, which was supposed to be locked. Not that she minded the walk; she needed the exercise. She had hardly been out of the house except for her visit to the bishop since Baldassare's death. Well, she had all but finished her embroidery commission. Perhaps tomorrow she would take it to the mercer in the East Chepe.

Having arrived at the Old Guesthouse and closed the gate behind her, Magdalene looked at the bell cord, thought of the purse William had left, and smiled. She was just about to turn her back and leave the cord inside when she remembered the message she had left for Bell. She glanced at the sun and decided she could not leave the cord inside. There was time enough for Bell to come.

He did not come, however, neither that afternoon nor even after the evening meal, by which time Magdalene was sure he would have returned to the bishop's house. She was furious, one moment calling herself a fool for having trusted Guiscard to do anything right, and the next, calling herself a worse fool for believing Bell would respond when she—a known whore—asked him to come. She was even more ashamed and enraged because she had waited long after dark, after Ella and Letice had gone to bed . . . and he had not come.

Fourteen

◦━━◦

25 APRIL 1139
EAST CHEPE, LONDON;
LATER, OLD PRIORY GUESTHOUSE

One good thing came of Magdalene's fruitless waiting for Bell—she finished her embroidery. The next morning when Bell still had not appeared after they had had breakfast, she wrapped her work in a clean cloth, swathed her head and face in her veil, and set out for the East Chepe. It was a long walk, across the bridge and up Fish Street to the Chepe, but since both sides of the bridge were lined with stalls selling all kinds of baubles, trinkets, and household wares, Magdalene did not mind a bit.

The cries of the vendors calling people to their stalls mingled with those of the sellers of sugared fruits and flowers, of hot breads, rolled savories, and yes, less fortunate women of her own profession. Not that one could concentrate solely on the proffered wares. Traffic moved along the center of the bridge, and a failure to dodge brought shrieks and curses and could result in bruises or real injury if one were too absentminded.

Magdalene bought a cup of violets in crystallized honey. Dulcie's were probably better, but there was a kind of joy in having a half farthing to spend and knowing she would not need to sacrifice some other desire.

That made the fruit all the sweeter. She stopped to look at embroidered bands ready to be sewn onto the collars and facings of gowns and shook her head firmly at the mercer's apprentice. They were poor things compared with her own work. Even Ella could do better.

A bolt of linen so soft and fine one could see through it on the next counter held her attention. She fingered the cloth, held it up to the light, pressed a fold of it against the inside of her wrist. A lovely, soft green that would have flattered her skin and hair, but when the journeyman murmured a price, and not unreasonable, she still sighed and turned away. She had no occasion for any garment made of such revealing cloth and never would have. The last thing in the world she wanted was to tempt a man.

That thought woke a small echo of her hurt over Bell's neglect, but she told herself she should be grateful for it. The light prick would save her deeper pain later—and one could not be sad in the midst of so much color and noise. In fact, before Magdalene was a third of the way across the bridge, she had forgotten her hurt and pique and was studying a pair of brass torchette holders that she thought would look very well at either side of the door of the Old Guesthouse. That time she stopped and bargained and came away with what she felt was a prize.

Fish Street distracted her in another way. Here, too, were stalls, but these were less attractive, with heaps of herring and mackerel, great mounds of cod, baskets of eels, piles of flounder. Magdalene's nose, inured to the smell of hard-worked, hard-riding, unwashed men, wrinkled against the overwhelming odor of fish. Far worse than the stalls was the gutter down the center of the street, where pigs and feral cats and dogs snatched at and fought over wares too ripe for even the poorest to buy, leftovers cast away amidst the dung and urine of horse and man.

Magdalene clutched her torchette holders under her

arm and tucked her veil firmly into her collar to free her hands so she could lift her skirt well off the ground. It took careful attention and quick footwork to get around the people haggling at the stalls, avoid stepping into the muck in the gutter, dodge the animals, and escape being splashed when others were not as adroit and landed in the sluggish puddles cursing and shouting. Next time, she promised herself, she would walk the extra street west to Gracechurch, where the shops were mostly those of pepperers and mercers.

She was cheered, however, by escaping with no more than a few small spots on her garments, and her interview with the mercer who sold her embroidery was also soothing. From her speech and manner, he had deduced that she was a lady of good birth who had fallen on hard times, or had a niggardly male guardian and was forced to sell her handiwork. That did not make him any more generous in payment for it, but he treated her with great courtesy, and it was a pleasure not to need to study a man to say just the right thing. He also had several more orders for her, one for an altar cloth.

To that offer, many months' worth of work, Magdalene shook her head. "I cannot do it for that price," she said.

"But the buyer will provide the cloth itself and all the embroidery thread, even the needles, if you desire."

Magdalene laughed. "Come now, Master Mercer, you know that half the beauty of my pieces is in the quality of the cloth, the thinness and rich dyes of the thread. I cannot trust another to purchase those for me. If the buyer wants the quality I produce, he or she must pay at least forty shillings. For that, I will provide cloth and thread and the very finest work, and either do the buyer's design or present a design of my own."

"That is too much," he said, looking disappointed.

"For my own work, I cannot take less, but I have a compromise to offer." From her purse, Magdalene withdrew samplers of Letice's and Ella's work. "These are the work of two of my women. It is not so fine as mine, but it is good. For the price you offered—the buyer to provide cloth and thread, too—your purchaser may have the work done by those women. If you like, I will leave the samplers with you to show. The other two pieces, the headband and collar band, I will do. Would you desire a matching design, or are these for different customers?"

"Matching." He fingered the samples she had given him and sighed. "If I raised the price to thirty shillings?"

Behind her veil, Magdalene smiled. "Keep the piece I gave you and show it with the other two. Then ask for fifty or sixty shillings and let the buyer wear you down."

He sighed again. "You are too aware of your own worth or not hungry enough," he said. "All right. Forty shillings, and let me have the design for it before next Monday. And let me keep these samplers. There are customers who cannot afford your work and might be content with these."

The smile he could not see broadened. If she got many more orders for embroidery—the mercer across the street had asked if she had any more he could sell— she and her women could make their claim to be embroiderers genuine, except that they could not pay the rent nor enjoy the kind of life they had as whores. Nonetheless, she thanked the mercer and agreed to leave the samplers with him.

With her pay in her pocket, a tittle though it was compared with what she took each week for her women's work, Magdalene felt a strong temptation to shop. It was as if the money she made as an embroideress was not real and called out to be used for pleasure.

She found a soft, gold-colored cap. Hanging from it were thin metal chains interset with bright stones; those would shine and flash through Letice's dark hair and lend an additional exotic touch while she danced. For Sabina, she chose a shawl of a soft, fine wool of a delicate rose color. Many of Sabina's clients wanted peace and comfort; that she should look like a woman beside a cozy fire was all to the good, and Sabina would relish the softness. For Ella, she picked a thin shift with delicate openwork around the neck and bright ribbon bows to show above a low-necked gown; the trailing ends of the bows would lie to each side of her high breasts and mark out their strong rise. And for Dulcie, a good white-linen head veil.

For herself, she bought fine wide ribbons, and hanks of thin thread spun so tightly that they shone. She smiled as she tucked those away with the brass torchette holders; she had bought only materials for her work and to adorn her house. It was too dangerous to adorn herself.

The sadder mood that such thoughts brought was dissipated as soon as she arrived at home just before dinner and heard that Bell had come after all. Magdalene was rather ashamed at the difference the news made in her feelings, and merely nodded. Sabina volunteered that he had not stayed long. He had said he must attend Baldassare's burial that morning and that he would try to go to St. Paul's afterward, as Magdalene had asked.

St. Paul's. Then he had believed her message and did intend to question Beaumeis, but it was likely too late now to extract extra truth from him, even if he had actually been shocked and shaken by the news of Baldassare's murder. It seemed more possible now that Beaumeis had committed the crime and his display of grief was overpretending. She was annoyed at having been taken in, but few men bothered to pretend for a whore. Still, she should have realized the shock he showed had been too great to stem only from surprise and regret at the death of a friend. That should have been more like Buchuinte's reaction, which rang true.

Did it ring true, Magdalene wondered, suddenly critical. Buchuinte had said he was too upset to go to Ella, but he had lingered as though he wanted to be persuaded to stay. And he had had the opportunity to commit the murder. He had been there in her house at the same time as Baldassare. Nothing would have stopped him from going to the church instead of going home when he left Ella. Only, why should Buchuinte wish to kill Baldassare? Certainly not to keep the bull from Winchester or the letter from the king. Still, there could have been some personal matter, some insult or crime Buchuinte had learned of since Baldassare's last visit. Magdalene shuddered, pushed the thought away, and displayed the gifts she had bought.

Everyone was delighted, but Ella, holding her new shift up and examining it minutely, said absently, "It is lucky he did not stay. He would have been even angrier when you had no gift for him."

"Who?" Magdalene asked.

"Sir Bellamy." Sabina hesitated. "I do not know whether he was annoyed or disappointed because you were not at home. He was not angry, precisely, but his voice was . . . stiff."

"Can I try on my new shift?" Ella asked. "And may I wear it when BamBam comes?"

"Yes, of course," Magdalene said, hardly hearing, and when Ella had gone, she asked, "What do you mean, stiff?"

Letice touched her arm. She had put on the cap with a smile of delight when Magdalene first gave it to her and her attention had seemed to be all on lifting her hair to watch the metal chains gleam through it. Now she fixed Magdalene's eyes with her own and acted out blows, choking, then clasped her hands tightly together.

"He could not have been so angry as to wish to do violence," Magdalene protested. "Sabina would have heard that in his voice, surely."

Poor Letice shook her head and showed her frustration, but she did not simply sit down and shrug with tears in her eyes as she so often did when she could not communicate. She tried again, even trying over and over to mouth a word with her dumbshow until, at last, Magdalene drew a sharp breath. Jealous, was the word.

"You think he was jealous?"

Letice breathed a great sigh and nodded.

"That could be," Sabina said. "That could be what I heard, that kind of constraint over anger in his voice."

"What can I do?" Magdalene cried. "The fool! How can a man be jealous of a whore? And I cannot refuse to let him in and talk to him. We *must* discover who killed Baldassare." She sighed and shook her head, remembering her underlying desire to see him, which had sent her to the bishop's house. "Oh, he is not the only fool! Why did I ask for *him*, leave a message for *him?* I hoped he would believe I only wanted him to discover whether Beaumeis was guilty, but doubtless he flattered himself the message was an excuse for us to meet."

Sabina protested that it was not Magdalene's fault, and Letice patted her and hugged her. Magdalene shook her head and sighed some more over her own folly, still unable to put aside all hope that she could come to some reasonable arrangement with Bell. After all, he had gotten over his first fury at learning that she still served William of Ypres, and it was the first time he had ever found her missing from the Old Priory Guesthouse. He would adjust to that, too, she told herself. He must accept the fact that she was free to work her trade if she wished.

Ella returned, proudly displaying her shift under a bedgown, and Dulcie brought in dinner. By the time they sat down to eat, Magdalene had put aside most of her anxiety, and she mentioned the new requests she had for embroidery. Ella and Letice were laughably proud of their skill, considering how little it earned in comparison to whoring, and they began to discuss new work they could do. The lively talk allowed Magdalene to plan what she would say to Bell when he did return and vow silently she would never again go to seek him out personally.

The first three clients arrived, took their pleasure, and left according to schedule; those three—a cordwainer, a dyer, and a woodworker—also had had guild meetings on Wednesday and had nothing to do with Baldassare. Of the second set of clients, BamBam came ahead of time because he intended to leave early; he was a wool factor who had to travel at dawn the following morning to collect sheared fleeces. He had been away on the same errand the preceding week, from Wednesday morning to Saturday, and his name could be crossed off Magdalene's list.

The two others had come soon after. Sabina's client was a horribly ugly but gentle man, scorned and derided for his looks by his wife. He had been introduced by a friend who valued him highly and hoped that Magdalene and her women could restore a spark of joy to his life. That hope had more than been fulfilled. He adored Sabina and had already asked Magdalene whether he could buy her and keep her for his own.

Letice's "guest" Magdalene thought must, from his complexion and halting French, be a fellow countryman; he had been brought to Magdalene's by a shipmaster and was apparently very rich. Although he had his own house on the north shore of the river in London, he always stayed the night. Something about Letice fascinated him, and he spent more time playing an odd, high-pitched little pipe and watching her dance than he did in her bed.

When they were all safely closed away and busy, Magdalene got a large, tight-woven white cloth and a thin piece of charcoal from her workbasket, pinned the cloth to the table, and began to sketch out a design for the altar cloth the mercer wanted. A lock-and-key border for the bottom of the cloth and a large cross in the center would bind together a pattern of interlocking square frames with rounded and barbed sides. Within the frames she would embroider pictures of various saints. It took some time to draw the squares with their convoluted sides, and she rubbed out more than once. When she came to the saints, all she could do was to sketch in some vague forms. The mercer would have to tell her which of the saints his customer wanted shown.

Magdalene sat back and looked at the design with considerable satisfaction. She lifted her eyes as she heard a man's sharp, impatient voice telling Ella to be good and that he would see her again the next Tuesday, and then the closing of the back door. Ella had not named him BamBam for nothing. Doubtless she had been urging him to stay longer, but it did not matter; although impatient, as usual, he seemed flattered, not angry.

Ella should now clean herself and straighten her room, but sometimes she forgot. Magdalene watched, saw the girl come back down the corridor, reenter her room. Magdalene's eyes went back to her design. She would use a fine, blue-dyed canvas for the background, she thought; she had seen just the right kind of cloth in the shop of the mercer across the way, too costly to buy on speculation, but now that she had a commission, she could please and profit her neighbor, too.

The bell at the gate interrupted her thoughts; this time she rose quickly, smiling. Ella would be ready for another client soon and would be delighted to serve him, since BamBam often left her unsatisfied. Magdalene again wondered why he bothered to pay two pence for Ella when he could get a common whore's service for a farthing. He never wanted to linger and play, she thought, as she went to the gate, that perhaps he disliked the filth or the danger of the common stew. He had the right to do what he liked with his own money.

She opened the gate, then gripped it tight. Another stranger! She did not recognize the man holding a dusty, tired-looking horse. "Yes, my lord?" she said, polite but distant.

"I have a friend in the Bishop of Winchester's Household who told me that I could get lodging for the night and most excellent entertainment at this house."

Magdalene raised her brows and let the man see she was examining him carefully. She did not remember ever having a client recommended by the bishop. No, not the bishop. He had said a "friend" in the Household, not the bishop himself. Most of the bishop's men were as abstemious as he himself was, but there were a few who were not, and one who was an infrequent and very shamefaced client. He could have . . . and there was Bell. Would Bell send her a client?

The man's voice was cultured, his French the kind spoken most commonly among the gentlefolk of England; his clothing was badly travel-stained but of good quality, and the sword belted around his hips had a hilt that glittered with gems on pommel and guards. Behind his high saddle was a thick, heavy roll, covered by oiled leather, that Magdalene guessed was his mail hauberk. Almost certainly a knight, and not poor. But where were his shield and helmet? If he had a place to leave those, why did he ask for lodging?

"Did your friend also tell you that your lodging and entertainment would be costly?" Magdalene asked.

"The cost is irrelevant," he said, but he looked over his shoulder at the road—at the mercer, who was watching from behind his counter, and at several men and women waiting to be served by the grocer, who had also turned to look. Suddenly he stepped forward, forcing Magdalene away from the gate. "Forgive me," he said quickly, "but I would just as soon not be stared at while entering your house."

"My price for lodging and a bed partner is five pence," Magdalene said, "and payment is taken in advance. An evening meal and breakfast are included if you desire them. There will also be shelter and fodder for your horse in our stable, but you will have to care for the animal yourself. I have no groom."

"You certainly do not try to entice a visitor," the man said, sounding offended.

"This is not a common stew," Magdalene replied without warmth. "We entice no one. To speak the truth, we have all the custom we need. . . ." She left the words hanging and glanced at the still-open gate.

Quite deliberately the man pulled his horse through and shut the gate. "My friend will be annoyed if he learns I have been turned away and must ride back to London to find lodging. I have other friends, too—" He fell silent abruptly, apparently seeing from her expression that far from being intimidated, she was about to order him out and call for help. "Wait." He smiled and held up a placating hand. "I am willing to pay."

Draping the horse's rein over his arm, he pulled open his purse and poured some coins out into his hand. Since Magdalene suspected he would not obey her, and at the moment she had no way to enforce her order, she did not bid him go. And then she saw among the coins a heavy ring, and a bicolored ribbon, red and probably white, although that was so dirty it looked gray, attached to a badge.

Magdalene pretended to watch as he picked out three silver pennies, a half penny, and six farthings, but she was trying in swift glances that did not long rest on the object to make out the badge. It seemed to be a simple cinquefoil; unfortunately, that sign appeared on so many shields that it meant little beyond that he was a member of a Household.

Her alarm was growing steadily. Why should the man put away his helm and shield and take off his badge and colors when it was plain he did not care that she saw the latter? If he was not hiding them from her, then from whom? Even as she came forward, hand outstretched to take the coins, a false smile on her lips, she determined to send Dulcie to collect a few Watchmen to sit in her garden until she was sure whether she would have to rid herself of this visitor by force.

No, not the Watchmen. If they attempted to interfere, a knight could likely overawe them. William . . . but

William was too far away. By the time Dulcie got to his lodging, it might be too late, and she herself dared not go out to hire a horse or a messenger; she did not trust what this creature might do, and Ella was too timid to resist. Bell. Bell was surely back from St. Paul's by now.

Having taken the money her unwelcome guest proffered, Magdalene directed him to the stable and pointed out the door of the house, which she entered. She hurried to her chamber, cut a small piece of parchment and wrote: "A man has come saying one in the bishop's Household recommended my house. I cannot believe this and do not trust him. Come and look at him—Magdalene."

This she folded small, sealed, wrote "Sir Bellamy of Itchen" on the surface, and carried out to the kitchen, where she pushed the note into Dulcie's hand. Seizing the maid by the shoulders, she said right into her better ear, "Take this message to Bell in the bishop's house. Bell. Bishop's house. Do you understand?"

"Bell at the bishop's house," Dulcie repeated, nodding.

By the time Magdalene came into the common room, Ella was standing by the table and admiring the altarcloth design and the man was standing beside her. Magdalene offered the ale she had brought from the kitchen and he accepted a cup.

"This is a strange thing to see in a whorehouse," the man said, gesturing toward the design and then sipping his ale. "Even such a whorehouse as this. What is it? A cope? An altar cloth?"

"An altar cloth, my lord," Magdalene replied, smiling at him because he had provided an opening to make clear her position. "As the friend in the bishop's Household may or may not have told you, I do not work as a whore anymore. I am an embroideress. I only make sure the women who do work here are not cheated or mistreated. This is Ella, who is ready to serve you."

"Indeed I am," Ella said, dimpling with smiles. "And I told him my name already."

"One moment, love," Magdalene said as Ella reached for his hand to lead him away. "Our guest looks travel-stained and tired. Perhaps he would enjoy it if you gave him a bath. I do not believe he is in any hurry."

"At an extra charge?"

"No, no charge. The service is included. I also assure you, you will have the tub all to yourself, except, of course, for Ella, who will wash your back and . . . ah . . . satisfy any other need."

"This may be worth five pence after all," the man said, and then smiled at Ella, who said she would get the water ready and tripped away.

Despite the remark, Magdalene was not happy. She was less and less sure any ordinary recommendation had brought the man to her door. So why was he here? Not for sex. Had he been lustful, he would have followed Ella to pinch and pat her while she filled the tub, and he had not.

"Since most of our clients are longtime friends who return again and again, I am sure they find their visits worth the price," Magdalene said, making herself smile.

"But some do not return," he said, watching her closely and then, when she only stared at him in surprise, he added, "My friend tells me that you had a great excitement here last week. There was a murder—Messer Baldassare, a papal messenger, no less."

Magdalene, who had just pulled a pin out of the cloth, dropped it. It rolled to the floor as she turned to face him. "No murder was done in this house," she said sharply. "The death took place on the north porch of the church of St. Mary Overy. It was nothing to do with us."

"But it was," he said, smiling. "Baldassare came through your gate, so he must have been here."

Magdalene fought to keep her breathing smooth. Who was accusing her of murder now? Whoever it was, she did not dare deny flatly that Baldassare had been in her house. She had admitted otherwise to too many.

"So the porter of the priory says," she remarked with what she hoped was a casual shrug. "But I did not see him go through the back gate, and between you and me, I think it impossible to get a saddled horse through that gate—you can look at it yourself if you like. However, the porter is a holy man and we here are whores, so who will believe *me?*"

"But he *was* in your house."

His insistence made her very nervous, but she could not be faulted if she told him the same story she had told all the others.

He listened, but shook his head. "But he was in here and could have left something. . . ."

Magdalene almost sighed aloud with relief. The pouch! He knew of Baldassare's pouch and wanted it. For himself? No. There was not about him the feeling of power and authority that hung about William of Ypres and the Bishop of Winchester. He was more like Bell, a man with assurance of his worth and knowledge of his purpose—a man with a powerful master. So he had been sent—but by whom? And how did his master know of the pouch?

Perhaps she could find out. Magdalene sighed heavily, exaggeratedly. "Another one looking for the lost pouch! I will try to answer all your questions at once. Yes, I believe Messer Baldassare was wearing a pouch, although I did not see it clearly, and no, he did not leave it here. The bishop's knight searched high and low for it. I am glad we dust our rafters and wash the back of our shelves because there was no spot from cellar to attic into which he did not pry."

The man laughed too heartily. "I did not come for the papal messenger's pouch. I did not know anything about it before you mentioned it. But I am curious about why he stopped here and what he said."

So she told him of Beaumeis's mischief and then

said, "Excuse me," and went down on her knees. "Pins are costly." And when she found it, she rose and began to fold the cloth.

"Will that not smear your design?" the man asked, as if eager to change the subject. "It is only drawn in charcoal and cannot last long."

Magdalene was not sorry to change the subject herself; she had thought of another way to pursue her purpose. "If I do not rub the cloth, the lines will remain, and it does not matter if it does not last. It is only to show the design to the bishop."

The deliberate untruth got an immediate reaction. "To the bishop," he repeated sharply. "I did not know you were familiar with the bishop."

"I am not *familiar* with him, but my Lord of Winchester has some hope of redeeming me. Thus, since I am a good embroideress, he is generous enough to provide work so I will not need to resort to whoring to fill my belly. I am very glad of his commission and wish to show him my design for an altar cloth for his chapel tomorrow."

Magdalene could almost see a sharp command rise to his lips; she certainly saw the effort it took to swallow it back and speak gently.

"Ah, I would prefer if you did not mention that one of his Household recommended this place to me. Winchester might not understand. I would not want to make trouble for my friend."

But he had hidden his colors and badge from the "friend," or was it from the others in the bishop's Household? Could his friend be carrying tales to . . . to whom? Winchester had many enemies. Magdalene could not take time to think about it; she needed to reply. She shook her head.

"We will talk about the altar cloth, not about the business of this house," she assured him. "Lord Winchester never asks unless there is trouble. I could not lie to the bishop, but I can promise I will give him no reason to ask about you."

She took the cloth and laid it on a shelf where it would be safe and was about to ask if he would like another cup of ale when Ella came back into the room. After a few exchanges, which left the man grinning, they went off together.

Magdalene immediately took the pitcher of ale back to the kitchen. The bathing room was just the other side of the kitchen and she would hear easily if Ella screamed. Although there were no untoward sounds from the bathing room, the longer she puttered about, the lower her heart sank. She was sure that Dulcie had had time enough to walk to the bishop's house, give Bell the message, and walk back with him. Either he was not there or he would not come.

She jumped with tension when she heard a door open, quickly turned her back, and bent over the fire to hide her face. But her breathing eased when she heard a familiar voice say, "Why not? I would be good to you, Sabina, you know that. Is it because of my looks?"

"My dear Master Mainard, you know that cannot be true. I cannot see your looks, and your voice tells me you look good and kind. I am always glad to hear you come and sorry when you go. I would be happy if you came more often and stayed longer. Indeed, if it is a question of the cost that prevents you, I could take less—"

"No! I would never deprive you. Anyway, it is not cost, it is time. I cannot get away to come here more often, and I do not only want to lie with you, although you have made me a man again when I thought that power was gone from me. Sabina, I need you where I can come and say a word to you and hear you answer me with the kindness that is part of you. Let me establish you above my workshop. You would have every comfort there—I swear it."

"I do not know," Sabina said sadly. "It is true I do

not like being a whore. If I sinned with one man alone, I would not be excommunicate, but I would have to leave Letice and Ella, whom I love. They are true sisters to me, which I never had. Oh, I do not know. I will talk to Magdalene and hear what she says."

"I will pay to free you. Anything ... almost anything."

There was a brief delay; Magdalene guessed that Sabina had kissed her client. Then she heard Sabina say, "I am not a slave, or bonded, but I cannot decide. Try to be patient with me."

He sighed. "I must go. I will be patient. There is no one like you, Sabina."

When Magdalene heard the back door close, she came out into the corridor and drew Sabina into the kitchen. "Listen to what goes forward in the bathing room," she murmured, "and tell me what you hear."

Sabina's ears were far keener than her own, and Magdalene went back to the common room so that the man would not find them all clustered together if he came out suddenly.

"Nothing unusual," Sabina said softly when she, too, had come into the common room. "Perhaps Ella was not laughing as much as usual, but I heard her speak and she did not sound frightened nor was she crying."

Magdalene sighed. To keep her hands busy, she had cut a section of deep crimson ribbon to the right length for the headband the mercer had ordered. In a low voice, she told Sabina about the visitor, her suspicions about him, and her anxiety because Dulcie had not returned with Bell. All the while, she used a decorative stitch to hem into place the blunt arrow formed by the turned-in corners of the ribbon, into which she had fixed another very narrow, matching ribbon for tying at the back of the head.

They had fallen into an uneasy silence until a door slammed open and the stranger's voice said, "Enough, girl. Empty out the bath or whatever else you want to do. I need to talk to the mistress of the house."

Sabina bit her lip. Magdalene stood up.

"That girl is an idiot!" the man exclaimed as he entered the room. He was wearing one of the bedgowns kept in the bathing room for guests and carrying his sword and clothing. He looked from Magdalene to Sabina. "I need someone to whom I can talk," he said. "Is this one an idiot, too? Why is she closing her eyes?"

"Sabina's eyes are closed because she is blind," Magdalene said. "Ella is simple, but not an idiot, and she has a great enthusiasm for her work. Most men like her very much."

"Well, I do not. I paid for a whole night, and I will strangle that one if I must spend it with her. So this one is blind, is she? I'll bet she has good ears. I'll try this one."

Magdalene drew breath to offer him his money back and invite him to leave. Before she could speak, Sabina shook her head and rose, putting out her hand. Her staff was not in its leather socket attached to the stool, however; she had left it in her chamber as she sometimes did when she did not intend to leave the house. Misunderstanding, the stranger seized her hand and yanked her toward him.

"Go and comfort Ella if she needs you," Sabina told Magdalene, and then turned her head toward the man who was pulling at her. "I am ready, sir. About what would you like to talk?"

"In your room," he said, letting her come even with him and walk to her door.

Magdalene heard her apologize over some small disorder in the room before the door closed; then she put aside her embroidery and went to the bathing chamber. Fortunately, she did not find Ella in tears, and after helping her empty the tub, she was able to step softly from the bathing room to Sabina's door. There she caught the low murmur of Sabina's voice, was about to walk on, and then stiffened with alarm. The man's reply was low and snarling. She pressed her ear to the door.

"You lie, whore! If you saw Messer Baldassare for only a moment, why are you crying? Did you kill him yourself?"

"No," Sabina sobbed. "He was only here for a short time, but he was a good man, a kind man. He knew just how to lead me from my stool to the table. I would never have harmed him. I weep because I am sorry for any man who died so."

"Liar!"

Magdalene was already reaching for the door latch when she heard the sound of a slap and a thump as Sabina, thrown off balance, fell. She flung the door open.

"Stop that," she snapped. "I told you I did not allow my women to be hurt."

"And how will you stop me?" he spat back and laughed. "What can you do? I am not afraid of your protectors. My master is more powerful than either William of Ypres or Winchester, who was *not* elected archbishop." He advanced on Magdalene. "You may curse the Bishop of Worcester for not agreeing to my lord's will. If he had not refused to block Winchester's advancement or we had known what the messenger carried or when he would come—or if you give me the pouch right now, I would not have to smash your pretty face."

"I do not have it," Magdalene breathed, backing away along the wall as if she were mindlessly trying to get as far from him as possible, but that made him turn to keep her in sight. "Really, I do not. I swear it. And why should your master care what was in the messenger's pouch?"

He laughed when she came up against Sabina's chest and reached toward the water pitcher but let her hand drop as if she knew throwing it could not save her. By then, the door was at his back. He did not notice Sabina squirming along the floor toward it . . . or did not care.

"None of your business why, whore!" He stretched an arm toward her, but she had got out of reach and leaned farther away toward the chest. "All whores are liars," he said. "I tell you now that what will happen to you for admitting you stole the pouch is nothing compared to what will happen if you do not give it to me. If you do, I will let you be—after a kick or two to abate your pride."

"I do not have it!" Magdalene whispered, raising a hand in a pleading gesture and dropping it.

"You do, and you might as well tell me *before* I smash in your nose and cut off your ears as tell me after the pain has broken you. If you do not tell me at once, I will break your fingers, too, beyond mending—so you cannot even embroider. You will starve in earnest if you do not give me that pouch immediately."

Fifteen

The man took a threatening step forward. The hand Magdalene had dropped with seeming hopelessness grasped the edge of Sabina's slop bowl and swung it viciously toward him. The dirty water sprayed into his face; the edge of the heavy bowl hit his cheekbone. He took one staggering step back, began to roar wordlessly with rage, and choked and gagged as the liquid running down his face filled his mouth. Even before he caught his breath, he started forward again, only to be propelled ahead a great deal faster than he intended by a violent blow in the back from Sabina's staff.

Blinded by the washwater, choked by the dirty liquid in his mouth, made breathless by Sabina's blow, and totally off balance, he still stretched his arms to catch Magdalene. But Magdalene was no paralyzed rabbit. She had dropped to the floor and scuttled sideways out of his reach, and he fell forward, the chest catching him just above one knee so that his momentum bent him almost double and his forehead hit the wall. Half dazed though he was, gasping for breath, he was a well-trained fighting man. He was still trying to twist around to lay hands on his prey when Sabina's staff came down once more, this time on the back of his skull.

In the open where she could swing the staff freely, the blow could have done much more damage. In the close confines of her bedchamber, it was only strong enough to bring him to his knees, dazed but not truly unconscious. With a tenacity born of desperation, he turned toward Sabina, flung up an arm, and caught the staff. He pulled, but he was on his knees, blocked by the edge of the chest, and could not exert much power in his twisted position. Sabina pulled back hard.

As soon as Sabina struck her attacker on the head, Magdalene had gotten to her feet and run into the kitchen to seize Dulcie's long-handled pan from its hook beside the door. She returned only a few heartbeats later during the tug-of-war. The man, now struggling to get a foot under him so he could rise from his knees but constantly pulled off balance by Sabina's fierce tugging, saw her. His eyes bulged with rage, but he did not dare let go of Sabina's staff, which, once free, could next be thrust into his eye or his throat. His mouth opened to shout, but it was too late. Magdalene had swung the cast-iron skillet, which came down on his head with a most satisfying thunk. He fell forward.

"It's all right, Sabina," Magdalene gasped. "I think he has lost his senses now." She breathed for a moment and then added, "I hope we did not make so much noise that Letice's client was alarmed."

"I do not think so," Sabina whispered, lowering the staff to the floor and leaning on it. "He shouted only once, and men do that while futtering. He was talking softly while he threatened you. Maybe he guessed there were others in the house who would come to your assistance."

Magdalene fought to control the trembling that threatened to make her helpless. This man could not simply be carried out and dumped in the street. There was a great deal to do, and it would all be harder without Dulcie.

"Love, if I gave you the pan, do you think you could hit him again if he moves? I must go see if all is well."

Sabina swallowed. "Yes. Just let me come behind him and feel out the distance between us. Then if I hear him move, I need only lift the pan and bring it down."

"Do not be too gentle," Magdalene warned, taking the man's sword from where he had leaned it near the head of the bed. "A knock or two on the head can do him little harm, but if he seizes you, I will have to run his sword through him."

"You need not worry," Sabina said, her voice harder than Magdalene had ever heard it. "I remember what he said he would do to you."

Now Magdalene was afraid Sabina would hit too hard. "Threats, love, threats. Do not kill him, either. It is a terrible nuisance to get rid of a body." But what if the blind girl missed? Then an idea came that would solve both problems. "Ah, wait. I will just tie his hands with his own cross garters and stick a sock in his mouth to gag him."

Having done as she said, Magdalene listened at Letice's door. All was quiet. Seemingly, Letice and her client had slept through any disturbance. She breathed a prayer of thanks that Letice's bed was on the far side of the chamber and went on. In the common room, Ella had apparently been unrolling and rerolling strips of ribbon from a stock Magdalene kept. Three strips were lying on the table, and Ella was just replacing a fourth in the basket.

"Come with me, pet," Magdalene said. "I need you to help me." She shepherded Ella into Sabina's room, where the girl stopped just inside the door, mouth and eyes wide. "He is not a nice man," Magdalene assured Ella, pushing her forward. "He hit Sabina and knocked her down and threatened to cut off my nose and ears. Now we must dress him so I can take him to William, who will punish him for trying to hurt us."

The trouble cleared from Ella's face, and she nodded. She remembered a previous time, in Oxford, when the king had been holding court and a group of men-at-arms who had been turned away tried to break in. A neighbor had sent his apprentice to William of Ypres, who had come with his troop and mended the invaders' manners so firmly that no other transgressions occurred.

Magdalene and Ella flipped the man over on his back and pulled on his braies, stockings, and shoes, since that could be done without untying him. Then Magdalene tied his feet together and tethered them to the bed so he could not kick. Thus hobbled, one of them could hit him on the head again before he could do any damage. Meanwhile, Sabina had untied his hands and dragged the bedrobe off him. Ella propped him up so Magdalene could pull on his shirt. He groaned and tried clumsily to seize her. Magdalene dropped the shirt, seized the pan from where Sabina had placed it on the bed and whacked him on the head again—just as the door opened.

"Magdalene!" Bell exclaimed.

"Didn't hit 'im hard enough," Dulcie remarked. "He'll be stirrin' again 'n no time."

"Hush!" Magdalene exclaimed, signaling for silence and keeping her own voice low. And then to Dulcie, "Thank goodness you are here." She handed Dulcie the pan. "Help Ella and Sabina get his clothing back on." She turned on Bell. "What took you so long? If you had come at once, things might not have gone so far."

That was not true, of course. Once Magdalene was sure that their unwelcome guest had come from a powerful master interested in the papal messenger, she had determined that the best place for him was in William of Ypres's hands. One way or another, she would have got him there; possibly force would have been needed anyway, but if Bell had come sooner, she might have been saved some terrifying moments.

"What the devil do you mean, what took me so long? I was in a cookshop eating a very late dinner since I had been at St. Paul's and all over London this afternoon. Dulcie had to find me, and I could scarcely run as I was to your house when Dulcie implied there was danger. I had to arm and get my horse. Who the hell is this?"

Magdalene glanced down at her women, who had tied the man's shirt and were maneuvering his tunic over his head. She drew Bell out of the room, closing the door behind her, and led him to the common room, where she gestured to the benches around the table. Flipping the tails of his hauberk out of the way with a practiced air, he sat down. Magdalene sat across the corner of the table.

She pushed the ribbons Ella had left on the table to one side and said, "I have no idea. He came to the gate saying a friend in the Bishop of Winchester's Household had recommended my house as a place to find lodging and entertainment."

"A friend in Winchester's Household?" Bell echoed, evidently astonished, then signed for her to continue.

"I knew at once something was wrong. No one from the bishop's Household has ever sent us a client. It is understood that there is to be a separation. I pay my rent, and usually that is our only contact. I tried to warn him off by saying that we were expensive but he pushed his way in and threatened that his 'friend' would be angry if I did not let him stay. That was when I sent Dulcie for you."

Bell grunted. "Even if he was not welcome, surely you did not need to knock the man unconscious."

"Did I not?" Magdalene explained what had happened.

"I see," Bell said, his voice thick with controlled anger. "So he knew about Baldassare and the pouch. From whom? And what master?"

"He gave no name, but he carries a badge in his

purse, a cinquefoil attached to a red-and-white ribbon."

"Beaufort!" Bell exclaimed instantly, and his teeth snapped shut. Then he said, "He must have come from Hugh le Poer, who is at the Tower of Montfichet."

"No, not from Montfichet. Did you not see how travel-stained his clothing is? And his horse was dusty and very tired. He had come a long way, not from just across the river in London." Magdalene drew a deep breath. "If that cinquefoil on a red-and-white ribbon is the badge of Beaufort, I think he came from Waleran de Meulan in Nottingham."

"From Meulan?" Bell echoed. "But how is that possible? Nottingham is over four days' travel. The murder was not discovered until Thursday morning. Why, the bishop did not even hear of it until Friday."

"But you told me the sacristan had sent his man to the abbot on Thursday morning. Could he have been told to stop at Montfichet? A message could have been sent from there. And this man said a friend in Winchester's Household had told him to come here. Could the bishop have spoken of the murder to anyone after we were gone?"

"I do not like this." Bell bit his lip. "You told the bishop that Baldassare gave you his name, so you knew that, but you did not know he was a papal messenger until the bishop mentioned it. No one at all in the priory *should* have known until I identified him."

"Except for the murderer," Magdalene said. "He would have known."

"Even so, even if the murderer sent a messenger at once, or the messenger was sent from Montfichet, there still would not be time enough for the messenger to get to Nottingham and this man to have come here."

"Yes there would," Magdalene said, "if the messenger had stopping places where he could change horses. William has arrangements like that."

"I suppose if he changed horses—two and a half or three days. Yes, that could be done. But why go to such effort? Could we have been mistaken? Could there have been something more important in the pouch than the confirmation of Stephen's right and possibly the bull of legatine power?"

"I have no idea." Magdalene shivered. "I do not even want to know."

"And what are we to do with him? You cannot simply toss him out into the street. If he is Waleran's man, he will come back with friends and burn you out . . . or worse. I could kill him, I suppose, but . . ."

"Oh, no, that is no problem at all. I am going to take him to William."

There was some argument about that, but it did not last long since Bell's objection was really only that he did not like the contact between Magdalene and Ypres. Magdalene's arguments were a good deal more cogent. William was best suited for extracting whatever information the man carried and disposing of him, whether back to his master or into oblivion. Nor would the fact that Magdalene had brought him to William betray any information to others. It was well known that William was her protector and natural that he should settle with any troublemakers in her house.

Having accepted her arguments, albeit ungraciously, Bell said he would get a cart to carry the man. To transport a man tied to the saddle of a destrier would draw too much notice, he said over his shoulder as he mounted his own horse, which he had left saddled.

While he was gone, Magdalene managed to saddle the unconscious man's destrier—with a peace offering of a rather dried and wrinkled apple. She and Ella were struggling to raise the rolled hauberk to the back of the saddle when Bell came back, divested of his armor and wearing a nondescript padded-leather jerkin over a heavy shirt.

He made nothing of lifting the armor, fastening the straps to hold the rolled mail while Magdalene ran back into the house to get the man's sword and scabbard, which she had almost forgotten, and check for anything else left behind. There was only a cloak, fallen behind a stool onto the floor when the women got his clothing. She snatched her own cloak and veil as well and ran back.

When she returned, Bell had pulled the blanket off the man and hoisted the unresisting body to his shoulder. Magdalene hurried over and threw the cloak across the limp form, lifting the hood to conceal the blindfold and gag and picking up the blanket.

As she seized the horse's reins with the clear intention of following, Bell protested, but she only said sharply that he should not be a fool. She was his pass to William's presence, which was not easy of access to just anyone.

Angrily, Bell tumbled the body into the waiting cart and tossed the blanket, which Magdalene handed him, over the man, who uttered a loud groan. Magdalene sighed with relief; she had been afraid he had been stunned too thoroughly. Bell turned, took the horse's rein from her, and tied it to the end of the cart.

Bell glared at her as he mounted to the bench but said nothing the curious mercer and grocer from across the street, who were both out serving customers, should not hear. Then, grudgingly, he gave Magdalene a hand up. When she was settled, he clicked to the sturdy mule and the cart moved forward. A thump came from the back of the cart. Magdalene jumped. Bell only looked over his shoulder to make sure that the back of the cart was well fastened.

When they got onto the bridge, however, he turned his head and shouted, "You lie quiet under that blanket or I will take a strap to both of you. Only reason I didn't take the hide off you yet was that your mother wouldn't let me."

With the sun near setting, the bridge was quieter than usual and Bell's voice carried. A few of the merchants and their customers looked around, saw the good cart

and handsome mule, the decently dressed man and carefully veiled woman, and laughed, imagining the mischief a pair of naughty children could get into. Magdalene leaned closer to him and spoke in a low voice as
if pleading the children's cause, but actually she was
telling him to turn right on Thames Street, that William
was lodging within the walls of the Tower of London.

At the gate of the inner bailey of the Tower, Magdalene gave her name, said she had a delivery for William of Ypres, and asked for Somer de Loo. After a
coin had exchanged hands, a messenger was sent and
eventually Somer de Loo arrived. He looked at the
heaving, mumbling blanket, at Bell, then at Magdalene,
and insisted she take off her veil, his hand on his sword
hilt. However, once he had made sure it was indeed she,
he gestured for them to drive in.

"What the devil are you doing here, Magdalene?" he
asked when they were clear of the gate. "What delivery?
And who the devil is this?"

"This gentleman is the Bishop of Winchester's
knight, Sir Bellamy of Itchen," she said, "and he was
kind enough to help me when the man in the cart hit
Sabina and threatened to disfigure me."

Somer frowned up at her as the cart trundled across
the bailey, not toward the great bulk of the White Tower
itself, but toward the king's palace, around which were
grouped several houses that were occupied by the great
nobles when the king held court in London. They
headed toward the last of those, one closest to the entrance to one of the wall towers, servants and retainers
on various duties or on their own business making way
as they passed.

"Why bring him to us?" Somer asked irritably.
"Surely—"

"If you will forgive me, I had rather tell the tale once,
and where there are fewer ears to hear it."

"That way, is it?" Somer said, eyes narrowing.
"William said if you came without his summons, it

would be trouble." He moved to the side of the cart to help Magdalene down and gestured toward the guard at the door. "It's all right. The lord wants to see her," he said and then told Magdalene, "The stair is just within, against the side of the building. Go up. He's waiting for you."

Magdalene shielded her face again, but she was uneasy about whether Somer and Bell would rub each other wrong and hesitated by the door. However, it was not Somer who raised Bell's hackles, and Magdalene soon entered the building. The hall was rather overfull of armed men, but only one or two glanced at her and, seeing a woman, looked away. Nonetheless, she was glad to get up the stair. The door was open, but she called from the landing.

"Come in, chick," William said.

He was wearing worn leathers under a sumptuous surcoat. Worried as she was, Magdalene could not help smiling. It was typical of William to dress for safety— the leather over a light gambeson would turn a knife and even protect against all but the most direct and violent sword blow—and at the same time dress for show, because the surcoat could be pulled together to impress an important visitor. He seemed to be lounging at ease in a large chair with arms as well as a back, positioned comfortably near a stone hearth in the middle of the room, but his hand rested on the hilt of his sword.

Magdalene went forward quickly, unwinding her veil and draping it loosely over her shoulders. "I am sorry to bring trouble to you," she said, coming close to the chair as he beckoned.

He gripped her around the waist and pulled her down so he could kiss her. "What else does anyone ever bring me?" he asked and laughed. "At least you are pretty to look at."

But he let her go quickly and stood up when the sound of heavy footsteps and heavy breathing came up the stairwell. Bell and Somer struggled into the room and to within a couple of arm's lengths of William before they deposited their burden on his bound feet. Somer continued to steady the man, who had been writhing as they carried him across the floor but seemed to realize that resistance was futile when they set him on his feet, and Bell pulled down the hood of the cloak and removed first the blindfold and then the gag.

"Raoul de Samur!" Somer exclaimed.

"You know him?" William asked.

"We are acquainted," Somer replied. "He was friendly with Henry of Essex and Camville and a few others in the king's Household, but I do not think he had any appointment."

"The king's Household?" Bell echoed. "Then why does he carry a cinquefoil badge on a red-and-white ribbon in his purse? The king's badge is a lion with blue and gold."

William of Ypres's eyes went to Bell, and Magdalene said quickly, "Sir Bellamy of Itchen, the Bishop of Winchester's knight. I sent for him when I realized this man—Sir Raoul, if Somer says so—intended to force his way into my house will I, nil I. Sir Bellamy lodges near the bishop's house, just around the street from us, so Dulcie could reach him quickly. You were too far away."

William had started to look offended when she said she had sent for Bell, but as she well knew, he did not really care deeply enough to reject a reasonable explanation. He nodded brusquely, but his attention was still on the man his occasional bedmate favored. Bell had now met Ypres's eyes. Magdalene held her breath and, at the same time had to fight against an impulse to giggle. Their expressions reminded her vividly of two dogs, bristles up, circling. But it was not in the least funny, really.

Then Bell bowed his head abruptly in a stiff sign of respect. "My master has ordered me to do what I can to discover the murderer of Baldassare de Firenze, who was my friend and his, and to find the pouch he carried."

"Most reasonable," William said. "I would be happy to help in any way I could, but I do not see what that has to do with Beaufort's man. And which Beaufort?"

"Why do you not ask me?" Sir Raoul put in.

All attention switched to the prisoner. "Very well," William said, "I will ask you. Who is your master and how did you come to know of the papal messenger's death and the loss of his pouch?"

"Very simply by visiting a friend I happen to have in the Bishop of Winchester's Household. I know him from times when the bishop and the king were on better terms, and—"

"Beg pardon, my lord," Bell interrupted. "That may be true, but if this man is carrying Beaufort's badge, he is no longer with the king's Household."

"Which is why I was carrying, not wearing, my badge," Sir Raoul snapped. "My liking for my friend has nothing to do with our masters and I wished to save him from just such suspicion as I see in you."

"That is possible," William said mildly. "So who is this friend who is a churchman of such pure spirit that he takes no sides between his own master and an avowed enemy, who gossips about important Church business to a most unclerkly friend, and then recommends that friend to the most expensive whorehouse in England?"

They could all see the struggle in Sir Raoul's face, but then, knowing he would tell one way or another and that his "friend" was already compromised because, no doubt, the bishop would winnow his Household to find who had a "friend" in the Beaufort Household, he shrugged and said, "Guiscard de Tournai."

Bell made a wordless sound, expelled from him by a mixture of outrage—but, he realized even as he felt it, not surprise—and enlightenment. He had always been a little puzzled by the richness of Guiscard's dress and the luxury of his lodgings, although butchers and physicians could become rich and might indulge a child; still, the answer had left him unsatisfied because Guiscard did not have that indifferent acceptance of wealth that a man born to it has. Now he understood. No doubt Waleran de Meulan paid well for information about the plans and activities of the Bishop of Winchester.

William flashed a glance at him, but plainly felt no impulse to discover what revelation Bell had had. He returned his attention to Raoul de Samur and asked, "And which Beaufort condones a friendship with his enemies?"

"The Bishop of Winchester is no enemy to Beaufort. Did he not arrange for Hugh le Poer to obtain Bedford—"

"This man did not come from Hugh le Poer, who is here in London, in the Tower of Montfichet," Magdalene said. "He has ridden a long way. Look at his clothing, William. And his horse was exhausted when he came to my gate, covered with dust and mud."

"Likely from Nottingham," William agreed. "It would be an easy transfer from king's hanger-on to Waleran's Household."

"I never denied that," Sir Raoul said quickly, although his eyes, fixed on Magdalene for a moment, said "bitch and whore" before he added with some bravado, "No reason why I should deny that I am Lord Waleran's man. No matter what you think, I had some personal business and got leave to come to London. You know it is a four-day ride from Nottingham. There is no way I could have known about the papal messenger when I started out. Curse me if I ever again do more than I am asked to do, but when I heard of the pouch, I just thought that if I could find it, my lord would be pleased."

There was enough sincerity in the last sentence to carry conviction to his listeners. William shrugged.

"Well, it should be easy enough to discover when you started, and in the meantime, you will have to remain a few days as my guest."

Sir Raoul paled visibly. William smiled.

"But, of course, if you make pleasant conversation— and do not in the future make trouble for Magdalene, her house, or any of her women—there is no reason for Lord Waleran to know what kept you. Searching for the messenger's pouch according to suggestions made by your 'friend' and the women of the whorehouse could take some time. It might be dangerous—or it might be profitable." He smiled again and turned his head to look at Somer de Loo. "You can cut his feet free and put him in my bedchamber. Find him something to eat and a pallet to sleep on—and put a chain around his neck. I will speak to him when I have time."

When the door was closed behind Somer and his prisoner, Magdalene said, "Be careful, William. That man has no more sense of honor than a snake."

He laughed heartily. "I am always careful, which is why I am still alive." Then the laughter was gone. "I made one real mistake in my life—and I am still paying for it—but I have been very careful since then." He suddenly shook himself, as a dog does to shed water, smiled, and looked at Bell. "So you are Winchester's ferret."

"And his bullyboy, too," Bell said, his nostrils pinching a trifle.

"I think—" Magdalene put in desperately.

William raised a hand. "No offense, Sir Bellamy. The bishop is a good man and your work is necessary, but that last word—bullyboy—puts me in mind that Magdalene should have one of those for the next few weeks, until the pouch is found or word can be sent to the pope and the instructions Baldassare carried be replaced."

"My clients—" Magdalene began again, but Bell's voice overrode hers.

"As of tonight, she has one."

William opened his mouth and then shut it and nodded. "Good enough. Your duty to the bishop falls in well with keeping an eye on Magdalene's house, and you will be more discreet than any of my men."

Magdalene detected a faint air of amusement under William's civil remark, but she hoped it was only because she knew him so well and that Bell would not notice. William, God bless him, was never jealous of her body. He accepted that she *was* a whore, and he could not care less who slept in her bed when he was not there. He could be amused by Bell's words and manner, by the knight's faint air of staking a claim; William had no doubts about her loyalty and fondness for him.

Nonetheless, to distract the men from each other, she asked, "Did I not prove today that my women and I can take care of ourselves?"

"So far, chick, so far, but we now have a murderer about. And speaking of that, my men can find no trace of that little rat Beaumeis on the road to Canterbury on Wednesday, at least as far as Rochester. I had a messenger from there not long before you came."

"Hmm," Bell said. "According to Brother Godwine, the porter at the abbey, Beaumeis was there on Wednesday. Brother Godwine believes he left before Vespers, although he thought he might have seen him later. However, Beaumeis did not go to his lodgings near St. Paul's."

"Could he have started for Canterbury at night?" Magdalene asked. "He said to me he spent Wednesday night on the road."

"Is he the kind to lie out under a bush?" William asked doubtfully.

"Not at all," Magdalene replied. "He is a most selfish and self-indulgent young man."

"Still," Bell said, "I think that is just what he did, although I will admit I cannot imagine why. I was at St. Paul's this afternoon and no one there has seen him since he left for Rome. He came back at top speed, too, because he was in his lodging Monday night. The woman who keeps it said he was sick when he came in and had fits of weeping."

"That was after he learned on Monday afternoon that Baldassare was dead." Magdalene frowned. "I told him when he came in, pleased with himself for having sent an unsuspecting foreigner to me. And I could swear he was truly shocked . . . although if he is as good an actor as Guiscard says . . ."

"Perhaps he is." Bell shrugged. "He was at Baldassare's burial on Tuesday morning and carried on as if he were the man's brother . . . or wife. I tried to catch him to speak to him, but Buchuinte stopped me to ask if I had learned anything new about the murder or recovered the pouch—Buchuinte thinks he could use Baldassare's letter of credit to pay for the burial and Masses—and Beaumeis escaped me."

"Guiscard told me Beaumeis is a skilled pretender, that he can counterfeit emotion, and that he used that skill with such fervor and fear that he induced Winchester to agree to ordain him on that last day of the conference."

"But why should he pretend so *much* grief over Baldassare?" Bell asked. "A little, yes. A few tears and head shakings for a friend with whom one has traveled for weeks and of whom one has become fond—that is reasonable. But Beaumeis drew too much attention to himself. He was white and shaking, utterly distraught."

"To prove he could not have killed a man he loved so much?" But the doubt in William's voice was clear.

"Because of guilt?" Magdalene suggested.

"That seems—" There was a noise at the door, and William looked up and said, "Yes?"

"The evening meal, my lord. Shall I bring it up?"

"Magdalene? Sir Bellamy? Will you join me?" William asked courteously.

Magdalene could think of nothing more horrible than

being trapped between Bell and William exchanging light conversation. While they were both engaged in serious discussion on a subject on which they were cooperating, they were safe. The moment they were just two men together, one or both would remember they had a bone of contention.

She shook her head. "Unless you feel that this conversation should be continued and could lead somewhere important, I would like to go home. There is no one at the guesthouse to deal with anyone who might stop by."

"You work too hard, chick," William said, frowning. "I want to talk to you about that someday, but it will have to wait. Do you want me to send a man—"

"I will see her home, my lord," Bell said.

That time William let his amusement show and Magdalene held her breath, but before Bell could react, William had risen and said to the servant waiting by the door, "I will come down and eat with the men." He waved the servant off and grinned at Bell, adding, "After that, perhaps I will have a little talk with the 'guest' Magdalene was so clever as to furnish."

As he came abreast of them, he gave Magdalene a rough hug and kissed the top of her head. When he released her, he gave Bell a friendly buffet. "Remember, I was there first. And don't try to teach your grandfather to suck eggs."

Sixteen

25 APRIL 1139

OLD PRIORY GUESTHOUSE;

ST. MARY OVERY CHURCH

There is no need at all for you to change your lodging to my house," Magdalene said somewhat stiffly when they were again in the cart driving the mule back up Thames Street toward the bridge. "As you saw, my women and I were well able to—"

Bell, who had been silently considering the interview with William of Ypres and unable to decide what he felt about it, turned his head sharply. "Are you telling me I am not welcome, that one of Lord William's men would be preferable to you?"

"I am telling you that my women and I do not need a guard."

"I do not believe you—and you do not believe it, either. Why do you not want me? Because you are William of Ypres's woman?"

"I am no man's woman, not William of Ypres's, not yours, not anyone's. I am a whore. I am *every* man's woman. William knows that, and until you know it, too, I do not want you in my house, glowering at my clients and making them uncomfortable."

"I thought you told me you were retired." His voice was low, ice-cold with rage.

"Whether I am or not makes no difference," she flung back defiantly. "I am a free woman, *femme sole* in law, nor will I have any ado with any man who thinks I can be his alone and wishes to deny me to other men."

The answer left him speechless, not with surprise because she had said as much before, but because he realized he had nothing he could offer as an inducement for her to give up her freedom. "I will protect you" was exactly what she was trying to avoid.

They had reached the bridge without speaking again and both started when a voice called a challenge. A lifted lantern showed a shock of filthy, unkempt hair, a raised cudgel, several dimmer forms behind. Bell called his name, identified himself as the Bishop of Winchester's man, said that he and his companion had been unexpectedly delayed. He named the sheriff of Southwark. The Watchman waved him on. At the other side of the bridge, Tom the Watchman knew Magdalene well, and they were spared further delay.

At her door, Bell jumped down and helped her to the ground. As she pulled the bell rope, he asked, "Are any of the clients who are due tomorrow yours?"

"It happens not," she replied coldly, "but I cannot swear that one to whom I owe a favor will not arrive. In any case, it is none of your business."

He smiled faintly. "In *this* case, it is. If you do not take any client to your bed, I can promise that I will not glower at them, nor even feel disapproving. And I really think that until this matter of Baldassare and his pouch is resolved, you should have a man to answer your gate."

As if to prove his statement, Sabina's voice, wavering with nervousness, called, "Who is there?"

"Bell and Magdalene," he answered.

"Oh, thank God," Sabina cried, and they heard the key in the lock.

"What has happened, love?" Magdalene asked,

pushing the gate open as soon as the latch lifted and taking a trembling Sabina into her arms.

"Nothing," Sabina replied with a sob. "But I am frightened to death and cannot seem to calm myself."

Behind her, Dulcie stood holding her long-handled pan. "Ella's as bad," she said. "When she 'eard th' bell, she ran in 'er room 'nd pulled th' covers over 'er 'ead. 'Nd Letice's been out twice wit' eyes big 's servin' plates."

"You win," Magdalene said to Bell. "We will make up the room you asked questions in. I hope you will keep your promise."

The question remained unanswered, largely because there was no challenge to it. Bell drove the cart back to the Bishop of Winchester's stable, took his horse and armor and clothing from his lodging, and returned to the Old Priory Guesthouse. There Dulcie and Magdalene had brought a bed down from the loft, set it up, and furnished it with a well-stuffed mattress and clean, if worn, linens and blankets. Since there were no other visitors that night and everyone was tired from tension and anxiety, they did not linger long after the evening meal but went to bed.

In the morning, Bell went to the bishop's residence. He told Guiscard de Tournai, who was presiding at the table near the entry as usual, that he wished to report his change of lodging. When Guiscard went to the bishop's chambers to announce him, fury swept Bell at his own stupidity. How could he not have noticed that Guiscard so often held that place? Well, he had noticed, but thought it a kind of silly pride, a desire to be known as Winchester's gatekeeper. Bell bit his lip. Perhaps Meulan was not the only contributor to Guiscard's purse. Others might want to know who came to see Winchester, and sometimes even learn for what purpose.

With some effort, Bell subdued the desire to pick Guiscard up and kick him out of the house. Simultaneously, he wondered if he could convince Winchester not to dismiss the man. If Guiscard were sent away, word would get back to Meulan. Would he connect that with Sir Raoul? Would that spoil William of Ypres's plans to use Sir Raoul? Bell's preoccupation permitted him to manage a civil nod as he passed Guiscard to climb the stair to the bishop's private apartment. The door was open; he entered and closed it behind him.

Winchester pushed aside a plate of cheese and smoked eels and looked up as Bell crossed the room. "You do not look happy, Bell," he said.

"Guiscard de Tournai is in the pay of Waleran de Meulan and perhaps others," he said, and went on to tell Winchester about Raoul de Samur's revelation of his "friend" and how he had been involved.

Winchester sighed. "I am very sorry to hear this."

He looked disappointed, and he had had so many disappointments recently that Bell became angry again. "Do you want him beaten soundly before I cast him out?"

"No, no." The bishop sighed again, then signaled Bell to get a stool and sit down. "The fault is as much mine as his."

"Do you mean, my lord, that you did not pay him quite enough to furnish him out in silks and velvets and diamonds and gold? I have not found you ungenerous."

The bishop put a hand on Bell's arm and patted it. "No, not that." He smiled thinly. "I knew he was venial and ambitious soon after he applied for a place in my Household and that I could not trust him enough to advance him and that he would likely resent that. I should have dismissed him, but he is clever and useful, so . . ." He shook his head. "But I am not a fool. I have known of his connection with Meulan for some time. However, the bond works both ways. To make himself more valuable, Guiscard has come to me from time to time with this and that tidbit. From the false hints and tales, I have learned much, and some tales he told were even true and still useful."

Winchester raised a brow as if daring a man of honor to find fault with his acceptance of Guiscard as he was and his use of the man. Bell laughed.

"I am greatly relieved," he said. "I had to tell you, of course, but I believe Lord William intends to release Sir Raoul on the understanding that he is to play Guiscard's role in Waleran de Meulan's Household. I suspect Lord William would not be pleased if Guiscard is dismissed."

The bishop shrugged. "I am sure Sir Raoul is not the first, nor will he be the last, that William of Ypres uses. And, to speak the truth, it is better for me if Guiscard is not exposed. I would hate to have to look for a new spy in the Household. Now, are you any closer to who murdered Baldassare?"

"Possibly, but not to his pouch—unless the murderer did take it and we can squeeze its whereabouts out of him when I lay hands on him. It begins to look as if Richard de Beaumeis might have killed Baldassare."

"Beaumeis?" Conflicting emotions passed over the bishop's face—anger, satisfaction, and then a reluctant doubt. "I would not think he had the courage."

"Panic can take the place of courage," Bell said and then stated his belief that Baldassare had recognized Beaumeis and divined his purpose, further explaining that Beaumeis would have been ruined and the archbishop besmirched. He told Winchester of Beaumeis's lie to Buchuinte about needing to leave for Canterbury, that William of Ypres's men had found no sign of him along that road on Wednesday, the fact that Brother Godwine had seen him in the priory at Vespers and possibly later, and the man's violent reaction to Baldassare's burial.

"Well, I cannot say I will be sorry if he is guilty," Winchester said. "But if he got the pouch, he will have destroyed anything that would benefit me, so I suppose

I will have to write to the pope and tell him—"

"Not yet, my lord, if a few days will not matter. I have not yet been able to lay hands on Beaumeis, although I have been to St. Paul's several times. He has not appeared there to take up his duties."

Winchester laughed shortly. "He has no duties. The bishop of the diocese must confirm his appointment—and as the acting administrator of the London diocese, I am not likely to do that. Perhaps when Theobald returns to England. Beaumeis can persuade him to confirm him." He bit his lip. "Could that fool have believed I would use the legatine power to override the archbishop's confirmation of his appointment and wanted to steal the bull to prevent that?" He laughed aloud, then sighed. "It would be a tragedy if Baldassare died because a stupid man believed me so small-minded."

"I hope not," Bell said, "but I am glad you told me he is not yet a deacon of St. Paul's. I will not waste my men's time watching the cathedral. I will just set a watch on his lodging. Meanwhile, because Waleran and his brother seem to believe Baldassare's pouch is in the Old Priory Guesthouse or that the women there know where it is, I will be lodging with them."

Winchester raised his brows again and smiled. "I see my warning has fallen on deaf ears."

Bell laughed. "No, you are quite right that she is tied most firmly to William of Ypres's purposes, but in this case, I cannot see that his purpose is different from ours. And I am not, much as I would like it, lodging in Magdalene's bed."

Winchester's frown returned. "I would not wish openly to cross Waleran or Hugh. They seek for causes of irritation and insult to report to the king."

"I am sure they will know nothing about what happened to the man who came to Magdalene's house. Ypres will take care of that."

"Very well." Winchester shrugged. "If you think it

necessary to lodge there, be sure to let Robert or Guiscard know where to find you."

Bell tensed to rise, but the bishop did not dismiss him, sitting quietly, his brow furrowed with thought. Finally he said, "Beaumeis . . . how I would like that . . . but it is known how little I love him. We will need to close all the doors through which he might try to escape."

"I am aware, my lord," Bell said. "I have set inquiries and found assurances that all but one or two of Magdalene's noble clients could not have been the killer. There are a few men of the city—Baldassare's friend Buchuinte, for one—who are not yet cleared, but when I lay hands on Beaumeis, I will know better what his excuses will be and how to counter them."

Bell was back at Magdalene's house in time for dinner, which he shared with the women. When the bell rang for the first client, he retired to his own chamber, leaving the door open so he could respond to any emergency. None occurred. When the men were all settled, he came out and spent a very pleasant afternoon idling in Magdalene's company. He retreated again when the men started to leave and the second set of clients arrived, among whom was Buchuinte. He came in full of a double outrage. Tuesday morning his servant had complained of being questioned about what time Buchuinte had come home on Wednesday night, and later that day, when he was at a guild meeting, his house had been invaded and most thoroughly searched.

Magdalene sympathized and soothed him, but when he and the others were safely ensconced with their bed partners, she came to Bell's room and shut the door behind her.

"Did you hear Buchuinte?" she asked.

He nodded. "The questioner was my man. The servant was too loyal to answer. Perhaps Buchuinte did not go directly home when he left here. The searcher? Likely Beaumeis, looking for the pouch."

"I agree," Magdalene said. "But why is he so desperate to have it?"

"I think because he needs Theobald's favor more than ever," Bell said. "Winchester will not confirm him as deacon of St. Paul's; he must convince Theobald to do it. I have men out searching for him and will ask when I have him."

Magdalene sighed. "Doubtless they will call you in the middle of the night. When the last man leaves, I will show you where the keys are kept."

The last to go was Buchuinte, who did not depart until very nearly full dark. He went out still grumbling about the invasion of his privacy and his property. Ella came from her room, also disgruntled, and pouted all through the evening meal because Poppe had kept talking about the questioning and the search of his house and had not been his usual energetic self.

Aside from that, however, Bell and the women ate their evening meal in peace. Afterward, to appease Ella, who was not tired enough to want to go to bed, Magdalene allowed them to be drawn into a silly game. In fact, because they had one deaf, one blind, and one mute player, it became far more amusing than anyone had expected. Soon they were all whooping with laughter, completely absorbed. However, some time after the church bells had rung Compline, Magdalene's head turned toward the window.

Bell immediately raised his head alertly, also listening. "What?" he asked.

"I thought I heard the bell at the gate."

Sabina uttered a soft groan, and Magdalene frowned. Even Ella looked disappointed over the interruption of their game. All listened intently, but the bell did not ring again. Giggles ran around the table as they picked up where they had left off, feeling both guilty and triumphant over ignoring a possible summons. Fortunately, the interruption did not spoil their fun and none were inclined to retire at their usual bedtime. In fact,

the hour was nearer Matins than Compline before the
last round was played. Magdalene, wiping away tears
of laughter, had just forbidden the start of another round
when a wild pounding on the back door began, accom-
panied by a man's hoarse screaming.

Bell leapt to his feet and ran to his chamber to get
his sword. As he came out, bared weapon in hand, he
found Magdalene, carrying a stout cudgel, coming up
the corridor and Dulcie standing at the kitchen door, her
long-handled pan in her hand.

"Who is there?" he shouted.

"Murderers! Murderers!" a hysterical voice shrieked.
"Open the door! You cannot escape! Open the door! I
will drag you to justice."

Magdalene and Bell exchanged wide-eyed glances.
"The *back* door," Magdalene breathed. "He must be
from the priory."

Dulcie may or may not have heard the voice through
the door or Magdalene's remark, but she must have
come to the same conclusion or decided no one would
stick a weapon in the window, because she went back
into the kitchen, opened the shutter, and peered out.

"It's that lunatic sacristan again," she said, slamming
the shutter closed in disgust and coming out into the
corridor. "Be he goin' t'ave mad fits ev'ry Wednesday
night?" Even as she uttered the complaint, she turned
to look for the key to the door. Then she remembered
that Bell had it. "Ye've th' key," she reminded him.
"Be y'goin' t'let him in and deal wit him so the rest of
us can get some sleep?"

"My God," Magdalene cried over the shouts and
pounding. "Could Brother Paulinus have lost his mind?
He was very disturbed when I last saw him in the prior's
house, but that was about the stolen pyx. Why is he
crying 'murder' again?"

The sacristan was still pounding on the door and
screaming that he must drag the murderers forth. He did
sound mad, but he had shown no sign of hysteria when

Bell had questioned him about Baldassare's death. Bell's heart sank. He could not believe that all of a sudden, a week after the event, Brother Paulinus would be precipitated into madness without cause. Something must have set him off. He propped his sword against the wall, making sure it would not fall, took the key to the door out of his purse, and turned the bolt.

As the door opened, the sacristan plunged through, fortunately right into Bell's arms because his eyes were fixed on Magdalene, his hands in fists swinging wildly. The full impact of a double blow on Bell's chest brought an *oof* from him, but did not stagger or shake him. In the next instant he had seized Brother Paulinus's wrists and controlled the man's madly flailing arms.

"Murdered!" the sacristan shrieked. "The church desecrated! Blood all over. All over."

"That was last week," Magdalene said, trying to keep her voice low and soothing. "Brother Sacristan, try to—"

"Murderess! Whore! Is nothing too foul for you? For a silver candlestick, you killed a good and holy man right at the altar." Brother Paulinus began to sob. "The altar, the very altar was desecrated with blood."

He began to struggle again and Bell folded him against his chest, holding him tight while his eyes met Magdalene's. For a long moment neither spoke, then Magdalene said, "Surely he is mad?" Tears ran down her face. "It could not have happened again. It could not."

Oddly, Bell's hard embrace seemed to have steadied the sacristan. He was weeping now, but not fighting Bell's hold, and Bell asked softly, "Who was killed, Brother Paulinus?"

"Brother Godwine," the sacristan replied, sobbing. "Who would kill so gentle, so kind, so holy a man?" He jerked in Bell's arms, so violently that he almost broke loose. "Only one inspired by the devil. Only a whore." He strained to look around Bell at Magdalene and the other women, who had come to the end of the corridor and were standing there, clinging to one another. "Murderers!"

"Not these whores," Bell said, tightening his grip. "Magdalene and her women have been under my eye— or under some man's body—since dinnertime. This must have happened after Compline, for the prior must have led services from the altar then. We were all sitting together from soon after Vespers, when I myself locked up the house, until we heard you at the door. None of these women can be guilty."

"They are! They are! You are lying to protect them because your lust has put you into the devil's power."

"The devil may have inspired me to lust, but not to lunacy," Bell snapped, patience all but exhausted. "The whores were in this house behind locked doors when the brother was killed. Forget them for a moment and tell me when Brother Godwine was discovered."

"Now, just now."

Bell's eyes widened. "You mean you discovered the body and ran here without telling anyone? And how did you get to this back door? How did you come through the locked gate?"

"The gate was not locked."

"But you locked it yourself, last Thursday," Magdalene protested.

"It is not locked now," the sacristan shrieked.

"Who has the key?" Bell asked, still gripping the sacristan but holding him away so he could look into his face. "It was locked this morning. I forgot and tried to use the back way, which is shortest, to go to the bishop's house. Then I remembered I would have to ride to St. Paul's and went for my horse—but I had tried the gate, and it was locked."

Magdalene shivered. "So sometime after Prime—you left between Prime and Tierce—someone unlocked the gate. But why?"

Bell looked across the sacristan at Magdalene. "So

someone could enter or leave the priory without passing the porter at the priory gate." He transferred his gaze to the sacristan. "Did you find the porter's keys?" he asked.

"I did not look," Brother Paulinus cried. "Brother Godwine was dead. Who should I ask for keys?"

Bell opened his mouth, then closed it and shook his head impatiently. "Never mind that. Brother Godwine's death must be reported to the prior and to the bishop. If I let you go, Brother Paulinus, will you go to the prior with this terrible news instead of trying to attack Magdalene, who is innocent of this?"

The sacristan, who had been intermittently straining against Bell's hold, again stood still. "Oh, no! I came here to bring the guilty to justice. You must come with me to stand before the prior and the bishop. You will repent your sin when you face your master, Sir Bellamy. You will tell the truth and let justice prevail over this harlot."

"I am very willing to come with you, and I will certainly tell the truth both to my master and the prior," he agreed and released his grip on one of the sacristan's arms. "Now"—he showed the sacristan the key he had thrust into his belt when he grabbed for his hands— "this is the key to the doors of this house. The front is already locked. You may go try it if you like. I will lock the back when we go out and keep the key. Thus the women will be confined within—"

"No!" Brother Paulinus cried. "She goes, too." He pointed at Magdalene. "Let her face the dead. God will raise Brother Godwine to point his finger at her. His wounds will bleed anew. God will prove her guilty."

Bell drew breath to argue, but Magdalene put a hand on his arm. "If it will content him, I will come."

She went to get her cloak and veil, accepting with a somewhat tremulous smile the hugs and kisses of her women when she passed. As they went through the gate, not only unlocked but flung open so hard that the front post had caught on the rise in earth at the verge of the path and stuck wide open, they could see that either someone else had independently discovered the corpse or the sacristan had not, after all, been alone when he discovered it. Lights were blazing through the windows of the apse, and the chanting of prayers mingled with sobs floated out to them.

The sacristan rushed through the north door, gripping Bell firmly with one hand and Magdalene with the other and crying out, "I have them! I have the guilty ones!"

The singing stopped. All the monks turned to gape as Brother Paulinus dragged Bell and Magdalene forward, pushing them up onto the low dais on which the altar stood and then prodding them around behind it. Magdalene drew a sobbing breath and huddled in on herself, pulling her veil higher over her face and turning her head away. Bell also drew breath, but he stepped forward and bent a little to look more closely.

The altar cloth was raised on one side to show an open strongbox under the stone altar table. Lying athwart the box—as if he had deliberately fallen there so the box could not be closed—was the body of Brother Godwine. His head was a bloody ruin, flattened and misshapen, and blood, no longer bright red but not brown yet, had formed a jellied pool in a slight declivity. Some blood had run down onto the floor of the dais; the streaks still had a slight liquid sheen, but the spatters that splotched the altar cloth and the exposed part of the stone altar table were brown and almost dry. The droplets, Bell thought, had come from the foot of the candlestick—the murder weapon—which had been dropped atop the corpse. It was thickly covered with blood and other matter. He stared at the candlestick.

"My God," he breathed, "he was struck so hard and so often that the shaft was bent." He went down on one knee to examine the weapon more closely and soon shook his head. "No, I see. No man's head could make such a mark."

There was a dent in the shaft where the candlestick was bent, the bright silver deeply scratched and a duller substance showing below. Gingerly, Bell picked up the murder weapon to look closer, then turned his eyes to the altar. Not far from Brother Godwine's head, the corner of the stone was chipped. Bell bent closer. A tiny sparkle of silver marked the edge of the chip.

Brother Patric, sobbing bitterly, had helped Prior Benin to his feet. His hands and the front of his robe were smeared with blood as if he had taken Brother Godwine's head on his lap. "Are you—" Bell began, but was interrupted by voices and looked across the church to see another weeping monk leading through the monks' entrance the infirmarian and two burly lay brothers bearing a stretcher and blankets.

"Brother Porter, rise up!" the sacristan cried out suddenly. "Show us the guilty one." And when the body did not move, he raised his hands, also bloodstained, to heaven. "God! God!" he wailed. "Is it because we are not strict enough in keeping Your law that You will not vouchsafe us this miracle? Let the dead accuse his killer. There she stands!"

"Brother Sacristan!" The prior's voice was rough with pain. "We have been granted free will so that we can solve our own problems. This killing is Satan's work, not God's, and we must deal with the devil ourselves." He turned his head. "Magdalene, why are you here?"

"The sacristan insisted I should come to confront the . . . the body." Her voice broke and she uttered a sob. "I am so sorry, so sorry, but it is nothing to do with me."

The infirmarian pushed past the group of monks standing around the altar and took his turn kneeling by the body. "He did not die when this was done," he murmured. "And what—"

Bell held out the candlestick.

Brother Patric cried out, "He was not dead? You

mean if I came sooner, you could have saved him?"

"No!" the sacristan exclaimed. "No! He was dead."

"How do you know?" Brother Patric gasped. "How could you bring the whore here so soon after Brother Elwin found him and ran for the infirmarian? You must have found him first, and instead of trying to save him, you went to accuse the whore. He died because to you, the sins of the flesh are—"

"He died because some thief beat in his head with this candlestick," the infirmarian said firmly, then sighed. "Be at peace, brothers. Even if I had come as soon as the blow fell, I could not have saved him. The skull was crushed. There is no mending that."

Seventeen

After what seemed an endless time of confusion, during which Brother Godwine's body was carried away to be laid out for burial and Bell had gone to give the bishop the news, Magdalene found herself seated on a stool in the prior's private chambers. Not far from her, also seated on a stool, was the prior himself, while the Bishop of Winchester occupied the prior's chair. Beside the bishop was Guiscard de Tournai with pens and ink and parchment, recording what each had said about the crime that would make it necessary to reconsecrate St. Mary Overy church. The other monks involved in finding Brother Godwine's body were also in the room, as was Bell.

The bishop, having stated that the most important task facing the monks was the purification and reconsecration of their church, then winnowed out the facts surrounding Brother Godwine's death with brutal efficiency. He listened with a stone countenance to the sacristan's hysterical accusations and then to Magdalene's soft-voiced defense and Bell's firm confirmation of her statements. He then agreed with the sacristan that Magdalene's profession was an evil—called it a necessary evil since men were imperfect creatures—and recommended that Brother Paulinus pray for Magdalene's soul in the hope of correcting her, instead of accusing her of crimes she could not have committed.

He then determined in short order that the sacristan had gone into the church to make sure that Brother Godwine had indeed checked that the safe box was locked and had locked the door to the north porch. Instead, he had found what he insisted was the dead body of the porter and had run to catch the thief and murderer before she escaped. He assumed she had been hiding in the church and had attacked Brother Godwine to get the key to the strongbox.

Bell had started to speak, but the bishop shook his head and he subsided. Brother Patric was next. He and Brother Godwine had gone to the gate after the Compline service to let out those from the neighborhood who had attended. At about a half candlemark after Compline, Brother Godwine had gone to the church to check the safe box and lock the north door—as they had been doing since the loss of the pyx. Brother Godwine had said he would pray for a while because he was troubled over something he had seen. When Brother Elwin came to relieve Patric at the gate about a candlemark before Matins, he had gone to the church himself. He did not know why, he said, sobbing again. He had just been uneasy. He had found the body and run to fetch the prior.

When all the times and the succession of events were straight, the bishop looked down at the bent candlestick, which, now cleaned of gore, lay on the table before him. The cleaning had made more apparent the fact that the silver was only a plating over a lead base. Winchester sighed.

"It hardly seems worthwhile to kill a man for a lead candlestick."

The prior, who had been looking at the floor and weeping softly, looked up. "It would not have been worthwhile if the candlestick was pure gold. But it is not lead. That is one of a pair of candlesticks that is solid silver."

The bishop smiled cynically. "Alas, sometimes those who give cannot resist magnifying the worth of their gift to the Church. It is a handsome design, but—"

"That pair of candlesticks was *my* gift," the prior said. "And I cannot believe that Master Jacob the Alderman, who was the goldsmith that made them, cheated me."

"I would not think so myself," Winchester agreed, frowning. "He is a man of spotless reputation and a great artist, too. I have used him myself for a chalice for my chapel here. Nonetheless, this candlestick is lead, covered with a thin coating of silver. Come and look, Father Prior."

The prior rose and approached the table, taking the candlestick in a hand that trembled with reluctance. Bell had followed him to the table. At first Father Benin seemed to be having difficulty even looking at what he held, his thumb running over the break that showed the base metal. But suddenly, as his thumb passed over the elaborate design, his eyes fixed and he began to examine the candlestick closely.

"No," he said, beginning to shake his head. "This is not my candlestick. The carving is all blurred. No, no, this is not Master Jacob's work. His was clean, every edge sharp and clear." He turned it upside down to look under the base and nodded with satisfaction. "See, no master's mark is here."

The bishop and Bell both leaned forward to look. "There is not," the bishop agreed.

Bell reached out for the candlestick, saying, "May I?" and took it from the prior's hand, twisting it this way and that. A moment later he said, "There is a mark. See, very small, in that corner."

Someone in the room drew a sharp breath, but Bell could not tell who, and a brief argument began about whether what Bell saw was a craftmark or some irregularity in the metal.

Bell turned his head, "Magdalene," he said, "you are used to making out small patterns. Come and look."

She rose with some reluctance, afraid she would not only see a mark, but recognize it. Then she thought of Brother Godwine's battered head. Her lips firmed. There had been no need for that. A single blow would have rendered Brother Godwine unconscious; then the thief could have taken whatever he wanted and gone away. She would not protect the man who had battered in Brother Godwine's head, client or no client. Besides, the man who made the candlestick was not necessarily connected with the murder. She lowered her gaze to the foot of the candlestick and shifted it to catch the light.

"That *is* a made mark," she said, concealing a sigh of relief. Despite all her reasoning, she was glad she did not know the sign—except for one thing. "I do not know the mark," she added, "but look here, just below it. Is that not an S? Could that mean Southwark?"

"It could mean anything," the prior said. "Some craftmasters can read. It might be the initial of his name."

"Hmmm, so it might," the bishop said. "Bell, tomorrow you should go to the Goldsmiths' Hall and speak to the guildmaster. He will surely know the names of all his members. It might be worthwhile to question those whose names begin with an S." He took the candlestick from Bell's hand and looked up at him. "So, Bell, what do we know? Is the man who wielded this the same who killed Baldassare?"

"If Baldassare was killed not for what he carried but for being in the church at the wrong time, it is possible. And the golden pyx did disappear from the safe box about the same time. But this seems far more an act of fear and rage. Baldassare seems to have stood talking to the man who killed him. Would he have allowed that man to come close if he had seen him stealing church plate?"

"You think this is a common thief, who hid in the church and when Brother Godwine knelt to check the safe box, struck him, took his keys—"

"Struck him with what?" Bell asked. "Brother Godwine was killed with the candlestick. Does that not mean that the safe box was open, the candlestick in the thief's hand, when Brother Godwine entered, possibly rushed at the thief, shouting? No, if that had happened, either the thief would have fled or he would have run *at* Brother Godwine, in which case the porter would have been struck out in the church, not behind the altar."

"Perhaps the thief was kneeling down behind the altar removing the candlestick," Magdalene said. Then her breath caught and she raised a hand to her lips.

The words had just popped out before she thought, because she had remembered vividly how she and Dulcie had lost sight of the monk who was returning the candlestick . . . the same candlestick? She glanced swiftly from the bishop to the prior to Bell, but if any had noticed her guilty reaction, he most likely put it down to her anxiety at having spoken out in such august company without permission.

Guilt flooded her. She and Dulcie had seen a monk with a candlestick the night after Baldassare was killed. That had to mean something. She should tell someone about it, but she did not dare, did not dare admit she had been in the church that Thursday night. She glanced up nervously and saw that Bell and the bishop were looking at her with approval.

"You are very likely right," Bell said. "Godwine may have walked right up to the thief before noticing him. And the thief might not have noticed Godwine coming if he were kneeling down looking into the safe box. Then Godwine exclaimed; the thief rose up with the candlestick in his hand—and struck."

"But that would mean the thief already had the keys."

Winchester's eyes moved to look at the sacristan, who leapt to his feet.

"I did not. I did not," he whispered, his eyes bulging.

The prior went and put an arm around his shoulders; Brother Paulinus was shaking so hard he would have fallen except for that support. "On my soul," the prior said, "I will swear that Brother Paulinus would sooner . . . would sooner visit a whore than steal from the church."

"If Brother Paulinus had visited the whore, he would have a much better case for accusing *her* of stealing," the bishop said dryly. "She would have then had a chance to steal his keys and make a copy."

"Make a copy," Bell repeated. "I have a fear that not only the key was copied. Father Prior, I think you had better look most carefully at the church plate. You said that Master Jacob made your solid silver candlesticks, but you thought this one was yours until you examined it closely. So, then, this is a copy of the candlestick you gave to the church. How many other items in the safe box are copies?"

"Oh, my God," the prior breathed.

He turned away as if to go back to the church, but the bishop said, "Never mind that now. Tomorrow will be soon enough to discover what has been stolen. More important now is to discover who had access to Brother Sacristan's keys . . . or yours."

"No one," Brother Paulinus shouted. "I kept my keys with me at all times."

"Now that cannot be so," the prior said soothingly. "You had them all on one ring and I know you lent your keys to Brother Cellarer when one of his was damaged, and to Brother Porter when he needed to get more bedsteads from storage. And you must have given them to the lay brother who assists you to take the plate out for cleaning."

"Knud," Bell said with satisfaction. "I knew he was hiding something." But even as he said it, his voice became uncertain. The bishop looked at him inquisitively and he shrugged. "Hiding something, yes," he said in reply to Winchester's expression, "but not something like stealing the church plate. Besides, it must cost something to have copies made and plated with silver. I do not think Knud—"

"If he sold a small item first," the sacristan said, breaking his silence for the first time, "something no one missed, that would give him a sum to start with."

"Shall I fetch Knud?" Bell asked.

The prior sighed. The bishop said, "I think you must."

"He does not know where Knud sleeps. Let Brother Elwin go," the prior suggested.

"Very well," the bishop agreed. He turned toward Brother Elwin. "But you are not to give him any warning or to tell him why he is summoned, nor even who summons him. I do not wish him to have time to think up lies. A shock often makes a man more likely to speak the truth."

In this case, the shock seemed more likely to make Knud incapable of speech. When he entered the prior's chamber, he was uneasy—as any lay brother might have been when summoned to his prior in the middle of the night—but when he saw the Bishop of Winchester in the prior's chair, he turned white and fell on his knees.

"I have not," he cried. "I have not. Not a word. Not a look."

"You are not summoned to answer for past crimes," Guiscard de Tournai said sharply, "but for present ones."

The bishop's eyes shifted briefly to Guiscard, then returned to Knud, and he asked, "Who is the goldsmith who made the copies of the prior's silver candlesticks?"

Now Knud's eyes and mouth were both wide open, but more astonishment showed than fear. "The prior's silver candlesticks?" he echoed when he was able to make his jaw and tongue work. "I do not know of any copies made, but I am only the sacristan's assistant. Who would tell me if copies were made?" There was a tinge of bitterness in the voice.

"You have cleaned those candlesticks often," Bell said. "Look at the one on the table. Is that the candlestick that you have cleaned every week?"

Brother Elwin helped the man up and he went and looked at the candlestick. "It looks like it," he said, glancing nervously at the bishop. Then he saw the crack showing the base metal. "I thought it was solid silver," he said.

"It was, which is how we know this is a copy," the bishop remarked.

"To whom did you give my keys?" the sacristan shouted. "Or did you have the safe-box key copied for your own use?"

Knud's face, to which the color had mostly returned, paled again. "I never gave your keys to anyone," he cried. "And I have no copy of the safe-box key. You can search me, search all my things. I am no thief!"

Bell thought there was honest indignation in the last four words. No thief. Yet the man was utterly terrified of the bishop's discovery of some crime. That certainly made him vulnerable to anyone who knew his secret. The sacristan?

The bishop sighed. "Unfortunately, in a place like this there are enough hiding places for an object the size of a key. We could prove nothing with a search, and we have a more immediate, more important, task for the lay brothers and monks. There has been another murder, and this time in the church itself. The whole church must be purified, washed and cleansed of blood and the desecrating presence of the act."

"Murder?" Knud was plainly horrified, but Bell thought he did not associate the murder with himself at all.

"Look at the mark on the base of the candlestick. Can you tell me whose that is?" Bell asked.

Knud took the candlestick and after a moment, shook his head. "I do not see any mark. The mark I know was in the center and boldly raised. I believe Brother Paulinus once told me it was the mark of Master Jacob the Alderman."

Wordlessly, Bell pointed out the small craftmark in the corner of the base and Knud stared at it, then shrugged. "I do not know whose mark that is, but I think it possible that there are two or three other pieces made by the same hand."

"God have mercy on us," the prior sighed.

Before Winchester could speak, the prior's secretary appeared in the open doorway. "It is time for Matins," he said, his eyes round, his face pale with distress. "We cannot pray in the church. Where . . ."

"Until the church is reconsecrated, in my chapel," Winchester said, rising. "Brother Elwin, do you and Brother Patric or others you trust completely keep close watch on Knud, even when he goes to the privy. I will have more questions for him some other time. Tomorrow, after Prime, we will begin to purify the church so that it can be reconsecrated before Sunday." He started for the door but stopped when he came abreast of Magdalene and Bell. "You may return to your house, Magdalene. I believe you have nothing to do with this crime."

"Thank you, my lord," Magdalene said. "May my women and I help with the purification? I know that Dulcie will wish to clean, and Sabina—she regrets her state so bitterly—she is blind, but—"

"Yes, of course you may. That you are excommunicate is no hindrance, and good works are good works. God and His Mother are merciful; perhaps the good work will lead to the redemption and the saving of a soul." A quiver moved his lips, and was repressed. "I am sure Brother Paulinus, who is going to pray for your souls, will be glad of a good work that would help make the church ready for reconsecration."

Magdalene had a little struggle with her mouth, too, but subdued the urge to grin, bowed, and turned away. Bell started to follow, but the bishop laid a hand on his arm. Magdalene, who had many causes to be grateful to Winchester, now had one more. She had been wondering how to conceal from Bell the fact that she was sending news of this second murder and the need to purify the church to William of Ypres. Fearing that Winchester would not keep Bell very long, Magdalene hurried down the path to the back gate.

Who had opened it, she wondered. Who had a duplicate set of keys to every lock in the priory? Brother Fareman had. No, ridiculous. The sacristan, of course, but . . . could it be that Brother Paulinus *was* mad and truly did not remember what he had done? At least this murder cleared Richard de Beaumeis . . . unless Brother Godwine had let him in and no one else knew. But he could not have escaped after the murder. The front gate was still locked. So who had opened the gate? And when had it been opened?

Magdalene lifted the latch of the back door and went in, only realizing after she entered that Bell had fortunately not relocked the door. She drew a sharp, anxious breath, then let it out when she saw the key to the front gate hanging on its usual hook; Ella had seen Buchuinte out and had locked the gate after him.

By then, the women had heard her. Dulcie rushed into the corridor, her pan at the ready. Letice was right behind her, carrying the longest and most vicious-looking knife Magdalene had ever seen. Sabina followed, clutching her staff, and Ella cowered last, peering nervously around the corner.

"What happened?" they all cried, almost with one voice.

Magdalene sighed. "Unfortunately, Brother Paulinus did not suffer a mad fit. Brother Godwine *was* murdered. It was dreadful, but the bishop came back with Bell. He listened and said we were innocent. He even gave permission for us to help clean the church, which was desecrated—"

There were various exclamations at this piece of news, but Magdalene gestured for silence and for a return to the common room. There she said, "I will tell you about it tomorrow morning. The cleansing is to begin at Prime, so we must all be up early. It will be best if you go to bed now and try not to think about this horror."

"Are you going to bed, too?" Ella asked. "Should not someone watch for the murderer? He could get in if the gate and the house are open."

"The murderer will not come here, love. He is not interested in us—you can go to sleep without worrying about it. I will douse the lights in here, but I will be awake in my own room awhile longer. I must write to William about the murder and hint to him that if Baldassare took the pouch with him and the murderer did not get it, then he must have hidden it in the church. And if the church is thoroughly cleaned, someone is going to find the pouch."

"How will William get the message?" Sabina asked. "You cannot go out in the middle of the night."

"Tom the Watchman will take it. He should be on his way home right now." She caught Dulcie's arm and said loudly, "You must catch Tom the Watchman before he gets to bed and bring him here—bring him to the stable. I will go there to give him a letter and explain what he must do."

"Tom the Watchman," Dulcie repeated. "To the stable."

"Take the key to the gate," Magdalene reminded her. "Lock the front gate behind you when you go out."

Dulcie nodded and left. Magdalene shooed the other women into their chambers, snuffed all the lights but the torchette over the front door, and hurried to her own room where she took a fair-sized piece of parchment from her drawer. At the top of the sheet she wrote,

"From Magdalene la Bâtarde of the Old Priory Guesthouse to Lord William of Ypres. It is after Matins on the tenth day following Easter Sunday. If you are well, I am well also, but all is not well in the priory of St. Mary Overy." She followed the warning with as succinct a description of the murder as possible—William would not be much interested in that or in the theft of church plate—and then moved on to the need for a purification of the church before it could be reconsecrated.

"Because Baldassare had been found on the porch," she wrote, "it has been assumed that he never entered the church, and I do not believe the monks ever searched there for the pouch. Also, they did not know until Sir Bellamy recognized the dead man that he was a papal messenger, and did not know they should look for a pouch. However, Baldassare did leave this house when the bells rang for the Compline service. If he entered the church quietly and slipped back into the darkness of the nave, he could have hidden the pouch during the service and no one the wiser."

She sat for a moment staring at the parchment. Perhaps she should not concentrate solely on the pouch. She frowned, passed the feather of the quill she was using between her lips, dipped it again, and then added, "I do not know whether you are interested in this murder or whether it would be worth your while to watch or join the cleansing of St. Mary Overy, but I felt you should know what was happening so you could decide for yourself out of knowledge rather than let matters slide, out of ignorance."

All the while she had been writing, she had had an ear cocked for the sound of Bell returning. Breathing a short prayer of thanksgiving because he had not, she folded and sealed her parchment. Her seal was unique; she used a small, very ancient brooch William had given her, engraved in low relief with a naked woman reclining on an odd-looking bed.

Letter complete, she snuffed her candles and stepped

out of her chamber, barely opening the door and closing it softly behind her. She could only hope that Bell would not come back before she did. If he saw the house all dark, he would likely lock the door and she would be locked out. Magdalene sighed. It would not be the first time in her life that she slept in a stable loft.

That last sacrifice was not necessary, however. When Dulcie returned, the door was still open and the older woman slipped quietly inside after giving Magdalene the key to the front gate. At the stable, Magdalene gave her letter to Tom the Watchman, walked him back to the gate, and bade him deliver the missive to William of Ypres's lodging in the Tower of London. She also gave Tom a silver penny, which made his eyes widen.

"The quicker Lord William has this message, the better," Magdalene said. "You know his colors?" The man nodded; he had delivered messages to William of Ypres before. "Be sure the letter goes into the hands of a man wearing William's colors and that you tell him quietly his master needs to know what is therein before this morning's Prime. You need not come back to say he has the letter. I expect to see Lord William himself or one of his men soon after Prime."

Eighteen

It was William himself who came, striding through the main door into the church as if it were another of his own keeps. He was dressed in mail, his spurs making a soft metallic scraping against the stone floor. Magdalene, attracted by the sound, gave him one glance and then turned angrily away. To Sabina, who was kneeling about midway down the chancel near the wall opposite to that on which the St. Christopher high relief was carved, she said, "Can you feel the edge of the lowest course of the stonework? Just wash along it down to the nave. I will then ask the prior whether he wants us to continue down the nave or do the other side of the chancel."

"I feel it. I will not miss any places, I promise."

"I know you will not, love. Do you have your pillow to kneel on?"

Sabina answered—Magdalene hoped in the affirmative, but she did not really hear her. She was furious with William. She had feared her letter would convince him that she had hidden the pouch in the church, but she had not expected he would appear dressed and ready to ride to the king as soon as it was found. Did he think she was going to fish it out and hand it to him?

Without a second glance, Magdalene wrung a cloth out in a bucket of water, stepped up on a stool, and began to wash the wall as high as she could reach. Behind her, a young novice was perched on a ladder scrubbing even higher, to where the arches curved inward to support the roof.

"Hey, chick!" William bellowed across the church. " 'Nother kind of good works, eh?"

Magdalene turned her head and bowed it. "Lord William," she murmured, but she did not step off the stool to move toward him.

To her intense relief, he did not veer toward her either, or address her again. He continued straight through the nave, passing her without another glance, heading for the dais, where the bishop was watching the prior carefully scrubbing at the bloodstains on the floor and the altar, from which the cloth had been removed. The safe box, Magdalene had noticed earlier, was also gone.

When William called out, the bishop abruptly stopped assuring Father Benin, for the fourth or fifth time, that no amount of scrubbing would completely remove the stains from the stone and that they no longer constituted a defilement. He looked out at the noisy newcomer blankly.

"Ho, Winchester," William shouted. "I was on my way to speak to Hugh le Poer in Montfichet and I heard about the trouble Father Benin had here. It was only across the bridge, so I thought I would ride over and ask if he needed any help. I could send men over from the Tower."

Magdalene stepped off the stool and bent to wash the chosen strip of wall down to where Sabina had already cleaned the stone course that met the floor. She bit her lip, feeling a fool, as she so often did when dealing with William. Almost everyone in Southwark knew he frequented her house and was her protector. Naturally, he could not ignore her. It was necessary for him to greet

her and then for him to pass her by as if she were just
one more of the large number of men and women from
the surrounding area who were cleaning as she was.
And how could she believe he would not have a good
and sufficient reason for being in full armor? Likely he
had a full troop with him, too. That would be only natural if he was going to speak to Waleran de Meulan's
brother.

William had reached the dais, and the prior sat back
on his heels, lifting a swollen-eyed, tear-streaked face
to him. "A thousand men could not remove the stain, I
fear," he said, his voice rough with weeping.

"Why do you wish to remove it?" William asked,
looking astonished. His harsh voice was loud above the
soft sounds of rags on stone and splashing, dripping
water. "Surely you have already cleaned away the pol-
lution of murder. You should not want to wipe away
the memory of the good brother's death also. Was he
not a martyr because of the sin of greed? The spilled
blood of war makes the earth rich and fruitful. Will not
the stains in the stone make more fervent your prayers
for escape from temptation and for the grace of mercy?"

Father Benin blinked, then stared up at William of
Ypres's coarse-featured face with its hard mouth and
cold eyes. Slowly his terror, his oppression of hopeless
grief, diminished. He had not been comforted by the
statements of the Bishop of Winchester, who knew the
rules of the Church as a scholar knows the rules of
mathematics but had little faith and little love of God.
But this! Such a sentiment could not come from so brutal a man unless it was God-inspired. A question rose
to Father Benin's lips, but Lord William had already
transferred his attention to the Bishop of Winchester.
The prior swallowed what he had wished to ask. Whatever had inspired Lord William was gone now.

"What happened?" Ypres asked. "Got a crazy story
of a gang of thieves that came to rob the church and
killed a monk while they were getting the plate. Did

they get it all? I could help with a chalice and an offering dish."

"It is not so bad as that," Winchester said. "We do not actually know whether anything was taken. What we do know is that some of the pieces that were solid silver and gold have been replaced by plated copies."

"Plated copies?" William repeated. "How can that be possible? The real piece would have had to be taken to whoever did the copying. I am no metalsmith, but if the plate of St. Mary Overy is anything like that of my church, it is ornate and could not be copied in a candle-mark or two. Would not the sacristan have noticed that a piece was gone before the copy could be substituted?"

"I had not thought of that, but you are quite right, Lord William," the bishop said.

"God have mercy on us!" The prior sighed as he got to his feet. "That means it *must* be someone in the priory, someone who would be able to remove the pieces, then return them while the goldsmith created the copies, and then bring the copies to replace the originals."

Stepping up on the stool again to begin washing another section of the wall, Magdalene had to struggle to keep her expression indifferent. That William! He had turned so he could see both Winchester and the prior; his back was to the church. No one could seem less interested in the cleaning process or expect less that anything would come of it. Moreover, she suspected he had about as much interest in what had happened to the church plate as he had in what the monks would have for dinner. It was the subject of primary interest to the bishop and the prior, however, and one they would be unable to resist talking about and speculating over. And if that topic failed to keep their interest long enough, she was quite sure that William would have another one ready.

Fortunately, providing another topic was not necessary. Father Benin would not have noticed, but Winchester might well have smelled bad fish if William lingered after discussion of the theft ended. As she began to wash another strip of wall, Magdalene found herself mentally urging more speed and less scrupulous care on the part of the workers on the other side. Probably that had not the smallest effect; however, before the prior had fully described the discovery of the fakes, the novice washing the opposite wall moved his ladder beside the St. Christopher relief. He wrung out his cleaning cloth, climbed three rungs, and cried out with surprise that something was lodged between the Christ Child and His bearer.

Magdalene could have cheered when William only looked from the prior, who had been speaking, to Winchester. It was the bishop who turned swiftly, stepped down from the dais, and as he saw what the boy was drawing from the hollow behind the Christ Child, almost ran to the foot of the ladder. By then, everyone in the church had stopped work to look, and it was safe for Magdalene to turn and stare with the others.

The prior and William had followed Winchester and were beside him as he reached up to take the pouch from the boy's hand. Winchester was staring at the complex knot of the cords that bound the pouch, and the prior bent his head toward it, too, sighing, "Sealed. It is still sealed."

Over their heads, William's eyes met Magdalene's for a brief, meaningful moment. Then he laid a hand on Winchester's arm and asked, "Have we any right to open this? Should it not be taken to the king?"

"This is Church business," Winchester replied immediately. "What has it to do with the king? If the archbishop—" He sounded as if he wished to spit, but his voice smoothed as he added, "—were here, it might be his right, but likely he is still in Rome—"

"Whatever must be done were better decided in private," Father Benin interrupted.

William and the bishop agreed at once. Each, Magdalene knew, had his own plans for the contents of the pouch, but both realized that their arguments had best be made out of public hearing. She returned to her scrubbing as the prior led the others not to the monks' entrance, but out the main door. Her surprise lasted only a moment before she realized that the prior wished to avoid the chapel where Brother Godwine lay—as Baldassare had lain before him.

The thought brought a pang of regret into the relief she felt over the discovery of the pouch. Her hope that the killer would betray himself either by searching for it in her house or trying to discover whether she knew what had become of it had not been fulfilled. No one had searched after the stable had been turned over . . . except Bell.

Magdalene swallowed and scrubbed harder. No. That was mad. Even if the bishop and Bell were both monsters, what reason could Winchester have to order Baldassare's murder? The messenger would have delivered the bull to him in any case. And neither of them could have any reason to kill Brother Godwine or meddle with the church plate.

William? No, she knew him well. He was likely enough to order a murder without a second thought, but she was ready to swear on her life that he had not known when Baldassare would arrive and had hoped, until she sent him news of the messenger's death, that Baldassare would come to Rochester and accept his escort to the king. And William would have no more reason than Bell or the bishop to attack Godwine.

She reached the bottom, moved her stool, rinsed and wrung out her rag, and began to wash a new area of wall. She hardly realized what she had done. All she could think of was that Godwine's death might have nothing at all to do with Baldassare's. Or it might. Godwine was the porter at the gate. He might have recognized someone who had come in that night and not left, or had done some other suspicious thing. Had not

Brother Patric said Godwine wished to pray over something that troubled him? But how did that fit with the open safe box? The faked plate? The candlestick used to kill him? Surely Brother Godwine had surprised a thief and died of it.

By dinnertime, Magdalene had got no further in her thoughts, but more than half the church had been purified and more townsfolk were coming in to help clean. Magdalene gathered her women and took them home to eat, rest, and welcome the day's clients. They found Bell waiting for them, tired and frustrated.

"We still have not laid hands on Beaumeis," he said to Magdalene as soon as Dulcie had disappeared into the kitchen and the other women into their chambers. "He did not show his face once at his lodging, nor in the cathedral, nor to any friend, nor in those haunts known to his friends."

"Maybe for good reason," Magdalene said, sinking down on the bench and wearily placing her elbows on the table. "He may have given up on getting the pouch when he did not find it in Buchuinte's house and fled, but one thing troubles me. I cannot imagine how he could have gotten hold of the keys of the priory. No one trusted him enough to lend them to him or, probably, to allow him even to touch them to do an errand."

"That may be true, but his absence from his lodging last night is very suspicious. And Godwine may have let him into the priory. How would we know now that Godwine is dead? Most significant is that he had the most compelling reasons to want Baldassare dead, for if Winchester did not get the bull, surely Baldassare would have spoken out about having carried it to England."

"But how could Beaumeis have gotten the candlestick?"

"I can guess that. Say Godwine went to look at the candlesticks because he had noticed something different about them. Remember he told Brother Patric he was troubled. Say he took the candlestick out and was examining it and Beaumeis came in with the intention of searching for the pouch. If Brother Godwine had been kneeling behind the altar, Beaumeis would not have seen him—whatever light he carried would have mingled with that of the altar lamp—and Godwine might not have noticed Beaumeis. If Brother Godwine then rose and saw Beaumeis, he could have challenged him, asked what he was doing, possibly even remembered that he had seen Beaumeis after Vespers on the night Baldassare was killed."

"Yes, I see." Magdalene shivered. "If Brother Godwine had put the candlestick down on the altar and asked Beaumeis his business, that little rat could easily have come over to Brother Godwine sure he could lie his way out of anything, but if Brother Godwine would not be satisfied and perhaps asked what he was doing so late in the priory on the day Baldassare was killed, Beaumeis might have snatched up the candlestick and. . . . He had killed before. I have heard it grows easier each time." She shuddered again. "I cannot imagine that."

"It is true, I assure you," Bell said, his mouth tightening into a grim line. "If Beaumeis had killed Baldassare, he would have found it easier to silence Brother Godwine."

"Do you think he has fled?"

"Yes, and I think I know where he went. I sent a good man to St. Albans. Father Benin told me that Beaumeis is a nephew—sister's son—to the abbot—"

"So that was why he was forgiven so many transgressions," Magdalene exclaimed. "I often wondered why the prior did not put him out. He was forever cheating and skipping classes to come here to whine about my prices." She shook her head. "I wonder what the abbot would have said if he learned what Beaumeis bought with the money he was given for living expenses." Then she frowned. "If he *is* there, I doubt the abbot will give him up to your man."

"I will leave that problem to the bishop. I know how difficult it might be to drag Beaumeis out of the monastery even if I can prove him guilty. The Church prefers to deal with its own, and he has been ordained a deacon. For now, I only want to talk to him, and I think the abbot will permit that. Knowing he is safe, he may even be willing to tell the truth, which is what I need to hear. I have made a good case for his being the murderer, but I have no evidence—except that he was in the priory the day Baldassare was killed. All the rest is guesswork."

Magdalene sighed. "Well, I suppose it is better that it be he than another. Let me go wash and dress. I think Dulcie will bring in dinner in a quarter candlemark."

Bell nodded. "May I join you for the meal? I meant to find something at a cookshop, but I had to tell the bishop about Beaumeis's absence from his lodgings and the result of my search for the goldsmith, so I came here. . . ."

"Of course. You are more than welcome."

When they had gathered around the table, however, to everyone's surprise, Ella did not seem to subscribe to that sentiment. She scowled at Bell and asked severely, "Did you not care that you left us in danger of our lives last night?"

"In danger?" Bell looked from one face to another. "Did something happen last night after Magdalene returned? I thought it was safe enough for her to walk through the back gate. The monks had scoured the churchyard."

"Nothing happened," Magdalene said, shaking her head at Ella. "I came home quite safely. I cannot imagine what Ella is talking about."

"The door was unlocked," Ella said. "You took the key and left us in an open house while a murderer is loose. He could have come in and slain us all in our beds. And I heard noises in the night and saw a light in the stable. I was so frightened. . . ."

"Someone was in the stable?" Bell asked sharply.

Magdalene sighed; that secret was out. "It was I, you silly girl." She turned her head toward Bell. "I sent Tom the Watchman with a message to William to tell him about the murder. I was trying to avoid frightening the others. I suppose the bishop told you that the pouch was discovered?"

"Yes, and that William of Ypres was there." Bell's gaze was definitely sardonic, but Magdalene met his eyes with bland indifference.

"Did Lord Winchester tell you what was in the pouch?" she asked. "I am so curious. We have talked about it so often. Were our guesses right?"

"Yes, in fact, they were, at least about the bull naming the bishop as legate. There was also a letter to the king. Of course, we do not know what it said, but since it is just a letter, the bishop and Lord William assumed it must be a confirmation of Stephen's right to be king. If the pope had changed that decision, he would surely have sent one of his cardinals to Stephen to explain what he had done and why."

"And did they decide to send the pouch to the king?" Magdalene asked eagerly, not because she cared, but to disguise her relief at having the contents described to her; now she would not need to fear mentioning what was in the pouch when she was not supposed to know. "I know William wanted the king to give Lord Winchester the bull to show his good will," she added. "He hopes to effect a reconciliation between the brothers."

"Well, he did not succeed in that. I was there by accident—I will tell you about that later—but Lord William and the bishop finally agreed to divide the spoils. Winchester kept the bull and Lord William took the letter and the remainder of the contents—letters of introduction and credit and some money—to the king."

Dulcie brought the soup tureen in just then. Ella got up to bring bowls from the shelf, and when she set them down, Magdalene began to ladle out the soup. Ella slapped the bowl down in front of Bell so hard that the soup splashed. Magdalene protested, and Ella said he did not deserve to be cosseted after leaving them exposed. It did not matter that no harm had come of it, she insisted. That was luck. Safety should not be left to luck. Magdalene bit her lip, hearing her own words come back at her. She had worked hard to train Ella into self-protective patterns and did not dare scold her for them now.

Bell seemed to understand, because he apologized between spooning up mouthfuls of soup. "I did take the key," he admitted. "And I forgot all about it. I will put it back on its hook as soon as I finish eating. I should have done that last night, but I thought I would come back with Magdalene. I could not because the bishop had work for me, and it is not yet done."

"Then you did not find the goldsmith?" Magdalene asked.

Bell sighed. "No. I was all over London this morning visiting craftmasters whose names begin with S. The Guildmaster gave me a list, but none of them knew anything about the chalice, candlesticks, and patens that have been copied. We even had the journeymen in and asked if any had done them as a side job—they were copies, after all—but no one seemed to be guilty or troubled. And Jacob the Alderman swears that the molds were destroyed after the candlesticks were cast. His reputation is too good to doubt his word, and frankly, I believed the others, too. None of their marks were anything like those on the copies."

"They would not be if the journeyman was lying about having done the work," Magdalene said.

"True, but I doubt they were lying. A metalsmith cannot simply rent a room and do his work there. The hearths and forges and tools for metalworking are not easily come by, so a journeyman who wants to do work on his own must do it in his master's shop. Again, metalsmithing is not quiet work, not something a man could do on the sly while his fellow apprentices and journeymen sleep."

"True enough, but I never thought the letter referred to a man's name. A master's mark *is* his name. It is placed so a work can be identified and those who like that work can order pieces from the same master. I put a mark into my embroideries; several mercers know it and can order work from me. You were right that it might signify a journeyman working under his master's mark, but it might mean something else, too. Most goldsmiths have their shops in London. What if a man established a place near enough for Londoners to buy from but where rents were much cheaper? Might such a man not put an S on his sign to signify Southwark?"

"Hmm, yes. You mentioned that before. I had forgot it, and the bishop said to try goldsmiths with names beginning with S. Well, there cannot be so many goldsmiths in Southwark. I think I will try here before I go back to London."

At that point Dulcie brought in a large pasty, a platter piled high with cold meat, and another with rounds of bread well smeared with dripping. There had been no time to prepare a hot meal, but all had excellent appetites because of their unaccustomed labor and no one complained when Magdalene served out generous portions. Conversation was also suspended while all devoted themselves to their food.

Bell went out as soon as he was finished, Ella pursuing him to the gate to get the key he had again forgotten. She returned after hanging it in its usual place, full of righteousness, and the other women dutifully hid their smiles until she went off to her room. It was not easy to get an idea into Ella's head, but once it was there—like avoiding knives and the river and locking the house—it was there for good. Magdalene then exclaimed with exasperation because she had pulled in the bell cord before they left to clean the church and had forgotten to tell Bell to push it out again. Letice wer to take care of that, and the rest of them cleared the table and set the room to rights.

They were hardly done before the bell pealed. Magdalene sighed. "God knows, I hope the church can be reconsecrated tomorrow and that this never happens again. I feel as if we have been running hard all day long and cannot catch up."

The client was Sabina's Master Mainard, and he came in with Letice, his hood, as usual, pulled so far over his head that his face was invisible and his greeting muffled. Sabina recognized either his step or the muffled voice, went to him at once and took his hand with real affection. Magdalene watched them go to Sabina's chamber, their heads bent toward one another.

"We are going to lose her," she said softly to Letice. "Between her pity for him and his kindness and passion for her, she will agree to go with him."

Letice cocked her head to the side, pointed to Sabina's room and made a cutting gesture, then a query gesture.

"Of course I will let her go," Magdalene said. "If she begins to hate her work, she will be useless here, and I think Master Mainard will give her everything any woman could desire. Her blindness is precious to him, and there are not many men of whom that can be said. But where am I to get another Sabina?"

Letice uttered her silent laugh, made a gesture of closing a door, then turned about and pretended to open another.

Before Magdalene could reply, the bell pealed again and she gestured to Letice and went to answer it. Ella's client was all agog at the news of the second murder and the desecration of the church. He stayed talking until the bell pealed a third time, when he finally went off to Ella's room. Magdalene felt as if she could not bear to make conversation with another person, but Letice came out to greet her client herself and brought him in, wiggling her hips and making suggestive gestures with her fingers. He did not even glance at Magdalene but followed Letice immediately into her room, leaving Magdalene to bless her woman's kindness and perception. She stared around blankly for a moment, knowing she was too tired and overwrought to work, and decided that this once she would indulge herself and lie down while her women were occupied with their clients.

She was asleep as soon as she removed her shoes, lay down on the bed, and pulled the coverlet over her. The knowledge of the two deaths weighted her spirit, evoking bitter memories, and pressed her deep into sleep. From time to time, she dreamed she heard a bell ring somewhere, but the sound was always cut off before she could force herself awake to respond to it, and she continued to sleep, hardly stirring.

Later, when she was less exhausted, she thought she heard Bell's voice saying her name, and she stirred sensuously in her bed. The call did not come again, however, and she sank back to sleep once more, but less deeply. Still later, she was dimly aware that someone had entered her room and started to force open her eyes, but a soft glow told her it was only Dulcie lighting her night candle. That troubled her, although she did not know why, and she was stirring toward wakening so that when a hand fell on her shoulder, she opened her eyes without shock.

Then she drew breath to scream, but it was too late. The light of the night candle gleamed on a drawn knife blade. A heartbeat later, a sharp prick warned her that the knife was touching her throat. A voice hissed at her.

"Shhh! Quiet! If you cry out, I will kill you. If you tell me what I want to know . . . we will see."

Nineteen

"Why do you not stay the night?" Sabina asked Master Mainard as his hand slipped out of hers and he reluctantly got out of bed. "The price is the same and you will be very welcome to me."

"I cannot, my love," he replied, his voice low with regret; she heard him walk across the room and take his clothes from the chest on which they lay. "I have already lingered far longer than I should. My wife will not be pleased. She will complain over my being late, but if I am away all night, she will make my life hell, even if my guild-fellows lie for me and swear that I was in their sight every moment. She will go to the priest, to the guildmaster, to my friends.... I would not care if she only cursed and accused me, but she insults them and rages at them."

Sabina sighed. She liked to feel Master Mainard's strong, warm body beside her. She liked it even more that he talked to her about everyday things, about an order for a special saddle, about the naughtiness of his apprentices, and a quarrel between two journeymen that had nearly come to a battle with wickedly sharp, curved leather knives. It was almost as if she were his wife and he were talking over with her the business of the day. He listened to her also, with grave intensity, when she suggested ways of gently curbing the apprentices and soothing the journeymen.

In the course of the talk, he had told her other things without realizing it. She never acknowledged those slips about troubles increased or fomented, debts incurred, but they had built for her a picture of the personal devil who was his wife. He might stay if she urged him, but he would suffer for it acutely. Sabina sighed again and rose.

She drew on a warm bedrobe, for the nights were still chilly, and opened the door. "Is there only one torchette alight near the door, Master Mainard?"

"Yes, my dear."

"Then I will let you out the front way because everyone else is gone and the street torches are there. I hope I did not keep you too long. I like to talk to you"—she laughed softly—"and to love you also. It is selfish of me to hold you when I know it might make trouble for you, but I never think of it until too late."

"If the trouble were only for me, I would not care. You have given me back my life, made me a man again. But others will pay, and I cannot bear that."

They kissed once more, and Sabina let him out, laying a hand on his arm and allowing him to lead her. That was something else about Mainard that bound her to him—he never seized her and pulled or pushed her; he even let her lead if she wished, never implying that she was helpless or stupid because she could not see.

When they reached the front door, Sabina drew Master Mainard toward her for one last kiss, then reached into the tall basket near the door and pulled out a sturdy stick with a bulge of straw matted with resin and fat at the top. She handed him the torch and stepped aside to allow him to light it at the torchette and open the door. As he closed it behind him, she stood there for a few moments thinking about his repeated offer to make her his mistress. Tonight he had offered her a contract, a legal lease on the apartment above his shop and a monthly stipend, "for services provided."

She let herself smile. The Church would duly register the contract, never asking what kind of services she owed. That would make it a sin for her to withhold her "service." Her smile broadened. Would that cancel the sin of cohabiting outside of marriage? She started back to her room, but her mind was so busy with her novel idea that she did not orient herself perfectly and brushed against the table when she reached it. Startled, she stepped away, lost her bearing and had to go forward cautiously, feeling for the wall of the corridor.

There was nothing to her right, but after a few steps, the fingers of her left hand just touched the edge of the shelves. Trailing her hand across the wall, she moved with more confidence, felt the door frame of Magdalene's door and then the door itself. The door? Closed?

A wave of uneasiness passed through Sabina. Magdalene never closed her door, unless Lord William ... but Lord William had not come. Likely he was gone from London altogether with Baldassare's pouch. And the door had been open when she went to fetch an evening meal for herself and Master Mainard a little while ago. She put her hand out to open it, then drew it back hastily.

What a fool she was. Bell must be in there. He had asked for Magdalene and sounded very disappointed when he heard she had gone to bed. He said he had something important to tell her. Sabina grinned. What she had heard in his voice made plain that the important thing he had to tell Magdalene was more ready to leap out of his chausses than off his tongue.

Still grinning, Sabina hurried past Magdalene's door, unwilling to eavesdrop on a private pleasure. Overhearing a client with one of the other women was one thing; one listened to make sure all was well. A private lovefest was no one's affair but the two involved.

As the thoughts went through her mind, Sabina heard and dismissed Letice's breathing, with its little characteristic whistle, and Ella's very delicate snore. As she was about to enter her own doorway, she stopped and uttered an irritated little snort; she had been so taken up with Mainard that she had forgotten to take the keys to lock the gate and the house when she let him out. That was the duty of whoever's client left last. Sighing, for she was tired, Sabina turned toward the kitchen where the keys hung—and stopped dead in the corridor. A different snore, not terribly loud but much heavier and more rasping than that of any of the women—and from the door beyond hers—told her that Bell was asleep in his room. Sabina stood frozen. But if Bell was asleep in his bed, who had closed the door to Magdalene's room?

———◦————

Magdalene looked at the gleam of light on the polished metal blade and breathed, "Who are you?"

"You do not want to know that," the voice murmured, now holding a definite note of satisfaction. "If you know, I will have to kill you. If you do not know ..." The last words were unsteady, doubtful. "Never mind," he continued. "Just tell me at once what you did with Baldassare's pouch and hope I will let you live."

The knife had withdrawn a little. It was no longer pricking her throat. Magdalene shifted away slightly and seized the edge of the coverlet, her hands clenching on it so hard that her knuckles whitened.

"The pouch?" she whispered. "But—"

"I do not want to hear that tale you told to everyone. It was a pack of lies—"

The low voice stopped abruptly and a hand fell over her mouth, tightening to form a gag, as heavy footsteps went by in the corridor. Magdalene made no movement and no attempt to call out. The hand over her mouth drew away. The dark figure leaned closer, his voice scarcely more than a murmur.

"I want that pouch now. I do not want to hear any lies. I know Baldassare slept here, and one does not wear a pouch in bed with a whore. Nor does a man like Baldassare leave so precious a burden in the open for a whore to pick over while he sleeps. He hid it here."

"No," Magdalene said. "He hid it in the church."

"You stinking slut," he hissed. "He did not have it when he came into the church. I saw—"

A very soft scratching sound told of fingers trailing across her door. They paused. The dark figure turned half toward the door and raised the knife higher in threat, but it was displaced by his movement and no longer directly over her. Magdalene yanked hard on the coverlet, striking away the hand that reached down to gag her, and flung the quilt toward her attacker, rolling across the bed, away from him as soon as the cloth left her hands. The man staggered back, trying to free himself from the fabric, which had fallen across his arms, and Magdalene screamed aloud.

Sabrina's shock had not lasted long. She had stepped into Bell's chamber and found his bed by the sound of his breathing. "Bell," she said softly, touching his shoulder, "wake up."

She was thrust away so violently that she staggered back and fell against the wall. As she righted herself, she heard the leather straps of the bed creak and then the scrape of metal against stone. He had grabbed his sword from the floor.

"Who?" Bell growled, coming off the bed.

Sabina stepped back, and then back again out of the doorway. She was about to say, "It is Sabina. Something is wrong. Magdalene's door is closed." But at that moment, Magdalene's cry rang out. Sabina instinctively moved away from the doorway through which she knew Bell would erupt. She was not wrong about that, but it was not Bell who ran into her. She was hit from the back and left side and flung down on the floor.

As Magdalene shrieked for help, she also grabbed the candlestick from her table, prepared to use the burning candle or the stick itself to ward off the knife. However, the attacker did not run at her. The moment she cried out, he turned and started for the door—but he had forgotten the quilt. That had fallen to the ground and tangled his feet so that when he tried to get away, he fell flat on his face.

Magdalene was so surprised that for one moment she just stood staring; then a gust of semihysterical laughter shook her. She put down the candle, which was about to fall from her hand, but, still whooping, was unable to make any other move. Less hampered than she by near hysteria, the man had managed to free himself of his encumbrance, fling open the door, and run out. Magdalene's laughter stopped abruptly. He would escape, and he must be the murderer! He had confessed that he had seen Baldassare enter the church.

Magdalene shouted again for help and ran for the door, snatching up the coverlet on the way, only to stop, gasping. The corridor was a scene of chaos. Two bodies squirmed on the floor while Bell, naked as a jaybird but clutching his sword, stood over them. Ella, holding a bedrobe to her front, had stopped in her doorway and begun shrieking. Letice, wearing a bedrobe and with knife in hand, was emerging from her room. While Magdalene, openmouthed, watched, Sabina, also shrieking, wormed her way out from under the man, who was again flat on his face.

"He has a knife," Magdalene cried in warning, but after that, unable to help herself, she began to laugh again.

The sound of laughter quieted Ella, who then stood staring from one person to another. Letice, seeing Bell was pinning the intended fugitive to the ground and that the erstwhile attacker was doing no more than shivering and crying, lowered her knife. Magdalene now reached down and pulled Sabina, who recognized her scent and touch, into her arms, where she fell silent. Still chuckling, she stood staring over Sabina's head at Bell and, with an appreciative expression, ran her eyes up and down him.

"You strip very nice," she murmured.

"You think this is funny?" Bell snarled. "If you don't like rough sex, don't take money from perverts."

"Sex!" Magdalene exclaimed, thoroughly exasperated. "Is that all you think of? Is that creature dressed for sex? Don't be a jackass. The only thing he pointed at me was a knife." Then she shrugged. "This is no time for your fancies. I think we may have our murderer. He told me he knew Baldassare did not have the pouch when he entered the church, because he had seen him." She turned to Letice. "Get some stockings, love, so we can tie him up."

"No, I did not. I did not," the man wailed. "I am at fault because it was by my design that Baldassare came to the church, but I did not kill him."

No one answered that. While Bell stood guard, Letice fetched several stockings from the ragbag and then pulled off the man's cloak. A sharp prod with Bell's sword made the sobbing creature put his hands behind his back; Letice tied them fast, then his feet.

"This is the second man we have tied up in a week," Ella said. "I do not like it."

"No, there is no reason for you to like it," Magdalene replied. "I do not like it, either. It is really nothing to do with us. It is because of the trouble in St. Mary Overy church, and I hope that is now ended. You can go back to bed, love."

"But what has Richard de Beaumeis to do with the trouble in St. Mary Overy?"

"Beaumeis?" Magdalene and Bell said together.

"I have seen the back of his head often enough to know it," Ella said, and added with uncharacteristic severity, "He is a silly man and very selfish. Often he did not wait for me but only took his own pleasure, even when I explained that he would enjoy it more if he waited."

Bell choked. Magdalene said, "Then he was punished, for he spoiled his own joy."

"I hope you will not let him come again," Ella said, turning away. "He always wanted more and said the price was too high for what I gave him."

"No, love," Magdalene said, and handed Sabina to Letice, who signed that she would sit with her; Magdalene nodded and Letice took Sabina into her chamber. Turning back to Ella, Magdalene said, "He will not come again. And I am going to close your door so our voices will not trouble you."

Ella yawned. "Good. All that scrubbing in the church has made my arms ache. I really want to sleep."

When she was closed in, Magdalene turned to Bell, who was starting to shiver. With another appreciative smile, she suggested—somewhat reluctantly—that he should dress and take Beaumeis to the bishop's house. Beaumeis immediately began to squirm and object. Bell whacked him with the flat of his sword and he subsided into sobbing.

"He must be questioned," Magdalene said, raising her voice over Beaumeis's whining protests, "but before witnesses who would have credence. What court, specially a Church court, would accept testimony from an excommunicated whore? And there must be two witnesses."

Bell grimaced, but he could not deny what she said. "I will take him," he agreed, started to turn away, and then shook his head, frowning. "No, you must come too. Other churchmen might not be willing to hear you, but Winchester will listen, and you know this little rat better than we do."

Magdalene started to protest and Bell held up a hand. "Not tonight. I do not think the bishop would be pleased to be wakened for what could easily wait for morning. Come to Winchester's house tomorrow morning soon after Prime. I know he must reconsecrate the church tomorrow, which will make a very full day for him because he has other business that cannot be put aside, but he must eat, too, so he will be able to squeeze us in while he breaks his fast."

Either the bishop had still been awake when Bell arrived with his prisoner or Bell had thought better of not waking him and explaining what had happened. In any case, Winchester was certainly taking the matter of whether Beaumeis had murdered Baldassare more seriously than merely asking questions while breaking his fast. When Magdalene arrived, she found what amounted to a court convened in the bishop's chamber of affairs.

Winchester sat at a long table, Father Benin on a stool beside him. Guiscard was at one short end, parchment, pens, and ink ready, and Bell stood near the other short end. Standing in a group not far from the door through which she entered were the sacristan, the infirmarian, Brothers Patric and Elwin, Knud, and the two brothers who were guarding him, whose names she did not know. Across the chamber near the window was Master Buchuinte.

The shock of seeing him made her hesitate as she stepped over the threshold. She was grateful for the veil that hid her face, although ten years of habit in not recognizing any client in public should have kept her expression unchanged. Fortunately, the monks had all turned to look at her, which was reason enough for her hesitation. Then Bell, wearing not only his sword but full armor, came forward and drew her to stand a little farther back, near the wall, at the short end of the table. No one spoke. A few moments later, the priest and archdeacon who officiated at St. Paul's entered the room.

They spoke briefly to the bishop and then went to stand beyond Guiscard, near Master Buchuinte, whom they both acknowledged with nods. The bishop gestured to Bell, who turned and went out.

They all heard Beaumeis before they saw him, wailing, "I did not! I did not!" Then Bell entered and went back to stand at the end of the table, where he could see the bishop, and two of the bishop's men-at-arms dragged Beaumeis into the room. They brought him to stand before the table, but the moment they released his arms, he fell to his knees.

"I did not kill Messer Baldassare!" he shrieked. "I did not! I did not!"

His face was swollen with weeping, and Magdalene could not help but feel sorry for him. The bishop glanced at him once, so coldly that Magdalene understood better why as many hated Winchester as admired him. Beaumeis shuddered and was still. The bishop looked across the room.

"Master Buchuinte," he said, "stand forth and say when you last saw Richard de Beaumeis."

So that is why he is here, Magdalene thought, listening to the story that was already familiar to her. Buchuinte explained how Beaumeis had come from the ship with Baldassare, refused to dine with himself and the papal messenger, claiming that he must ride at once to Canterbury with news from the archbishop. The priest and the Archdeacon of St. Paul's then stated, with some reluctance, that Beaumeis had not come to St. Paul's that afternoon. Last, Brother Patric reported that Beaumeis had been seen in the priory before Vespers and had said he had come because he missed his old school and wished to attend the Vespers service.

"Richard de Beaumeis," the bishop said, "do you admit that the testimony of these men is true?"

"Yes," Beaumeis said. "I was at St. Mary Overy priory, but that does not mean I killed Messer Baldassare."

"Then why did you admit to Sir Bellamy of Itchen

last night that you were responsible for Baldassare's death?" the bishop asked sternly.

"Only because he went to St. Mary Overy church on my word. I never hurt him. I never came near him," Beaumeis shouted.

"And why did you send him to St. Mary Overy?"

There was a silence. Bell took half a step forward, and Beaumeis said sullenly, "I told him that you wanted the papal bull naming you legate to be delivered in secrecy so your enemies in the court could not cause trouble."

"And to whom was the bull to be delivered? Neither I nor any member of my Household received a message to come to the church that night."

Another silence. This time the bishop did not wait for Bell to move but himself said sharply, "Well?"

Beaumeis's head dropped. "I intended to receive the bull," he whispered, and then, louder, almost indignantly, "There was no harm in it. It could not have mattered to you if you received the bull a few months later, and Archbishop Theobald would by then have been known to his bishops, and . . . and. . . ."

Winchester unloosened his jaws, which had gritted together, and asked, almost mildly, "Why should we believe you did not kill Messer Baldassare? You wanted the bull. You wanted it badly enough to come to the Old Priory Guesthouse last night and threaten Magdalene with a knife." He turned his head. "Come forth, Magdalene la Bâtarde and tell us what happened."

Lowering her veil so that her face could be observed, Magdalene described being wakened by the knife pricking her throat and described the remaining events of the previous evening. The priest of St. Paul's moved uneasily. Magdalene's lips thinned. She knew he was going to ask haughtily why anyone should believe the word of a whore over that of an ordained deacon of the Church. Before he could speak, the bishop turned baleful eyes on Beaumeis.

"Is what the whore has told us true?" he thundered.

Beaumeis cowered and began to weep again. "What if it is?" he sobbed. "She is only a whore, and I thought she had stolen the pouch from Baldassare."

Winchester shook his head. "Are you trying to tell me that Baldassare left a whore's house without noticing his most precious possession was missing? Do not take us for idiots! You thought he trusted you so little that he had preferred to leave his pouch in a whore's care and she had hidden it after she heard he was dead. But he had not. Baldassare might visit a whore, but he had faith. He had placed the pouch in safer hands, in the church. The pouch was found behind the statue of St. Christopher and the Christ Child yesterday morning."

"That is impossible!" Beaumeis exclaimed, his weeping checked by surprise and disbelief. "I saw Baldassare enter the church from the north door. I was far back in the nave because I did not want him to see me, but there were torches and tapers in the chancel and I could see him. It was a mild night. His cloak was thrown back. *He did not have the pouch.* There! There is the proof I did not kill him. Why should I kill him if he was not carrying the pouch I wanted?"

Magdalene's breath drew in sharply. She knew what Beaumeis said was true. She saw Bell's head turn, his eyes flash a glance at her, saw that he also knew Beaumeis was speaking the truth, and that he had always suspected the pouch had been hidden in her house and later moved to the church.

Winchester must have known too, but his expression did not change, nor did he look toward her. To Beaumeis, he said, "Ah, you admit you were there and you noticed that Baldassare was not carrying his pouch. You must have asked him for it and killed him because he would not tell you where it was. Then you began to search for it. When Magdalene reported the murder, she told me her stable was searched, nearly torn apart."

"But that was before," Beaumeis protested. "I came in through the front gate before it was locked and searched the stable. I saw the horse there. That was how I knew Baldassare *did* stay in Magdalene's house."

Father Benin looked startled. All the monks moved restlessly, and Brother Paulinus uttered a squawk of protest, but Brother Infirmarian hushed him. The bishop did not acknowledge their reactions and they subsided, realizing that Magdalene must have told him the truth; he only gestured to Beaumeis to continue.

"I thought Baldassare would have hidden the pouch in the stable, not wanting to bring it into a whorehouse. I thought I could get it and get away without ever meeting him in the church, without ever taking the chance that he would recognize me."

"But he did recognize you when you came to ask for the pouch, so you had a double reason to silence him."

"No, I did not. I did not. I never came near him," Beaumeis cried, beginning to sob again. "I never had a chance to ask for the pouch. I told you. I was in the back of the nave and I saw he did not have the pouch, but I could not approach him. He had stayed near the north door, waiting for the monks and those who came to the service to leave. I had to wait, too, of course, and I was thinking, how to disguise my voice and who I should say I was. And it was dark, because when the monks left, they took their torches and tapers with them, so I was feeling my way forward when I saw a light coming from the monks' entrance."

Everyone tensed with interest. Father Benin and several others in the room drew breath sharply. Another witness, even another suspect, would be welcome. All knew of the grudge Winchester held against Beaumeis. All were sure they had been summoned to listen to Beaumeis so they could testify that he was guilty and that the bishop had not punished him to satisfy his own spite; and all feared everyone would say they bowed to Winchester's will only because they feared him.

Perfectly aware of his audience's emotions, Winchester asked eagerly, "Who was it? Did he see Baldassare?"

"I do not know who it was." Beaumeis sounded exhausted now, almost indifferent. "One of the monks. He wore a robe with the hood pulled well forward. And he did not see Baldassare at first. He just walked across the chancel to the apse, went behind the altar, and started to stoop down."

Although he was disappointed that Beaumeis could not identify the man, Winchester was not completely dissatisfied. Once a miscreant reached exhaustion, he was very likely to tell everything he knew, being more eager to escape the questioning and rest than to save himself.

"Your eyes must have been accustomed to the dark by then." Winchester made his voice sharp and accusatory. "The light from the altar lamp and his taper should have been bright enough for you to see him clearly."

"It was, but his back was to me and I could not see his face or why he was stooping. But Baldassare must have seen him, because he came forward and said, 'So it is you. Well, I suppose you know what you are doing. Wait here. I will go and—' Then the monk jerked upright, hushed him, and hurried toward him. He said, 'I can explain it all.' And Baldassare said, 'You do not need to explain. I understand very well.' The monk then put his hand on Baldassare's shoulder and urged him toward the north door. He was holding the light out and it guttered, and Baldassare was in the way. I still could not see his face."

"How unfortunate." The bishop's voice was cold.

"It is the truth. I would tell you if I could." Beaumeis burst into tears again. "God's curse on him for killing Baldassare and laying that burden on my soul. I meant no ill, only to help Archbishop Theobald, who is a good man." His voice checked; he glanced at the bishop's face and shivered, and his eyes moved around the room like those of a hunted animal. Then suddenly he burst out, "It was the sacristan. I was afraid to speak before. I was sure you would not believe me."

There was a dead silence. Every head in the room turned toward Brother Paulinus. Father Benin rose from his seat, but the bishop put a hand on his arm and he stood still.

"I *was* in the church that night," Brother Paulinus said. He spoke calmly, without the frantic excitement that had marked both of his visits to Magdalene's house and his accusation of her in the prior's chamber. "I had been walking in the cloister after Compline service, and when I entered the slype, I thought I heard voices in the church. Naturally, I looked in the door, and I thought I saw a gleam of light moving, so I lit a candle and went in. I think I called out, 'Who is there?' but I cannot swear to that. No one answered, but a breeze almost blew out my candle and I realized the north door was open. I went and closed it."

"You did not look out?" the bishop asked.

"No." A touch of color stained the sacristan's pallid cheeks. "I thought it was a pair of sinners seeking a dark and quiet place. I thought I heard running as I came close and believed they were gone, so I only caught the edge of the door and swung it shut." Then every bit of color faded from his face until it was whiter than bleached parchment. "Are you telling me that when I went to the door, the papal messenger was bleeding his life away on the north porch? Have I killed two men by my carelessness and mistaken zeal?"

"No, Brother Paulinus," the infirmarian said firmly. "Both had taken fatal wounds at the hands of their murderers. Nothing you could have done would have saved either one."

"Perhaps," the sacristan said and took a few steps forward to confront Beaumeis more closely. "I was not the man who spoke to Messer Baldassare or the man who went out with him and stabbed him on the north porch. I will swear it on a cross heated red. Will you swear on a burning cross that I was the man you saw, Richard de Beaumeis?"

Beaumeis had shrunk away and would not meet the sacristan's eyes. Between the two, Magdalene knew she would choose the sacristan, much as she disliked him, as the truth-teller. She suspected that everyone else in the room felt the same, and it was clear from the way Beaumeis was almost panting for breath that he knew he had damaged his own cause by accusing Brother Paulinus.

The bishop, however, had little patience with religious fanaticism; his voice was cool when he said, "We have not yet come to such an impasse as to need a trial by ordeal. Can you offer any support at all for this tale of yours, Beaumeis?"

"What can I offer?" Beaumeis cried. "You are condemning me because you hate me."

That was true enough to make everyone uncomfortable. The bishop glared. The priest and the Archdeacon of St. Paul's looked at the floor or their toes. The monks drew closer together and whispered among themselves.

Emboldened, Beaumeis continued. "I was *trying* not to be seen. I—" He started to shake his head and then drew in his breath. "Oh, wait. Brother Godwine saw me going out the gate. He said, 'I thought you left at Vespers.' I had said I was leaving after Vespers. I did not answer, but he will be able to tell you—"

"Brother Godwine is dead," the bishop interrupted. "He was murdered on Wednesday night."

"No!" Beaumeis wailed, growing even paler. "I was not even here Wednesday night," he gasped, his eyes nearly starting from his head and his body shaking so hard that he almost toppled over. "I was with my uncle, the Abbot of St. Albans. No! You are only trying to frighten me into confessing what I have not done, because you think I did you a despite." He was sobbing hopelessly, and then he did fall, folding in on himself and collapsing to the floor.

The bishop turned to Bell, his face hard and angry, clearly about to order the knight to bring Beaumeis to his senses by any necessary means, but the prior spoke first.

"If what he says about being in St. Albans is true, he could not have killed Brother Godwine."

"That is still no proof that he did not cut Baldassare's throat." Winchester's voice was calm, but the rigidity of his expression betrayed his fury.

Father Benin bent and put a hand on his arm. "My lord," he said softly, "you need real proof, hard proof. He is such a nothing that no one here really believes he could have murdered Baldassare. Even if you bring him to confess . . ."

The prior shook his head and went around the table, clearly intending to see to Beaumeis. There was an instant of breath-held tension and then the bishop turned his head and looked at Bell. Bell in turn beckoned to the men-at-arms and told them to take Beaumeis back to the chamber in which they had kept him and keep him there.

"He was once in my keeping," the prior said; his voice held apology for crossing the bishop's will, but also the determination of a martyr, and he went to his monks, where he told the infirmarian to follow and do what he could for Beaumeis.

Bell drew a breath, waiting for the thunder of Winchester's rage to explode, but the bishop sat like a graven image and Bell finally came around the table, bent close and said, "My lord, I have sent a trusty man to St. Albans and he will discover the truth of this, but I am afraid it *is* true. I must tell you that my men have been through all the clothing Beaumeis had in his lodgings. None were stained with what could be blood, and the woman who rents to him and does his laundry says she has found no worse than mud and vomit on his garments and nothing missing since he returned from Rome."

Without speaking, the bishop rose, possibly to leave the room, but when he turned, he saw Magdalene. To her surprise, he said, "You know Beaumeis best, I think, despite the fact that he lived with the monks in the priory. To them, he always tried to pretend virtue; he did not think enough of you or your women to pretend. Do you believe what he told us?"

Magdalene sighed. "My lord, I hate to admit it, but I do. Perhaps he is even a better actor than Guiscard said, but that tale was very convincing. I would swear he really did not know the pouch had been found in the church or that Brother Godwine had been murdered. And what he did when Baldassare was killed is just like his actions last night. He made a plan, but the moment a little thing went wrong, he ran away. Still, he is a dreadful man. I shudder to think what he will do if he is confirmed in office as a deacon."

The rigidity of the bishop's face eased. "Oh, I do not think that will happen. Even if he can prove himself innocent of murder, his attempt to steal a papal bull is no light fault. I think even his uncle will not object if I arrange for him to retire for many years to some monastery, perhaps as a lay brother."

"That might be worse for him than being hanged."

Magdalene could not help smiling as she offered that sop to the spirit of vengeance, but she had really lost interest in Beaumeis. The murderer was still not marked and she and her women were still at risk—and Winchester might be less interested in identifying the murderer now that the pouch was found and he had his bull.

"If Beaumeis is not guilty," she went on before the bishop could move away, "and if what he said is true, it is clear that Baldassare knew the man who stopped beside the altar. My lord, do you remember that the safe box was under the altar?"

The bishop looked confused. "The safe box? But

what has that to do with the pouch and Baldassare's murder?"

"Perhaps everything," Bell said, leaning down again and keeping his voice low. "What if Baldassare was not murdered for the pouch but for chancing upon someone he knew was stealing, or about to steal, the church plate?"

"I see," the bishop said, sitting down again. "I see."

"But then—" Magdalene's voice was loud with excitement as what Beaumeis said finally made sense. Hearing it, she put a hand over her lips and looked hastily around the room.

She expected to see every churchman staring angrily at the whore who was shouting at a bishop, but she was mistaken about that. The monks were far more concerned about whether the Abbot of St. Albans would blame them for what had happened and were indifferent to her. All except the sacristan were clustered around Father Benin, and even the sacristan was not paying attention to her; he was standing a little apart, staring down at the floor. The Archdeacon of St. Paul's was beside Guiscard, reading over his notes of the interrogation, and the priest was holding Buchuinte—who Magdalene thought was looking longingly at the door— by the sleeve and talking earnestly.

The bishop, who was twisting his neck to look at her, asked kindly, "But then what, Magdalene?"

"Now I understand that conversation Beaumeis related," she said, stepping to the other side to be out of Bell's way and coming closer. "If it was the thief who killed Baldassare, those two were talking to each other but about entirely different things. When the monk said he could explain, he meant he could explain what looked like a robbery. And when Baldassare said he understood, he must have meant he knew you did not want the bull delivered in a public way that would incite your enemies, but the thief thought he had seen him stealing. So when Baldassare said, 'Wait here,' meaning he would fetch the pouch from where he had hidden it, the monk panicked, drew him out of the church, where sound, if Baldassare cried out, might carry . . . and killed him."

"Except for one thing," Bell put in, his eyes bright with revelation. He drew a deep breath and said, "My lord, if Baldassare was killed for recognizing the thief, the thief could not have been a monk. How would Baldassare know a simple monk? Bishops he knew, and some of the important abbots, for it was to them he carried the pope's messages, but a common monk?"

Magdalene's eyes widened. "And I know more certainly it could not have been a monk of St. Mary Overy priory because Baldassare had never previously visited either the church or the priory. He told me so, and had to ask me before he could be sure the church he saw from my gate was St. Mary Overy."

"Not a monk." The bishop looked up from one to the other. "Must we seek throughout England for the murderer?"

"No, indeed," Bell replied, now smiling grimly. "If the thief is the murderer, I will have his name very soon, or if he gave a false name, a good description of him. Remember, my lord, I reported to you yesterday that I had found the goldsmith who made the copies of the stolen plate. I would know now who had brought him the originals and ordered the copies, except that yesterday I could not ask him any questions. He had been attacked that very morning—"

Magdalene gasped, and both men looked at her. "The morning after the craftmark had been discovered. Could that attack have been a coincidence?"

"I did not think so," Bell said, looking a bit smug. "I left four men to keep a guard on the goldsmith, so he should be quite safe."

"Yes, but . . . but . . ."

Magdalene's glance flew around the room, and she drew a deep and calmer breath when she saw that no one was paying any attention to their little group or trying to listen to them. The sacristan was still deep in his own thoughts, and not pleasant ones judging by his expression; the prior and the other monks were listening to Brother Elwin urging something on Brother Patric; and the priest and archdeacon were now arguing with Guiscard about the way he had phrased something in his report. Reassured, she turned to Bell, who was frowning.

"Well? But?" He was a little annoyed, thinking she was about to raise an objection.

She waved a hand at him to indicate he should lower his voice. "There is no need to tell everyone about the goldsmith. Do you not remember there were only a few of us who knew a craftmark had been discovered? Do you not see that it must have been one of the people in the prior's chamber when we talked of that who tried to silence the goldsmith? And we are all here again— except for the priest and the archdeachon." She looked up at Bell. "How badly was the man hurt? Is he awake yet? Could he be carried here on a litter?"

"I do not know, except to say he was not hurt to the death. I asked and was told he would recover. But I can find the answers to the other questions quickly enough. I will send a man to my guards and they will bring him, if it is at all possible."

Now Magdalene turned eagerly to Winchester. "My lord, is there any way you could keep all of us here until the goldsmith arrives? If he has before him most of those who were near when Brother Godwine died and he can pick out one as the person who ordered the copies made—"

The bishop nodded curtly.

Twenty

28 APRIL 1139
THE BISHOP'S HOUSE, SOUTHWARK

Before Bell could look for a messenger to send to the goldsmith's house, the man he had sent to St. Albans to ask about Beaumeis accosted him and reported that Beaumeis *had* been with his uncle from Tuesday evening until midmorning of the previous day. The man-at-arms seemed a bit disappointed when Bell merely nodded over what he had thought was startling information, but he had come across another tidbit. He thought it less important, but it got the reaction his first news had failed to produce. Bell's lips parted and his eyes widened.

"Are you sure?" he asked.

"Yes, indeed," the man-at-arms said, and recited what he had done.

"So." Bell pulled a coin from his purse to reward the man for not being afraid to go further than his strict instructions, but he did not explain why he was so pleased, then dismissed his man.

He stood for a moment digesting what he had heard, now certain they would find the plate stolen from St. Mary Overy church in St. Albans. He had started to turn back to tell Winchester when another man-at-arms, one of the guards he had left to watch over the goldsmith, spoke his name. His heart sank heavily because the fact he had learned was not proof of guilt—they needed the goldsmith's testimony—but the man relieved his fears by telling him that Master Domenic was right there in the bishop's house.

"When 'e slept off th' potion th' 'pothecary gave 'im 'nd woke up this mornin', 'e wanted t' know what we was doin' in 'is 'ouse 'nd who we was. Then when Michael told 'im we was the bishop's guards sent t' be sure 'e weren't attacked again 'nd give 'im yer message 'bout the craftmark, 'e got all excited like and insisted on comin' 'ere."

"Well, no harm's done." Bell smiled. "I was just about to send a man to you to ask if he was well enough to be carried here. I gather that wasn't necessary."

"No, sir." The guard grinned back. "Fact is, we 'ad a time keepin' up with 'im. Real eager to get 'ere, 'e were."

That information was rendered superfluous while the guard was speaking. A short, tubby man with a large bruise on his temple, a very red nose, and marks of its dripping on his sleeves, had got to his feet as he saw the guard approach Bell and now came forward.

He sniffed richly and then said in a rather thick, hoarse voice, "So the bishop saw my copies and found my craftmark. I am very pleased, indeed I am. Master William, the clerk who ordered them, did not want me to put a craftmark on because they were copies of Master Jacob the Alderman's work, and I agreed that it would be wrong to put my mark where he put his, as if the work were mine, but they were *good* copies, well done, and I thought it could do no harm to put my small mark off in a corner."

"No harm at all, Master Domenic," Bell said, suppressing a grin. In fact the mark had done much good. And then, masking what was important to him in politeness, he said, "I hope you did not lose anything to the man who attacked you. Did you recognize him?"

The goldsmith began to laugh, then bent his head quickly to sneeze into his sleeve. "One does not recognize thieves," he said, wiping his nose; he sniffed again, then looked thoughtful. "No, I lost nothing, although not through my own wariness. I did not suspect him. He did not look around to see what was most valuable, as a thief might, but came right up to the table where I was working and struck me. At least so says my apprentice, who ran out to see why I had fallen."

"But you did not see or remember his face? Did your apprentice see him?"

"No, he wore a scarf over most of his face under his hood. I suppose I should have suspected then, but I had such a dreadful cold that I guess I just thought he had a bad cold, too. Luckily, my carelessness did not cost me. He did not even seize the pieces in the window, which he could have done as he ran. And of course I thought nothing of a man wearing a monk's robe. With the archbishop's palace right behind my shop, as it were, we have monks and nuns aplenty passing by, and even stopping in. Of course it has been very quiet since Archbishop William of blessed memory died, and the new archbishop may not . . . who knows if he will use Lambeth Palace as much as Archbishop William did? So when I heard that the Bishop of Winchester was interested in my work, I hurried right over."

Bell was disappointed that the goldsmith was unable to recognize or describe his attacker, but he had plenty of time to recover from the disappointment as the man rambled on and on. The fact that the attacker had taken nothing indicated that he was more interested in harming the goldsmith than in stealing, which made him no common thief—unless he was a particularly inept and timid one. Bell wondered whether the attacker knew he had not hit the goldsmith hard enough to keep him stunned and so fled without stealing.

"I am surprised you were able to come here if the

thief struck you hard enough to knock you down and render you unconscious," Bell remarked.

Master Domenic grinned at him. "Ah well, God works in His own wondrous ways. As you may guess, I was not overly pleased when I woke with a sore throat day before yesterday, nor when the tisanes and potions did not stop the cold from spreading to my head. It ached so much yesterday morning that I wrapped a poultice in a warm, woolen cloth around my head under my hat. That shielded me from the full force of the blow—and it was a strong one, for it knocked me off my chair and stunned me, even with that protection. I was helpless, but fortunately my apprentice came running so quickly to see what was wrong that the thief had no time to steal."

And no time to deliver several more blows and finish the job, Bell thought. The goldsmith had no idea of how lucky he had been. Maybe when he realized it, he would be a little less cast down to learn that the bishop had not summoned him to order work. But Bell decided he had better not tell Master Domenic anything about that yet. He did not want the man sullen with disappointment.

"If you will wait just a moment or two more," Bell said, "I will go in and tell the bishop you are here. I know he wishes to speak to you, but I told him you had been hurt, so he might not be expecting you so soon."

"I will wait upon his lordship's convenience very willingly," Master Domenic said, and sniffed liquidly again.

Bell went back through the door just in time to see the bishop lean from his chair toward Magdalene, who was now seated on the stool the prior had vacated. Bell froze for a moment, struggling to conquer an insane impulse to pull his master away, made even more insane by the fact that he knew Winchester took his vows of chastity very seriously. He could not speak for an instant, and then kept silent because the bishop was obviously in the middle of a conversation.

"Do not be so hard on him," Winchester said. "His manner is irritating, but it is because he is too aware that he is not so well-born as the others, who are mostly second, third, and fourth sons of noblemen—like Bell. His grandfather was a butcher—"

"Oh, dear," Magdalene said, trying hard not to giggle. "Think of being a butcher's son and trying to maintain your dignity against all those noble-born cockscombs."

The bishop smiled. "It was not so bad as that," he said. "The butcher had grown rich, and his father had come up in the world. He was a physician, and a good one. He was my own physician until he died some years ago."

Bell suddenly stiffened to attention and his glance flashed across the room. However, the bishop's voice had been low, no doubt because he did not wish to waken curiosity about his easy conversation with a whore, and no one in the room was taking notice. Brother Patric was listening with an expression of mingled joy and anxiety to what Father Benin was saying; Brother Elwin and some of the other monks were nodding agreement, and the infirmarian had a hand on Brother Patric's arm. Knud had moved to stand nearer the sacristan, who was staring across the room at a window, his face pallid and stone hard. Buchuinte was now listening intently to the priest of St. Paul's and nodding, while the archdeacon seemed to have won some argument, because Guiscard was using a pumice stone to smooth over a line he had scraped off the record he was writing.

"A physician?" Suddenly the laughter was all gone from Magdalene's voice, and Bell turned to look at her. Her eyes had become unnaturally large as she stared at Winchester. "A physician," she repeated. "My lord, was he always meant for the Church, or did he first study to be a physician?" she asked urgently.

Bell stared at her, startled again by the quickness of her mind. She never forgot anything, it seemed, and saw the significance of the man's first training.

"What does it matter?" Winchester asked, puzzled but also slightly amused by her interest.

"It does matter, my lord," Bell said, coming quickly to the table and leaning forward across it to speak softly. "I cannot remember whether I troubled you with a description of Baldassare's death wound, but it was delivered in one clean stroke by a man who knew just where to put his knife. That wound always made me doubtful of Beaumeis's guilt. I thought it must have been dealt by a man accustomed to bearing arms—and I wasted a great deal of time discovering where Magdalene's noble patrons were on that night. Fool that I was, I never thought that a butcher or a physician would have the same knowledge."

Winchester's face had frozen, the half-smile still on his lips. "He did study to be a physician," he said, the smile disappearing into a grimly set mouth. "It gave him Latin and made him specially good at writing a clear letter of explanation. He wrote more simply than a clerk trained in theological disputation. I told you I knew his father and that he had attended me. He was a good man, and when he came to me and asked if I could find a place for his son because the young man hated being a physician, I was glad to do it."

"Then he would know exactly where to put a knife," Bell said even more softly, nodding. His eyes flicked around the room again, came back to Winchester, and he took a deep breath. "And there is no one in St. Albans for him to visit. His mother died two years ago."

"Two years ago," the bishop repeated.

"Well, my lord," Bell said, still softly but now with a brisk intonation, "we will have proof very soon, I hope. The goldsmith I was about to send for came all on his own and is waiting in the hall without."

"Came on his own," the bishop repeated, as if he did

not understand what Bell had said. He was a little pale and had some difficulty preventing himself from staring.

"Yes. Master Domenic knows we found the craftmark. He is very proud of his copies and thinks you wish to order more work from him."

"This is no time for worrying about a thief. We must—" Winchester blinked and shook his head, seeming to remember that the thief and the murderer were almost certainly the same person. "Did he name the man who ordered the copies?" he asked eagerly.

"A Master William, a clerk, he said."

The bishop's face showed his anger and disappointment. "But there is no Master William—" He stopped abruptly and uttered a bark of laughter. "I am so surprised and shocked that my wits are wandering. Of course he would give a false name. Very well, bring in the goldsmith."

While Bell and the bishop had been talking, Magdalene had risen, pushed the stool under the table, and stepped back against the wall, now a foot or so to the right of Winchester. In rising, she had stepped on the trailing edge of her long veil so that it fell on the floor. Her mind was on the discussion they had had and she absently picked the veil up and stood staring down at it, holding it loosely in her hands without draping it over her head again. She was as shocked as the bishop, hardly able to believe the near conviction she shared with him and Bell. It seemed strange to know someone so long and never suspect that kind of evil in him.

She looked up but was careful not to stare. And it was strange also that so momentous a truth had been uncovered without in the least affecting anyone but those who had uncovered it. Everyone else seemed most innocently occupied with his own immediate concerns. Then the door opened and Bell quietly ushered in a tubby man with a red nose and a blue bruise on his temple. Placing himself so that his body shielded the goldsmith from casual scrutiny, Bell guided him toward the table. The prior turned to look, but Magdalene thought he could see little except the back of the man's head. The prior looked anxious, but there was reason enough for that if he thought the bishop was going to be diverted to business other than the reconsecration of his church.

Master Domenic meanwhile was bobbing a whole series of bows to Winchester and babbling in an awed whisper about how much he was honored by the bishop's approval of his copies.

"They were good copies," the bishop said, also quietly. "At first we could not tell them from the originals."

No guilt disturbed Master Domenic's expression; in fact, he beamed. "Oh, were they compared? I did not know that would be possible. I knew the originals were Master Jacob the Alderman's work and were borrowed and had to be returned quickly, but I thought . . ." His brow wrinkled. "Surely Master William told me the copies were to go into his master's chapel in Oxford. Oh, well, it does not matter. As long as you saw them, my lord, and appreciated the work."

"Oh, indeed I did," Winchester remarked dryly. "They were brought to my attention"—irresistibly his head was drawn around, and his eyes fixed for a moment before he went on—"by some very unusual circumstances."

The goldsmith had naturally followed the direction in which Winchester had looked. "Why, there is Master William," he said with pleased surprise, his voice much louder than it had been when he spoke to the bishop.

In that moment, Guiscard de Tournai looked up from the parchment on which he had been trying to squeeze the priest's and archbishop's phrasing into a space too small for it. His expression changed the goldsmith's pleasure into doubt as he realized that "Master William" should not be scribing at the Bishop of Winchester's table, but in Oxford with his copies of the candlesticks.

"I only wanted to express my gratitude, Master William, for bringing my work to the bishop's notice," Domenic said, his voice now somewhat tremulous with uncertainty and his eyes shifting swiftly to gauge the bishop's expression.

"You fool!" Guiscard shouted and snatched up the knife with which he had sharpened his quills.

The roar of his voice startled everyone into immobility, except Bell, who thrust himself between the goldsmith and Guiscard, pushing the tubby man back so hard that he staggered well away from the table. Bell started to draw his sword, but Guiscard had no interest in a worthless revenge. He leapt instead for the bishop, right past Magdalene, who was as frozen as anyone else, and before Winchester could move, he had seized the bishop's head in his left hand and with the right pressed his knife, which was small but very sharp and with a keen point, to the bishop's neck, just under the ear where a big vein pulsed.

"Stand still and be silent," Guiscard hissed. "I assure you one more death will not trouble me at all. One move, one shout for help, and the bishop dies. And you need not think I do not know that if I kill him, I will free you to kill me. I will die anyway if I cannot use him to help me escape, so I will either be free or take him with me."

"My son—" Father Benin whispered, stretching out a hand.

"Shut your mouth and stand perfectly still," Guiscard snarled and shifted his eyes to Bell, who was scarlet with rage and frustration, frozen with his sword half drawn.

"You"—his lips curled down in bitter distaste— "strutting peacock, go out and order the bishop's litter to be brought to the door. When it comes, you will raise the curtain on the side facing this door, I will get in with the bishop. You will lower the curtain and then walk with the litter to my lodging. There you will go in and get from the chest at the foot of my bed the bags of coin and—"

"I will need the key," Bell said, sliding his sword fully back into its sheath and placing both empty hands on the table. "And do you want any other valuables? The candlesticks? The golden pyx?"

"They are not in the chest. I am not such a fool as to keep them. . . ." Guiscard's voice faded and his hand tensed so that a small bead of red blossomed on the bishop's neck where the knife pricked him. "Oh, you think you are so clever, that you have tricked me into admitting that I stole those things." He laughed. "Why should I deny it? I will either be safe and far out of your reach . . . or dead . . . very soon. Neither way will lying be of any benefit to me." He laughed, but not hard enough to move the knife from its position. "Half the pleasure of taking the things was doing it under all your noses. And all of you cared so little for me that you did not bother to discover that my mother had died, so I had a perfect place to dispose of my gleanings."

"It must have been . . . amusing." Bell's eyes flicked to Magdalene, but not for long enough for Guiscard, whose attention was mostly on Winchester, to notice. "I suppose the whore let you in and out through her gates so you could enter the priory in secret anytime you liked."

Magdalene bit her lip in mingled hurt and fury, but she had sense enough to be silent. She was entirely too close to Guiscard to want to attract his attention. One thing she was sure of: He would be as happy to kill her as to leave her standing. Then she realized he had discovered he enjoyed killing, and even if he escaped safely, he would not let Winchester live. Her hands tightened on the scarf she held and she twisted it, tears misting her eyes.

"I would not trust a whore!" Guiscard had spat. "Not that one, who will cheat an agent out of his just fee and whine to the bishop about it. She would have run to

Winchester the moment I asked." He laughed again, a little more heartily. "You are all such fools, even the so-wise, so-powerful Bishop of Winchester. I had copies made of all the keys to the Old Priory Guesthouse when I showed her the place."

The bishop twitched, and Guiscard gripped his head tighter.

"Of course," Bell said, very quickly. "I forgot you held the keys to that place. But it could not have been so easy to get the key to the priory safe box."

"But it was." Guiscard raised his brows superciliously. "It only took a little planning. Brother Knud was a priest, but he has a little secret; he is a bit too fond of little boys. When he was sent to the bishop for punishment, I received the charges against him and offered him the alternative punishment of being the sacristan's lay brother in St. Mary Overy. Naturally, I came now and again to make sure he was doing well. We talked about his duties, so I knew the days and times when he cleaned the plate. Once I came when he had just begun to clean. The key was on the table. I said I saw he was busy and went away—with the key. When I returned, he was almost finished with his work and I had a copy. If he suspected"—Guiscard smiled across the room at Knud, who had fallen to his knees with his hands over his face—"I knew he would never mention it to anyone."

"I thought Knud knew more than he was saying," Bell said. "I intended to question him again, but . . ."

He leaned farther forward over the table, as if totally absorbed in what Guiscard was saying. He seemed to be putting all his weight on his hands, which should immobilize him, but Magdalene saw how the table cut into his thighs and she realized he was balancing himself against it so that his hands were really free. Unfortunately, Guiscard was no more deceived than she.

"Stand back," he snarled, and the red bead marking

the point of his knife against the bishop's throat enlarged into a thin trickle of blood.

Bell straightened up. "Sorry," he said. "I was—"

"You thought you were distracting me by letting me talk and were about to leap on me. You are a fool. I am not. You were misled because I was willing to talk, but I have time, until the bells ring for Tierce. There are several ships in the river that will sail on the tide. I thought it would be safer to wait here, but you are getting too cocky."

"Ships?" Bell echoed, eager to distract him.

Guiscard laughed once more. "How surprised you look. I have kept myself informed of every sailing on every day we were in London for near a year. Safe is better than sorry, but I am afraid you will make a mistake and I will have to kill Winchester before—" He cut his words off and added quickly, "I would rather get away than kill him. You had better go and order his litter now, and do not warn those in the outer room, either, or call your men. You may succeed in stopping me, but the bishop will be dead before I am."

Magdalene had held her breath when Bell leaned forward. She had seen from the angle of his body that he intended to throw himself across the table and try to push Guiscard to the right, toward her and away from Winchester. Although the bishop had not apparently moved, she thought she had seen a shadow under his chair shift very slightly, and she hoped he was setting his feet so he could lunge away from the knife.

Guiscard had been too wary, however. Worse, Magdalene knew the abortive effort had fixed his attention on Bell so firmly that Bell would not be able to try again to attack him. She caught her lip between her teeth and bit down hard when Guiscard's slip about not wanting to kill Winchester "before" confirmed her fear that he intended to murder the bishop no matter what. And if Winchester were dead, her easy life and prosperity might also be over—and one of the few churchman who had at least tried to be fair to a whore would be lost. Bell, too, if Guiscard could somehow manage it.

She stood as still as the stones themselves against the wall, hardly breathing. Guiscard did not care enough about her now to try to hurt her, but if she interfered, she would be the only one close enough on whom to vent his rage. Was it worth the risk to try?

"The key to your chest," Bell said desperately. "You never gave it to me."

He moved an open hand slowly toward Guiscard, who instinctively started to relax his grip on the bishop's head. But he did not make that mistake, either, and instead, shouted, "Out! Get the litter!"

In the same moment, never having answered the question she had asked herself, Magdalene took two steps forward, threw the scarf she had been holding between her hands over Guiscard's head, and yanked him toward her with all the strength she had.

As she pulled, she screamed, "Jump!" at Winchester, who showed himself as brave as he was clever. Instead of trying to wrench himself to the left, away from the prick of the knife but against the pressure of Guiscard's hand, he rose straight upward, knocking his heavy chair backward with the force of his movement. The knife scored a long line down his neck, but because Guiscard's left hand had lost its grip on his head as he rose, he was able to lean away from the pain, and the blade did no more than slice the skin.

When his victim and safe-conduct tore free of his hold, Guiscard knew he was dead. Unable to find better prey—he knew the bishop's layers of rich vestments would armor him against the blade of the little knife, and that the bishop was no physical weakling—he turned on Magdalene as he tore the scarf from his head.

"Bitch! Whore!" he shrieked, striking at her face. "No one will ever wish to lie with you again!"

She raised her arms instinctively to protect herself, felt the sting as the sharp blade pierced through her sleeve to cut her arm. She tried to back away, but he was upon her, dragging her arms down, screaming obscenities. She saw the knife rise, realized it was aimed for her eye, and tried desperately to fight his grip and free herself.

Then he screamed wordlessly and she was able to pull her head away. The knife came down, but only slid against her neck, which was covered by her gown. And then he fell away altogether, and she was looking at Bell, who had a long poniard dripping red in his hand.

"Are you hurt?" he asked.

"No," she whispered, backing so she could lean against the wall.

"Give her the stool or she will fall," the bishop said, and Bell pulled the stool out from under the table and set it beside her so she could sink down upon it.

"And you, my lord, are you hurt?" Bell asked anxiously. "I am so sorry. Fool that I am, I thought he would go for Master Domenic." He bent and righted the bishop's chair. "Sit down, my lord. I will fetch the infirmarian."

"Is it safe to leave Guiscard without a guard?" Winchester asked, sitting down rather heavily and looking at the body on the floor.

"He is dead, my lord," Bell said. "I am sorry about that, too. I did not mean to kill him, but in a fight . . . I had no time to draw my sword, and when I hold a knife . . . habit and training, my lord."

Magdalene had closed her eyes at first, but they snapped open when Bell said Guiscard was dead. She could see only the side of Bell's face, and his eyes were down, looking at the bishop, but they flicked once sideways to her and she knew he was not at all sorry. He *had* meant to kill, and he meant it because Guiscard had been threatening her.

Then her eyes closed again. She did not faint, nor did she slip off the stool, but she was not really conscious of what was happening around her—beyond a blurred and indistinct sound of voices coming and going—until someone lifted her arm. She uttered a low cry because the movement made her aware of the ache.

"You said you were not hurt!" Bell's voice, low and angry.

She opened her eyes, saw the bishop still in his chair, now with a bandage around his neck, the infirmarian loosening her sleeve, which was marked with a wide stain of blood, Bell behind the monk, bending forward to see her wound, his face anxious. Drawing a deep breath, she looked down. Guiscard's body was gone. Raising her eyes, she saw that Master Domenic and Master Buchuinte, the priest and the Archdeacon of St. Paul's, the prior and the monks—all except for the infirmarian—were also gone. On the table near her was a pot of salve and more bandages.

"It was only a small cut," she said.

"It bled enough," Bell retorted.

"The knife touched a small vein," the infirmarian put in, "but the bleeding has stopped now, and it assures a clean wound." As he spoke, he reached for the salve, applied it gently, and wrapped her arm in the waiting bandage. He came upright and looked at her carefully. "Hmm. There is another small spot near your neck. I think the point just touched you there. Take the salve and apply it if you need it."

He would not ask a whore to loosen the neck of her gown, Magdalene thought, suppressing a smile. But at least he had been willing to treat her. Still, he was quick to turn away, gathering up the bandages and another small pot, which he put into a leather bag, and walking around the end of the table. When his bulk no longer blocked the bishop's view of her, Winchester turned in her direction.

"You saved my life, Magdalene," he said, "at some risk to your own. I am very grateful. But why?"

"Because you are *willing* to be grateful to a whore, my lord," she said, and smiled.

He laughed. "And how am I to reward you for so great a service?"

Magdalene shrugged. "In a sense, you owe me nothing. I am afraid I did not think so much of your life, my lord, as of how much harder my own would be without you. Nor do I really remember thinking clearly that I *would* do this thing. I—I just did it."

Winchester stared at her for a moment, then said, "I do not like a sense of obligation hanging over my head."

She laughed and shrugged again. "If you feel so, my lord, then money is always useful to a whore. The more I have, the closer is the day when I can leave my work."

"Ah, you should not have said that." Winchester shook his head, but he was smiling. "It might make me parsimonious. Not for greed, at least not *mostly* for greed, but because I am not so sure that I want you to leave the Old Priory Guesthouse." He sighed ostentatiously. "However, I know it is a sin for a churchman not to try to wean a whore from her lechery, and I owe you for a great increase in the prior's peace of mind also."

"The prior?" Magdalene repeated, surprise giving her a small spurt of strength, which permitted her to keep her eyes open and not sag back against the wall.

The bishop struggled with his mouth and kept himself from grinning. "The prior will be rid of the sacristan, who is much chastened. This day has finally hammered home to Brother Paulinus that his hatred of you and your work has led him to excess and to misuse of his power as sacristan. He has requested permission to give up his place to Brother Boniface and go back to the mother house to restore his soul."

"Brother Boniface?" she breathed, and then bit her lip to keep from laughing.

Brother Boniface was as much the opposite of Brother Paulinus as a monk could be. Although he loved the buildings of the priory and would see to their welfare devotedly, he was round and jolly and one of the few monks who was an occasional patron of her house. She had sense enough, however, to look down and say no more, hoping the bishop would not realize she knew Brother Boniface. And at last she was able to yield openly to the exhaustion that was turning her bones to water. Sighing, she allowed herself to fall back against the wall and close her eyes.

"She needs to go home and rest, my lord," Bell said.

Winchester nodded. "Yes. I would like to go above and rest myself, but I must reconsecrate the church." He sighed. "I think I will need my litter to get there."

Bell smiled. "At least you will sit in it alone, without a knife at your throat. I was getting so desperate I was wondering if I could thrust my sword in and skewer Guiscard without giving him time to skewer you. I'll go and tell the men now."

Magdalene simply sat, hoping the bishop would not speak again. He did not, and slowly the aches and tremblings of her body that resulted from the shock eased away. At first the fading of her reaction left her even weaker and more flaccid, but by the time she heard the sound of Bell's footsteps returning, she was already feeling better. Nonetheless, she continued to sit with closed eyes, leaning back against the wall as Bell helped the bishop to his feet and, she assumed, lent him a strong arm to lean on as they made their way to the litter.

She expected Bell back, but he did not come and she wondered if the bishop had forgotten her and ordered Bell to accompany him. Well, it did not matter, she thought. She would be better off if he avoided her in the future. He had killed one man already, partly because of her, and she was afraid there would be more if he continued to desire her. Enough! She opened her eyes and got to her feet.

"And where are you going, Mistress Magdalene?"

She smiled, a bit wryly when she realized that the time between his leaving with the bishop and his return

was less than her eagerness for his return had made it
seem. "I was going home to rest and to put on a clean
gown. I do not want to frighten my clients by being
covered with blood."

"Sit down again. I will see if I can find a litter for
you. I think—"

"No, thank you. I am quite well enough to walk, and
I do not think anyone will object today if I go through
the priory grounds, so it is not far."

He watched her make her way slowly but steadily
enough to the end of the table, then came and offered
his arm. She hesitated momentarily, remembering that
she really should not encourage him, and he dropped
his arm and turned his face a little, almost as if she had
slapped him.

"I am sorry I did not stop him before he was able to
hurt you," he said. "I have failed most thoroughly, for
if not for you, Winchester would have died."

All practical considerations flew away in the face of
Bell's pain. She hastily took another step toward him
and took his hand. "Don't talk so silly. How could you
have guessed what Guiscard would do? I thought he
would be enraged and go for the goldsmith, too, but he
may have noticed Master Domenic when you brought
him in and got over his first rage and terror. Likely he
was planning what to do all the while Master Domenic
and the bishop were talking."

Bell sighed. "Perhaps. Still, I should have—" He
shook his head, raised his arm, and placed her hand on
it. "Are you sure this is support enough?"

She smiled up at him. "Yes. If I tire, we can stop in
the churchyard . . ." Her voice drifted away. "I think we
should stop. I would like to visit Messer Baldassare's
grave."

"He is avenged," Bell said through thinned lips as he
steered her out of the bishop's chamber and started
through the hall. As they neared the outer door, he

added, "The Church does not take blood vengeance, but I am no churchman."

His voice was cold and hard, yet Magdalene felt a great lightening of her spirit. Yes, Bell had killed apurpose, and one reason had surely been because Guiscard had attacked her, but he would have done the same for the bishop or for any other person in danger. Moreover, the small injury done her could easily have been avenged—more than avenged—by whatever punishment the Church decreed for murder and Guiscard's threat to the bishop. It was *Baldassare's death*, not the attack, that had called for blood and made Bell tilt his knife at just the angle that would find Guiscard's heart.

They spoke no more until they had passed through the priory gate—Brother Elwin, as she had predicted, only nodded at her as he opened for them—and into the graveyard. For a few moments more, they were silent, looking down at the wooden marker.

"The bishop is having a fitting gravestone carved," Bell said softly. "There is a Latin verse praising Baldassare's devotion to his duty."

"It should praise his intelligence and good nature, too." Magdalene raised a hand to wipe her eyes. "He was a good man, and a kind one. I know we are not supposed to question the will of God, but why? He did not die for *any* reason, just by the accident of coming into the church at the wrong time and because Beaumeis was too great a coward to call out. Perhaps if he had taken the pouch—"

"He hid it in your house, did he not?" Bell's voice was accusatory.

Magdalene turned her head, her eyes now dry and defiant. "I could not admit that, not even to the bishop. Stop and think of the result if Winchester had demanded that I give him the pouch after the messenger was murdered."

Bell's face, which had been angry, suddenly went blank. Then he drew her away from the grave and began walking toward the gate to her house. After a moment he asked, "Were you really thinking of Winchester when you hid that pouch in the church?"

"And myself." Now Magdalene's voice was hard and cold. "Winchester would have had to admit how he came by the pouch, and I and my women would have been accused of murder. That would not have done the bishop any good, because he is known to be my landlord. Would not all say he was the most likely one to bid me murder Baldassare? Never mind there was no reason in the world for him to do so, for Baldassare was bound to give him the bull in any case. But blaming the bishop would not have helped me, either, for I would have been gutted and hanged for the crime, no matter who gave the order. I am a whore and thus guilty, remember."

"I know why you did it," Bell said, waving dismissal of her reasoning, "but I thought you could have trusted me. You told William of Ypres."

"I did not! I told William that Brother Godwine had been murdered, the church would have to be purified, and since Baldassare had not hidden the pouch in my house, it was possible he had been inside the church, had hidden it there, and the cleaning might expose it. If he guessed what you guessed, he gave no sign of it. And since William is not one to cry over spilt milk, I doubt he cares how the pouch got into the church. It is enough that he was there when it was discovered."

"Well, he did not hint to the bishop that there was any doubt about who hid it—not that it matters; Winchester knows now, but obviously he will not make an issue of it, or of anything else that might cause you trouble. And anyway, he got what he wanted. Lord William did try to convince him of the benefits of bringing the pouch to the king intact and allowing the king to bestow the bull, but when Winchester said flatly he would not accept it from the king without the pope's special order, Lord William agreed that the bishop should take the bull. Winchester sweetened that by suggesting that he would not announce receiving the bull or use it until it was absolutely necessary, so that the king would believe it had been sent by a different messenger."

Magdalene sighed. William had not got everything he wanted, but he had the letter confirming the king's right, and he had a fascinating story to tell. He would be back in full favor—for a time, anyway.

"I am delighted to hear they came to a peaceable agreement," she said. "Is that where you were when we were all scrubbing the church? Acting bodyguard for the bishop lest William lose his temper and take the bull by force?"

Bell laughed. "No, I heard by accident. I was waiting to report to the bishop about my search for the goldsmith who made those copies of the church plate. Neither Lord William nor Lord Winchester even noticed I was in the bishop's private closet. I spoke at once, but they both waved me to wait. Thank God they seem to trust me to hold my tongue"—he looked surprised and shook his head—"which I have not done. God help me, talking to you, Magdalene, is like talking to myself."

"And what you said will go just as far. I am accustomed to hearing what is dangerous to know. If William can trust me, you can."

"Oh, yes, unless my interest conflicts with his." His voice was bitter.

They had stopped by the gate; the latch lifted readily and Bell swung it open. Magdalene passed through, then turned back to face him.

"William has a right to my loyalty. He has been my patron, my protector—my lord, since you will understand that term best—for over ten years. I am no man's woman, not even William's, but I do put his interests above those of others. If you cannot understand and accept that, I am most truly sorry."

There was a little silence. Bell watched her as if he

expected her to slam the gate in his face and walk away. Finally he said, "I suppose you want me to gather my things and go back to my former lodging."

Magdalene looked up at him over the gate and put out her hand to keep it half open between them. He had *not* killed Guiscard over her. He had *not* flown into a rage over her repeated statement of her obligation to William. Maybe training would tame him. She smiled.

"Not unless you cannot bear to live among us any longer, or you think the bishop would disapprove. I would miss your company, which I enjoy. And it is comforting to have a man in the house whom we can trust to defend us. I will gladly exchange that for the cost of your board. *If* you can remember that I am a whore and can belong to any man for only his five-pence worth of time, you are welcome to stay . . . if you wish."

"You said you were retired."

"So I am, but that does not change what I am."

He grinned. "Now that Baldassare's murderer is taken, I will begin in earnest to convince you that total retirement is not so blessed as you think."

"I look forward to the contest," she said, laughing.

The twist of Bell's lips in response was sour, but he stepped through the gate, shut it behind him, and walked companionably beside her to the back door of her house. Both reached for the door latch simultaneously and their fingers touched. She snatched hers away, which restored Bell's good humor and he laughed aloud. But he did not try to follow his advantage. He lifted the latch and opened the door, looking down at her, his eyes sparkling.

"We will both enjoy the contest, I think."

About the Author

ROBERTA GELLIS has a master's degree in medieval literature and another in biochemistry. She is the author of numerous novels and the recipient of many awards, including the Lifetime Achievement Award for Historical Fantasy and the Romance Writers of America's Lifetime Achievement Award.

Roberta Gellis lives in Long Island with her husband of over fifty years and her Lakeland terrier, Taffy.